I0645157

Figure 92-Don Pawlitschek

I authored this novel after having a dream about it. It then wrote itself, or at least I had an outline in mind when I started. Sometimes, the sneaky little characters would take off on their own. Like it or not, I found it best to follow them along.

It took me five years to write it and three years to edit it. (I flunked spelling in school and got a D in English!) I rewrote and edited the book at **LEAST ~~TWENTY, TWENTY-ONE, TWENTY-TWO,~~ TWENTY-THREE TIMES, AND NOW HAVE THE ERRORS DOWN TO** *"WHAT THE @#$%^&*0_@#$%^, !!!!!!"* which I'm sure you will find.

TO

____

____

____

____

Don Pawlitschek – (Popps Dundee)

____

Donald Pawlitschek

The Dash

Does Enduring Love Conquer All?

Donald Pawlitschek

PrintCast News L.L.C.

18014 499th Ave

Lake Crystal, MN 56055

Donald Pawlitschek/PrintCast News LLC
18014 499th Ave
Lake Crystal, MN 56055
www.printcastnews.com
507-546-3448

First Edition
Book Layout © 2017 BookDesignTemplates.com
Cover Design by Donald Pawlitschek
The Dash/ Donald Pawlitschek -- First Edition.
ISBN 978-0-9992279-2-3

Dedication

To My Wife, Korrine

To My Children-

Andrew Pawlitschek and his wife, Sara,

Jennifer Pawlitschek,

Heidi (Pawlitschek) Zalusky and her husband, Pat,

Sarah (Pawlitschek) Beauregard and her husband, Brett,

Ben Pawlitschek and his wife, Sara

To My Grandchildren,

Solomon Pawlitschek, Allejandra Pawlitschek, Sienna
Pawlitschek, Malachi Pawlitschek, Azariah Pawlitschek,
Arabella Pawlitschek, Cyrus Pawlitschek,

Mathew Zalusky, Josef Zalusky, Charles Zalusky, Sophia
Zalusky,

Zachariah Beauregard, Lukas Beauregard,
Abigail Beauregard

Lily Pawlitschek, Aaron Pawlitschek, Arden Pawlitschek,
Margaret Pawlitschek, Elizabeth Pawlitschek,

May you always follow the light! Remember the_Dash!

"God first, then Family, then Work, then Church."

Donald Pawlitschek

Prior Poems, Stories and Scripts

Poems

A Soldier I Once Be
Cowboy
Cow Pie
Echoes of My Mind
Family
Favorite Grandchild
Freedom Gate
Fifty Is Nifty!
God Is Love
God's Art
He Touched Me
How Quaint
Just A Drop More
Peace March
Sands of My Mind
Sixty-Five
Some Girls Dance.
South Dakota Lady
Stuff
Talk to Me
Thank You
The Fight
The Love of One
The Puppy
Our Father

Humor

Bib Speaking
Bib Speaking Jen
Chucky
Crotch Fans
I Wreck
It Was a Great Party

Little 42, the Four-legged Chicken,
Up Comedy Routine
Knute Vol 1, 2, 3, 4
Knute's Letter to Boys
Knute's Letter to Mathew
New Yorkee Snow Knute
Rufus 1
Rufus 2
Surgery
Ting Tang Walla Walla Bing Bang
Questions for Grandpa
Zigadee

Stories

Angela's Eyes
Bertha Struggled
Bible
Chubby Nun in A Tree!
Class of 59
Crime Does Not Pay (TV script)
Director's Notes 1, 2, 3, 4, 5, 6, 7, 8
History of Auctioneering
I Weep
Letter to John
Little Stone Church Singers
Marriage
Meanest Mother
Oscar Teeterdink
Our Father
Papaya and Maple Syrupul
Remember the Good Times
The Worst Christmas
Vet PTSD

Photo Credits

Figure	Item	Photo Credits
Figure 1	Octagon Dance Hall	Wikipedia
Figure 2	Helicon Tuba	Wikipedia
Figure 3	Cimbalom and performer.	Dreamtime
Figure 3a	Young Eliska	Don Pawlitschek
Figure 4	Brown Swiss Cow	Don Pawlitschek
Figure 5	Holstein Bull	Wikipedia
Figure 6	Windmill	Wikipedia
Figure 7	Bulls Nose Ring	Unsplash
Figure 8	Roma Horses	Dreamtime
Figure 9	Racing Horses	Dreamtime
Figure 10	Mack AC Truck at Coal Yard	Public Domain
Figure 11	Map Litomysl to Karvina	Google Map
Figure 12	Inside Mack Ac Truck	Public Domain
Figure 13	Hand Crank	Dreamtime
Figure 14	Hand Crank Wiper	Wikipedia
Figure 15	AhooGaa Horn	Public Domain
Figure 16	Mack AC Truck	Public Domain
Figure 17	Acetylene Headlights	Public Domain
Figure 18	Saint Wenceslas Shrine	Public Domain
Figure 19	Babbling Brook	Don Pawlitschek
Figure 20	Army Tents	Public Domain
Figure 21	Dvur Olsiny Hotel	Dvur Olsiny Hotel Historic
Figure 22	Dvur Olsiny Hotel Bunkhouse	Dvur Olsiny Hotel Historic
Figure 23	St. Peter of Alcantara Church	Wikipedia
Figure 24	Mute Swans	Dreamtime
Figure 25	The Woods	Don Pawlitschek
Figure 26	A Buchty	Dreamtime
Figure 27	The Dark Figure	Unsplash
Figure 28	Entrance to the Room	Dvur Olsiny Hotel Historic
Figure 29	Eliska's New Home	Unsplash
Figure 30	Gunnysack	Don Pawlitschek
Figure 31	A new Baby	Don Pawlitschek
Figure 32	Babushka	Don Pawlitschek
Figure 33	The Barn	Don Pawlitschek
Figure 34	Road to the Farm	Don Pawlitschek
Figure 35	Wooden Thread Spool	Don Pawlitschek
Figure 36	Horse Harness	Dreamtime
Figure 37	Roast Goose	Unsplash
Figure 38	Pumpkin Pie	Unsplash
Figure 39	Map Litomysl to Karvina to Skoczow	Wikipedia

Donald Pawlitschek

Cover

Gypsy and Child — William-Adolphe Bouguereau, Public Domain
Sunset on Lake Elysian — Don Pawlitschek

Back

Mack AC Truck Public Domain
The Chateau   Dreamtime
Helicon Tuba   Wikipedia
Andela At Five Don Pawlitschek

Thank you to the folks who reviewed and commented on this book.

Ron Alfolter
Jennifer Pawlitschek
Deloris Smestad

Chapter 1

THE DANCE

Litomysl, Czechoslovakia, Sat April 15, 1916
Why does a headstone cause us to reflect on the dates thereupon?
April 1st, 1898 – Sep 1, 1965
Just the birthing and the dying show. Is that all that the dates tell?
Or does the story hide in the dash between?

~~~~~~

</div>

From the ashes of rotting oak leaves springs forth, the sweet smell of a lilac splashed spring.

In the waning daylight, not quite dark nor full light, a tall figure shuffles along. Flashes of lightning from the last rolling thunderstorm reveals a tall man clutching a large black case. A tattered black hat, wet with rain and sweat, droops over his uncut blond hair. Soaked to his skin, his coarse, hand-spun shirt outlines his tight muscular body.

He walks with stiff, awkward movements, stumbling and mumbling to himself, "No want do. -- Papa say do, so me do. -- No place at home, -- make own way. -- Mama want stay. -- Papa say go -- find what to do. People -- laugh -- say me dumb -- Me stay home, but papa say -- Go! Try!"

Figure 2 Octagon Dance Hall

For fifty years, the first wedding dance of the season was always a big affair, and tonight is no exception. It is held in the Tanecní dum (dance house), a large octagon, unpainted building. Strung around the outside, wrap-around porch, are bright kerosene lanterns swinging from dainty silver chains.
~~~~~~

The lanterns flash and paint dancing shadows on the walls. This porch is the perfect place for young lovers of all ages to stroll, hand in hand, sometimes closer; lovers hoping for a lantern to run out of fuel, so to steal a kiss in the darkness or sooner.

From the door of the dance house, the lively music of a Roma band drifts out across the wet grass. The fresh night air paints an extra touch of melancholy on the music. A rain-soaked haze hovers over the newborn grass; tulips and daffodils tentatively peek at the evening sky.

A group of young men, members of the Freikorps gang*, stand in a circle on the dance house steps, smoking cigarillos and passing a bottle of brandy around while waiting for the opportunity to have some fun.

With faltering steps, the tall man steps on the first wet step, slips, trips, and falls to his knees. One suspender of his overalls slides off his shoulder and falls to his waist. He struggles to get up, rolls on his back, still gripping his black case. He tries to rise, but a filthy Freikorps foot is pressed down on his shoulder.

Ales Baum, the gang leader, spits and sneers down at the man from the top step. "What's a matter, clumsy fool, too much Slivovice (plum brandy)?" He bends over the wet man and blows a circle of smoke in his face.

"Ah -- ah -- no -- steps -- slip -- slippy." The man fervently peeks up at the gang out of the corner of his eye, then tries to stand up again.

The rest of his group crowds in. The odor of brandy, beer, and cigars, is all rolled up in a blanket of week-old sweat, emanates from them. One member gives the man a nudge with his foot. "Let us peek in your case."

The desperate man holds on with both hands and pulls his case closer as he stands up. "Ahh -- ah -- is -- tuba."

Ales snorts. "Ha! Listen guys, listen to the dummy! Tuba? Hell, only a big man can play the tuba! A smart man! It ain't you. We will try it."

__Freikorps__ (Free Corps) German voluntary armies formed in German lands

Ales raises a small swagger stick and raps the confused man's knuckles. The man howls in pain, steps back and drops his tuba case.

Ales grabs the handle of the case and jerks it away. The man mouths words, but no sound comes out. He tries again to retrieve his case, but each time he reaches out for it, the Freikorps pass it off to another gang member. Hooting and laughing, they prod the man, again and again, savoring the enjoyment of their perverse pleasure.

The man moans, "Oooh -- No take -- no take!" He wrings his hands together, rocks back and forth, and examines his shoes.

"This is no fun! We need more brandy," Ales said. "Let's go, men! Here's your damn piece of junk!" He throws the case at the man's feet. Sheets of music and a badly dented Helicon tuba roll out on the ground.

Figure 3 Helicon Tuba

Ales snarls. "Those are stinking gypsies in there; they won't let you play with them; you're a Czech and a damn poor one. They won't mix with a tongue-tangled fool." The strutting gang slaps each other on the back, congratulates each other for another victory won, and swaggers into the dance.

~~~~~~

The man picked up his papers and horn, placed them back in his case, climbed the steps, and peeked in the door. Then he slipped into the dance house, pasted himself against the wall, fidgeted from foot to foot, clutching his case to his chest.

Building his courage up, the man carefully, step by faltering step, resumed his journey into the dance house. An odorous wave of stale beer, week-old cigarette smoke, and unwashed sweat floated on the humid air. It hit him in the face as the room exploded with music. The bewildered man shuddered, peered around the hall, and blinked his eyes, adjusting to the bright light.
~~~~~~

Inside the large octagon room, lanterns hung in a crazy quilt order, splashing puddles of light on the well-worn dance floor. Warped floorboards, thanks to a leaky roof, curled and marred the floor.

Rather than fix the floor or the roof, the frugal dance house owner gave the warped floor a liberal dose of powdered dance floor wax. The boisterous dancers paid no heed to the occasional stumble. They were having too much fun dancing, drinking, and whooping it up.

The confused man edged his way up to the ticket counter at the entrance to the dance floor. "In -- please," he mumbled.

A short, thin woman, a cigarette dangling between her left-over, two front teeth, gave the man a quick smirk. "Hello, handsome," she cackled and blew smoke. "Tickets are two korunas (Czech Money) for beer, three korunas for the dance, and a little fun later costs ten korunas."

The woman rubbed her hand up his arm, twirled her bleached blonde hair with her other hand, showed her best ten-koruna grin, and winked at him. "What'll it be? Get out of those wet clothes? Treat you to a good time!"

"Aoo -- me, -- need -- look -- band -- how much -- that?

"Don't have no looking price! Five koruna gets you a ticket and a beer! And a discount for later. What'd ya say?" Her sagging face lit up with a nauseous suggestion of temptation, almost erasing her deep wrinkles.

"Aah -- five koruna -- me do." The man laid his money down.

"Good, don't forget about it later. You won't regret it!

The man weaved through rows of randomly placed, mismatched tables and chairs. Making his way to one side of the band, he sat down at a deserted corner table next to the men's bathroom. Wrinkling his nose at the odor emanating from the bathroom, he swatted flies away and set his black case on the table. *Papa always say, "Zuba, go to dance house, get a job. What me do here? -- Me want to farm, not play tuba. Make money. Playing the tuba in the barn for cows, don't put no koruna in your pocket; it just irritates the pigeons."*

Up on the bandstand, a Roma family band played. A young girl stepped down from the bandstand, slapping a tambourine in her hand and beating out a staccato rhythm. A green satin blouse shimmered as she swayed to the music; long black hair floated around her shoulders in ringlets. Her pale skin shone from her perspiring efforts as her fiery dark eyes cast out 'come-hither, maybe later,' glances.

Peeking above the case, Zuba closely watched the whirling Roma girl. Whenever she came near him, she flashed a pretend smile and coyly waved to him. He wasted his return glance by quickly lowered his head behind the case. When she turned away, he raised his head and eyed her. *Maybe find a girl like her -- Me don't talk no good. She's Roma. -- Not allow me to see her. No girl want me. All girls in Litomysl laugh at me. What me do here?*

Zuba's eyes followed her every move. The curve of her body, the gold hoop earrings, and her uncharacteristic, pale skin. Her sensual nature cast a spell of desire over him.

When she came near, his eyes quickly counted the squares of the checkered tablecloth. A whiff of her lavender splash water engulfed him, signaling her nearness. It snared him. His heart beat faster, his breath caught in his chest, and he trembled. *If only, -- but Papa said: "Zuba, stay with a simple woman that cook good. The wedding night lasts just two, three days, cooking stays longer."*

On the dimly lit bandstand sat Bolda Danka, the father, a broad, muscular man with dark curly hair. He covered his head with a bright red headscarf. He nodded in time to the music as he strummed a brightly painted guitar.

Figure 4 Cimbalom

Florica Danka, the mother, wore a yellow headscarf, a colorfully embroidered vest, and she pulled her salt and pepper dark hair, back into a bun. She sat behind her Cimbalom, her playing sticks racing over the instrument.

Their daughter, the one who danced past Zuba, is Eliska Danka. Front and center, constantly in motion, keeping the party going with a swagger and a wink. Wearing a colorful purple scarf wrapped around her raven black hair, large gold hoop earrings, and a gay yellow hip scarf around her waist, she sang, played the fiddle, and pounded a mean tambourine. When not

Figure 3a Young Eliska

performing, she timidly sat quietly behind her mother.

Eliska's short, younger brother, Hanzi Danka, squeezed out tunes on his scratchy, squealing accordion. He wore a red and gold embroidered vest and a colorful blue satin shirt with billowed bishop sleeves. Hanzi wrapped his head with an orange scarf. He smiled and winked at any girl that caught his eye.

Around Florica's feet were her one-year-old, curly-headed twin boys, Luca and Stevo, crawling on the floor. The instruments they played were wooden toys made by Bolda.

Jacob Conkova, the only non-family member, covered his balding pate with a white scarf and wore the plain clothes of a farmer. He played clarinet with a sour disposition. Between songs he complained that his pay wasn't enough for his skill level.

The inebriated dance house owner staggered up to the bandstand. "Hey, gypsy! Play some Czech music with the tuba beat!"

Bolda shrugged his broad shoulders, "We can't! Got no tuba!"

The owner blew a puff of smoke and pointed his cigar at Bolda. "Well, damn it, better get one, or you can pack up and get out of here. Who da hell do you think you are? I hired you; you play a good old polka!"

Bolda glared at the owner, "Maybe, you pay us, and we leave."

The owner wiped his hands and sweaty forehead with a dirty towel and slung the towel over his shoulder. "Pay you? Like hell I will! Get a tuba, or get your gypsy asses out of here! You have ten minutes!"

Bolda stood up, doubling his fists. Florica reached over and grabbed her husband's sleeve and pulled him back to his chair.

"Now, now Papa, please be patient; we need the money," Florica cried.

"I know. We played all night already, damn gadjo*, trying to cheat us."

Eliska interrupted, "When I was out dancing, a big gadjo was sitting in the corner. He might have a tuba. Seems slow, though."

Bolda placed his guitar down and stood up to see the man better. "He's not Roma. We don't mix with his kind. Bad enough to play for these gadje*, we can't let them in the band. Probably can't play a lick. He has no Romanipen* and looks like the mule's rear end."

"Just this time," Hanzi said. "We need the money awful bad, awful bad. Eliska ask him! Please, Papa, she can do it, watch and see."

Eliska retreated behind Florica. "No Papa, please! I'm afraid to talk to him. He peeks at me; that's bad enough. When I look at him, he puts his head down, kinda sneaky. I can guess what he's thinking. You can't trust gadjos; they are only interested in one thing."

"Don't be afraid, Eliska; I'll be close by to protect you," Hanzi cajoled.

"No!" Bolda replied, "It is not proper. I promised Eliska to Jacob!"

"Oh Papa, ask him if he plays, just this once," Florica interjected.

Bolda rubbed his chin whiskers, "All right, but Hanzi, you do it. If it doesn't work, I can kick him out, and Hanzi, get to the point, don't be jabbering so."

*gadjo Anyone who is not Roma. *gadje non-Roma plural.

*Romanipen - Roma adopted the Romanipen code to survive in certain circumstances, such as the persecution they suffer when assimilating into a foreign society. Following this code helped the Roma preserve their ethnic identities and values in each country where the Roma lived.

Hanzi twirled his little black mustache between his fingers, adjusted his vest, and ran across the dance floor. Coins, dangling from his belt, tinkled out a rhythm on the way to the table. "You got a name, big man?"

"Ah -- Zuba,"

"What do you have in your case?"

"Tu -- ba."

"Zuba! Zuba with a tuba, it works, it works," Hanzi tweaked his mustache again. "Are you hiding a horse or your lunch in there too?"

Zuba slowly raised his head from behind the case but wouldn't look Hanzi in the eye. His mouth shaped words and finally stammered out a weak moan, "No -- No, -- horse."

"Well, you are something else," Hanzi said. "Why do you have your black hat pulled down over your ears? Your ears cold? Bet you have big ears! Big ears! Stick right up through the hat, I bet. You know what? I'll cut holes so they can stick out. Some holes, so the ears stick out, that's what I'll do." Hanzi drew a small silver dagger from his vest. "It's the thing to do. See this?"

Zuba's words tumbled around in his mouth. Sweat beaded on his upper lip and dripped on the table. "Ah. -- No -- doon do -- dat!"

Hanzi raised the silver dagger. His teasing tone now took on a hard edge. "I'll cut you some holes. Let the ears stick out. You will look like a donkey pulling a hay rack! A hayrack, I tell you! Just a big old donkey! Can you hee-haw like a donkey? I hear nothing else out of you."

Hanzi reached for Zuba's hat, but before he laid a finger on the hat, Zuba wrapped each of Hanzi's childlike hands in each of his big hands. "No- do," Zuba said. "No, -- hurt -- hat."

"Let me go, you... you... before I kick the devil out of you!" Hanzi screamed and kicked at Zuba.

Zuba stood up. Squeezing Hanzi's hands in an iron grip, Zuba raised his arms toward the ceiling. Painful concern crept across Hanzi's face as his feet left the floor, and his dagger clattered away.

"No -- do -- dat," Zuba said. "Me -- no -- want -- hurt -- you."

"Let me down, you, you ... I'll stomp the devil out of you, I say! You will wish you were a donkey when I get through with you; put me down, and you'll see," Hanzi stammered, as his eyes flitted from Zuba's face to the bandstand. *Where is papa? Help me.*

Zuba shook him. "Make -- no -- trouble?"

"Put me down, or I'll throw you against the wall. That wall over there. Right through, and I'll mop this place up with you, bust you up, stomp you into the mud," Hanzi wailed.

Zuba stood perplexed, not knowing what to do next.

Hanzi blubbered, "You better be careful; I'm small but tougher than old horse leather, rougher than old dry corn cob, I say! I don't take no sass from a gadjo." By this time, Hanzi's eyes watered, and he blinked a punctuation mark with every word he said. "Papa, please come! Help me!"

"You -- no -- gonna -- do -- dat -no more?"

"Let me go before I really get mad; I can get sore, you know. There will be hell to pay, I tell you! I just wanted to see if you are a tuba player. And you jump me!" The pain in Hanzi's hands went from 'damn, that hurts' to 'passing out' pain. "Papaaa!"

At the mention of the tuba, Zuba's face lit up with a 'Christmas morning' grin. He relaxed his grip, and Hanzi fell to the floor.

"I -- play -- tuu -- ba -- good," Zuba said.

Bolda heard Hanzi's call for help. He ran over and sized the large man up. "I might teach you a lesson!" He hesitated, picked Hanzi up, and brushed off the dance floor wax from Hanzi's back. "Are you all right?"

"I'm all right! Don't fight him, Papa," Hanzi said, trembling and rubbing his bruised hands. "I scared him, so he put me down. I was teasing him, and I guess he can't take it."

Bolda shook Hanzi by the shoulders, "Did you do anything to start this?"

Hanzi squirmed and dodged the question. "Papa, you know what? I found out he don't have no horse in the case; he has a tuba!"

Hanzi babbled on, "Just what we need! And in a place like this, Papa, not his lunch Papa! A tuba! He said he plays it too! So, he says. Maybe just blowing steam. Should we try him, Papa? If he can't play it, at least I tried. Right, Papa?"

Bolda eyed Zuba warily but stayed out of the reach of the big man's long arms. "I don't know; seems daft in the head. Play the tuba? Don't think so. That takes a man with thinking skills. Do you play by ear? We play by ear, no music on paper."

Hanzi peered around from behind Bolda and giggled. "With those ears, he should do a bang-up job, simply great. Play on either side, I bet. Hee-Haw, Hee-Haw, you play by ear, big guy? Huh, no way," Hanzi said.

"I -- play -- tuu -- ba -- gud," Zuba said, a note of calmness and pride crept into his voice.

Bolda slyly glanced at Zuba and stated, "Well, I tell you what, we need a tuba player in the band. You must try out, of course. I need to hear you play. What you say?"

"Me -- play -- tuu -- ba -- gud -- me -- show. -- come tomorrow and -- play for you." Zuba pulled his hat down on his head, his trembling hand grasped his tuba case, and he turned to leave. *Need to -- get out of here. Go back to farm. Me showed Papa. Me come here. -- Leave before me wet pants.*

Hanzi spit on the floor. "Tomorrow? Wait until tomorrow? I told you he was blowing steam. Bet he never comes around again,"

Zuba stopped, turned back bewildered, "No -- me -- come."

Bolda winked at Hanzi and said to Zuba, "Well, we'll do it right now. Just a tryout, no pay mind you,"

Zuba glanced at the dance floor. A crowd had gathered and stared at him. The bucket of courage he had filled up, while walking the seven miles to the dance house, now quickly leaked dry.

"Oo -- me -- doon -- know -- lots -- of -- people -- see -- me -- doon -- know -- Oo -- no." Zuba moaned.

"Don't worry, we'll put you in the back; all anyone will see is your tuba. You can hide back there," Bolda said, waving at the bandstand.

"Ya, way back, out in the yard or by the lake! Is that far enough away?" Hanzi chuckled and sneered to no one in particular, "I told you he is a big bag of air. He can't play the tuba a lick." Zuba cashed in his last scraps of courage and replied, "Me -- play -- tuu -- ba -- gud -- me -- show," Zuba nodded at Bolda. "Me -- show -- right -- now."

"Go to the bandstand. I've got business to attend to. I'll be right back," Bolda said, relieved that things might work out.

Bolda found the dance house owner leaning against the wall, leering at a barmaid and rubbing her back. She reluctantly pretended to accept the unwanted attention as she calmly smoked a cigarette.

"We have a Czech tuba player; can we get paid, please?" Bolda said firmly, trying to show the owner that he was in charge.

The owner didn't look up but kept rubbing the barmaid's back. "What tuba player?"

"Right up there! He's taking the tuba out of the case?" Bolda said.

"OK, I'll pay you after the polka," said the owner, still nibbling on the barmaid's left ear.

"All right, you better," Bolda said.

Bolda walked back across the floor, climbed the bandstand, and sat next to his wife, Florica.

"Did you get a tuba player? Is the owner going to pay us now?" A worried Florica asked.

"Yes, we get paid after the polka," Bolda said, through his clenched teeth.

"The tuba player, is he any good? A little slow, I think we should forget about him," Eliska said, retreating further behind her mother.

Bolda picked up his guitar. "He'll be all right; we'll keep the big ox around long enough to get paid,"

"All right, big fellow, can you play the Praha Polka?" Bolda said.

"Ya -- Farewell to Prague – sure -- need -- valve -- oil first." Zuba reached behind his chair to get the valve oil from his instrument case.

When he did this, Jacob Conkova slipped up and stuffed a large rag into his tuba. Zuba oiled and made sure the valves slid up and down to perfection. "OK – me ready!"

The band launched onto the music, and Zuba played. The usual sound of the booming tuba sounded like a constipated cow. Zuba hesitated, took his lips from the mouthpiece, and said, "No -- sound." A frustrated Zuba examined his tuba thoroughly.

Jacob guffawed, slapping his knee, "See the big ox, he can't make a noise with his mouth or tuba!"

"Jacob, please don't; we will lose the money. He might be all right," Eliska said quietly.

"I want to have a little fun with this gadjo; what's the matter with that? You soft on this man-child? Mind your own business, woman," Jacob muttered. His eyes burned a contemptuous stare at her. "We aren't married yet."

"I'm sorry to upset you, but if he can't play, we don't get paid. How is that any good?"

"We don't need him."

"We need him; shut up, Jacob!" Bolda hissed under his breath.

Bolda stepped up and pulled the rag from Zuba's horn and threw it at Jacob. "Here's your trouble. Trouble begets trouble, doesn't it, Jacob?"

Zuba's face blossomed a bright red, his mouth moved, but not a word escaped. *Me so dumb --in front of the beautiful lady -- What me do here? -- should be in the goat barn; that's where me belong, in the goat barn. – Me? -- A great tuba player? -- Will my horn talk for me? -- With a rag in it? -- Didn't even see it. -- Me dumb enough to jump high in a room with a low ceiling.*

Eliska, sensing Zuba's turmoil, spoke up, "It will be all right. Never mind Jacob; he means well but sometimes doesn't think too far ahead. Just play your horn; you will do fine."

Zuba's face beamed; a warm rush came over him. *She say me do okay.*

"Are you ready to play Zuba?" Bolda asked, casting a stern glance at Jacob.

Zuba's mouth froze in a silly grin; he nodded and lowered his eyes. He raised his tuba mouthpiece to his lips and played. "Bom bump Bom bump Bom bump Bom bump Bom bump Bom bump Bom bump Bom bump."

The band joined in, and the Praha Polka was on its way. When the song finished, all were pleased that the polka had gone well, but no one said a word to Zuba. All except Eliska, she nodded and gave him a "thumbs up."

Upon seeing this, Jacob burned with rage and jealousy. He threw his clarinet in the case and spit on the floor.

Bolda left the bandstand to find the dance house owner and collect his money. After finding him, he came back with a handful of cash yielding five hundred korunas.

"That's it for tonight, let's go home," he said to the band, and then he paid Jacob fifty korunas.

Jacob said, "I bet you will pay me more when I am your son-in-law, eh?

"I paid you fair. We agreed." Bolda said.

"I carry the band; I should get more," Jacob replied.

"We could play without you next time, and you get nothing; that's fair too," Bolda snapped.

Zuba was putting his tuba away when Eliska timidly approached him. "Thank you. You play well."

A red flush crept up Zuba's face, slipping up his forehead, under his blond hair; his breath came gasps as he tried to speak, but a nod was his only reply.

Jacob pushed himself between Zuba and Eliska. "You know we're to be married, don't you?" he said to Zuba, as he pulled Eliska tightly to him. "My Papa paid half the dowry, already, and Bolda arranged it."

"Oh Jacob, please don't cause trouble. You are my intended, and we will marry." Eliska said. "Zuba wasn't flirting; I was nice because he helped us out. Nothing wrong with that, is there?"

"Just so he knows which way the crow flies. I'll have nobody messing with my bride-to-be. I saw how he watched you when you turned your back! I won't allow him to talk to you again! Do you hear me?"

"Talk to me? He hasn't said a word! He won't even look me in the eye!"

"You know what I mean!" Jacob jabbed his finger in Zuba's chest, "and as for you, you big dumb donkey, stay away, or I'll place a curse on you."

Bolda came up and intervened. "Jacob, will you escort Eliska home? We're stopping at grocers and be home later. Remember your manners!... Hanzi, are you coming?"

"Well, I thought, I'd stay awhile, see there's this girl. What a girl, she keeps making eyes at me, smiling at me, dances every dance, and slows down at the bandstand." Hanzi drew a deep breath and continued, "I have to talk to her. Won't take too long. I'll be along quick. You'll see, just say hello. Just hello, it won't hurt, will it? No, it shouldn't. OK, Papa? What you say, Papa? I won't be long!"

"All right, all right! You wear me out. Just don't get into any trouble."

Zuba stood off to one side, fidgeting with his head down, and he muttered to Bolda, "Yu. -- Like. -- way --me -- play?"

"It was all right, I guess, an audition! No pay!"

"Me -- play -- again -- with -- you?"

"Ya, another time, in the summer. I'll let you know." Bolda dismissed him with a wave of his hand.

"Me -- play -- tuu -- ba-gud."

"Yeah, sure, another time," Bolda packed up his guitar and walked out. Zuba clutched his tuba case under his arm, and with his head down, he stumbled out of the dance house.

Jacob and Eliska picked up their instruments and strolled, arm and arm, out the door. They were walking down a wooded dirt path that led to Litomysl. Ales Baum and his Freikorps gang followed behind. When Jacob and Eliska entered a tree-covered part of the lane, the gang surrounded them.

"Hey gypsy boy, how about sharing the korunas they paid you tonight?" Ales snarled, hands on his hips, with his gang backing him.

"Go away and leave us be." Jacob clutched Eliska by the arm, and they continued walking.

"Why don't we take it and share your girlfriend too?" Ales grabbed Jacob by the shoulder, twisted him around, and pulled back his fist, preparing to strike Jacob.

"No! Run Eliska!" Jacob cried, as he twisted loose and ran down the path.

"Wait, don't leave me," Eliska cried out, running after him.

They ran for several yards when a low-hanging tree branch caught one of Eliska's gold earrings, ripped the earring from her ear. She screamed, whirled, and tumbled to the ground. She lay, petrified, her ear bleeding as the Freikorps surrounded her.

Jacob turned, hesitated, and then ran away yelling, "I'll get help!"

"Oh, such a pretty gypsy you are." Ales held his hand out to her. "Here, let me help you up."

Eliska hesitantly took his hand. With a quick jerk, Ales pulled her up and into his arms. "Now there, isn't that better, sweet gypsy girl? You have nothing to worry on. Ooooh, your poor little ear, it's bleeding." He reached down and pulled Eliska's skirt up to her ear, exposing her slender legs. "Let me dab it with your skirt."

"Now, aren't those lovely legs? They are as good as any German girl. Hey boys! They say gypsy girls are put together differently than our girls. Let's see!" Ales's garlic breath was in Eliska's face as he reached under her skirt, but before he went any further, Eliska kneed him in the groin.

"Ooh, you gypsy bitch!" moaned Ales, dropping to his knees, holding his groin with both hands. "Boys! Toss her around! Soften her up!"

The Freikorps grabbed her, one Freikorp on each arm, formed a circle, and tossed her from one gang member to another.

"Toss her good!" Ales moaned as he stumbled to his feet.

Eliska flew around the gang, screaming. Frequently, a gang member stuck out his leg and tripped her to the ground. Each time she fell, they'd grab her by the arms, jerk her to her feet, and throw her around the circle again.

Meanwhile, still in the dance house, Hanzi was in earnest conversation with the girl who had caught his eye. Hearing his sister's screams, he raced out of the dance house and saw that Eliska was in trouble.

He reached inside his vest to get his knife, but it was still on the floor of the dance house. Without hesitation, he raced to help his sister and leaped on the back of the biggest gang member.

Hanzi wrapped his arms around the man's neck and held on for dear life. "Leave my sister alone, or you will be sorry; you'll be sorry you messed with my family. I got you now. Do you give up? You messed with the wrong guy, I tell you. Give up, I say!"

"Eldric! Hartmut! Kill the little bastard; then we'll have a go at his sister." Ales moaned, still holding his groin.

The two gang members pulled Hanzi off and threw him to the ground and kicked him violently.

A large man stood by the outskirts of the group; he hesitated and then stepped into the circle. "Doon -- do," Zuba stammered. "Leave -- be!" He paused again. *They no stop. What do now? -- Maybe bulldog. -- No want hurt -- Maybe separate them like two hogs fighting.*

Eliska screamed, "Please don't hurt Hanzi, please!" Her screams awoke a fierce fury within Zuba's heart. A wave of anger swept over him as he cried out, "No More!"

He stepped behind Eldric, and Hartmut grabbed Eldric's collar in one hand and Hartmut's collar in the other hand, and with a quick tug, he pulled both backward. Off-balance, they flew behind Zuba, rolling butt over teakettle, on the ground.

"Get the stupid fool! Kick him good!" Ales yelled and charged Zuba. He head-butted Zuba in the stomach, but Zuba didn't flinch. With one mighty push to the back of Ales's head, Zuba sent the gang leader, face down, to the ground.

Zuba turned and wrapped his arms around two more gang members, a headlock with one arm over each of their necks and squeezed. "No -- more -- hurt!" He let go of the bulldogged gang members. They gagged and bent over, holding their throats.

Zuba grabbed them by the seat of the pants and shoved them into the rest of the gang, collapsing the entire gang into a pile of squirming arms and legs. Hanzi, not to be outdone, jumped into the fray and delivered a few well-placed kicks.

The Freikorps gang hesitated, sensing they were in over their heads; they picked up Ales and ran off.

Hanzi strutted, spit, and yelled after them. "Run, you cursed Germans. I told you not to mess with me! May the crows peck out your eyes, and the dogs pee on your beds!"

"Are you all right? I showed them didn't I Eliska?" Hanzi helped his dazed sister up.

"My back hurts, and I twisted my leg," Eliska replied shakily.

Zuba picked up Hanzi's headpiece and handed it to him.

"Zuba, where? ... How?" Eliska said.

"Oh, he helped a little, holding my scarf, so it doesn't get dirty. You know how wild I get when I get mad." Hanzi strutted, swinging at imaginary foes.

"I think he helped more than that, dear brother." Eliska brushed herself off. "Thank you, Zuba."

Zuba hung his head and stared at his shoelaces. He tried to speak, but only a slight croak came out.

"Sounds like you swallowed a frog in the fight," Hanzi teased. "Zuba is a zaba, a frog."

"Now be kind Hanzi, he helped us twice tonight. He is a velky tichy zaba (big silent frog)," Eliska said, a teasing glint flickered in her eyes. She put one hand on Zuba's arm and placed her other hand in his work calloused right hand. "Will it hurt your feelings if I call you a big silent frog?"

Zuba stood silently, heart-pounding, longing to look at her, to talk to her, but his eyes pondered the pebbles on the ground. *Lavender splash water smells good* -- He dropped her hand and reached to take her other hand off his arm. *Shouldn't touch me. -- me should be hurt. -- Call me a big silent frog. -- that kinda nice, -- me like -- Wish me could tell her.*

As Zuba's hand rested on Eliska, Bolda, Jacob, and a group of Roma men ran up.

"Take your filthy hands off of my daughter, you fool!" Bolda lashed out with his walking stick hitting Zuba's arm.

"Are you hurt, my love?" Jacob said, rushing to Eliska's side.

Eliska pleaded with her father, "Stop Papa! Zuba helped us. If it weren't for him, I'm afraid of what could have happened." She glared at Jacob. "Where were you, my husband to be? Where were you when I needed you? When the Germans jumped us?"

"Oh, the best thing to do was to get help; see how well it worked out?" Jacob unashamedly denied his cowardice.

"I whipped them, Papa! I got mad! Bang! Boom! Bam! I lowered the boom," Hanzi proclaimed.

"Yes, Hanzi, I bet you did. Now, take your sister home, have Mama treat her ear," Bolda said.

Eliska clung to Hanzi's arm with one hand while holding her side with the other. She limped along beside him on their way home. Jacob hurried to catch up, and when he did, he reached out his hand to Eliska, and she slapped it away. "See how well that works out," Eliska snapped.

Bolda faced Zuba and stamped his walking stick hard on the ground, "It's best you not come around Eliska no more. I'm grateful for your help, but we Roma can handle it. There wouldn't be trouble if I hadn't let you play in the band. Understand? Roma and gadje don't mix."

Zuba hung his head, nodded, and turned away before Bolda could notice the tears in his eyes. *Done it again. -- Always mess up. -- Why can't me stay with my people even though they make fun of me? Me deserve it. -- am so dumb!*

~~~~~~

Chapter 2

THE BULL

Palzek Farm Outside Litomysl Czechoslovakia Sun, April 16, 1916,

A sweaty Petr Palzek was frantically chasing a Brown Swiss cow, trying to get her into the milking barn. He called out to his wife Emilia and son Zuba.

Figure 5 Brown Swiss Cow

"Will somebody help me get this damn cow back in the barn?"

Zuba was behind the barn, repairing the windmill used for pumping water and grinding grain. Wiping his hands, he ran toward his father's voice.

Figure 6 Windmill

Coming around the barn, he came to an abrupt halt, face to face with a large Holstein bull.

This colossal beast has escaped from the Antonie Dusek farm on the far hillside.

The bull resented this detour. He was on a quest to capitalize on his romantic intentions.
~~~~~~

The sleepy-eyed cow, with the same lovelorn feelings, moaned a mournful moo.

The swinging tail of the angry bull had smeared his feces on his rump. Snot snorted out of his nostrils as the lovesick bull pawed the ground, threw dirt and manure up onto his vast black and white back.

Figure 7 Holstein Bull

The frustrated bull bellered, raised his tail high, lowered his head, and charged! Zuba scrambled for the fence, but he tripped over his feet and fell into a long wooden water trough and then rolled behind the trough. Zuba hid as the angry bull attacked from the other side. The fierce animal rammed his broad head hard against the trough, lifting it off the ground. The trough fell on Zuba, dousing him with brackish water. The bull pushed and pushed, pinning Zuba between the fence and the trough.

"Help, -- help!" a battered Zuba cried out.

Petr came around the corner with a wooden staff in his hand. He raised his muscular arm high above his six-foot height; brought the staff down with one swift blow to the head of the Holstein bull, diverting the bull's attention from Zuba.

Antonie Dusek had inserted a large steel ring through the bull's nose just for such of an occasion. Petr grabbed the nose ring with both hands, and with all his might, jerked it upward. The beast gave out a wild bellow, whirled, and raced for home. When the bull spun, Petr's hand was trapped in the nose ring, and the rampaging animal drug him along.

The unbearable pain in the bull's nose caused him to turn to attack the demon holding onto his nose. When the bull turned, Petr could release his hand from the ring.

With the pain removed, the bull forgot about Petr. Tail high, the bull charged across the field back to the Dusek farm.

"Are you hurt, Zuba?" A shaken Petr pulled his red bandana out and carefully wiped Zuba's cut lip. "Any other hurts?"

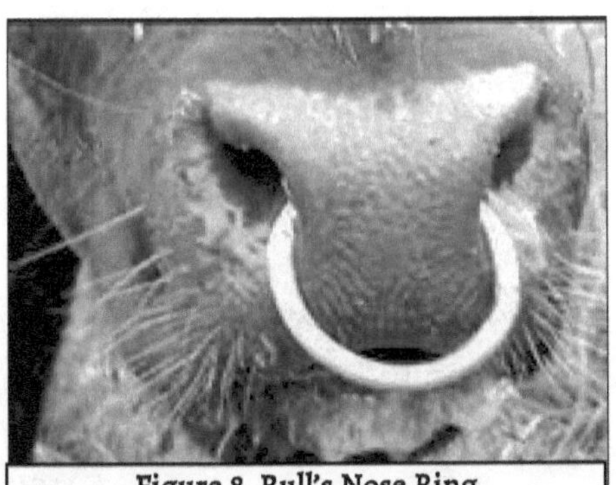

Figure 8 Bull's Nose Ring

"No- Papa -- shook up -- a little. That -- one -- mean -- bull."

"Ya, but he makes good calves. We must get him back in the late summer to breed the cow."

Petr brushed manure from his overalls and pulled his hat down tight on his head. "Help me get the cow in the barn, and then we go eat. First, we clean up by the well. Mama will get upset if she sees the mess the bull made of us. Don't tell her about the bull! She worries too much now."

Entering the house, the smell of chicken soup and sauerkraut met the men. Zuba's mother, Emilia, bustled around the combination kitchen and dining room. She was round and squat, made for traction and not speed. Her graying hair was pulled up into a tight bun. Her big floral apron, attached to her ample waist, covered a plain sackcloth dress. She was, as Petr loved to say, "husky, but nice to have around to keep a body warm at night." Whenever he said this, she'd lovingly rub Petr's bald head and plant a kiss firmly on top.

"Clean the manure off your shoes outside, put it in the flower bed, wash up quick, time to eat," Emilia admonished them as they entered. She was used to the smell of livestock in the house, but her floors must be clean. The Palzek family sat and bowed their heads and intoned the prayer.

The table was heavy laden with cabbage soup, chicken with sauerkraut, big glasses of milk, and a plum cake that finished the meal. No sound filled the room except the melody of slurping.

Finally, with a big burp from Petr, the meal finished. Emilia beamed. She knew her husband enjoyed the food when he ended it with his improvised thunder praise.

"I wish we didn't have to work on Sundays," sighed Emilia as she cleared the table.

"Ya, but the cows need milking, and everything needs feeding. Even Jesus said, Get the donkey out of the well on the Sabbath," Petr said, proudly quoting the scriptures.

Zuba chuckled, "I bet he would have -- left the cow in the pen -- if he knew the bull was loose." He knew he had misspoken when Petr gave him a hard stare. Petr held a finger to his lips and shook his head, no.

"If Jesus can walk on water, he can handle a Holstein bull, don't be disrespectful," Emilia said playfully, pulling Zuba's ear.

Then Emilia scurried off to the nearby kitchen sink, with her arms full of dishes pressed against her ample bosom. She halted, frozen, as worry crossed her face. "The bull was loose?"

"Oh ya, nothing to worry on; I said a little prayer and shooshed him back to the Dusek place. Easy as pie!" Petr responded calmly.

Emilia stared hard at Petr. "When I shoosh up and bake a pie, I don't get no cut lip and tear the seat out of my overalls!"

Petr changed the subject. "It will be good when we have Petr Jr. home, from the army, to help farm. What do you think of that, Zuba?" Petr rubbed his bald head and passed the sauerkraut to his youngest son.

"That's good Papa, -- the oldest should take over."

"Ya, it's right, but what about you, Zuba?"

"Me go to town and work for the coal company, -- they need mechanics, -- me talk to foreman at church -- can get hired. Pays better -- than farming." Zuba's confident words were misleading. *Have to be brave. -- Not enough farm here. -- Don't want, leave. -- was born here.*

"Litomysl is seven miles away. So far, you go. You sure?" Emilia's motherly worries showed on her weather-beaten face. Zuba was her baby. Even at six feet two and two hundred and forty pounds!

"Ya Mama, me walk it easy," Zuba said. *It's -- only way. Petr Jr.is the oldest, he married a nice girl in town, and they move to the farm. -- me be in the way.*

"Oh, do you have to go so far? You can stay and help out here," Emilia threw a worried glance at Petr.

"He'll do just fine; he's a Palzek, isn't he?" Petr boasted. "There's a time when the chick needs to leave the nest. Remember how we were when we first met? I said, we run away. My Papa said, slow down, everything in its time." Petr took a big pull from his pipe and continued, "Now is Zuba's time. Take your tuba along. You might play some. I bought my first cow with what I earned playing my tuba."

Emilia came to Zuba's chair and stroked his back. "You know what the doctor said; don't get too excited cause you don't talk no good."

"It be OK, Mama," Zuba remembered the long journey to Prague. *-- A whole week, -- doctors stick wood in my mouth and ears -- tell different words for me to talk, -- the more they did, the less me could.* "Selective mutism*," *doctors said, "he might grow out of it, but not likely, just keep him calm."*

The big city, tall buildings and fancy people, fancy clothes. -- Look at me and my plain country clothes. -- Turn away. -- Don't want go from home. Noises scare me and hurt my ears. -- How get by? -- nothing for me here.

~~~~~~

*Selective mutism: This is the consistent failure to speak in social situations. Persons with this condition can speak and understand the language but do not speak in certain situations. This is often thought to be shyness, lack of intelligence, or rudeness to others. A child can be silent at school but speak freely at home. The condition interferes with educational or job advancement.

However, many persons with selective mutism have above-average intelligence, are creative, love art or music, and have empathy and sensitivity to others' feelings. A strong sense of right and wrong are all trademarks of this disorder. ~~~~~~
~~~~~~

Chapter 3

RUNAWAY

On the Road to Litomysl Czechoslovakia, Mon April 17, 1916

Zuba finished packing his clothes when Emilia scurried in. She carried a big bag of apples, smaller packages of dried goat, stuffed dumplings, and pickled eggs.

"Just a little something for the road," she said, wiping her tears on her apron. "Now, you stay with Aunt Dominika. Here are twenty korunas I save for you. Don't spend it foolishly!" She pinned the money to the inside of his shirt.

"Ya Mama, -- me miss your cooking." *Sure, miss you taking care of me.*

"Don't forget to change your underwear at least once a week," Emilia admonished. She was still fussing over her youngest son as he walked out the door.

The day was hot, the road dusty, as Zuba made his way toward

Figure 9 Roma Horses

Litomysl. He walked six miles and had eaten all the food that his mother fixed for him. He was kneeling and drinking water from a wayside stream when the rumble of horses and a wagon approaching shook loose ripples on the still stream. Standing up, he saw the horses racing toward him at a breakneck speed.

"Papa, you drive too fast!" Eliska screamed.

"Never mind, girl, I know what I'm doing," Bolda replied angrily. "You sound like your mother." Bolda slapped the reins again, and the horses surged forward.

There was an unseen washout in the road ahead, a deep rut caused by the run-off of the melting winter snow.

The horses leaped it with ease, but the wagon wasn't so lucky. It crashed down into the washout and bounced back up again, tipped up sideways on its two left wheels, and Bolda flew off into the bushes along the roadside. After he fell, the wagon righted itself, and Eliska fell backward, over and behind the seat. She tried to reach the reins but couldn't keep her balance and kept falling back into the wagon.

Figure 9 Racing Horses

Zuba heard her screams and saw the driverless wagon, pulled by the terrified horses, coming toward him. He planted himself in the middle of the road and waited until the horses were next to him. As they raced alongside him, he jumped up and grabbed one of the frightened animals around the neck. Unable to stop the horses, they dragged Zuba down the road. The heels of his new work boots threw up clouds of dust, plowing furrows along the ground. *"O Mother, Mary, what me got into?!"* Zuba prayed, but there was no time for praying; the horses were fast approaching, a curve in the road. A curve that a sensible man would only drive at a slow speed, not at the breakneck pace they were going. Boulders lined one side of the road, and a nasty drop-off on the other would soon force the issue.

It was now or never! Zuba tried to pull himself up onto the back of the horse that was dragging him.

He slid back off from the sweaty horse. Zuba tried again, but the slippery horse made it hard for him to secure a handhold.

He finally grabbed a piece of the harness and climbed on. Inching his way up the neck of the horse, he stuck his finger in one of the horse's nostrils and his thumb in the other nostril, squeezed hard, and pulled the horse's head back toward him.

As he did, Zuba reached over with his other hand and snagged the reins of the second horse. He pulled hard on the reins, leading to the bit in the second horse's mouth. When Zuba pulled the first horse's nostrils back, the horse stumbled and fell. The second horse also fell, throwing Zuba off. Zuba landed hard on his back. The wagon overturned, and Eliska fell out, landing on Zuba.

Zuba lay moaning on the ground, mouth full of dirt. *That no good idea. -- Something soft and warm is on my chest. -- O Lord, a horse fell on me! -- me smell sweet lavender splash water. --- Eliska???*

Embarrassed, Zuba sat up quickly, and a dazed Eliska rolled unceremoniously onto the ground.

"You -- aw - right?" Zuba stammered.

Befuddled Eliska, her black hair falling over her face, dirt on her arms, and a torn dress, sat up, "Where did you come from?"

Zuba's face reddened, "You -- in -- trouble -- me give -- hand. You -- OK?

"I'm all right; my head hurts, is there blood on my face?"

"Just -- a -- hurt -- above -- eye," Zuba pulled a red bandanna out of his back pocket and reached up to wipe the wound on Eliska's eye. Eliska pulled away at his touch.

"Me -- sorry. -- bandanna -- clean. Mama -- give -- me."

"No, it's not that, it hurts; where's Papa?"

"You -- the -- only -- one -- on -- the -- wagon."

"He fell off on the road; we have to find him!"

Zuba and Eliska ran back down the road. They called for Bolda, stopping every five feet to part the bushes and peer underneath.

Hearing a low moan coming from the undergrowth, they parted the bushes and found Bolda, with his face pressed into the ground.

"Oh, Papa!" Eliska screamed. "Are you all right? You're not dead, are you?" She grabbed Zuba by the arm, "Oh, do something, Zuba, please do something!"

Zuba carefully rolled Bolda over, put an arm under him, and helped him to sit up. Dirt painted his face and blood crusted in his black hair, and a trickle of blood ran from his mouth.

"Oh, Papa! Are you dead? Oh, no, Papa!" Eliska gently slipped her arm under Bolda's head and wiped the blood from his mouth. She pulled a small leather pouch from inside her blouse, opened it and took out a pinch of a white powdered substance, and rubbed underneath Bolda's long nose.

Bolda moaned and opened his eyes. "What happened?" He said, puffing, spitting out blood and dirt.

"I told you, you were driving too fast." Eliska wiped dirt from his face. "Are you all right?"

"I think I wrestled a bear," Bolda groaned, "My arm hurts."

"Oh Papa, this is bad; the arm is sticking out funny," Eliska said.

"It -- broke," Zuba added.

Bolda shakily rose to his feet and glared at Zuba. "What are you doing here? I told you to stay away from Eliska!"

"Papa, don't!" Eliska exclaimed. "Zuba stopped the horses and helped me!"

"Are the horses OK?" Bolda looked around, still dazed, "and the wagon?"

"Horse -- break -- leg," Zuba stammered. "Me can -- tip -- wagon -- back -- up -- all right?"

"Come on, Zuba, let's get the wagon up, hitch the other horse to it and get Papa to a doctor." Eliska brushed the dirt off Bolda's back.

Bolda leaned on Zuba and Eliska as they carefully escorted him over to the overturned wagon.

One horse was struggling to free himself from the tangled leather harness. The other horse lay quiet, gasping and shivering.

Eliska reached into Bolda's vest and pulled out a long dagger. "Here, Zuba, cut the horse loose?"

Zuba did as asked. He untangled the harness and helped the unharmed horse back on its feet. He reached under the side of the wagon and, with a mighty heave, righted it back on its wheels.

"Oh Zuba, what about the poor horse?" Eliska said. "He's in pain; can you help him?"

"No -- fix," Zuba said. "Get -- you -- Papa -- to doctor."

They loaded Bolda into the wagon, and Eliska climbed into the driver's seat. She grabbed the reins, and with a "clisk, clisk," sound from her mouth, she drove the wagon towards Litomysl.

"Thank you, Zuba," Eliska cried out over her shoulder. "Thank you so much! Goodbye."

"Ya, sure," then Zuba murmured, "She could have left me ride along with her!" He shrugged his shoulders and waited until the wagon was out of sight and then whispered to the fallen horse. "Me sorry but got to put you out of -- misery." The dazed horse let out a fearful whinny. Zuba firmly gripped Bolda's dagger and, placing one foot on the horse's neck, reached down, and cut the horse's throat. The horse kicked futilely as the blood gushed from the poor beast's neck, soaking Zuba's new shoes.

~~~~~~
~~~~~~

Chapter 4

THE FIRST DAY IN TOWN

Litomysl, Czechoslovakia Tues, April 18, 1916

The village dogs yipped and licked at Zuba's blood-soaked shoes. He kicked at the dogs as he walked up the dusty Litomysl street. He came to a small stucco cottage. A stone walkway, worn from years of use, wound its way to the front door. Along each side of the walkway, cheerful petunias splashed out a colorful greeting. A lilac bush in the front yard wafted its fragrance, calling wayward bees.

Zuba pushed the slatted wooden gate open, its rusty hinges protested, and a bell tied to the gate tinkled. He debated knocking on the door. *Me look terrible.* He brushed his clothes. *Clothes dirty and torn. Blood all over my new shoes.*

He brushed his clothes off again, reached up, and gave the wooden knocker a light knock. His hesitant door knock brought an elderly lady to the door. She wore a plain sackcloth dress; her gray hair hung loosely around her shoulders; she bore a striking resemblance to Zuba's mother.

"Saints be praised, Zuba! Come in; you must be tired. Are you hungry? I've nice blood sausage and sauerkraut in the oven," Aunt Dominika Palzekova* chattered. "You're hungry, aren't you? Sit. Sit down. How are you doing? Is you folks all right? Are the crops good? I miss your mother."

"You -- ask -- questions -- fast -- Let -- me -- catch -- breath," Zuba replied, laying his hat on the table beside him. "Ever -- ting -- good. Me -- comes -- for a job at -- coal company."

"Well, I declare, Zuba, you will talk my leg off, and my good one at that," Aunt Dominika laughed heartily, cutting up the blood sausage. "You will stay in the spare bedroom, won't you? It's nice to have someone to talk to. When does your job start?"

"Me start -- to -- morrow."

"Well eat, I have fresh bedding in the guest room; you can sleep there."

Note: *In Czech, the married woman adds 'ova' to her husband's name. Dominika married Georg Palzek, so her married name was Palzekova, not Palzek.*

~~~~~~

The next day, the sun was a faint lemon glow in the eastern sky as Zuba walked the mile to the coal yard. Once inside, black choking coal dust swirled in the air, kicked up by Zuba's shoes, but mainly from the trucks coming and going. The yard was at the end of Nadrazni street on the northwest side of Litomysl. Railroad trains, loaded with coal, sat on the tracks that ran close by.

On the other side of the yard was the Loucna River, where the drivers washed the coal trucks and made them ready for duty. Huge piles of coal were arranged in rows, each piled

Figure 10. Mack AC truck in the coal yard.

according to the quality of the coal. Massive Mack trucks, belching exhaust, lumbered in and out.

They carried their loads of coal to Prague and other parts of Czechoslovakia. Sky punching cranes dumped the coal into the waiting truck boxes.

Zuba dodged back and forth between the trucks on his way to the superintendent's office. It's five AM, one hour before his interview time. Zuba is prepared to earn his keep! *Papa say, "Without work, there are no cakes. He who's late won't be fed." Eating is my favorite thing.*
~~~~~~

Zuba entered the dingy coal office. A single light bulb cast a pale-yellow light across the room. He walked over to a wooden bench, sat, and waited. *It was early when me got up. Didn't sleep good. Dominika's bed too soft.* Zuba's head slumped, and he fell into a nodding sleep.

A woman entered the office at five-thirty and hung her scarf and coat on the coat rack, next to several wet, rain slickers. Smiling, she tip-toed to the sleeping Zuba.

"Oh, by Sara E Kali (Saint Sara)! Who do we have here?" she said. "A sleepy frog!" Reaching out, she slyly tipped Zuba's hat off his head. Zuba awoke with a jerk and gazed into the green eyes of Eliska. He blinked his eyes, trying to wipe this dream away, but the sweet scent of her lavender splash water tickled his nose. He stood up, knocking the wooden bench over.

Eliska blushed at his reaction, "You sure make a bunch of noise for a tichy zaba (Silent Frog). Let me help you set the bench back up. I'm sorry I startled you, here; let me get your hat," Eliska sweetly said as she reached down to pick up a Zuba's hat.

Zuba reached for his hat, and Eliska brushed against him. Their hands met, and her warm body pressed against his. The moment sent a shock through Zuba. He stumbled backward, reached out to steady himself, and he grabbed Eliska's arm.

They both fell over backward to the floor, toppling the coat rack over. Insult was heaped on injury as the wet, coal-encrusted rain slickers followed the rack down on top of them.

As they untangled themselves, a small, bald man walked through the office door. "Jezís Marja (Sweet Mother of God)," he said, as he stomped across the room. "What in the hell is going on? Did he hurt you Eliska?"

Eliska, sitting next to Zuba, laughed an embarrassed laugh, "No, I'm all right." She stood up, rubbing her posterior. "This is Zuba, and I was teasing him, and we kinda, accidentally, eh, probably, knocked the coat rack over."

"Well, I hope you behave more like a lady. I took a risk, having a Romani girl as my helper, but I owed your father a favor." the man said.

"Did you say Zuba?" the small man squinted over his glasses. "I'm supposed to have a new man by that name. Are you the mechanic?"

"Ya -- me -- me -- is," Zuba answered, looking up from the floor.

"Well, get up, you big ox! I don't know if I can use you if you are this clumsy. Do you have the hiring papers?" the man curtly said.

"Ya -- me -- does," Zuba replied, "in -- hat -- to give -- Josef Jelinek."

"I'm Josef Jelinek, so where're the papers?"

"In -- hat -- here -- somewhere," Zuba said. *Why does this happen? -- Beautiful Eliska will think me a fool. -- lose job before hired.*

"Here -- they is -- me -- sit -- on -- hat," An embarrassed Zuba said.

Josef scrutinized Zuba's papers, knowing that he needed to hire Zuba. The last mechanic quit yesterday, and Josef direly needed a mechanic to keep the trucks moving.

"Well, you might work out," Josef said. "Suppose we try you out at five korunas per hour (about twenty-five cents)."

"But -- your -- hiring -- man -- said -- you -- pay -- ten -- koruna -- a -- hour," Zuba pleaded.

"That was last week. We have plenty of mechanics this week, so we're paying less now," Josef said as he shuffled a stack of papers.

Behind Josek, Eliska held up both of her hands with all the fingers outstretched and mouthed the word 'ten.' "Zuba will make a fine workman. Give him a chance!" she said forcefully.

"Mind your business Romany; I'll decide," Josef snapped back. "I suppose we could try you at eight korunas an hour. How about it, big fellow?"

"Someone -- lied -- me -- don't -- belong -- here," Zuba replied. "Maybe -- try -- the -- other -- coal -- company."

"Oh, all right, ten korunas it is," Josef mumbled, "You better earn your keep!"

Eliska winked and flashed a victory sign at Zuba. A red flush crept across his face. "Oooh-- Ya -- OK." *Hope my heart not jump over the edge of my bib overalls.*

"Your first job is washing trucks. Find one of those rain slickers that fits you and get going," Josef commanded. "I'll take five korunas out of your pay for it... Eliska, get this office back in order. Pick up the damn pile of raincoats!" ~~~~~~

Chapter 5

TROUBLE AT HOME

Bolda Danka home, Litomysl, Czechoslovakia, Mon, Jan 1, 1917

On the far side of town, surrounded by makeshift houses with rusty, corrugated, metal roofs, sat the Bolda Danka home. The Dankas did their best to brighten up the two-room house with fresh whitewash, but no amount of whitewash could cover the smell of poverty. No flowers adorned the dirt walk to the house, replaced with white rocks painted with the left-over whitewash. A pushcart parked to one side of the walk had a broken handle. On the other side of the walk, broken furniture strewn on the ground had weeds growing up through the legs.

Inside the home, stray wood smoke from the cookstove had smudged the walls a dirty gray. The only wall decoration was a small crucifix. In the corner, Florica had wound dried flowers around a statue of a black woman, a shrine to Saint Sara. Bare wooden floors, worn by years of traffic, showed deep cracks and creases. Roaches made their home underneath it and raced across it in the dead of night. On the far wall was a series of shelves, one for each family member, a futile attempt to provide order.

Eliska sat at a wooden table surrounded by four worn chairs. She caressed a small cedar box over and over, drinking in the red-orange color and breathing the dark rich aroma.

Bolda sat next to Eliska, mending a horse harness and smoking his pipe. "What do you have there, Eliska?"

"Zuba has made it for me for Christmas, Papa."

"Zuba the dumb gadjo? Isn't it bad enough we have him in our band? Why do you make friends with him? He doesn't talk right, stumbles around, leave him be!"

"He's good to me; saved me from those Freikorps boys and the horse runaway too. Remember?"

"How can I forget? I lost a good horse, and my arm still hurts."

Bolda wagged his finger at Eliska. "Don't get so friendly with him. I think you feel sorry for him."

"Oh Papa, he's not so bad. We work at the coal yard, and he's lonely like me. He comes in the lunchroom every day for Bratislavsky Goulash and Garlic Soup. We just sit and talk, well, I talk, and he nods and stutters. Sometimes I give him the stuffed eggs I make. He likes them."

Bolda took a long pull on his pipe. "All the same girl, he's not a Roma, and I promised you to Jacob. He paid me half of the dowry. Once you marry, you won't have time to be lonely."

Eliska lowered her eyes and mumbled. "Oh, Jacob is all right, I guess, it's just that...," Eliska then blurted out. "He acts as if he owns me. He never even gave me a Christmas present. He said we would marry in the spring; then I'll have him, the best present ever."

Bolda put away his harness mending tools. "Ya, he rubs me wrong, too. He gets puffed up with pride. But I am sure his family will have the rest of the dowry. I've given my word. He will make a good husband. His father is rough on him, and his mother has had no easy way. I don't think Jacob knows how to act around you. He's good to his mother, though, and so I think he will be good to you."

"Papa, I'm afraid of him. He has a mean streak."

Bolda admonished Eliska, "Don't sass him like you do me. You should forgive his pompous ways. Forgiveness is the Roma way, especially at Christmas. How could we live together if we didn't learn to forgive each other? Remember the Christmas song, 'Roma Forgive'?"

Eliska got up and put her treasured cedar box away on her shelf. "But Papa, why can't I find a younger boy, a nice boy who would care for me, and we could have a good family, like you and mama?"

"A family is good, but marriages are arranged. Parents know best. We have been doing it this way for a long time." Bolda said.

Bolda talked on, "It's tradition and the Roma way, and it works good. That's how Mama and me got married, and we get along great, and our family is happy. Aren't you?"

"Ya Papa, I guess you are right. You only want the best for me. I love you."

Bolda hung the harness on the wall and put on his hat, preparing to leave. "I love you too, girl, but things go better when we Roma stay together and apart from the gadje." Bolda stopped and pointed his pipe at Eliska. "It is best not to blow in the bear's ear."

~~~~~~

Chapter 6

THE PALZEKS OBJECT

Palzek Farm Outside Litomysl Czechoslovakia, Mon, Jan 1, 1917
The winter sun tumbled through the cottage window. Zuba had spent Christmas with his parents and now was packing his bags to return to the coal yard in Litomysl.

"Joyfulness is half your health," Emilia Palzek said as she helped pack Zuba's suitcase. "Are you doing good work?"

"Ya Mama, -- me –the top mechanic at -- coal yard," Zuba proudly exclaimed. "They give -- me ten korunas -- raise for Christmas. Me now make twenty korunas an hour -- two hundred and forty korunas -- a day, Mama!" *Course, -- Me the only mechanic!*

"You are such a good boy, Zuba," Emilia exclaimed. "Soon, you need to look up a wife to settle down. Have you met any sweet girls?"

"No, -- no, -- no, -- Czech -- girls but -- there's a -- Romany girl – she pretty -- and smells good too. She treats me like a friend and smiles at me and -- me play the tuba -- in her -- Papa's band."
~~~~~~

Emilia wrung her hands. "Oh, I hope you don't get mixed up with no Romany girls. You know how they are. They steal chickens, beg for handouts, dance around like they are crazy, and pray to that Black Sara."

"Black Sara -- is a saint in the -- Catholic Church, Mama." Zuba protested.

"Well, it's not the same Catholic church we go to. They are different."

"Just -- friends -- Mama. She pledged -- to Jacob Conkova -- and they gonna -- marry. Her Papa -- doesn't like me much -- He only needs -- a tuba player -- for the beer hall."

"Well, it worries me, those chicken thieves may trick you. Don't tell Papa! He wouldn't be one bit happy! He doesn't trust them and watches them like a hawk when they come around every spring, sharpening knives, hay sickles, and mending the horse's harness. We're always missing chickens when they leave."

"Mama -- the hens go -- out in -- the grove every -- spring -- to lay eggs and hatch out their chicks. A fox -- gets -- some of them. The rest show up sooner or later."

"Well, all the same, Romany are no account, and you shouldn't be sleeping in the same barn they are."

"Ya Mama," Zuba said sheepishly. *It won't make no difference. Can never have the love of pretty Eliska. -- We couldn't get married. -- Better put foolish thoughts out of my head. -- Why would a beautiful girl like Eliska marry a big, tongue-tied fool like me?*

"You hurry now. Be off with you, say hello to Aunt Dominika," Emilia said.

She stood on her tiptoes and placed a tender kiss on Zuba's cheek. "Are you coming home on Fat Thursday for the holy week at Easter?"

"Ya, -- Mama," Zuba said.

"Remember, you are Czech, and she is Roma. Oil and water don't mix." ~~~~~~

Chapter 7

THROWN TOGETHER

Coal Yard Office, Litomysl Czechoslovakia Mon, April 30, 1917

"God in heaven, what next? Eliska! Go get that big ox, Zuba! Have him come to the office right away! And be quick about it!" Josef yelled out, peering over his wire-rimmed glasses.

"Yes Mr. Jelinek," Eliska said. She grabbed her coal-soaked slicker and ran out in the pouring rain. Hurrying across the coal yard, she dodged coal wagons, and skipped over the deep potholes of black coal-soaked water, then slipped and fell on the slippery entrance to the coal yard repair shop. Picking herself up, she brushed small black chunks of coal from her hair and straightened her slicker.

Upon entering the building, she met Yanick, the supervisor.

"Well, what a nice little plum cake!" Yanick said, sizing her up and down. "What have we got here! You come around to see me?"

Yanick grabbed Eliska around the waist and pulled her to him. His hot beer breath was right in her face.

"Please leave me be!" Eliska pleaded, "Mr. Jelinek needs Zuba."

"Oh, it can wait awhile. What'd ya say? We go over behind the lumber pile and talk?" Yanick said, pulling at Eliska's arm. "I heard you Roma girls want to have fun."

"No, Mr. Jelinek needs Zuba right away," Eliska replied, trying to twist away. "Zuba! Where are you?"

"The big ox will take all day to get here. Let's go behind the lumber pile. What do you say, little gypsy girl? I hear gypsy women are friendly." Yanick again pulled on Eliska's arm and grabbed at Eliska's breast.

Zuba shuffled up, "Me -- here -- what -- you -- want Eliska? -- Why you -- grab at -- her -- Yanick? Not nice! Let -- go!" Zuba strode up to his boss and glared down at him.

Before Yanick released Eliska, she faced him and kicked him in the shin. Yanick howled and hopped back, rubbing his leg.

Eliska snapped to Zuba, "You don't always have to come to my rescue; I can take care of myself. I don't need you to jump in and help me. Who are you, a big Saint Bernard dog?"

Zuba stood, perplexed, "Me, -- sorry. -- me didn't -- mean."

Eliska cut him off, "Never mind! Mr. Jelinek wants you! Come quick!"

"Ya -- ya," Zuba replied. They crossed back across the coal yard and entered the office.

"It's about time you got back! Where in thunderation have you been, girl?" Josef cried. "Did you bring Zuba?"

"Ya, he's outside cleaning his shoes off," Eliska said.

"Cleaning his shoes off! Look at this office! The yard outside is cleaner!" Josef roared, "Do you suppose you could clean up around here?"

"But I thought I was to tally up the shipping papers and the production reports?" Eliska replied.

"Of course! Clean up after that! Tell that fool of a Zuba to come in!"

"Come quick Zuba!" Eliska called out.

Zuba entered and walked up to Josef's desk. Remembering that he had forgotten to take off his hat, Zuba pulled his wet hat from his head and said, "Here -- me -- is."

Josef jumped up and grabbed the papers that Zuba's rain-soaked hat was dripping on. "What's a matter, are your ears as slow as your mouth? Back up and quit dripping on my papers! Now, go pack a bag." Josef handed Zuba a map. "Tomorrow, you go to the mine at Karvina. Take the Mack AC truck. Load your tools. They have several trucks not working. Take extra chains for the chain drives and more hard-rubber tires."

"How -- me -- get -- there?"

"Just follow the damn road or use that map! You can read a map, can't you?" Josef cried in exasperation.

"Never -- saw -- no map before -- me -- don't -- read -- no good." Zuba stammered.

"Oh, good Lord, you need to be there by tomorrow night! It's 130 miles; it will take you six or seven hours. Why do I get saddled with the fools?" Josef moaned. "I must send someone with you. But who can I spare?" Josef pondered and rubbed his chin. "Eliska, are you done with the tally sheets and production reports?"

"Yes, Mr. Jelinek, now doing the floor; I'll be done at quitting time,"

"Never mind the damn floor, I'm sending you with Zuba to Karvina; you can spend the overnights at the Olsiny hotel. I'll send enough money to eat on and for each of you, to have a room. Go home. Pack your bags for at least a week. I'll wire the Mine Supervisor to put you to work straightening out their production records. Now, off with both of you. Be here bright and early tomorrow morning."

"But... but Papa won't like this. I can't go alone with a gadjo." Eliska stammered.

"He likes the money you make, doesn't he?"

"Yes."

"Then he better like this."~~~~~~

Chapter 8

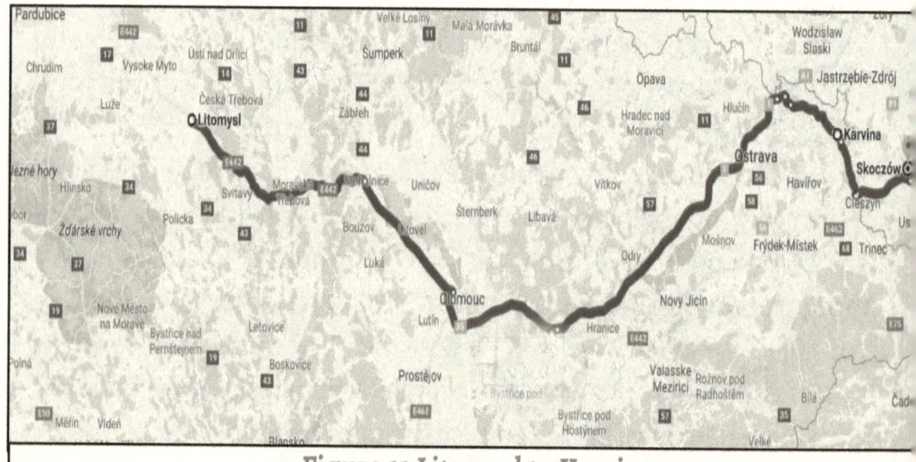

Figure 11 Litomysl to Karvina

ON THE ROAD

Coal Yard Litomysl, Czechoslovakia, Tues, May 1st, 1917

There is little coal dust in the air at four in the morning. Heavy frost on the grass signaled a late spring, a brisk day with a pale orange kiss from the sun in the eastern sky.

Zuba met Eliska as they entered the coal yard gate. "Good -- morning -- Eh -- eh -- Eliska." Zuba removed his battered hat and blushed. Eliska stood before him in her green cotton dress and a yellow babushka (scarf) tied around her head. A pink blush kissed each cheek, emphasizing the nip in the air.

"So, how is the silent frog this morning?" Eliska teased, with a faint smile tickling her lips. "I see you found your way here all right,"

"Ya -- me -- was -- up -- at -- three -- packing," Zuba replied.

"I hope you packed good. Have you got enough clean underwear for a whole week?" Eliska giggled.

Zuba's red flush bloomed again and crept up his neck to the top of his head. "Yaa -- extra -- pair -- My -- Sunday -- underwear -- Girls -- no -- talk -- on -- those -- things."

"Listen, who do suppose washes the underwear? I wash Papa's and my brother Hanzi's underwear all the time. I've seen men's underwear before! Are yours something special? Do you have pink polka dots or something on them?" Eliska teased.

"Oh, oh-- better -- go -- to -- the office." Zuba hurried on toward the office, leaving Eliska standing at the entrance to the yard.

Eliska laughed playfully. "Hey, wait for me, we go together, remember?"

Josef Jelinek was already in the office. He handed Eliska a thick briefcase stuffed with papers. "Here, take these to the supervisor; it costs a fortune to mail them... Zuba, load the Mack truck and be on your way."

Zuba loaded the truck and pinned his Saint Christopher medal prominently to the dash. Eliska climbed into the doorless cab.

"Hook -- strap -- across -- door -- opening. -- The company -- too cheap -- to buy doors," Zuba walked to the front of the truck and grabbed the crank. "When -- me -- crank -- turn -- magneto* -- lever -- on!"

Figure 12 Inside Mack AC Truck

* ***Magneto*** *To start and run the engine in a truck, you need electricity to fire the spark plugs, which ignite the fuel in the cylinders, causing the pistons to move. By cranking the engine, the magneto turns, creating electricity for ignition. There isn't a battery, so there is no electricity to power lights or start a vehicle with an electric starter.*

Zuba put the hand crank* into the hole in front of the truck and

Figure 13 Engine Hand Crank

gave a mighty twirl. The engine sputtered, squirmed, and stumbled to a stop.

"Did -- you -- turn -- magneto -- lever?" Zuba yelled.

"I didn't get a chance."

Zuba whirled the crank again. "Now!" Zuba shouted.

The engine again sputtered, shuttered, and stopped. A frustrated Zuba glanced up as Eliska turned the windshield wipers* back and forth.

"Not -windshield -- wiper -- lever -- the -- one -- by -- the -- steering column."

Zuba again made another mighty heave on the crank. "Now!" Zuba shouted. A loud ahoogaa sound emanated from the side of the truck as the engine snickered, burped, and stalled.

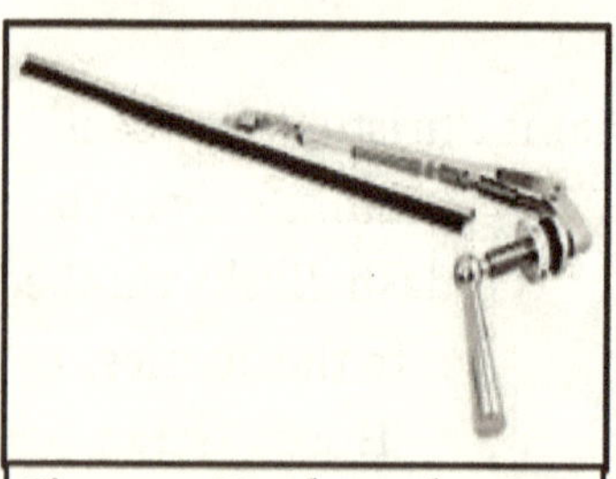

Figure 14 Hand Crank Wiper

"Not -- the -- ahoogaa horn -- just pull -- the -- lever down!"

Figure 15 AhooGaa Horn

Zuba again gave another mighty tug on the crank. "Now!" Zuba shouted. The engine once again stuttered, belched smoke, and went back to sleep. Zuba stomped over to the cab door and glared in at Eliska. Eliska sat with a bewildered expression on her face. "What did I do wrong this time?"

Crank -Without a starter, the only way to start an engine was to push it and engage the clutch or crank it. To start the vehicle, you inserted the crank through a hole in the front frame into the engine, the crank connected to the end of the crankshaft. Turning the crank by hand, turned the engine over, the magneto supplied the spark to ignite the gas in the pistons starting the engine, hence the phrase, "crank it up!"

***Windshield Wiper** - Mary Anderson invented the first windshield wiper in 1903. In her patent, she called her invention a "window cleaning device." Operated via a lever from inside the vehicle, these windshields wiper resemble the windshield wipers found on cars today.*

"Close -- glove compartment -- door and -- here's -- the -- lever," Zuba said as he pointed to the magneto lever.

Eliska repacked the gloves and the driving goggles in the glove compartment. She closed the compartment door with a hearty slam. "Why didn't you say so?" she said testily.

Zuba resumed his position in front of the truck and again gave another mighty heave on the crank. "Now!" Zuba shouted.

The engine roared to life, throbbing to a mighty hum. Zuba stepped up on the running board and slid into the cab. Eliska's lip quivered, and tears streamed down her cheeks. "That did it. This is the first time I was in one of these contraptions. We go around in Papa's horse and wagon."

"Well horn works, -- windshield wiped clean -- the gloves -- needed repacking," Zuba replied, trying to console Eliska.

A startled smile crept across Eliska's face. The smile spilled into a giggle and then into a deep, hearty laugh. Zuba thought Eliska was laughing at him; then he realized what he said made Eliska laugh.

Zuba chuckled, "Is kinda funny, isn't it?"

Eliska couldn't stop laughing. "It's funny, and you didn't stutter and stammer. Does it always work that way?"

"Ya -- me -- guess-- so," Zuba said self-consciously, "Me -- talk -- good -- when happy and -- with a friend."

Zuba pushed down on the floorboard clutch, grabbed the gear stick, and selected a gear. "Forward we -- go!" he shouted as he pushed the accelerator pedal down, the engine roared. He let out the clutch. -- And they raced backward!

"We'll be on the road a long time if we go in this direction." Eliska laughed.

"Ya, I guess so, me try again," Zuba said, laughing heartily. He grabbed the gear stick, found the proper gear, and the truck lurched forward.

The slowly rising sun gave off a fiery blaze, supplying enough light to see the road. The coal company didn't allow the truck drivers to use the acetylene* headlights because it cost too much, so they waited until it was light enough to drive. Now, Eliska and Zuba were on their way to Karvina.

Note: Introduced in 1915, the Mack Model ACs had a radiator mounted behind the engine to minimize accidental damage. It made a distinctive front-end design. During World War I, British soldiers liked the toughness of the trucks, so they nicknamed them 'Bulldog Macks.'

**Figure 16 Mack AC Truck
Notice the Chain Drive on the rear wheels**

Acetylene headlights *-The first vehicle headlamp, introduced during the 1880s, used acetylene and oil as the old gas lamps. The two substances fueled the headlamps also, but improving the existing systems was impossible because of the high costs of both. They were praised for their resistance to air currents and harsh weather such as snow and rain, but electric lamps soon replaced them.*

Figure 17 Acetylene Headlights

~~~~~~
~~~~~~

Chapter 9

A MUDDY RIDE

On the Road to Karvina Czechoslovakia Tuesday, May 1, 1917

"Only -- 130 -- miles -- to -- go!" Zuba yelled out over the roar of the big Mack truck engine. "We -- get -- by -- dark -- seven or six hours."

The road stretched out before them, rolling through the wooded hills of the Beskydy Mountains. Mile after mile melted behind them as they chugged along the roadway. Recent rains have left the road in sad condition. Zuba dodged the many mud holes, but sometimes there were too many. Eliska continually reached up to the overhead wiper lever and cleared the mud from the windshield.

"You could miss a few of the puddles. I could break my arm running these wipers?"

"Ya -- me -- try-- but -- road -- not -- so -- good."

After they drove for 2 hours, it rained again, and Eliska lowered the canvas tarp rolled up over her door frame.

"Need -- to -- lower -- mine -- too," Zuba tried to untie his tarp from above the door frame. In doing so, he removed one hand off the steering wheel and steered the big truck into a group of low-hanging bushes growing along the road.

"Zuba, you'll kill us. Get back on the road!" Eliska screamed. "Let me get it for you!" She leaned over Zuba and untied the canvas. Zuba felt her breast press into his shoulder, and her warm breath flowed past his ear. The lavender splash water was intoxicating.

"Me-- me -- me -- me," was the most that Zuba could stammer. Suddenly he swerved the truck and yelled, "Big -- mud -- hole! -- Ahead!"

When he swerved right, Eliska flew left, halfway out the cab. She was desperately gripping the canvas tarp and the door strap. Zuba wrapped a big arm around her and pulled her back into the cab.

Eliska had lowered the canvas tarp, but Zuba's warning came too late. The most recent mud hole, which couldn't be missed, splashed mud over the front of Eliska's dress.

"Can't you talk any faster or drive any slower? I almost fly out the door. Mud all over my dress! Could've got out of the way if you talked faster,"

The truck lurched down the muddy road. Steering was of no avail as the truck sunk to its axles in the deep ruts made by vehicles passing through. Once in the ruts, it was impossible to steer right or left. The only choice was to follow along.

"Slow down!" Eliska screamed.

"If -- me -- slow -- down we -- stuck! -- Hang tight -- gotta -- get -- through -- this -- muddy section. Ahead is -- a wayside shrine -- to – Saint Wenceslas. We -- stop there."

"I hope he's in today; he might clean my dress," Eliska said, smiling with a chuckle in her heart.

"Don't -- make -- no fun. Saint -- Wenceslas -- is-- saint patron -- of -- the -- Czech," Zuba blurted out. "Him and Saint Christopher -- get -- us down -- the -- road -- safe."

"Well, they couldn't hold a candle to Saint Sara E Kali, the Black Sara, who guides Roma travelers. She rowed out to the three holy Mary's, who were adrift on the stormy sea, and threw her dress onto the water and miracles! The dress turned into a raft, and she brought the three Marys safely to shore." Eliska said, smarting back. "St. Christopher only had to cross a little creek. Saint Sara had the whole ocean to deal with. So, what do you think of that?" Eliska proudly proclaimed.

"Don't know -- what you talk on -- but -- when -- we -- at -- shrine, -- be quiet -- don't -- get Saint -- Wenceslas – mad. -- We have enough troubles."

It was noon when Zuba pulled the truck onto a grassy knoll next to an alcove containing a statue of Saint Wenceslas.

It stopped raining; the skies cleared. A bright sun beat on the knoll, heating the air like steam rising from a bubbling kettle. A haze of evaporation was squeezed out of the wet grass, painting the warm breeze with the smell of lilacs and lavender.

A small brook tumbled and gurgled inside a ravine behind the shrine. Flocks of blackbirds and finches drank and splashed in the stream.

By the side of the brook, the willows grew in gay abandon, their green leaves shimmering in the freshly washed sunlight. The willows were alive with songbirds tweeting their songs of longing for each other. The bird's melodies blended with the gurgle of the babbling brook and the sighing of the breezes in the willow trees to create a symphony. Finer than any symphony in Prague or Vienna!

Figure 18 Saint Wenceslas Shrine

Zuba climbed down from the truck and reached behind the seat and pulled out his knapsack. "Here -- good -- place to eat -- dinner -- Eliska -- get yours out -- and we sit on -- bench -- and eat."

"Look at me, at the mud on the front of my dress. What will they say when we get to Karvina?"

Zuba pulled his bandanna out and wiped off Eliska's face, and then he lowered the bandanna to clean the mud off her dress.

"Never mind! I can take care of it," Eliska pointedly said to Zuba.

"OK," replied the red-faced Zuba. "Me -- sit -- here -- and -- eat."

They sat in silence, ate, and soaked in the spot's beauty.

"Know what, Zuba?" Eliska exclaimed. "St. Sara threw her dress into the water; that's what I'll do. The brook is nice and clean. It should get the mud out. I'll go down to the brook and wash my dress."

Eliska jumped up and ran toward the stream. "You stay here! Don't peek! I'll wash and dry it on those bushes down there. It will take a while. Promise me you won't peek!"

"Ya, -- Ya, me be right here -- hurry! -- We still have three hours to go," Zuba said, his red face now glowed a bright orange.

Eliska skipped lightly down to the brook, slipped her shoes off, and waded into the cold rushing water. She pulled her dress off and rinsed the mud off in the sparkling waters, wrung it out and hung it on a nearby bush to dry. She sat on the grassy bank and hummed along with the chorus of twittering birds perched above her. A song about birds and babies; her lilting voice blended perfectly with the surrounding sounds. The balmy sun caressed her, and the early morning journey had sapped her energy. She nodded and lay back on the sweet grass and closed her eyes. *Just a quick nap, a minute or two, I'll be ready to go when the dress is dry.*

Figure 19 Babbling Brook.

Zuba finished the last of his bratwurst sandwiches when Eliska screamed, "Oh no, go away!"

Zuba leaped to his feet, and as he ran down to the brook, he slipped on the wet grass, fell, and slid, feet first, into the rushing water.

"Me -- help -- you!" Zuba cried, wiping his muddy hands on his shirt.

"No! Turn around; I'm not dressed. It's a snake, but he's gone now."

Zuba came to an abrupt stop, turned on his heels, and climbed back up the slippery hill. Falling, struggling up, then falling, struggling up again, he finally made it back to the rest area.

He wiped the mud off his knees, poured the water out of his boots, and sat down to eat the rest of his lunch.

"Oh no, go away!" Eliska screamed again.

Zuba leaped up again and ran toward the brook. He slipped, his feet left him, and he landed on his stomach on the wet grass and slithered down the slope.

"Me -- is -- comin!" Zuba cried as he slid, headfirst, into the brook.

"No! Stay away until I get my dress on!" Eliska cried.

Zuba came to an abrupt stop at the bottom of the brook. Shaking the water off, he crawled out of the brook and again, up the slippery slope of the hill. He muttered, "Sometimes I don't know whether to come or went."

"Get away!" Eliska screamed again.

Zuba, halfway up the hill, stopped and stood motionless. "You -- need -- to -- get -- rescued?" He yelled back.

Eliska shouted back, "No, the snake went into his hole!"

"Good -- cause -- me -- awful -- tired." Zuba climbed the rest of the way up, flopped down on the wooden bench, and faced the statue of Saint Wenceslas. He murmured, "I know why -- you never -- married."

Eliska dressed and climbed back up the hill. "Zuba! You are wet and muddy! What have you been doing?"

"You call -- and -- me -- come -- rescue -- you -- then -- me don't rescue you, so -- me go back up -- pour water out of boot -- and then you call -- and me go again -- to rescue. -- me fall in the brook -- but you don't -- need be -- rescued --so -- me don't -- rescue you -- me go back up -- and here me sit. -- No more rescue for me!"

"Well, come on! We can't lie around the entire day. Times a wasting. Let's get going!" Eliska declared. A soggy Zuba and a dry perky Eliska resumed their trip to Karvina. ~~~~

Chapter 10

AT KARVINA

Karvina, Czechoslovakia, Coal Fields Tuesday, May 1, 1917

Mining around Karvina began in the 19th century with the development of ironworks and railways. The outbreak of the First World War brought a record-breaking increase in coal production. The entire district was militarized, and the Czech Army was now in charge.

~~~~~~

Zuba and Eliska lumbered thru the narrow streets of Karvina in the overheated Mack truck.

"We -- have -- to -- get -- water -- for truck radiator. -- Where -- we -- to stay?" Zuba said, gazing at the maze of cobblestone streets ahead of him.

"Mr. Jelinek said, follow Polni Road to the army post. The army has been in charge since the war in Germany. They will tell us where to go," Eliska replied.

Zuba followed the road to the end, where it widened out to an open field, across which stood neat rows of gray, canvas tents. Entering the gate, Zuba pulled up to a row of hastily constructed wooden buildings. A bored guard slouched by the entrance and eyed them suspiciously.

Figure 20 Army Tents

Zuba stopped the truck next to a long-handled water pump. "Me get -- water -- for -- truck. -- Find out where -- go."
~~~~~~

"We're to see a captain about fixing trucks and where we're to stay," Eliska informed the guard.

The guard eyed Eliska up and down, "You have the papers, gypsy girl?"

Eliska gave the guard a hard glare, "Yes, here they are!"

The guard looked the papers over and then motioned with his thumb, pointing it at a large wooden building. "Inside!"

Eliska entered the building and walked over to a large desk where a fat captain sat. He glanced up and peered at Eliska through dirty spectacles that caressed his bulging eyes.

He resumed sorting through a pile of papers. Looking up again, the captain remarked, "We don't need no damn trinkets or potions today, gypsy girl. How did you get in here? Be off before I sic the dogs on you."

"I am not selling trinkets! Josef Jelinek sent us to help you with the paperwork and Zuba to fix your broken trucks." Eliska snapped back.

"A gypsy, and a girl no less! You? Help us with the paperwork? Ha! What the hell is that old Jelinek is trying to pull this time?" the captain roared. "Must be a joke!"

"No, it's true, here are our papers," Eliska replied as she pulled the papers out of her bag and slammed them on his desk.

The captain rocked back in his chair and scooped up the papers. "I suppose the mechanic is a gypsy too. All he can do is fix a damn horse!"

"No, Zuba is a gadjo, not a Roma, and a great mechanic," Eliska replied. Looking down, she kicked hard at a ball of lint.

"All right, the repair shed is on the other side of the camp. The mechanic can go there. You come here first thing in the morning. Now git, you're making my head hurt."

"Where are we to stay?" Eliska asked.

"Stay? How about a tent? You gypsies like sleeping in tents, don't you?"

"But Mr. Jelinek said we would have a hotel," Eliska glared at the captain, "I know he sent money to you for it because I wrote out the authorization.

"Well, it might be here somewhere," the captain blustered, taken back by the determined girl. "Ah, here it is, a room at the Dvur Olsiny Hotel. You don't mind sharing a room, do you?"

"Mr. Jelinek said we would have two rooms; he sent enough money. What are you trying to do, line your pockets?" Eliska demanded.

Beads of sweat broke out on the fat captain's forehead as he tried to wiggle around the sassy girl's accusations.

He again glanced down at his paperwork, "Oh, here it is! I guess I didn't see it before." He pulled out a voucher, signed it, and threw it at Eliska. "Here's your damn voucher! Now get the hell out of here, make sure the two of you are back at seven in the morning. I won't put up with any gypsy loafing, you hear?"

Eliska turned and left the room, smiling. *It's nice that a Roma girl can give a fat gadjo a taste of his own medicine.* ~~~~~~

Chapter 11

THE HORSE ACADEMY

Olsiny Hotel, Karvina Czechoslovakia, Tuesday, May 1, 1917

Zuba, Eliska, and the Mac truck bounced over the cobblestone streets of Karvina as they searched for the Dvur Olsiny Hotel.

It was pitch dark, and Zuba lit the acetylene highlights. He muttered, "Jelinek not -- here. We got -- to see."

Finally, Zuba and Eliska arrived at a sign saying, 'Dvur Olsiny Hotel.'

"Here!" Eliska cried.

"You -- sure -- this place? ---It looks like a horse farm," Zuba said.

"Smells like one too; leave it to Mr. Jelinek to get the cheapest place in town," Eliska commented.

"You check-in. -- me bring bags," Zuba said.

Figure 21 Dvur Olsiny Hotel

Eliska walked into the lobby of the hotel. The lofty ceilings and the rough-cut support beams of the hotel entryway suggested that it might have been a barn at one time. It looked like a barn, which, of course, it was! The primary business of the Dvur Olsiny Hotel was a horse-riding school. The management had added a bunkhouse to the stables for guest rooms.

Behind a large box, an oats bin to be exact, sat Pesek, the check-in clerk. A small impish boy of about 16 was also the stable boy and maître d' of the dining room. "Checking in?" Pesek said without looking up.

"Yes, please," Eliska replied.

Pesek wiped his hands on his shirt and turned the registration book toward her. She signed the book, and after Zuba came in, the stable boy took them to their rooms.

"Welcome to the Dvur Olsiny Hotel, Breakfast at 5 AM and supper at 6 PM. If you hurry, you can still get something to eat," the boy rattled on as he unlocked their rooms.

"Here we are, here are your keys." Pesek handed the keys to Zuba and stood with his hand outstretched after Zuba took the keys. Pesek cleared his throat and said, "You forget something?"

A bewildered Zuba looked at the boy. "Ah, -- sorry." Zuba tipped his hat and shook the outstretched hand of Pesek.

Pesek spit on the floor, "Damn cheap plowboy, don't even know how to tip!" He turned and stomped out of the room.

"Why did you make him angry?" Eliska asked Zuba.

"He -- said me don't -- know -- how -- to tip -- but me tipped -- my hat -- like always do," Zuba replied. "Does -- this -- look all right?" he said as he tipped his hat to Eliska.

"Looks fine to me. Sometimes these folks need learning about manners," Eliska replied. "Let's get something to eat!"

Zuba and Eliska entered the dining hall. There were eight round tables with six chairs each. A wine bottle with a candle stuck in the top was an attempt to show class. Eliska picked a table in the center of the room. "Looks OK here," she said.

"It make -- me nervous -- can -- we -- sit -- in corner?" Zuba said.

Figure 22 Dvur Olsiny Hotel Bunkhouse

"What's the matter? You afraid people will see that you are with a Roma girl?" Eliska snapped at him.

"Oh no -- me -- happy to sit with -- you. Everybody, -- can crowd in -- on me in the center," Zuba replied, watching the room out of the corner of his eye. "Guess -- me be a little silly."

"Well, silly or not, who's to care if I get something to eat?" Eliska said. "Where's the menu?"

"Menu? What -- menu? What -- do -- it look like?"

"It's a list of all the things they can cook up and serve us. There it is at your elbow," Eliska replied. "What do they have to eat tonight? Read it to me."

Zuba picked up the menu and fumbled with it. "I can't -- tell what -- they cook -- it doesn't -- look like any -- writing -- me saw in -- nun school."

Eliska took the menu from Zuba's hands and whispered, "Well, first you have to have the menu, right side up. You had it upside down." Eliska glanced over the menu. "Tonight, they have Bratislavsky Goulash (Bratwurst in sauerkraut soup), Vareniky (Stuffed Dumplings), Fried Calf's Brains, and Fried Carp Goulash with Peppers. What would you like?"

"I guess -- the Bratislavsky -- Goulash -- be all right," Zuba replied.

Pesek, in his cleanest grease-stained apron and a small flop hat, strolled to their table. He remarked, "Well, if it ain't the big spenders. Are you ordering something or just tipping your hat again?"

"Yes, we'll have Bratislavsky Goulash with bratwurst and Fried Carp Goulash with Peppers," Eliska snapped.

"Great, be right back," Pesek turned and reentered the kitchen.

"I hope he washed his hands after he worked in the stable," Eliska chuckled.

"Ya -- he kinda -- smelled like -- home," Zuba deadpanned. "Mama always -- make us -- wash our hands."

Eliska broke out in a hearty laugh. "Bet you never thought the smell of manure would make you homesick!"

Zuba and Eliska still chuckled when Pesek returned with their food. He slapped the goulash in front of them and retreated to the kitchen.

"Well, at least we won't have to smell him during our supper," Eliska chuckled.

"How -- you -- learn -- to -- read -- good? Me -- thought Roma -- didn't want no learning in -- school," Zuba said, as he cut up his bratwurst smothered in sauerkraut.

"Well, we put more stock in wisdom as opposed to writing," Eliska replied. "Mama taught me. She learned from her sister Kizzy, who married a gadjo. I never met her; none of the Roma will talk to Kizzy. Mama sees her at the market once in a while, and they slip away to talk some. That's how Mama learned to read." Eliska looked over at Zuba. "How come you can't read?"

"Me -- don't read no -- good -- me went to the -- nun's school -- one year. ---Sister Jarmila say -- me shy -- no smile -- no look at her. They -- say, -- go home, -- say, -- couldn't learn me. -- it's all right -- Papa need -- help on -- the farm. No, -- like being around -- the other kids -- especially the girls," Zuba said.

"What's a matter with girls? We smell better than the stable boy, don't we?" Eliska teased.

"Oh ya, -- sure do -- but -- girls make -- me nervous -- hard to talk to -- make fun of -- me talking," Zuba replied, slurping his soup and not looking up.

"Do I make you nervous, Zuba?"

"Ah -- ahh ah-a -- not too much now. You nice, me like you," Zuba replied and blushed a bright red.

"I like you too, even if you almost talk my ears off," Eliska joked. They finished their supper and went to their rooms. "Sleep tight, don't let bed bugs get you. I have a hunch there may be some," Eliska said.

~~~~~~
~~~~~~

Chapter 12

THE CROOKED CHURCH

Olsiny Hotel, Karvina, Czechoslovakia, Sunday, May 6, 1917
The sun rose brightly and kissed "Good Morning" to the gently rolling hills of the Beskydy Mountains. The area was resplendent with hundreds of miles of trails, secluded valleys, thick coniferous forests, mountain streams, bubbling, babbling brooks, and large, quiet dams.

A light breeze rustled in the tender limbs of the newly opened oak leaves. The church bells rang as Zuba and Eliska made their way along the cobblestone streets of Karvina to the Saint Peter of Alcantara Church*.

Figure 23 Saint Peter of Alcantara Church

"I've never been in a gadje church before," Eliska said, as they peered into the brightly lit interior of the church. "I -- thought -- you said you -- Catholic?" Zuba replied.

"We are, but we don't have to go to a building to talk to God. Roma talk to him as we walk along, whether doing dishes or making music; he is always with us. We talk to him through his mother, though. Sometimes a priest will come around for a baptism or a funeral."

Note: The people built Baroque Saint Peter of Alcantara Church in 1736. The ground settled because of the coal mining under the church, and the church now leans southwards. After 40 years of mining, the surface had sunk and tilted the church southward.

Zuba and Eliska entered the church and stood wide-eyed, peering at the high, arching ceiling. The interior, painted in different shades of white, set off the large crucifixion painting hanging over the altar. Decorations from May Day were still at the foot of the altar.

After mass, as they left, Eliska said, "Am I dizzy, or is the floor not straight?"

"Ya, -- stable boy said -- church sink -- a little," Zuba replied, taking Eliska's arm. "Coal mine -- right underneath the church. ---Propped it up good, -- me think."

"I don't like going to your Catholic church. I'd rather stay outside and talk to Mother Mary my way," Eliska replied. "I like to be on the level ground!"

They walked back to the Olsiny hotel as the bright May sunlight twinkled and danced around them. They entered the courtyard, and Eliska asked, "So Zuba, what are you going to do with the rest of your day?"

"Me take -- nap," Zuba replied.

"Oh, you can sleep when you're dead," Eliska teased. "Do you know what would be fun? We could get a couple of horses out of the stable and have a picnic. There's a big field behind the hotel, a pond, and some woods. We could take smoked carp, bread, and stuffed eggs. Wouldn't it be fun?"

"Ya -- me never -- been -- to -- picnic. ---What -- me do?" Zuba asked.

"Oh, there's nothing to it. We'll go over by the pond, put a blanket on the ground, eat our food, and talk a little. Even take a short nap. We could go for a walk in the woods and see all the baby flowers. They should be up by now! This will be great fun!" Eliska said.

"OK, sure -- as long as -- you know -- how to do it," Zuba replied. Eliska's enthusiasm had won him over, and the thought of food and a nap didn't hurt either.

"Good, I'll get the food, and you get the horses from that sassy, stable boy. Get good horses now, don't let him give you a swayback horse, and don't take any of his horse manure!" Eliska joked.

"Why not? -- Horse -- manure be -- good for those baby flowers -- you like. Mama always -- put it on her strawberries."

A silly grin crossed Eliska's face as she teased Zuba, "You have strange customs on the farm. I eat strawberries with cream and honey on them."

Zuba bantered, "Not for ---—eat! We put ---—on the strawberry plants to make ----—grow better. City girls don't know much about the farm, do you?"

"We know enough to swat a big farm boy when he makes fun of us!" Eliska replied as she punched him in the arm. "Now, no more foolin! Let's get things together and go on that picnic."

When Zuba came out of the stable, Eliska was waiting with a big basket under her arm. They mounted their horses and sauntered to woods in the distant corner of the field. Dismounting near a small pond, they saw a pair of swans gracefully floating on the water.

Figure 24 Mute Swans

"What kind of birds are they?" Eliska asked.

"They -- mute swans -- don't -- talk no good."

"Just like you, eh, Zuba?" Eliska teased.

"Ya, -- -but me don't -- float as -- good as they do," Zuba replied.

"Here, help me with the blanket and get the basket off the horse. I'm hungry," Eliska ordered.

They rolled out the blanket on the ground and spread out the food in one corner and sat next to each other in the other corner. Zuba sat with his back to Eliska, too afraid to turn and look her in the eyes.

"Here, Zuba, turn around, see at what the cook sent us. Some Stolní víno (Table wine)," Eliska said. "We have it at home once in a while, at Christmas and Saint Sara's day. Let's make this a special day too. What should we call it?"

Twiddling his hat in his hands, Zuba turned toward Eliska. "El -- Eliska Sunday! You, -- swan that can talk. Ya, a swan, like you, -- with me," Zuba lowered his head, surprised at what he said.

Eliska reached out to Zuba, placing one hand on each side of Zuba's face. "You are the sweetest man. We have so much fun together. Why do you always hang your head when you talk? You are handsome and a good friend. I love -- ah -- like you. I feel safe when you are near me."

Upon hearing that, Zuba sat with his head down in awkward silence. Eliska gently raised Zuba's face and gazed into his eyes. Tears were streaming down Zuba's cheeks. "Nobody ever -- -say that -- before --. They always make—up fun on me."

"Oh, Zuba, don't let what other people say get you down. They don't know you as I do," Eliska replied. Tenderly, she pulled Zuba close to her, embraced him, and rubbed the back of his head.

Zuba sobbed. A river of emotion burst from his heart. "Guess -- no good -- for man to -- cry," Zuba said with his head still on Eliska's shoulder. "Me don't know -- where that comes from."

"We Roma have a saying; a tear in the eye is the wound of the heart," Eliska replied while rubbing Zuba's head. "So, the wound in your heart must be deep."

"I have a way to heal that wound," she said as she lifted Zuba's head and kissed him on his wet lips. "Does that help?"

"A little," Zuba replied. He wiped his eyes and then, with a wry smile on his lips, he whispered, "Another -- couple times more -- might -- fix it—really good,"

"Too much candy will make you sick, and then you wouldn't enjoy the carp sandwiches," Eliska replied as she playfully pushed Zuba away. "Open the víno! I'm hungry!"

After the meal was over, Eliska and Zuba packed the remains of the food in the basket.

"Let's -- go -- see those -- baby -- flowers of -- yours," Zuba said, rising to his feet. "Sun -----warm ---day wasting."

"Oh, you're in a hurry to get back here and take your nap," Eliska said.

"No—no, me really like flowers," Zuba protested. "Let's go -- what you wait for? They won't -- be babies -- for long!"

"Oh, all right here, give me your hand and help me up," Eliska replied.

Zuba reached out and helped Eliska up. After she was up, she gripped Zuba's hand. "Do you mind if I hang on to you? I've never been in the woods before. There may be a wolf in there."

Figure 25 The Woods

"You -- worried about -- Jacob? --Your promised?"

"Not that kind of wolf. Forget him; he's not here; I am!"

"OK, better hang -- on tight -- till we -- come back," Zuba replied.

They walked, hand in hand, exploring the pathways around the pond and in the nearby woods. The sun filtered through the overhead canopy of leaves, whispering a song of spring. The song roused the sleeping Ferns, Hyacinths, Snowdrops, Crocus, and Crested Iris into a standing ovation. Eliska picked yellow Aconites and wound the gay yellow flowers through her raven black hair.

The flowers sparkled like diamonds. Eliska pulled baby blue Scylla and decorated Zuba's hat with them. "They go so nice with your blond hair," she said. They lingered at a fallen log watching a rusty little squirrel searching for his buried treasure, lost under the snow until now. Eventually, they wandered back to their picnic site.

"Well, no wolves, I guess," Eliska said.

"Ya, me protect you -- real good, -- didn't me?" Zuba said, with a smirk.

"Yes, you did, and as your reward, you take your nap. I will sing a little," Eliska said and sang a light, lilting melody. (Dark Eyes)

> *Blue eyes, sweet blue eyes,*
> *Burn-with-passion eyes, how you hypnotize!*
> *How I adore you so, how I fear you, though.*
> *Since I saw you glow! Now my spirit's low!*
> *Darkness yours, conceal mighty fires, real,*
> *They, my fate, will seal, burn my soul with zeal!*
> *But my love for you, when the time is due,*
> *Will refresh anew like the morning dew!*
> *No, not sad am I, nor so mad, am I,*
> *All my comforts lie in my destiny.*
> *Just to realize my life's worthiest prize*
> *Must I sacrifice for those ardent eyes!*
> *Blue eyes, sweet blue eyes,*
> *They implore me into faraway lands*
> *Where love reigns, peace reigns*
> *Where there's no suffering, and our love is not forbidden!*

Zuba lay down on the blanket, slid his hat over his face, and was fast asleep. An hour passed. Eliska picked a yellow dandelion and tickled Zuba's nose. Zuba swatted it away like a fly. Eliska leaned over, tipped Zuba's hat up, and kissed him. Zuba stirred and reached up and pulled Eliska to him. They kissed for a long, passionate moment. Suddenly, Zuba realized he wasn't dreaming and sat upright.

"Sorry -- me thought -- me -- dreaming. Didn't mean --—grab you," Zuba stammered.

"It is all right. Maybe your dreams are coming true," Eliska responded coyly.

"Ya sure, -- looks like -- rain -- we better -- get back quick," Zuba replied, dodging Eliska's statement.

They mounted the waiting horses and sauntered back to the hotel.

~~~~~~

Chapter 13

A SAD WAY HOME

Back to Litomysl, Czechoslovakia, Saturday, May 12, 1917

"Hurry Eliska, we have to be back at Litomysl by dark," Zuba cried, knocking on Eliska's hotel room door.

"Just about ready. Is the truck all loaded?"

"Ya sure. Yesterday!" Zuba replied.

Eliska appeared in the doorway with her hair askew. "I didn't even have time to comb my hair! I didn't sleep too well last night."

"Me neither, -- don't want to -- go back," Zuba said.

"Well, it will be nice to see Papa and the family, but I'll miss you," Eliska said forlornly. "I'll only see you when you come to work or play in Papa's band. I wish we could go for walks and a picnic again! That was so much fun."

"Ya, me too, -- but your Papa and Mama -- and my folks -- say—it wouldn't be ---ok to do," Zuba replied.
~~~~~~

"Well, no matter, I'm supposed to marry Jacob Conkova. He has already paid Papa half of the dowry. And that's that," Eliska said.

They loaded their belongings into the Mack truck, and Zuba cranked it up. Eliska found the right levers, and soon the truck was humming its familiar low rumble.

The rising morning sun smiled over the mountain as they drove off. They sat in silence as mile after bumpy mile passed. Finally, they arrived back at the wayside shrine to Saint Wenceslas.

"The cook sent sweetbreads and apples with us. Should we eat now?" Eliska mumbled.

"Ya, but -me not ---much hungry," Zuba said.

"Well, we should stretch our legs," Eliska said as she stepped down from the truck.

As they walked to the shrine, Zuba reached out and took Eliska's hand. Eliska clung to Zuba's hand with both of hers as they strolled along. Eliska stopped and gazed into Zuba's eyes. "Zuba, I love you!" she blurted out.

Zuba was silent for some time. "Me -- me love you too. -- me -- hoped -- you -- would -- love me."

"Oh Zuba, what are we to do?" Eliska said, as she started to cry.

"Nothing to do -- you live -- in your place, and me live -- in mine. -- —Be no good -- with our families," Zuba replied, "and you are -- promised."

"Well, I didn't make a darn promise. My Papa did! -- He didn't even ask me!" Eliska replied angrily.

"Your Papa has the right, -- me guess," Zuba replied.

"Well, I love you, doesn't that matter?"

"It matters a -- lot to me -- but make -- no difference."

Eliska wept softly, and then the weeping turned to sobs. Her shoulders shook as Zuba pulled her close to him and put his big arms around her.

"There now, dear Eliska, -- my wound ---crossed over to your heart. -- Don't cry so, it be all right. -- God works in strange ways, my Mama always says.

Eliska looked up at Zuba and kissed him on the lips. The embrace continued for the longest time, and finally, reluctantly, they pushed away from each other.

"We always have the wettest kisses," Eliska said, as Zuba dabbed her cheeks with his big red bandanna.

Eliska took the bandanna and clutched it to her breast. "Can I keep this?" She asked. "Whenever you see me, I'll have this bandanna on; then you will remember I love you."

Eliska reached up to her neck, unhooked a gold chain with a cross on it, and gave it to Zuba. "My grandmother from India gave me this cross. It means good luck. I want you to have it and wear it and think of me."

Zuba turned the cross over and over in his big hands. "This cross is -- beautiful, but -- what are the little -- crooked crosses engraved on it?"

"They mean good luck and well-being," Eliska replied.

"I -- wear it -- all the time, -- close to my heart -- where you will always be," Zuba replied.

They held each other until Eliska said, "It's no use in hurting each other any further. We better get going, Zuba. We have to be back to Litomysl by dark."

"Ya, I hope the trip goes real slow," Zuba sighed.

Eliska laid her head on Zuba's shoulder as they drove back to Litomysl.

<center>~~~~~~</center>

Chapter 14

SWEET TREATS

Coal Yard, Litomysl, Czechoslovakia, Tuesday, May 15, 1917

Zuba entered the coal yard office. "Good morning, Eliska. Is Mr. Jelinek in yet? -- me need get -- repair orders."

"No, but he will be here soon. I guess he's late. How come you're so early today?" Eliska asked.

"I think -- it -- someone's birthday today," Zuba said slyly.

"Oh, who could that be?" Eliska answered.

"Why yours, -- am me right, or did me mess up -- and wish you on a wrong day?" Zuba replied, embarrassed.

Eliska answered with a smile, "Well, when you turn seventeen, you get to tease a little more. The Roma considers a girl a woman when we're past 16." Eliska whirled around, and threw her head back, posed with one arm on her hip. "Do I look like a woman to you?"

"Ya -- you sure -- then some," Zuba said, admiring the shapely woman before him. "But why you, -- have two different colored socks on?"

"Oh, leave it to you to see my feet, can't you see the rest of me? I was in a hurry to dress just right, and I couldn't decide which ones to wear. They must be mixed up." Eliska leaned to one side, trying to see what Zuba was holding behind his back. "So, what do you have for my birthday?"

"Why? Was me supposed to get you something?" Zuba said, smiling.

"Well, no -- but did you think of me?" Eliska asked.

"This morning -- me walking to work -- and dogs were barking."

"You thought of me as a barking dog?"

"Well, let -- me finish. me was -- wondering what the dogs were -- barking about, so me looked and -- they bark at a -- squirrel with a bushy tail."

"A bushy tail made you think of me? Do I have a bushy tail?"

"No, me -- me. -- me. -- me. -- How me get myself -- into these things?"

"So, a barking dog and a bushy tail remind you of me?"

"No, you don't understand. -- The squirrel sits -- on the fence chatter -- at the dogs."

"So, a barking dog, a bushy tail, and chattering remind you of me. This isn't getting any better!"

"Hush, -- be quiet -- till -- me -- get done," Zuba chided Eliska. "The squirrel was -- all perky, and -- didn't take no sass from anyone. -- That's what reminded me of you -- and your bushy tail!"

"Well, you walked a long way to get to the end of a story! What are you holding behind your back?" Eliska replied, still trying to see around Zuba.

"Oh, -- me got a backache. -- Aunt Dominika wrapped -- - up poultice -- to make it better," Zuba said.

"Here, let me look at it. Roma are good at fixing a poultice," Eliska replied, grabbing the cloth-wrapped package. She unwrapped it quickly and said, "This does not look like a poultice. What is it?"

Zuba spoofed, "I told Aunt Dominika -- me had friend -- at work -- who had a birthday -- today. She made -- some of her sweet fruit buchtys* for a friend. -- me brought them for Josef -- it's his birthday, isn't it?"

"You can't fool me; you brought them for me!"

"You -- are one with a birthday!"

Figure 26 A Buchty

Note: A Buchty is a fruit-filled pastry made with little squares of dough with apples or raisins stacked in the center. Then the four corners are pulled up over the fruit to the center and baked. A Buchty looks like a small square pie. You hold it in your hand to eat. Also called a Kuchen or a Kolach.

"Will you sit with me at lunch, under the tree, and we can share these?" Eliska asked as she handed the day's repair orders to Zuba.

"Be there -- when -- whistle blows," Zuba replied as he reached out for the repair orders. He took the papers with one hand, then reached and held Eliska's hand with his other hand. Just then, Josef burst through the door. Zuba dropped Eliska's hand as Josef roared, "Damn trains, they take all day to get across the road. I must have stood there at least a half-hour!" Joseph glared, over the glasses perched on his nose, at his two employees. "What the hell are you two standing there for? Don't you have any work to do?"

Zuba whirled and headed for the door. He turned and looked back at Eliska, who was standing behind Josef. She blew Zuba a kiss and mouthed the word "Lunch!"

Time creeps by when lovers are apart. It trickles on like cold honey pours. When lovers are together, time is a twinkle in the eye.

The dinner whistle blew. The whirring and clanging noise of the repair shop stopped as the men picked up their lunch sacks and sat down on the floor to eat. Zuba grabbed his sack and made a hasty exit out the door. He met Eliska at a picnic table under the only tree in the whole coal yard.

Eliska brought rags, wiped the seats down, and laid a few cleaner ones down as a tablecloth. They sat on the same side of the picnic table. Eliska's delicate leg pressed tightly against the grease-stained work overalls of Zuba.

"You -- better -- not -- do!" Zuba stammered.

"Why not! It's my birthday, and I like to do that," Eliska replied, pressing her leg still closer.

"Ya, but -- but you -- get -- dress full of -- coal dust and grease," Zuba stammered.

"I wear a black skirt every day because of all the coal dirt around here. Nobody will know the difference."

They sat silently, eating the sweet buchtys, enjoying each other, all along, avoiding the sadness they felt.

At 12:30, the whistle blew, summoning everyone back to work.

"Time to go," Zuba said, as he stood up from the picnic table.

"That was too quick!" Eliska replied. "You will play in the band on Saturday night, won't you?"

"Don't think me should. ---Nobody like me -- you can play without me," Zuba replied.

"Nonsense! I like you, and you play good. It's a gadje beer hall, so we need the tuba. So, you come, OK?"

"It -- hard to be around -- you -- knowing -- you are to -- marry Jacob -- me. -- me -- could cry; it hurts in -- my chest -- bad."

"I feel it in my heart too, but what is, is…. When I'm married, I can't sit with you and eat sweet buchtys." Eliska laid her hand on Zuba's arm. "So, we have such a little time left, then we go our separate ways. We must make the best of this time."

Eliska became pensive. "After that… we can only see each other from a distance. But even apart, our hearts will be together… Hurry now, back to work! We both need these jobs!" Eliska replied.

They both turned, heads bowed, tears in their eyes, and trudged back to work. ~~~~~~

Chapter 15

THAT RED BANDANNA

Dance House, Litomysl Czechoslovakia, Saturday, May 19, 1917

The music was loud, and the lights were low. A crowd of merrymakers sat at tables arranged in straight rows leading from the edge of the dance floor to the back of the room. Another assortment of party-goers sat or stood at a long bar. The rousing clink of beer glasses echoed. Round after round disappeared down thirsty throats. Another big Saturday night for the gadje.

Bolda's little Roma band played with fury. Their polkas and waltzes kept the people always on the dance floor. Zuba and his tuba anchored the group, supplying a steady beat to keep everything moving.

When the music stopped, Eliska, still wearing Zuba's red bandanna, said, "Zuba, thanks for the solid beat. It's great to sing to!"

Zuba smiled a crooked smile and hung his head.

"Don't praise him too much," Bolda whispered to his daughter. "He will want more money, and that's less for us."

"Oh, Papa, don't be that way. He works hard and doesn't cause any trouble," Eliska replied.

"Ya, but he is just a dumb gadjo if he can't stick up for himself. Who am I to care?" Bolda snorted. "By the way, where did you get the red bandanna?"

"Just a friend, Papa."

"What friend?"

"Oh, Papa, can't I have any secrets?"

Bolda's face softened and flashed an 'I love you daughter' smile.' "Oh, I suppose girls need to have their little secrets."

Hanzi and Jacob noticed the red bandanna and how Eliska had defended Zuba. Hanzi came around and stood before Zuba. "Well, big fellow, how often do you dump the spit out of that horn? I bet there's a lake in there. A lake, I tell you, a big lake! Bet you got a fish in the lake too, a fish, I tell you," Hanzi taunted on, amused by his cleverness.

"I don't want to be around when he dumps it. I always knew he was full of spit, horse spit," Jacob joined in. He smiled at his tailored use of words and the obvious references.

Zuba sat and said nothing. He held his precious tuba and emptied the spit valve. Jacob stood up and said, "I have a big announcement to make!" He took out a leather bag from his clarinet case and handed it to Bolda. "Here's the rest of the dowry. Now Eliska and I can get married."

Bolda took the bag and held it high. "There's to be a wedding. My beautiful daughter Eliska and Jacob are to wed! Open a bottle of víno, so I can toast to Jacob and seal the deal."

Florica hugged her daughter and stroked Eliska's head. "My sweet, you will be a wonderful wife. May you bring us many grandchildren."

Hanzi jumped up and down. "A wedding, a wedding so much fun we'll have at the wedding! Dancing, singing, a little víno. Such fun we will have, all night we'll sing, dance, kiss the girls and drink víno," Hanzi said.

Jacob reached over and grabbed Eliska's hand and pulled her close.

"Don't pull me so hard. I'm not an old cow!" Eliska cried.

Jacob leaned over and whispered in Eliska's ear, "I'll teach you respect after our wedding night!" He gave her arm a hard twist as Eliska tried to pull away.

"I am not your property," Eliska growled.

"Don't give me any of your sass! You will be after we marry. I know how to handle a smart-mouth wife! I'll handle you like my father handles my mother!" Jacob replied.

Zuba sat frozen, staring at his shoes, hugging his tuba. A sinking feeling in his stomach accented the helplessness he felt. He could do nothing to help his beloved Eliska.

"It is best that the wedding be as soon as possible. I set a date for the wedding as Saturday, June 30," Bolda proclaimed. Everyone except Zuba and Eliska cheered. Jacob drank down the vino, grabbed Eliska, and kissed her hard on the mouth. "It's legal to kiss you now," Jacob said.

Eliska pulled away, wiped her mouth, and looked longingly across the bandstand at Zuba.

Zuba's tear-filled eyes met hers, echoing the ache of their broken hearts. ~~~~~~

Chapter 16

ZUBA CONFESSES

Palzek Farm, Litomysl Czechoslovakia, Sunday, June 3rd, 1917

The Palzek kitchen echoed with the sound of slurping and burping. Odors of chicken soup and sauerkraut hung in the air. "It's good you are with us again, Zuba," Emilia remarked, setting another bowl of pork hocks on the table. She stroked Zuba's head. "How is your work going?"

"Good, lots of trucks need to fix. -- They bring them from -- Karvina on the train. They are all broken down -- from the coal mines," Zuba replied.

"A horse don't never break down!" Petr snorted.

"Ya, but the Mack truck -—hauls as much as ten horses and don't need all the hay or -—scoop the manure," Zuba replied. "They talk about making a repair shop at Karvina -—then the work slow down a little."

"You are not going to Karvina; are you Zuba?" Emilia said, horrified at the prospect of her baby boy moving so far away.

"Well, sometimes -- me wish to get -- far from -- Litomysl, but don't think so," Zuba replied.

"What you need is a wife! That will make you stay at home at night and keep you working days. Have you seen any cute girls? There must be lots there in town," Petr teased his son.

"Well, there's one, but she is promised to another," Zuba replied.

"She isn't married yet. Win her away! Us Palzeks are charmers!" Petr boasted.

"Well -- that -- is not -- the problem," Zuba said.

"Well, what is it, then? You got a good job, take a bath once a week, are handsome, so you are a prime catch," Emilia said. "Does she like you?"

"Ya, we like each other a lot," Zuba replied.

"Can she cook? Remember, the wedding night don't last long. Good cooking does," Petr chuckled. He gave Emilia a gentle swat on her ample posterior. "So, what is the big problem?"

"She's -- she's -- a -- Roma," Zuba replied.

Astonishment swept Emilia's face as the silverware she was carrying slipped out of her hands and clattered to the floor. She crossed herself with the sign of the cross. "Oh, sweet Jesus, no! Not a gypsy girl!"

Petr slammed his silverware on the table. "What in hell are you doing messing with a gypsy girl? They steal, have no honor, always dancing and singing. Good for nothings. I taught you better!" he roared.

"But Papa, -- she -- sweet, -honest -- me, -- me, -- me, -- love her!" Zuba blurted out.

"Better let sleeping dogs lie, rather than sleeping with dogs!" Petr snapped.

"It don't -- make no difference, she -- is promised, -- they set the wedding -- we knew being together -- would come to -- no good," Zuba said with tears in his eyes.

"Good, it's settled. Look for a Czech girl next time," Petr said, as he cooled off.

Emilia went to Zuba and pulled his head to her soft bosom. "My poor baby, it's hard enough to be in love, but when a gypsy girl steals your heart, it's awful. I'll pray to Saint Wenceslas to heal your heart. Now eat before the food gets cold."

Petr wiped his mouth, let out an enormous burp. "You find a Czech girl and make us proud; don't shame us with a gypsy girl."

Zuba got up from the table. "Me -- not -- hungry, me want to lie down for a while, and then go back to Litomysl." ~~~~~

Chapter 17

ELISKA CONFESSES

Danka home, Litomysl Czechoslovakia, Sunday, June 3rd, 1917

The sun poured through the lone window of the two-room house. In the corner of the entry room, stacked boxes holding all the possessions of this Roma family were piled together to make a makeshift closet. In the cramped quarters of this ramshackle house, there isn't a lot of room for belongings. Fortunately, they didn't have many.

Florica Danka and her daughter Eliska were preparing Sunday dinner.

"Hurry, Eliska; the sausage is cooked. Put the eggs in the pan, so they are ready at the same time," Florica instructed Eliska. "I am so excited that you and Jacob are to wed. It will be a wondrous wedding. I sent a message to all the families of the clan, and everyone is coming. It will be a wonderful day!"

Eliska was quiet as she broke the eggs for frying. Her heavy heart was throbbing, and happiness was a distant thought.

"Why so quiet this morning, don't you feel well?" Florica said.

"I'm all right, it's just... I'm afraid about this marriage. I don't love Jacob, so it may not be good," Eliska said.

Florica called to her twin sons, "Luca! Stevo! Go out and play for a while. I need to talk to Eliska." The boys roared out of the house, one chasing the other, riding their wooden stick ponies.

Florica turned to Eliska. "It will be all right; you are just nervous about being with a man. You're a virgin, aren't you?"

"Yes, mama, of course!

"Well, a girl will always have some hesitation. It's only natural. I'm sure you are worthy, and Jacob will be proud to have you," Florica replied, reassuring her daughter.

Eliska cried, "But Mama, I don't love Jacob."

Florica pulled Eliska close to her, "Now, now I didn't love your father when we were married either. But it was the best, my Papa was right. After a baby or two, you will love Jacob with all your heart!"

Eliska sobbed in her mother's arms, "Jacob has a mean streak. Do you see the bruises on my arm? They are from when he grabbed me. It still hurts!"

"Well, if he hurts you, he will have to answer to Papa. After the wedding, you will be under his mother's care until after the first baby. Then you will be a full wife."

The sobbing daughter buried her head in her arms and cried that much louder. "But Mama, I love someone else!"

"You love someone else?" Florica said incredulously. "Who could it be? Which family is it?"

"He is not Roma, Mama."

"Not Roma! Do you mean a gadjo?"

"Yes, Mama."

"Saint Sara, help me. Who is he?"

"Zuba."

"Zuba, the stumbling mute?"

"Ya Mama."

"That's even worse. Did you lay with him?"

"No, Mama."

"Well, good! A Roma can't marry a gadjo! Aren't you thinking? You would be banned from the family!"

"I know, I know," Eliska sobbed, "but I love him so, he is good to me and loves me too, not just to get me to the wedding bed."

"Roma can't have any relationship with a banished person, not even greetings! We must avoid crossing their path. Remember my sister, Aunt Kizzy? She married a gadjo. Nobody has had anything to do with her since then. She is dead to us. Do you want that?" Florica said.

"I know, but you talk to her at the market and have tea with her."

"Hush girl, lest your Father hears you. Kizzy is my sister and dearest friend. If the clan knew I saw her, I would have to explain myself before the Kris (Roma Judicial Council). That wouldn't be good."

Eliska stepped back from her mother. "O Mama, what am I to do? I love Zuba so much, and I love you so much. Why must I choose?"

"It's the way of the Roma, and it's a good way. It has kept us together."

"If I love one, I lose the other."

"If you go to the gadjo, the Roma will banish you. It's best you marry Jacob. Don't bring shame on the family."

Eliska hung her head; *shame or the pain of a broken heart is a tough choice to make.* ~~~~~~

Chapter 18
IT'S BEST YOU GO

Coal Yard Litomysl, Czechoslovakia, Monday, June 4th, 1917

The coal yard was slick on a rainy Monday morning. Coal trucks loaded to overflowing rumbled out the coal yard gate, dropping chunks of coal along their lumbering way and splashing through rivulets of black slimy water.

Zuba and Eliska arrived from different directions; dodged the loaded coal trucks as they made their way to the coal yard office.

When Zuba approached her, he took his hat off, "Morning, Eliska!"

Eliska didn't raise his head when she replied, "Morning, Zuba."

They walked on in silence together, and as they approached the office. Zuba spoke, "Did -- your -- weekend -- good?"

Eliska kicked a small piece of coal, "Not so good."

"Why?"

"I told my Mama, I loved you. She had a fit."

Zuba turned his hat edge to edge and said, "I told my Mama and Papa too -- they tell me -- forget you -- find a nice Czech girl."

"I'm sorry I got us into this."

"You -- did -- nothing wrong. -- me the -- one -- that -kissed you."

"I kissed you first."

"No matter, -- there will be no more kisses for either of us."

"Oh Zuba, I hurt so. If I love you, I throw the love of my family away."

"You can't do ---it better to marry Jacob. Me nothing to lose your family for."

Eliska cried, "It's not right! It's not fair! Don't I matter? It's all about the family and the good of the clan!"

Zuba placed his big hand on Eliska's shoulder, "Family is important -- to both of us. It's best you go -- your way, and me go mine."

When they had arrived at the coal yard office, Josef Jelinek was already there. "Zuba! Put your damn wet hat on the table and come to my office. I don't want you dripping on my papers again."

Zuba complied and stood before Josef's desk. Josef shuffled the papers around while Zuba stood and waited. "I have a big opportunity for you. Would you like to transfer to the coal mine in Karvina? They liked your work when you were there. They want you there all the time," Josef said, looking up at Zuba, trying to assess his reaction. Then he added, "Now you don't need to go because I still need you here. Frankly, I don't want to train in another rookie like I did you. But the big boss said they would give you a five koruna per hour raise if you come. How does that sound?"

Zuba's eyes widened, "Me -- me, -- me, don't know -- Got no way to get there."

"You can take one truck with a load of supplies," Joseph said.

"Well, don't know. -- me like to think -- on it some."

"Let me know tomorrow. I have to tell the boss if it's OK."

"Ya, sure."

Zuba turned and left the office, strode across the office waiting room. Eliska waved a faint wave of goodbye at him, but he didn't acknowledge it.

Zuba reached the front door, he grasped the door handle and he paused. *This is the answer.* He whirled around and strode back into Josef's office. "Me take job, -- when me leave?"

Sadness washed over Josef's face. "Well, I said you don't have to go! You are my best mechanic, and I'll give you a five koruna raise here."

"This -- be best," Zuba said. "When leave?"

"Saturday, June 30th. You would start work on the first of July."

"Ya, me do that."

Zuba left Josef's office, then paused at Eliska's desk. He slowly ran his hand along the desk edge and, without looking up, said to Eliska, "This is best."

A bewildered Eliska said, "What is best?"

Zuba said nothing as he turned and walked out of the office. ~~~~~~

Chapter 19

Uncomfortable Music

Dance House -Litomysl Czechoslovakia Saturday, June 9, 1917

The dance went on for four hours, and the Bolda Danka band finished with their last set. "Play the Praha Polka," a drunken man yelled as he spilled beer on the edge of the bandstand.

"OK, we play it next, right after this one," Bolda said as he waved the little band into action.

"Gypsy! Don't forget, or I'll kick your ass! Can't trust no damn gypsies! I suppose they want me to grease your palms, so they can play the good old Praha Polka," the man yelled, spilling more beer on the dance floor. "Here, here's a koruna now play the damn polka," he said as he tossed the koruna at Bolda.

Bolda stiffened at the words of the man. Florica touched his arm. "Papa, hold your temper. Let's play the polka, and he will go away."

Bolda picked up the koruna and tossed it back at the man, "Go buy yourself some white willow aspirin. You'll need it in the morning."

Then he said under his breath, "I don't take money for insults from no damn gadje fool."

The band played a rousing version of the polka. The drunk man tried to dance but stumbled, passing out on the dance floor. Two bartenders grabbed him under each arm and escorted him out the door.

The little band finished the last set and put their instruments away. Jacob and Eliska had stepped down from the bandstand. Jacob leaned close to Eliska and whispered, "How are the wedding plans coming along. I can't wait to dance a little and get you to the marriage bed."

Eliska ignored his comment and announced, "Zuba is leaving the band. He got a job at Karvina. We'll miss you, Zuba."

Zuba said nothing as he continued wiping off his tuba.

"Well, good riddance. He never was much of a musician," Jacob said, "Who needs him? We played without him before and can do it again."

"Well, we'll not get any more gadje beer halls and a lot less money in your purse without him. I hope you're satisfied!" Eliska said.

Jacob grabbed Eliska around the waist and pulled her close to his chest. He nuzzled his lips up to her ear and whispered. "Quit defending that fool, or I'll teach you some manners. Or teach him some manners, whichever comes first."

Eliska tried to pull away from him, but he held her in a vice-like grip. "You're hurting me!" Eliska cried.

Zuba saw what Jacob was doing, and anger flared up inside him. *This is none of my business. She is his intended, but he should treat her better.*

"Let me go!" Eliska cried, pushing away from Jacob.

Jacob pulled Eliska tighter. Zuba could stand it no longer. He put his tuba down and stood up. *I'll hold Jacob in a bear hug and see if he likes it.* Zuba jumped off the bandstand and headed for Jacob, but before reaching Jacob, Bolda stepped between Zuba and Jacob. "I'll take care of this," Bolda growled to Zuba. "It's none of your business."

Bolda turned and grabbed Jacob by the back of his neck and the seat of the pants.

He lifted him until Jacob was standing on his tiptoes.

Bolda growled, "Let Eliska go, you dog." Jacob released Eliska, and then Bolda swung Jacob around and grabbed him by the lapels of his coat. "You will treat my daughter right, or I'll stomp the meanness out of you. Dowry or no dowry, we have our ways. You cannot be the head of the family by pain. Do you understand me?"

Jacob pleaded with Bolda, "Yes, Bolda, I didn't mean to make.... you mad," he blubbered, "Zuba thinks he's Eliska's patron saint or something. I had to show him that she is mine!"

Bolda spun Jacob around and barked, "She is yours, now don't be a jealous fool! Earn her respect, or you will have a sour marriage."

Jacob's red face showed nothing but hate as he looked over Bolda's shoulder and glared at Zuba. If looks could kill, Zuba's funeral would have been yesterday.

Bolda gave Jacob's jacket a good shake and commanded Jacob, "Cool off you damn fool! You better figure out how to control yourself, or you will answer to me!" Bolda released Jacob, and Jacob slammed his clarinet into its case and left the dance.

Bolda turned to Zuba, "I'm glad you are going. You are nothing but trouble. See the pain you caused my family. I know you have feelings for Eliska, but no way will I ever consent to you with my daughter. Now leave, we've got enough troubles."

"Me -- me -- sorry -- me didn't mean to cause -- trouble. -- Just pay, and me go," Zuba said sheepishly.

"Pay you? After all the trouble you have caused. You are lucky I don't throw you out the door. Git! I never want to see your face again!"

Zuba meekly picked up his tuba and walked to the dance hall door.

Eliska sobbed in her mother's arms. "It's not fair to cheat Zuba out of his earnings."

"Hush, child, your Papa, knows best," Florica said as she stroked Eliska's head. "The Roma way and the gadje way will never mix." ~~~

Chapter 20

GOING AWAY

Coal Yard Office, Litomysl Czechoslovakia, Friday, June 29, 1917

A shiver ran up Zuba's spine as he entered to get his morning repair orders. *I don't want to -- see Eliska; I come early, leave quick.*

Eliska was already there, working since first light. She wore the same green satin blouse that she had on the night they met. Zuba's big red bandanna proudly adorned her neck.

She handed Zuba his work orders, whispering. "I suppose you will leave tomorrow early?"

"Ya, me take -- the truck home to the farm -- to get my things and load up for Karvina and leave Saturday morning."

"I'll miss you, Zuba," Eliska said, wiping her red eyes as she shuffled through a pile of blank forms.

Zuba turned away, unable to look at his beautiful Eliska. He strode to the door, stopped, but didn't look back. A dam of emotion lay hard on his heart; if it broke, she would see his tears. *Don't want to make it any harder than it already is.* "Me -- too, but -- best -- me go, don't want -- to make -- no more trouble -- for our families," Zuba said.

"You didn't make the trouble. They did. We did nothing wrong to love each other."

"No -- matter -- that's what is. -- if me could, me would marry you -- and hold you for the rest of my life. -- But we -forget -- each other. You want -- gold cross back?"

"No, never! You keep it. Then you will remember, I love you," Eliska said, weeping.

Zuba didn't turn back to face her. He stood, head low, waiting for something, anything, that would change the situation. He couldn't bear to walk away from her. It felt like his feet had melted into the floor.

Eliska wiped her eyes, jumped to her feet, and hurried over to Zuba. She slipped her arms around his waist and laid her head on his back.

"I love you. Take me with you!" Eliska blurted out.

"Me -- me -- can't, it -- wouldn't -- be right. What we do? -- We need -- two places to live. Where -- money come from?"

"If we are married, we can live together. I can cook, wash clothes, and love you. We'll get by; I don't eat much."

"It not-- work. Don't you see? -- We no good together -- no matter -- the love we have."

Zuba pulled her arms from his stomach, turned, raised Eliska's tear-stained face to his and kissed her on each of her eyes, then on the lips. "Now, no more tears and -- no more wet kisses."

Zuba walked to the door, stepped out, hesitated, and slowly closed the door.   ~~~~~~

Eliska worked late before trudging the quiet streets of Litomysl to the Roma village. Only a lone lantern on a lamp pole lit her way. As she approached the Danka house, Florica opened the door. "It's late, Eliska, supper is still warm, come, eat before you go to bed,"

Eliska paused and said, "I would like to sit outside a while in the cool night. My heart is troubled, and I need to think and maybe pray a little."

"Don't be long; lock the door when you come in."

Eliska sat on a wooden bench next to the door. She lowered her head and cried softly. As she sat there, a dirty, dark-faced little urchin came skipping along the street. Her clothes hung in tatters, and a ragged babushka wrapped her head. She skipped gaily, bouncing a small rubber ball, humming a musical soliloquy. An angelic smile danced on her dirt-streaked face. She smiled sweetly at Eliska and said, "Hello."

"What are you doing out so late, little girl? You should be at home!" Eliska said.

"I am home," the girl answered. She threw the ball in the air, and when it came down, she clumsily bounced the ball with both hands.

"You are home? I've never seen you before. What's your name, child?"

"I have many names; most don't matter now."

"You speak in riddles. Where are your parents? Where is your home?

"My last home was Germany before that Egypt. Parents are gone," the child said. She picked up her ball, rolled it over and over in her hands, and sat next to Eliska.

"You confuse me. Egypt is a long way away."

"I didn't confuse you, love confused you," the girl said, throwing the ball up in the air and trying to catch it, missing it, and then chasing after it.

"Love has given me nothing but hurt. I am not confused about that."

"You can't leave love, nor will it leave you. You cannot keep love unless you share it. When hate eats love, love dries up. Love blows away in a whiff of breeze, then is smothered by the dirt. When kindness rains on the dirt, the seeds of love will again sprout, growing to a trickle, to a stream, then to a rushing river."

"The only rushing river I get is the tears that I cry," Eliska said.

"Tears wash your soul clean. That's why God made them."

"What makes you such a know-it-all, little girl? You can't be over eight years old."

"I am older than you."

"Older than me? I don't think so!"

"In your dreams, I see fathers dying, mothers weeping, children wandering, love dying. Have you seen that?"

Eliska sucked in a deep breath as a perplexed look crossed her face. "No, I guess I haven't."

"You will before you come home. It will come soon enough. Grab love now and hang on for all your worth."

"You are a strange little girl. You must be hungry; would you like something to eat? I can get it for you," Eliska said.

"That would be nice."

"Good! Stay here. I'll be right back." Eliska entered the darkened house and went to the cupboard, took out bread and honey.

Florica got up, "Are you still up? What are you doing?"

"I'm getting something to eat for the little girl outside."

"A little girl, at this time of the night?"

"Come and look" Eliska took the bread, and Florica followed behind as they went back outside. "Here, little one, some nice bread, and honey......... Where are you?"

Florica stepped out of the house, "There is no one here, Eliska. You must be dreaming. I know your heart is troubled; maybe sleep will help."

"But Mama, she was just here! It was no dream! How could it be?"

"Hush child, you are tired. Tomorrow will be a better day."

~~~~~

Chapter 21

PLEASE TAKE ME ALONG

Litomysl to Karvina Czechoslovakia, Saturday, June 30, 1917

Figure 27 Dark Figure

It was pitch dark when Zuba entered the coal yard. He lit the acetylene headlights, and they shone on the maintenance building ahead of him. He drove the truck into the building and began loading everything that he was to take to Karvina.

While loading, he glimpsed a dark figure in a dimly lit corner of the shed. *It must be my imagination.* He packed the new chains on the floor of the truck box, placed his two gunny sacks of clothes on top, and then his tuba so that the tuba wouldn't get crushed. His heart was heavy; his mother had cried and held on to him as he left. *Mama, Papa. And me love Eliska.... It hurts to leave her behind.*

Zuba's thoughts were interrupted as a dark figure stepped out of the darkness with a bag on his back.
~~~~~

Just a beggar, looking for a handout, but they can be dangerous. Zuba reached into his toolbox and pulled out a big wrench. Holding it over his head like a club, he faced the man. "What -- do you want? You no belong here!"

Slowly, the figure advanced on Zuba. Zuba raised his wrench higher in the air and backed into the glare of the headlights. *Want to see him! There might be more of them here.*

The figure stepped in, bathed in the glow of the headlights, and Zuba started to swing the big wrench.

"No! Don't, Zuba, it's me, Eliska!"

Zuba hesitated and stared at the dark figure. It was Eliska, dressed in a man's black pants and a shirt with a black coal miners cap on her head! "What? -- What? -- You do here? Me just about hit you!"

"If you did, it might take all the pain away. ..... I want to go with you."

Zuba dropped the wrench and clutched both of her shoulders, "We talked on this, -- it's not to be."

"Please, I need to be with you now!" Eliska insisted.

"You know -- we can't -- be together."

"It doesn't matter anymore. I've already shamed my family by wearing men's clothes and running away. My father must give the dowry back, and that will make him furious."

"It -- can't -- work!"

"We can make it work!" Eliska pleaded.

Zuba softened, "Won't your family worry?"

"Yes, but I left them a note."

"Don't -- know if this -- a good idea."

"I love you, Zuba."

Zuba was quiet for a moment, then his resolve stiffened, "It not work! -- Why -- you not listen? -- Go home!" Zuba shouted at her.

Eliska's shoulders sagged as she heard the words.

She had pinned all her hopes on making Zuba understand. Gazing into his eyes, she mumbled, "I love you Zuba, with all my heart and soul."

Zuba swallowed hard, "Me too, but it -- not work, listen now!" Zuba said as he turned his back to her.

Eliska tried one more time to change Zuba's mind. "All I hear is my heart beating, and between every heartbeat, there's a tiny echo saying, I love you, I love you, I love you."

Zuba was quiet, pondering her statement, "There only be -- pain."

"I have more pain than I can stand. I've lost my family, and my heart aches for you. How can there be any more?" Eliska said, weeping openly.

Zuba's heart was in his throat as he reached for Eliska and pulled her close. His big arms engulfed her and wrapped her in a cocoon of love. "Me sorry -- you hurt -- it -- my fault. -- Do you know -- what you are getting into?"

"All I know is I love you and want to be with you," Eliska replied.

Zuba was silent, turning this over in his mind. *How are we to live? -- don't deserve her. -- Will she stay with me?*

Finally, he decided, and he calmly stated, "If you come -- we marry and by a priest. -- Will you -- marry me?"

"Yes, Zuba, oh yes Zuba, I'll love you forever more."

Zuba pulled her close and kissed Eliska's tear-stained lips. "Looks like a -- lifetime of -- wet kisses." ~~~~~~

Chapter 22

THE ROOM

Karvina Czechoslovakia, Saturday, June 30th, 1917

Zuba and Eliska drove all day Saturday, arriving at Karvina as the sun was setting. They entered the Dvur Olsiny Hotel and booked a room. Pesek, the stable boy, was again at the front desk. He smirked and said, "Oh, the big tippers, eh, want two rooms again?"

"No," said Zuba, "one."

"The two of you can't stay in the same room. You married?"

"No," Zuba said, "but we -- will -- soon -- be, -- just -- give -- one room."

"If you're not married, I should charge you extra fifty korunas. You'll get the room messed up. I'll have extra work," Pesek said, leering at the couple.

"We go to another hotel," Zuba said, as he turned and walked away.

Pesek jumped over the desk and caught up with Zuba and grabbed him by the shirt sleeve. "No. No, wait. I can help you. There's a room over the stable. Nice and clean, but hard to rent. I could rent it for... for.... the same price as a room here and you both could stay there. It's quiet except for the horses. What you say to that?"

"Let's take it! Zuba, it will be all right," Eliska said.

After paying Pesek, they put their sacks of clothes in the room and ate supper in the big dining hall. During the meal, Zuba yawned and nodded. After nodding off for the third time, he awoke with a start. "Long day, -- sleep -- be good."

"But Zuba, tomorrow is our wedding day. We need to celebrate!"

"Oh ya -- sure," Zuba turned to Pesek, "Bring us -- Stolní víno wine!

"Oh Zuba, can we afford it?

"Just a couple glasses, -- we have to -- celebrate!"

Pesek brought the Stolní víno, carefully wiped two glasses off with his soiled apron, and poured the wine with a flourish. "There you are my two lovebirds. It's on the house!" Pesek took a small candle out of his pocket, set it in the middle of the table, lit it, and bowed.

Eliska and Zuba thanked him, and after he left, Eliska spoke, "You know what we should do? Get close and link our arms together, and I'll give you some wine from my glass, and you give some from your glass. Do you want to?"

"Ya, -- me guess.

They linked arms and looking into each other's eyes, and they took turns giving each other a sip. After each sip, they whispered, "I love you."

They sipped slow and daintily, prolonging the moment until the glasses were empty.

Eliska broke the silence first. "We should get to sleep, Zuba; tomorrow is our big day.

"Ya, me guess," Zuba answered.

They got up from the table and, hand in hand, went to their room. "How will we do this, Zuba? There's only one bed! I can't lie to you before we're married," Eliska said.

"You take the bed, me -- sleep -- in the truck box -- need blanket," Zuba said.

Eliska dutifully brought Zuba a blanket. She lingered before Zuba. "Maybe a kiss to prove you are not still mad at me for coming along?"

"Me not -- mad at -- you, just worried -- this -- not be a good idea."

Eliska made an exaggerated lip pucker and batted her eyes at Zuba. "Just a little kiss to tempt you as to what is to come?"

Figure 28 Entrance to the Room

"How -- can -- you be-- silly when -- me worried?"

Eliska smiled a smile that was more bluff than bravado. "It'll work, I promise. We'll make it if we're together."

"Hard to believe -- tomorrow maybe wake, and this be -- a dream. -- was -- afraid -- to even think -- you could -- love me. -- And now -- here you are."

"Believe it. Now, stop talking and kiss me, or we'll never get any sleep!"

Zuba pulled her into his arms and lifted her until her feet dangled in the air, then kissed her tenderly. ~~~~~~

Chapter 23

SLEEPING ON CHAINS

Karvina Czechoslovakia, Sunday, July 1st, 1917

Eliska rose early. She rubbed lavender splash water behind each ear and then carefully brushed her long ebony black hair until it shone with a silky gleam. Rubbing charcoal on her eyelids, she darkened them to the perfect shade of sultry. A cool translucence danced on her skin when she powdered her face in cornstarch. She reddened her lips with beet juice mixed with bacon grease. A double aphrodisiac for a man!

She dressed in a flowing black dress and a green satin blouse and positioned each piece exactly right.

She tucked Zuba's big red bandana carefully over the shoulders of her blouse and into her bodice. Her black hair entwined around and through her gold earrings. The sparkling earrings dangled from her ears as she shook her hair to get the perfect tousled look.

Smoothing out any lingering wrinkles from her dress, she stepped out into the sultry July morning. Head erect, she bounced along on springs of happiness, giving a lifting dance to her step. Just like a child skipping along. A smile crept across her face as the sunlight gently warmed her blouse. She tiptoed up to the Mac truck and gently tapped on the truck box. "Zuba, sleepy head, wake up! The sun is up! Come quick, time to go to church!"

"Me hear you, but this pile of chains me sleep on, -- feels good -- me sleep a little longer." Zuba's voice echoed from deep in the truck box.

"Don't you dare, it's our wedding day, get your best clothes on, we're going to the Saint Peter of Alcantara Church!" Eliska cried out.

"You mean these clothes?" Zuba said slyly, as he stepped around the front of the truck wearing his best blue chambray shirt and bib overalls.

"You fooled me. You are dressed."

Zuba stood transfixed at the sight of the slim beauty before him. "Ya, me -- was awake since -- sunup, those -- chains are -- hard to sleep on. Hope you -- slept well in my -- nice soft bed," Zuba stammered.

"It was all right, but I'd sooner snuggle up to you."

"How do me look? -- This is my best clean pair of overalls."

"You look very handsome. Let's go!"

"Maybe a kiss -- before we go?" Zuba suggested.

Eliska stood on her tiptoes and kissed Zuba longingly.

"You taste—good!"

"Next thing you will tell me that I remind you of food."

"Ya, breakfast!"

"Well, let's go," Eliska said as she grabbed Zuba's hand, pulling him toward the church.

"Wait, me got something -- special for you," Zuba said as he pulled a bright bouquet of yellow daisies from behind his back and presented them to Eliska.

"Where did you get these?"

"Over there, at our picnic spot -- next to the -- swan pond. Long walk, but me need -- work the kinks out. A little nervous -- me think."

They hastened up the street to the church with the crooked floor, Saint Peter of Alcantara. After mass, they approached the priest.

"Father -- you have time -- to marry us?" Zuba said, hat in his hand.

"Of course, I can do it next month with the other August weddings. You time to plan the arrangements and have marriage instruction."

"Oh no, Father -- we need to get -- married right away!" Zuba said.

"What's the big hurry?" The priest asked.

"We don't -- want baby to come -- before we're married," Zuba said.

"So that's the way it is, is it?"

Zuba hung his head, "She wouldn't -- let me alone, -- she kept -- following me and -- so here we are."

Eliska crossed her fingers and squeezed Zuba's arm hard. She looked away and rolled her eyes.

Father hesitated and said, "Well, if that's the case, I suppose I better do it right away. But first, are you both Catholic?"

Eliska and Zuba both nodded yes.

"First, the instruction, and I'll marry you." The priest spent over an hour explaining the duties of man and wife and how the children should be raised. He married them, blessed them, and said, "When is the baby due? Do you want to arrange a baptism date?"

"Not right now, -- we haven't slept together yet -- may take time -- but we'll let you know," Zuba said

"I thought you said a baby was coming?" The bewildered priest replied.

"Oh yes, a baby might come -- but got to get married first. Then -- lots of babies. Maybe big business for you," Zuba said matter-a-factly.

The priest walked away, scratching his head, and smiling.

On the way back to the hotel, Eliska held firmly to Zuba's arm. "I think you fooled the priest Zuba," she said, smiling.

"Ya, but me didn't lie -- me no want to sleep in the truck box for a whole month! -- me said it plain. It's not my fault -- he no understand. Did you want -- to wait that long?"

"I don't want to wait another minute. Let's hurry to the room, pull the shades, and pretend that it's night."

When they arrived at their room, Eliska removed her blouse and skirt. She stood before Zuba with nothing on but the red bandanna. "Zuba, get undressed!"

"It's -- kinda -- light -- in -- here, -- maybe -- wait -- till -- dark."

"You're just bashful! Let me help you," Eliska said. She slowly unbuttoned Zuba's shirt and ran her fingers over his muscular chest.

"Do -- me have -- to take -- everything off?" Zuba stammered.

"Oh, No! You can leave on the gold cross I gave you."

Zuba's heart beat faster and faster. His passion rose as she touched him. Their lips met, and Zuba picked Eliska up, carried her over, and laid her on the bed. He lay beside her and kissed her. "Do you think it's too light?" Eliska whispered.

"Dark -- enough."

They spent the afternoon in bed, alternating between sleeping and making love. In the late afternoon, Zuba was sound asleep as Eliska sat on the edge of the bed and sang softly,

"Blue eyes, sweet blue eyes."

"Burn with passion eyes, how you hypnotize!"

"How I adore you so, how I need you, though,"

"I've seen you glow! I've seen your show!"

"Darkness yours conceal, mighty fires, real,"

"Now my fate will seal burn my soul with zeal!"

"But my love for you, now the time is true,"

"Will refresh anew like the morning dew!"

"Blue eyes, sweet blue eyes."

"They implore me into faraway lands."

"Now love reigns where peace reigns."

"Now, there's no suffering. Our love is not forbidden." ~~~~~~

Chapter 24

THE SOUND OF LOVE

At the Cottage Karvina Czechoslovakia, Sun Aug 15th, 1917

~~~~~~

Is the sound of love a well-turned phrase or a loving glance?

~~~~~~

The young couple stayed above the stable for a week. Each night was more passionate than the night before. They moved when Zuba rented a small one-bedroom cottage in the coal miner's section of town. It was at the end of a cobblestone street and surrounded by other decrepit houses.

Dirty children used a wagon wheel rim to play a vigorous hoop and stick game on the sidewalks. Once clean and neat, the surrounding houses were smudged in various shades of black, gray, dark, and dingy. No one bothered to whitewash them anymore, as the coal dust and the smoke from the cookstoves made it impossible to keep the houses clean.

Zuba worked six days a week at the mine's repair shop. Eliska busied herself, making the little cottage into a cozy home. She wiped the windows clean of coal stain. The interior of the house was bright and comfortable. She sewed curtains from the gunny sacks that had held their clothes. Simple, but the warmth of love shone through. In the far corner sat an old coal cookstove. A rough-hewn table surrounded by two dilapidated chairs graced the center of the kitchen, all discarded by the family across the street.

Figure 30 Eliska's New Home

She covered the table with a clean white tablecloth and placed a vase of her dried wedding daisies right in the center. As a finishing, welcome touch, she planted petunias in the window box.

Figure 29 Gunnysack

Eliska hummed a quiet song as she busied herself around the hot kitchen. Supper was in the oven, and the table set. Singing under her breath, she often peeked out the window looking for Zuba. They married a month and a half ago, and life is wonderful. She loved the way he loved her, and his tenderness toward her came as a pleasant bonus. Even with his kindness, she knew he was strong enough to care for and protect her.

Eliska felt a deep ache as she thought of her family back in Litomysl, but she never regretted marrying Zuba. She wrote a letter to her family asking for their forgiveness but had not received a reply, nor did she expect one. She helped Zuba write a letter to his family but had not received an answer from his family either.

The hot August sun was sinking low when Zuba came through the door. Eliska wiped her sweaty forehead on her apron, lunged into his arms, and planted a kiss on his lips.

"Ah, wet kisses again, me see," Zuba said, smiling a satisfied smile, "what's for supper?"

Eliska playfully swatted him with her wooden spoon. "You come home, and all you think of is food?"

"Ya, me could smell your cooking all the way down the street."

"Oh, you know what we're having?"

"Ya burned carp, scorched apples, and fried water," Zuba teased, "Me thought the house was on fire."

Eliska swatted him again, "I cook good. I always see a clean platter in front of you when you get done eating!"

"Me eat it just because me love you -- me afraid of wooden spoon!"

Zuba sat at the dinner table, and Eliska swatted him again. "Wash your hands. They were full of grease and coal soot. Don't dirty my tablecloth!"

Zuba ambled over the washbasin, poured water in, grabbed the lye soap, washed his hands, and sat back down. "What's -- white tablecloth for? You -- save it for special occasions."

"This is a special occasion!"

"It is? -- What?"

Eliska was quiet. A shy smile pulled at the corners of her mouth. "Eat your supper, and then I'll tell you."

"Oh, me have something special for you too," Zuba replied.

Zuba ate his supper with relish and, when finished, wiped his plate with a piece of bread, then let out a large burp. A legacy from his father!

"Your thunder praise is loud for burned carp," Eliska remarked.

"Ya, dat was good."

"Now, what did you bring me?" Eliska asked anxiously.

Zuba reached into his bib overalls chest pocket and pulled out a small brown package wrapped with a string. "Me couldn't get you a wedding present, so me made this."

"Oh, you were present enough," Eliska giggled, unwrapping the package carefully. She made sure not to tear the paper.

Eliska could use it again. The string she wrapped up and put in her apron pocket. She opened the last fold of the paper, and her eyes grew wide. "What is this, Zuba? Is this the cross I gave you?"

"No, -- Another one me made for you."

"It looks the same, but where did you get the gold? We can't afford it."

"Remember when we left Litomysl? -- Mr. Jelinek call me to office?"

"Ya, for more orders, I thought."

"Mr. Jelinek had a guilty conscience. He came to me -- and confessed he had been underpaying me. The priest told him in confession to make it right. So, he gave me three gold korunas. Me made it from one of them." Zuba said proudly.

"Oh Zuba, it's glorious! But we should use the koruna for something we need more."

"Don't worry. -- it be fine. -- Don't put no sorrow on my gift."

Eliska was visibly pleased: she walked over to Zuba and kissed him. She took his hand and placed it on her tummy. Eliska smiled slyly, "Now, here's a gift for you. What do you feel?"

"A fat tummy. me think you put -- on weight."

"Women usually do when they have a baby."

"Some women just get fat and no baby! -- You probably are eating too much," Zuba said, going back to wipe his plate with the bread.

"I'm eating for two now!" Eliska said earnestly.

A puzzled look crept across Zuba's face, "Why -- eat for two?" After he said these words, he dropped the gravy-soaked bread onto his plate. His head came up, his eyes widened, and his mouth dropped open. "Eating for two? -- Are you -- are you -- are -- we -- a baby?"

Eliska let out a squeal, "Yes, Zuba, I am with child!"

Zuba leaped to his feet, sweep up Eliska in his arms, and whirled her around the tiny kitchen. Zuba laughed and yelled. "Me gonna be a Papa! Me gonna -- be a Papa! Me gonna be a --!" Then he became silent. *How could me support a child? How to live? Shouldn't have made the gold cross.*

"We may need extra money," Zuba said. He continued, "The foreman wants -- people to play in the company band. Me don't want -- do it because -- practice on Sunday after mass. -- means less time together if me do. -- But now maybe."

Eliska placed her arms around him, kissed his neck. She put her head on his chest. "Oh Zuba, Sunday is our only day together," she quietly said.

"Ya, but me must."

"Well, whatever you think is best." ~~~~~~

Nane chave, nane bacht. (If there are no children, it is bad luck.) Romani proverb.

~~~~~~

Chapter 25

A LOVING GLANCE TURNS INTO A LEGACY

Cottage, Karvina Czechoslovakia, Mon March 11, 1918

The morning March sun poured through the kitchen window, burning off the rising fog from the melting spring snow. Trickles of water tumbled into the cracks and crevices in the street, percolating into the ditches surrounding the village.

Eliska, now big with child, stood at the coal stove fixing Zuba's breakfast. Zuba came into the kitchen, pulling his suspenders over his broad shoulders. He walked up behind Eliska and kissed her on the neck. He slid his hands around her big belly. "Good morning Eliska! How -- our baby this morning?"

"Busy as a rabbit running from a fox. Jumping around all over the place. We'll need the midwife quick. I talked to Mrs. Novak. She will come when the time is due."

"Ya, her husband said -- can come anytime. -- Knows what to do, -- she got six kids."

"I don't care how many kids she has had; how many has she delivered?" Eliska snapped back.

"Now, now, no get anguish, -- she the best midwife in Karvina. You said she stopped and -- talked to you last week."

"I know. I like Mrs. Novak, but I guess I'm a little afraid."
~~~~~~

"Don't worry, pray to Saint Sara. Me sure she will come. Saint Zuba will be there, -- Saint Wenceslas might come too." Zuba replied playfully.

Eliska swatted Zuba with her wooden spoon. "Did they ever deliver a baby?"

"Saint Zuba delivered lots of calves, pigs, and a litter of puppies -- Does that count?"

"That's reassuring if I have a puppy!" Eliska replied, holding onto her large tummy.

"It be all right, -- women do this all the time, -- me get a couple of days off to help -- when the time comes," Zuba reassured her.

"You better hurry, or you will be late for work!"

Zuba finished his breakfast porridge, got up, pulled on his coat, and put on his black hat. He grabbed his lunch sack and left, getting only a short way, when he heard Eliska scream. He whirled around and re-entered the cottage. Eliska squatted by the table, holding on to the edge with both hands.

"It's time! Get Mrs. Novak, the water broke!"

"Ya -- ya. -- me -- go -- to—who?—who -- you want?" Zuba said.

"Don't talk! Go get Mrs. Novak!" Eliska screamed.

Zuba hurried along the street, stopped at a house, pounded on the door with the name of Novak painted on it. A portly, older woman came out. "What's the matter?"

"A baby -- a -- baby -- here it comes," Zuba stammered. He turned and started back down the street.

"Wait a minute, who are you, and who is having a baby?" Mrs. Novak called to Zuba.

"Me! -- me-- having a -- baby! Come quick -- now!" Zuba replied frantically. He grabbed Mrs. Novak by the hand and pulled on her.

She twisted her hand back, "You called on the wrong Mrs. Novak. You want Clare Novak; she lives across the street. She's a midwife."

Zuba tipped his hat, twirled around, and mumbled, "Me sorry," then crossed the street and stumbled to the house shown.

He pounded on the door, yelling, "Me having -- a -- bab -- a baby! -- Come -- quick -- now come!"

Clare Novak opened the cottage door, "You must be Zuba. Eliska told me you would come. Is it her time to deliver?"

"Ya -- ya -- come quick! -- Now -- hurry!"

"Now, don't worry, it will be fine. It takes a while, especially with the first one. I'll be right there," Clare Novak said.

"But -she's a—Roma -- things -- are -- different!" Zuba stammered.

"Believe me; it works the same, no different."

"Me -- worried -- about -- the -- baby!"

"It's all right to worry. Eliska is a strong young woman, and her hips are set right. There will not be any trouble," Clare replied.

"You -- ever -- deliver a -- Roma baby before?"

"Yes, I have!"

"Do -- they—have horns?"

"What! Where in the world did you get such an idea?"

"The guys in -- the repair -- shop told—me it might happen."

"You tell those jokers to stop sticking their wrenches up their noses. Grease musta soaked into their brains!"

"But. -- But -- they said -- when a gadjo marries a Roma -- the baby has horns!"

"Listen, I've delivered Roma, Czech, Polish, German and French babies. It's all the same, and not one set of horns did I see."

"Was a Czech married to a Roma?"

"I am married to a Roma. None of our six children have horns. A couple of them are bull-headed, but no horns!"

Zuba let out a sigh of relief. "Me guess -- should not be fooled by -- those fellows funning me."

Mrs. Novak packed up her kit, and with Zuba trying to keep up, they hurried back to the cottage.

Entering, they saw that Eliska had placed a blanket on the floor. She was squatting over it, holding on to the edge of the table.

"Good, you are ready," Clare said as she examined Eliska. "Zuba, go outside and chop wood for the stove!"

Zuba stood baffled, "But we -- burn coal -- in the stove?"

"Never mind asking questions! Do it! Don't stop until I get you!"

Zuba dutifully put on his hat and left for the woodpile.

"Now we can get down to business. I don't need a man around, underfoot. If he sees what you go through, you will never have another baby," Clare said, chuckling.

Clare continued, "We women have to be tough to keep the family going. Where is the string I asked you to save?"

"Oh, it's in my apron," Eliska said, nodding to her apron hanging on the chair.

"Good, now push!"

Eliska's face contorted in pain. A low moan escaped her lips. Sweat beaded her forehead as the labor increased in intensity. When the head of the baby appeared, Clare laid Eliska on her back on the floor. With help from Clare, the baby was born. Clare raised the baby by the feet and gave a sharp slap on the baby's bottom. The child let out a gurgle, then a startled cry.

"Good, it's a healthy girl!"

Clare laid the baby on Eliska's stomach and retrieved Eliska's saved string from Eliska's apron. Clare tightly tied the string, close to the baby's belly, around the umbilical cord attached to Eliska. Then she tied another string around the umbilical cord, two inches away from the first tie. Finally, Clare cut between the two strings, cutting the baby loose from Eliska.

"Good, the ties are holding, no bleeding!"

Clare wrapped gauze around the baby's stomach to hold in the belly button.

She cleaned the baby's eyes and smeared them with a solution of liquid silver. Clare laid the baby in a wooden cradle Zuba had made, then she helped Eliska up and into bed.

"You stay in bed for a while, don't worry about bleeding. I tied the cord. The afterbirth can come quickly or in a few hours. There shouldn't be much more bleeding."

Clare wiped Eliska's sweaty face. "You did a good job! You have a beautiful baby girl!"

Eliska lay quietly in the bed, pale and drawn. Her lower lip quivered when she spoke. "Has Zuba seen the baby?"

"Not yet. I'll get the baby ready and call him when you have rested. He will be glad she doesn't have horns."

"Horns? Why did he think the baby would have horns?"

"Oh, it's a stupid gadje tale. Zuba's worker buddies said the Roma race was made when the devil mated with a woman from India. Don't worry; I set him straight. It'll be all right. You have a good man there."

"I know he is," Eliska sighed weakly as she fell off to sleep.

Three hours passed, and Zuba has chopped every log he could find. Exhausted, he sat on the chopping block and contemplated the future. *What now? A baby to support? Don't have enough for ourselves. -- Need more money. Can sell one of the gold coins. —Is it a boy or a girl? A boy would be nice to take after me, maybe talk better, be smarter, and read better than me. –if a girl, she would be -- as pretty as Eliska. That -- be nice. -- Oh, me don't care if the baby is healthy. And if not, me still love it with all my heart.*

While he was pondering this, Clare came out, "You follow me now. The baby is here." Entering the cottage, Clare picked up the baby and gave it to Zuba. "Here's your little girl."

Zuba's eyes filled with tears. "How -- me -- hold her?"

"Cradle her head with one hand and her little bottom with the other," Clare replied.

Zuba cautiously took the baby in his arms and pulled her to his chest. "A little -- girl -- with blond -- hair, -- blue eyes -- and oh so pretty."

"Now, she is still greasy, but don't wipe it off until she is nursing good. It protects her from losing too much moisture."

As Zuba tenderly cradled the small child in his big arms, he tiptoed over to Eliska and knelt by the bed. Eliska slowly opened her eyes. "Oh Zuba, you are here. Have you seen the baby?"

Zuba gently placed the baby on Eliska's chest. "Right here -- you did a good job -- making her."

"Well, you had a part in it too," Eliska replied as she unwrapped the baby.

"All me did was chop wood," Zuba said sheepishly.

Eliska chuckled, "Yes, I know. I mean, we chopped wood, really good, nine months ago,"

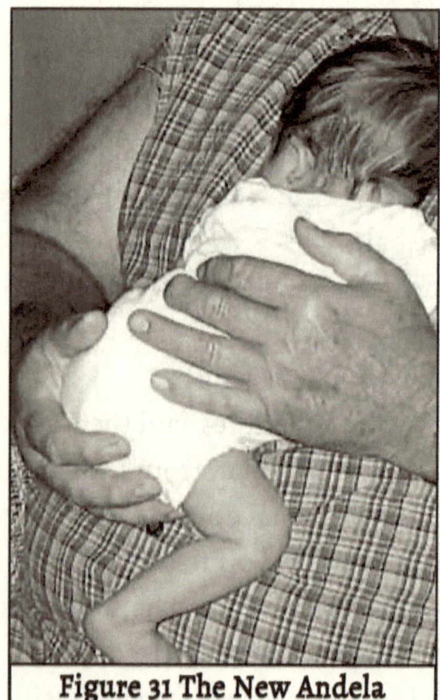

Figure 31 The New Andela

"We burned coal nine months ago," Zuba said, puzzled.

"Never mind, I'm sure the wood will burn in the stove and keep us warm as well as the coal," Eliska said, giggling as she counted the baby's toes and fingers.

"They're all here! See the blue eyes, just like yours, and the blond hair will last," Eliska said proudly.

"Ya --is -- for sure!" Zuba answered gleefully.

Eliska chuckled, "And no horns!"

"Oh no, you -- hear about the horns. -- Sometimes me -- so dumb. -- Sorry -- me think that."

"What would you do if the baby had horns?" Eliska teased.

Zuba chuckled, "Me thought on that -- me couldn't think of any good use for the horns—may be easier to keep a hat on—in a windy day."

"I wish I had my wooden spoon now," Eliska replied. "I'd fix you."

"Oh, me almost forgot -- here's a present -- for the baby."

"I do the work, and the baby gets the present? It isn't fair," Eliska pouted wryly.

Zuba unwrapped a small piece of wrapping paper and took out a gold cross. "Here -- me made for her."

"Oh, Zuba, it is so beautiful. Just like mine! But she is too little to wear it now. She might get it tangled up."

"Me thought that too -- so me made a small cedar box -- to keep it in and—with extra room for more stuff."

"What are we to call her Zuba? Eliska said.

"Me like Andela," Zuba said

"Me too, that means a messenger from God," Eliska said.

"It settled --then," Zuba said.

"Oh, Zuba, a message of our love, from God. I love you so!"

"Me -- too."

A decrepit room in a poor neighborhood. Zuba worries about getting by. Two different people, now truly one. They came together and formed this small child, now suckling at her mother's breast. The adoring father looks on. His big hand strokes his beloved wife's head, his other hand protectively resting on the newborn child. This drama goes on forever. It still is and always will be.... The richest scene in the world. ~~~~~~

Chapter 26

BACK ON THE FARM

Cottage, Karvina Czechoslovakia, Fri, Dec 20th, 1918, 8 months later.

Zuba played with Andela. "Here you are, my little baby girl. Chatter for me, Kali-Koki (DA-DA) sweet girl. God, bless you -- tiny, baby girl, my sweet Andela," Zuba said. Andela sat on the table in front of Zuba and held a rattle made from a cow's horn. Zuba had filled the horn with pebbles and stretched a piece of leather across the end. He bound it so that when Andela shook it, it rattled. When it rattled, she let out squeals and giggles.

Playfully, Zuba wrapped Andela's head in a big scarf. "There you are, my little babushka* this will keep your little head warm."

Zuba looked lovingly at Andela and wrapped his arms around her. "We're going to Litomysl to see your -- grandpa and grandma. Better not forget the doll -- Eliska made for you. You can't go to sleep without it."

After saying the words, a mantle of sadness swept his face. *He remembered his mother's letter, asking that he come home. Antonie Dusek's bull, the one that chased Zuba, caught his Father Petr when his back was turned, crushing him against the barn wall and severely injured him. He was in a coma, and the doctors did not expect him to live.*

Eliska came from the bedroom with a large gunny sack. "I hope I haven't forgotten anything. Did you pack the diapers for Andela?"

"Ya, everything we own. Should me load -- chairs and the table too?"

"Somebody's been eating too many smart aleck berries!" Eliska snapped. "We'll be there a week through Christmas, I don't want to wash clothes at your mother's. I better take my wooden spoon along!"

"No, not -- wooden spoon!" Zuba cried in mock horror. "Don't beat me again! -- me be good!"

"You better," Eliska suppressed a hesitant laugh as a look of concern crept over her face. "Do you suppose your family is still mad at us for running away and getting married?"

"Ya but wait till-- they see what we make!" Zuba said, swinging Andela in the air. Andela giggled and cried out in silly glee.

"Put her down! She will wet her diaper and never get to sleep if the two of you don't quit horsing around. Is everything packed?"

"Ya, long ago! We wait-- for at least an hour!"

"You have not! Let's go before I get the wooden spoon."

Figure 32 Babushka

** Babushka is a scarf folded into a triangle and worn on the head. Babushka is also what they call elderly women in Russian society. The scarves come in a variety of fabrics and patterns. A babushka keeps hair out of food; use it as a pail to collect berries or eggs or protect the wearer from the elements. A babushka banishes bad hair days.*

They cranked the Mack truck that the coal company wanted them to drive back to Litomysl. Zuba, Eliska worked the magneto lever, and the truck roared to life. Eliska pulled a heavy horsehide blanket up over her legs and up over Andela, who was sitting on Eliska's lap. Zuba wore a bulky woolen coat, an ushanka* pulled over his ears, and a shawl wrapped around his head. Large leather mittens covered his hands. They lowered the side curtains, hoping to block out December's icy stare. They were on their way. Somber thoughts and cold feet will be their lot for the next five or six hours.

**Ushanka is a Russian-style fur cap with ear flaps tied up to the cap's crown or fastened over the ears. ~~~~~~*

Chapter 27

A COLD WELCOME

Palzek farm, Litomysl Czechoslovakia, Sat, Dec 21, 1918

The Mack truck chugged into the Palzek farm. A family farm for many generations, it was now sadder and more run-down than Zuba

Figure 33 The Barn

could remember. A barn door hung by one hinge on the barn. Stacked up piles of manure, waited to be spread on the farm fields. Zuba surveyed the farmstead, and he couldn't remember when it looked this poorly. He jumped out of the truck and stamped his feet to get the blood circulating again.

Zuba's mother, Emilia, burst out of the farmhouse and ran with arms outstretched to Zuba. She held Zuba. Tears welled up in her eyes. "I've missed you, my son. You should write more often."

"Ya Mama, me know, -- but me no write no good."

Emilia held her youngest son for the longest time. She looked cautiously past Zuba, up at the pale faced Eliska still sitting in the truck. "Is that her?"

"Yes, Mama, that is my wife."

"Does she know how to get out of the truck?" Emilia asked sternly.

"Ya Mama, -- she afraid."

"Why? We don't eat gypsies, do we?"

"Oh, Mama, please be kind, -- you will love her as me do, -- once you get to know her."

"I doubt it. Quick, come in the house. It's freezing out here!" Emilia said as she hurried back into the house.

Eliska handed, the blanket wrapped, Andela to Zuba and again pulled the horsehide robe up around her. "I'll stay here; I can tell when I am not welcome. Go warm the baby."

"Please, Eliska, you come, you -- freeze out here!"

"I'll be colder in the house."

"Come in for a while, -- me no want you to freeze your feet. -- if it gets too rough, we leave -- OK?"

"You promise we'll leave if I ask you too?"

"Ya, me will."

"Oh -- All right."

Eliska reluctantly got out of the truck, but her knees wouldn't support her; fear and cold had set in, and she shook uncontrollably. Zuba carried Andela in one arm and helped Eliska. They made their way along the snowy path to the house and entered the warm kitchen of the farmhouse. Emilia had her back to them, busily stirring a pot on the stove. Without turning around, she bid them sit at the table.

"I have stew cooking. Been waiting for you for over two hours. What took you so long?" Emilia said.

"Mama, it was good going to Litomysl, -- but the snow was thick on the road to the farm. -- The truck got stuck every mile in wet snow. -- me had to scoop away; -- Too bad me not have the horses; they could get through easy."

Figure 34 Road to the Farm

"Well, Papa told you no truck could beat the horses," Emilia said. She brought the stew over, dished up two dishes, and placed them on the table. Holding a loaf of buckwheat bread against her bosom and using a sharp knife, she cut large slices and lay them next to the butter crock.

"What you have there, Zuba?" Emilia said, pointing to the blankets that Zuba was holding.

Zuba set the blankets on the chair and unwrapped them, revealing a sleeping Andela. "This is your granddaughter, Mama. This is Andela."

"Me? -- My? -- Granddaughter? -- I didn't know you had a child!" Emilia's eyes grew large as she reached over to the sleeping child and touched her icy little cheeks. She wrapped her calloused hands around the child's face, warming Andela's cheeks. Her anger melted. She turned to Zuba, tears streaming down her face, and asked, "Is it all right if I pick her up and take her by the fire?"

"You should ask her mother," Zuba said, as he nodded toward Eliska.

Emilia hesitated, then humbly asked Eliska, "Is it all right if I take your child by the fire to warm her?"

"It is not just my child. She is our child, Mrs. Palzekova. We're married. You are a Zuba's mother, and it's your right to hold your grandchild."

Emilia picked up Andela and hoodled her as she walked to the kitchen stove, where she unwrapped Andela. "Oh, she is so pretty, so sweet. Wait till Papa sees you; he will be joyful. It will wash away the hurt he has in his heart. He is...." Emilia hesitated in mid-sentence. She gazed longingly at the bedroom door.

"Where is Papa?" Zuba asked. "Can me talk with him?"

"He is in there; he has been asleep ever since the bull butted him. The doctor calls it a coma. He may never wake up again," Emilia said, as she clutched the sleeping Andela tight to her breast.

Zuba walked across the room to his mother and put his arms around both her and his daughter. "Sorry Mama, me wasn't here. Maybe me see him?"

"Ya, it won't do much good. Papa just lies there."

~~~~~~

Zuba entered the darkened bedroom, turned up the kerosene lamp, and knelt by his father's bedside. As his eyes adjusted to the light, he saw that his father's weather-beaten face was now much paler; his strong hands and body were limp and smaller than he remembered. Petr's breathing was short and irregular. Zuba reached out and stroked his father's head.

"Papa. -- Can you hear me?"

No answer came, not even a flicker under the eyelids.

"Oh, Papa, please come back. We need you. What is Mama going to do if you leave her?"

Zuba's big shoulders shook with his silent sobs. He lowered his head in prayer and asked God to heal his father.

Zuba made the sign of the cross, sighed, and whispered, "Thy will be done," and left the room.

~~~~~~

Chapter 28

WARMING RELATIONS

Palzek farm, Litomysl Czechoslovakia, Sun, Dec 22, 1918

Zuba entered the kitchen. "Me fed the cows and -- horses, slopped the hogs, and here's a basket of eggs," He stamped the snow from his boots, took off his cap and woolen coat. Emilia was busy making breakfast. Eliska had finished nursing Andela and was helping set the table.

The two women talked little, and when they did, it was about Andela. There was empty chatter about the weather and the best way to cure the croup in a child. Eliska told about the home remedies her family used, and it surprised Emilia that they were much the same as her remedies. Andela crawled around on the floor, playing with a couple of wooden sewing thread spools that Emilia gave her.

"Sometimes the best toys are the simplest," Emilia joked.

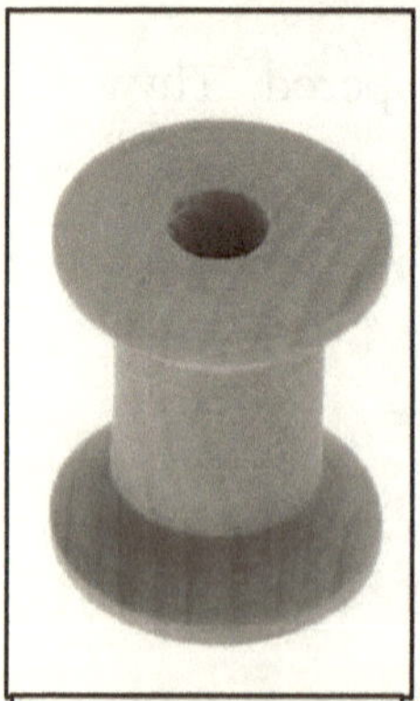

Eliska still felt uncomfortable but decided it was best to stay the night and leave after breakfast.

"Come, eat now Zuba, you must be hungry after the chores," Emilia said, placing eggs and sausages on the table.

"One horse was looking at me kinda funny when my stomach growled. Me think he was afraid -- me might eat him on the spot!" Zuba deadpanned.

"Zuba, thank you for coming. I don't know what I would have done if you didn't come. Antonie Dusek and his boy come and help, but the snow makes it hard to get here," Emilia said, rubbing her son's back.

Figure 35
Wooden Thread
Spool

"Where is Petr Jr.?" Zuba said.

"The army called him back for a while, but he should be back by spring. He said the Polish and the Czechs are arguing about the coal fields there at Karvina. Have you heard that, Zuba?"

"Ya, Pole miners talk on it, but maybe -- no fight."

"Oh, I hope not. We need Petr Jr. here on the farm. His wife Janel took a job in Litomysl to help get by. They want children, but -- the good Lord hasn't seen fit to bless them yet."

They continued to eat their breakfast. When Eliska got up to change Andela's diaper, Zuba reached out and put his big hand around his mothers. "What do you think of my little Andela?"

"Oh, Zuba, she is so sweet. I love her to pieces. Maybe you stay a day or two longer, at least through Christmas?"

"Well, it depends on Eliska, Mama. Are the two of you getting along?"

"Oh... maybe...... we get along, I guess...... she is not so bad as I thought she would be. She is a caring mother, and that is good. I don't believe...., we'll ever be friends, though," Emilia murmured.

"Mama, she is so good to me. Nobody but you and Papa ever treated me nicer.... You try a little harder, for my sake, please?"

"Ya, I try."

As they were talking, a loud moan came from the bedroom.

"Papa must have woken up!" Emilia cried excitedly, as she rushed into the bedroom.

Petr's eyes opened, and he looked around the room, "Where am I?"

"You are in your own bedroom!" Emilia said.

"How --?" A dazed Petr said.

"Antonie Dusek's bull butted you. How do you feel?"

"I hurt all over."

"Zuba is here."

"What's he want? Money! I suppose. Did the damn gypsies fleece him good?"

"No, you are wrong, he is fine. He brought his wife and another surprise. I'll get him!" Emilia said and jumped up and hurried out to the kitchen.

"No, don't!" Petr pleaded, but Emilia was already out the door.

Emilia burst into the kitchen and called to Zuba, "He's awake, Zuba! Awake! Grouchy but awake, he wants to see you but is too proud to ask. Why don't you take in sweet Andela and see him?"

"Are you sure it be all right? -- it may upset him more."

"Hush now! Talk to your Papa!"

Zuba entered his father's bedroom and walked over to the bed. "Hi Papa, it's Zuba."

Petr said nothing, looking straight ahead, avoiding Zuba's eyes.

"Me sorry you hurt Papa. -- That bull is mean. Does it hurt a lot?"

"Some," Petr replied, "but not as much as a son that won't listen to his Papa."

"I'm sorry me hurt you, Papa. Me thought it was right. Me have to live my life too."

Zuba picked up Andela and held her up for Petr to see. "This is Andela Papa, your granddaughter!"

Petr weakly looked at Andela, "I have a granddaughter? I -- don't know what to say -- What's her name?"

"Andela!"

"That's a good strong name. She is pretty, takes after your side of the family, I expect."

"Ha, Papa! You should see her mother! -- Can me bring her in?"

"You mean that gypsy girl in my house?" Petr said, angry again.

"She is my wife Papa, she treats me good, and me love her dearly. Could you meet her for me, for just a moment, please, Papa?"

Petr was silent as he turned this over in his mind. Andela crawled up on his bed and pulled on the end of his nose, with a slobbering "Brrrrrr" with her mouth. Petr couldn't help himself. He smiled a slight, reluctant, 'Why did you have to do that?' smile. "I suppose you better get your wife in here before this child pulls my nose off!"

Zuba brought Eliska in and introduced her to his father.

"How are you, Mr. Palzek?" Eliska said as she smiled her best apprehensive fake smile.

Petr looked at Eliska, "Well, I got to say this much, Zuba, you have a good eye."

Eliska blushed when Petr made that comment.

"But I still think you have made yourself a bunch of trouble. But you made that haystack. Now you must sleep in it. The wedding vow is forever, no matter how tough it gets. Do you two hear me?"

Both Eliska and Zuba said, "Yes, we do."

"I am tired. Send your mother in, will you, Zuba?"

"Yes, Papa."

Zuba and Eliska, with Andela in her arms, walked out of the room and quietly closed the bedroom door. ~~~~~~

Chapter 29

A Needle in A Haystack

Palzek farm, Litomysl Czechoslovakia, Wed, Dec 25, 1918

The dawn brought a sunny Christmas day. The bright snow causes one to peek out through half-closed eyelids. Zuba unhitched the horses and put them in the barn. Now, back from Christmas mass, he was looking forward to Christmas dinner. Emilia had taken Andela to the house. Eliska stayed behind and was helping Zuba hang the harness on the barn wall.

"Are you hungry, Eliska? Mama is a good cook, too," Zuba said excitedly.

"Ya, she is. Do you think she likes me?"

"She sure likes Andela! Her pride, -- will soften enough to like you too."

"I hope so; she is a good woman. You know, in Roma tradition; I would have been her helper till the first baby came."

Zuba brushed the horses down. "Me used to dream-- about having a girl in the hay-- in this barn." Zuba said wistfully.

"You did, did you? Was she as pretty as me?"

"Ya was you!" Zuba replied as he pulled Eliska to him and kissed her.

"Does the smell of horse manure always make you romantic?"

"Ya, me guess, -- like on our honeymoon!"

"Then I can save on buying my lavender splash water."

"How?"

"Wrap some horse manure up. We'll take it home. I'll dab little behind my ears before we go to bed."

"Now you -- funning me."

"Oh? You are not. Not! Not! -- Having any fun with me in the hay today. Do you hear me? It's too cold!"

"Me, -- warm you up!"

"The hay will be itchy!"

"Me scratch --itch!"

"It will take too long to find each other with all these clothes on."

Figure 36 Horse Harness

"Like a needle, -- in the haystack."

Eliska whirled and walked out of the barn. "If I had my wooden spoon, I'd swat you!" She said, all the while smiling. "You better come. I can smell the dinner from here." *Food and loving are all a man thinks of.*

They hurried to the house. Emilia had Petr seated at the kitchen table. She had placed a wool blanket on his shoulders and another on his lap and pulled his fuzzy farm cap tight over his bald head.

Andela sat on a box, on a chair, next to Petr. Emilia tied Andela around the waist to the chair to keep her from falling over. Petr, drawn and pale, beamed as he dangled a bunch of metal horse's rings on a leather string above Andela's head. He shook them. They tinkled, and Andela let out a squeal as she reached for them.

Petr pulled them away, and they both broke out in joyous laughter.

The game was still going on when Zuba and Eliska entered the kitchen.

"You teach my daughter-- new tricks, Papa?" Zuba asked, smiling.

"Ya, she learns faster than you did! See how quick she grabs on the rings before I pull them away?"

"You are slower -- than when I was a baby, Papa."

Emilia wiped her hands on her apron, came over to Petr, placed her arms around him, and hugged him tightly. "Fast or slow, I'm glad he is back."

Emilia looked at Eliska and said, "Would you help me bring the meal over to the table?"

"Ya, Mrs. Palzekova," Eliska replied cheerfully.

"Thank you, Mrs. Palzekova, but you can call me Emilia or Mama?"

"I think I like that; you can call me Eliska?"

"Is it all right if I call you, daughter? I don't have one of my own."

"It would make me proud," Eliska said.

Eliska, fearful that Andela might grab a hot platter as they brought them to the table, told Zuba to untie and set her on the floor, by the bed, with her favorite toys.

These actions dismayed Petr, but he saw the wisdom of it and said nothing. He tied the horse rings to his chair. He directed his attention to Zuba. "Your daughter has given me a heartworm! Into my heart like a worm in an apple."

Zuba straightened up and grinned, proud and relieved.

Over by the bed, Andela pulled herself up and stood, reaching back for the horse rings. She let out little cries, a series of whimpers. "Eh, eh, eh, eh, eh?"

Petr turned his chair and faced Andela, "Do you want to play some more? Well, you walk over here." Andela bounced up and down, still clinging to the bed. Suddenly she took one hesitant step, then another, then another until she reached Petr. She grabbed hold of his pant leg. Petr clapped his hands and laughed, "I guess she won't take no for an answer."

"Just like her mother," Zuba said, merrily, *proud to be around when my baby girl makes her first steps.*

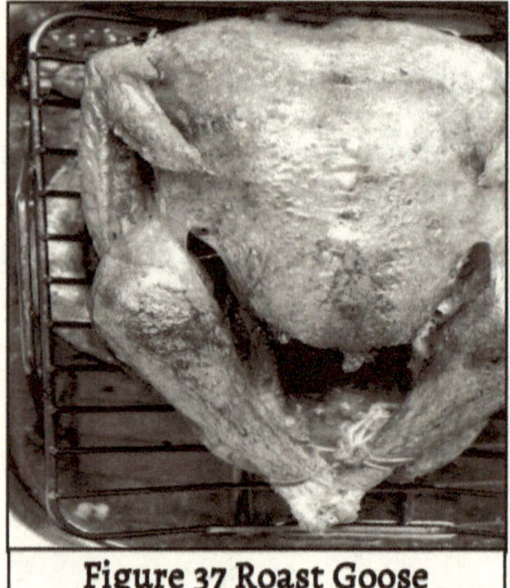

Figure 37 Roast Goose

The ladies dished up the food and Emilia then proudly brought the golden-brown Christmas goose to the table. She asked Zuba to carve it and then directed Petr to say the prayer.

Petr prayed, "Dear Lord, it is good I can say this on your birthday. Mary got her son then; now I have mine back. And he came with his Mary, Eliska, but they came in a Mack truck and already had a baby."

Petr looked up. A mischievous gleam danced in his eyes, "But they would have been more here quicker on a donkey like yours, Lord. Your creatures are better made than what a man makes. Bless this food, this house, and the people in it. Bring Petr Jr. home safely and give us peace. Amen."

Figure 38 Pumpkin Pie

The sound of a family eating together, in love and peace, is the only sound the world needs to heal its wounds. ~~~~

Chapter 30

FROZEN TEARS

Palzek farm, Litomysl Czechoslovakia, Thurs, Dec 26th, 1918

Crystal floating feathers of snow drifted lazily about, as Zuba loaded the truck to return to Karvina. The sky was gray and overcast with splashes of blue sunshine. At ten degrees below zero, a person better work fast.

Emilia brought out a large food basket filled to overflowing with Zuba's favorites. "You be hungry before you get home," she said.

Eliska bundled Andela up, and they climbed into the cab of the Mack truck. Then Zuba, with Eliska's help, started the truck. They had said their goodbyes at the breakfast table. They did not say goodbye to Petr as he slept fitfully, and Emilia asked them not to wake him. She would tell him of the goodbyes. Christmas day had tired Petr out.

The evening before, Petr called Zuba into the bedroom. He told Zuba to go to the closet and to get out his prize tuba. He held it lovingly and gave it to Zuba. "Here; take it, got no wind no more. You play it better than me, in that band of yours. I won't ever play again."

His father's resignation shocked Zuba. Petr never gave up on anything. Zuba nodded his head, thanking him. Choked up with emotion, unable to speak, Zuba kissed his father goodnight and left.

Horse traffic had packed down the snow on the road back to Litomysl, making the road hard and easy to travel. Eliska sat brooding, holding Andela close. She had been moody all morning and snapped at Zuba when he tried to hurry her. When they were within a mile of Litomysl, Zuba asked her what was wrong.

Eliska turned her face away from him and broke her tear-filled silence when she said, "Christmas is always a time of forgiveness for the Roma." Eliska spoke no more for several minutes, "Do you suppose Papa and Mama would see me if we stopped? Do we have the time?"

Eliska hesitated as a puzzled look crossed her face. "What do you think they will say?" Eliska sniffled and gazed out the frost-covered windshield. "Oh, never mind, let's go!"

"No, we stop. -- You try! Me sure they love you," Zuba said, "We take time, -- it's early."

Eliska sniffed as she nodded her head. "Yes."

"You cry a lot lately. Eliska, is there something else?" Zuba said.

"No! Drive the darn truck!" Eliska snapped.

Eliska directed Zuba to the Roma village; Zuba parked the truck at the gaily painted entrance, and Eliska cautiously entered. As she walked to her parent's home, there were people out and about, but when Eliska came close, they turned their backs to her or hastily re-entered their homes. She arrived at her parents' house and knocked on the door.

Hanzi answered the door. "What are you doing here? That gadjo throw you out? Go away before Papa sees you."

"Is Mama home?"

"She is no longer your Mama. It's Florica to you. She's busy, I'm sure! Go away! You shamed the family! Papa must give the dowry back. Now everybody in the village looks down on us."

"I'd like to see Mama!" Eliska insisted.

"She's not home!" Hanzi snapped.

An excited voice from inside the house called out, "Who's at the door, Hanzi? Tell them to come in. It's Christmas; our door is open."

"Your door is not open to Eliska, is it?"

Florica came to the door, her face drained of color. "Eliska, what are you doing here? Papa banned you from ever seeing us again."

"I had to see you, Mama. I am sorry for any hurt I caused you and the family. It's the Roma way, apology, and forgiveness at Christmas."

"Don't tell me the Roma way," Florica replied angrily. "You forgot that when you ran away with that gadjo!"

Florica lowered her voice and whispered, "Now go, before Papa wakes up. He'd be plenty mad to find you here."

"Oh Mama," Eliska cried out. "Please!"

"I not supposed to have no more to do with you. We must think of the family. What will the Council of Kris (Roma Judicial Council) say?" Florica said sadly and closed the door.

Eliska stood sobbing at the closed door. "Mama, please! I am married and have a child! A little girl! Don't you want to meet your own granddaughter?"

From within came the sad, muffled voice of her mother. "I'm sorry, it's best... I don't know those things."

"But Mama, how will we ever....?"

Florica's voice quivered. "Write to Aunt Kizzy and tell her your troubles. She is in the same boat as you are. Then, I can find out from her."

Eliska, head down, stumbled the long walk back to the truck. She climbed back in and sobbed. Zuba reached over, trying to console her. It did no good. She cried with great gasps of air. "Why can't there be any peace? We did no harm! We're good parents to Andela, and now another baby on the way will make it harder."

"Ya, we are. -- And -- and, -- Did you say -- another baby -- on the way?" Zuba asked incredulously.

"The warm July nights brought on another baby,"

"Why didn't -- you tell me?"

"You work so hard, and there's hardly enough money to live on. I wasn't sure, but it's been three months now and I am sure. How are we to make out with another baby?"

"Maybe me better take -- band job, it pay -- forty korunas, but -- be awhile before me get back. -- The band go to -- Skoczow Poland Music Festival. -- Company want to make big impression -- think it help to -- get new coal areas." Zuba looked at Eliska intently. "Will you be all right -- when me go?"

"I don't want you to go,........ especially now. But we need money. It'll be all right; the baby won't come until March. Clare Novak is close by. I'll be ok."

Eliska leaned back in the truck seat, clutching Andela tightly. *What lies ahead? The Romas say, "The world is a ladder, some things go up, and others go down." .... That's little comfort now..... The ups never come, and the downs get deeper....* She shivered as her tears froze on the frayed collar of her coat. The day was colder than any day she had ever known.

~~~~~~

<div align="center">

Chapter 31

BAD TIDINGS

</div>

The Cottage, Karvina Czechoslovakia, Thurs, Jan 2, 1919
Zuba returned home from work and took off his coat. He rubbed his icy hands together, slipped up behind Eliska, and kissed her on the neck. Eliska stopped her cooking and laid her head back on Zuba's shoulder. "Mmm, that was nice, but no more warming your hands on my tummy!" Eliska said with mock sternness. "Oh, Zuba, there's a letter from your Mama!" Eliska pulled a letter from her apron and handed it to Zuba.

"Would you read it, please, -- bet she talks on Christmas," Zuba smiled contently, unwrapping his neck scarf.

Eliska opened the letter with a quick slice of her kitchen knife. She read the message, and concern washed her face. "Zuba, you better sit."

"What is it, woman?"

"Your Papa is dead!"

"Dead? How?"

"Here, I read the whole thing," Eliska replied.
Dear Zuba, Eliska and Sweet Little Andela,
It was such a wonderful time at Christmas. Papa and me is happy you come. I am sad to say Papa never waked up after you left, the day after Christmas. There was no way I could get a hold of you. The letters are slow.
~~~~~~

We had the funeral in three days, as required. Petr Jr was here and a comfort. I am glad Papa got to be with you and your family and make his peace with you. He was holding on for that. God bless you, Zuba, for bringing peace to him.

He dearly loved your Andela, and he thought Eliska was nice too, and I know he always loved you.

Don't worry about me, son. Petr Jr will run the farming come spring. He left for the army right after the funeral, but he said he'd be back soon. Antonie Dusek's boy will care for the livestock till then, so I won't have to worry about them. I know it is a long trip here, but if you see fit, come home sometime. I love you!

Mama

PS: Don't Forget to Bring Andela and Eliska!

Zuba sat still, his head low, and he was softly crying. Eliska came up behind him and put her arms around him. "I'm sorry for you, my love. I think he was a good father."

"Ya, he was. me should have been there for Mama."

"Her letter said she understood."

"Still,.... should have been there."

"Sometimes, when the ones we love are hurting the most, we can't help to fix the hurt," Eliska replied. *I love my family, but the hurt is still alive. We just go on with life, and perhaps it comes better in the end.* ~~~~~~

Chapter 32

DID WE MOVE?

The Cottage, Karvina Czechoslovakia, Wed, Jan 22, 1919

Zuba came into the cottage. He set a small wooden box on the table in front of Eliska. "Here! This -- ready for new baby."

"The baby won't be here until March. Are you in a big hurry or something?" Eliska teased.

"Me know, -- but had time, and -- was thinking about Papa. It helps if -- keep hands busy," Zuba replied, hanging his tattered wool overcoat and his felt hat on the hook by the door.

Eliska opened the box and took out a gold cross on a leather string. "Oh, it looks like Andela's and my cross."

"Ya, I hope so, -- gotta eat and get ready -- leave early now."

"What's the big hurry? Skoczow Poland is only 32 km (20 miles) away."

"Need leave early -- after get there, need to dump -- a load of coal at the depot before -- go to the festival. Each band member -- takes a truckload -- we scoop the coal off -- That be all day." Zuba went to the bedroom and came out with his old tuba. "On Thursday we practice -- Friday and Saturday, we -- play festival. Me be home on Sunday. At least, -- no have to argue with border guards -- Karvina now in Poland, so no border."

"I thought we were in Czech lands?"

"Don't you remember -- stopping at a border station on the way back -- from Litomysl?"

"I guess my head is someplace else."

"Me glad -- you got it back!"

"Did they move our house too?" Eliska asked coyly.

"No! -- Since last November, -- we on Polish land."

"I don't feel Polish," she said matter-of-factly.

"Well, -- you are."

"I thought it was colder since we moved."

"We didn't move, -- the border did!"

"We were Czech, and now we're Polish, right?"

"Now woman! Don't -- try to figure out! Them damn big shots in -- Prague are doing it -- just to mix us up."

"Well, what do I care if they leave us alone. Kiss me, my silent frog, and be on your way. There's lots of coal for the fire and enough to eat. We'll be all right," Eliska replied.

Zuba leaned over and kissed Eliska, then placed his hand on her growing tummy. "Sleep well little one, -- Papa be back real quick."

He crouched down next to Andela, who was sitting on the floor, pulling toys out of the little wooden box he had made. "You like them wooden spools Grandma -- give you, don't you, and them horses rings, ya?"

Andela babbled, "DA, DA, Bye, Bye."

Zuba picked her up and gave her a big hug, and with a long kiss, he set her down. With a wave to Eliska, he turned and walked out the door.

Eliska's cheerful mood changed as the door slammed. *We have never been apart for more than a few hours since we were married. Now he will be gone for over four days.* A cold shudder swept through her and settled in the pit of her stomach as she reflected. *I must be brave; he will be back soon, nothing to worry about.*

She shook off the feelings of apprehension, pulled her shawl tighter around her, and turned to mend clothes. ~~~~~~

Chapter 33

BAND FESTIVAL

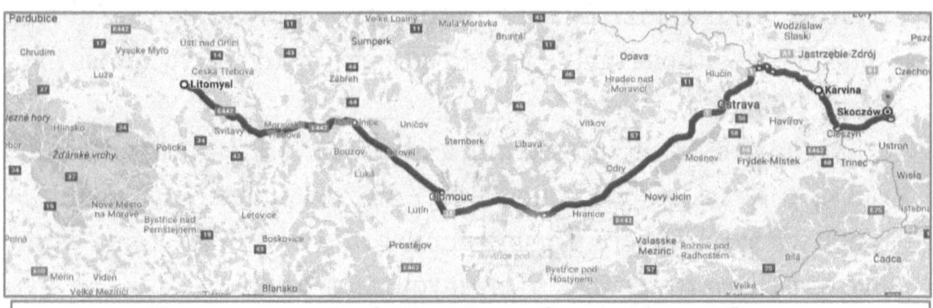

Figure 39 1919 Czech Map Litomysl to Karvina to Skoczow

Skoczow Poland, Wed, Jan 22, 1919

Eight, fully loaded, coal trucks lumbered into the train depot at Skoczow, Poland. After shoveling the coal off of the coal trucks, Zuba and his fellow musicians parked the vehicles behind the depot. They then walked to the Karell hotel, 10 minutes away.

The Karell hotel was an old 18th-century hotel and meeting place, where the band festival was held in the ballroom every year. There were two bars attached to the hotel, one outside the ballroom and one off the registration desk. It was the hotel of choice for coalfield workers, wayward peddlers, gypsies, and various other types of characters. A high standard of admission wasn't needed if their money was right.

The musicians made their marks at the registration desk and were assigned their rooms. They dropped their suitcases in the dingy rooms but kept their band instruments with them. Zuba had brought his old tuba leaving his father's tuba, at home. Playing his father's tuba still brought painful memories.

When supper was over, Zuba strolled to the ballroom where they were to practice tomorrow. He entered a big barn-shaped room with wooden floors, polished by years of dancing. A smell of stale beer, floor wax, and cigar smoke lingered in the air.

On the dimly lit bandstand, several musicians were setting up their instruments. They would play at a dance tonight that is a prelude to the contests on the following days.

As Zuba got closer, the musicians looked familiar. Squinting, he realized it was Hanzi, Eliska's brother, and Jacob Conkova. Zuba spun about without saying a word and hastily retreated across the dance floor.

But too late! Jacob spotted him and jumped from the bandstand, ran up to Zuba, grabbed him by the arm, and pulled him around. "Look who we got here. The big dumb gadjo who steals Roma women. I've waited for the chance to meet you head-on."

As Jacob spoke, he reached into his pocket and doubled up his fist around a roll of coins. He swiftly pulled his hand out of his pocket, and he took a mighty swing at Zuba. The unexpected blow hit Zuba alongside his jaw, his eyes blurred, and he fell to his knees. Jacob raised his leg high and aimed a knockout kick at Zuba's head, but Zuba warded off the blow with his raised left arm.

Jacob again tried to kick Zuba, but by this time, Zuba had regained his senses and was ready for him. As Jacob kicked, Zuba grabbed his out-stretched leg by the ankle and lifted it high. Jacob crashed to the floor and rolled over several times. Zuba got up and grabbed Jacob by both ankles and swung him around and let loose. Jacob, on his back, legs spread wide, slid across the polished dance floor.

He struggled to get up, but he fell back down and rolled, ass over teakettle, into an unceremonious heap against the bandstand.

Hanzi jumped from the bandstand to help Jacob, but when Jacob came sliding across the floor, Hanzi remembered the earlier encounters with the big man and lost his courage. He resorted to doing his fighting with his mouth. "You cursed ox. It's dark. You ought to get back beneath your bridge! May the dogs pee in your bed. I'll place a curse on your manhood, so it never talks again. You don't want to mess with me! I'll take you apart and put you together backward." Hanzi's rants continued as he helped Jacob stand.

Zuba stood tall, rubbed his bruised jaw, turned, and left the ballroom.

Jacob and Hanzi slunk into the adjacent bar to lick their wounds.

"Damn, gadjo took my woman!" Jacob growled, rubbing his sore back. "If he is gone, Eliska is mine, and I only pay half the dowry cause she has been with a man. Let's wait for him in the alley and cut his throat."

Hanzi was uneasy at the thought of killing a man, but he didn't want Jacob to sense his hesitation. "You sure you want to do that? We're in Poland, and the gadje are tougher here than at home. If they caught us, they would string us up or worse. Killing him is not a good idea," Hanzi said.

"Maybe you're right if we could just get rid of him," Jacob mused, nursing his brandy.

A tattooed bartender with a dirty apron leaned on the bar and said, "How much are you willing to pay to get rid of him?"

"Can you do it? Is it easy? How soon can you do it?" Hanzi said.

"Sure, nothing to it," the bartender said, "I do it all the time."

"We don't want him killed. Just have him go away," Hanzi said.

Jacob became very interested. "How would you do it?"

"I got a way to put him on a boat going to China or America. You will never see him again. It won't cost a lot, but you'll be rid of him."

"How much?" Jacob said.

"Thousand korunas," the bartender said, "and he is gone forever!"

"Thousand korunas is a bunch of money."

"Well, take it or leave it."

"We must talk it over," Jacob replied.

The bartender left to wait on other customers.

"We traveled from Litomysl for this job to put money in our empty pockets," Jacob said. He turned to Hanzi, "They are paying each of us two hundred korunas. How about you come in with me on this? Then, we only have to raise another six hundred korunas."

"Two hundred korunas? I don't want to get rid of him that badly!" Hanzi said. "Where will you get the rest?"

"Bolda still has the dowry I paid. With Zuba gone, I'll only pay half the dowry for Eliska because she is used. Bolda must return the other half. She is damaged goods, but I can live with that. How about it?"

"Oh no, if Mama or Papa found out I did that, I would have to go before the Kris (Roma Judicial Council)," Hanzi said. "Further, I need the two hundred korunas."

"You know I have a well-to-do Papa, don't you? He gave me six hundred korunas. I am only supposed to use it in case of an emergency." Jacob said. "I think this might be an emergency. He is on his last legs, and when he goes, I inherit it anyway. Help me now, and I'll double your money back to you within one year. Four hundred korunas for two hundred invested, now what you say?"

Hanzi thought it over, "Make it six hundred for two hundred, and you got a deal."

Jacob glared at Hanzi and finally spat in his hand and reached out to Hanzi, "Deal! Shake on it. Now, call the bartender back."

Hanzi called the bartender back and told him they would do it and made the arrangements for the money. "That's it, eh bartender? Is everything ready?" Jacob said.

"Almost," the bartender said. "Have the money here tomorrow night, then get him to the bar by railway depot."

The bartender continued, "We'll grab him there and load him on the train. He'll be in the Baltic seaport in Szczecin, Poland, by Friday night. Can you have the money by then?"

Jacob rubbed his hands together, "Ya sure!"

"How are we to get him to the bar?" Hanzi said.

"We'll figure it out," Jacob replied, nodding to the bartender.

"Good, have him there tomorrow night at 9 PM. We'll take it from there," the bartender said.

Jacob rubbed his hands together, "Boy, this is good. Eliska will be mine. Soon she will warm my bed!" ~~~~~~

Chapter 34

THE POLISH WAR

The Cottage, Karvina Czechoslovakia, Thurs, Jan 23, 1919

On 23 January 1919, at 11:00 AM, in Cieszyn Silesia, Polish commander Franciszek Latinik and Czechoslovak officer Josef Šnejdárek met. The Czechs gave the Polish an ultimatum to evacuate the area to the Biała River in less than two hours. When the Polish didn't respond, the Czechoslovakia army attacked at 13:00 (1 PM) to seize the territory. The Czechoslovakia army moved quickly and took Bohumín then Orlová and Karvina. Polish troops retreated to the river Vistula.

<div align="center">~~~~~~</div>

Andela was down for her afternoon nap. It was late afternoon, and Eliska was busy sewing a patch on Zuba's overalls. *That man could rip his clothes if he tip-toed through a pussy willow patch.* Eliska had made it through an entire day without missing Zuba, more than once or twice. Every hour! The nights were the worst as he had always been by her side. His loud snoring irritated her at first, but she learned to love it and felt secure when she heard it. Just like one loves to listen to the purring of a favorite cat.

Eliska could still hear his low rumbling sounds as she rocked back and forth in her chair. Slowly it dawned on her that the rumbling wasn't in her imagination.

Louder and louder until the rumbling turned into a continuous roar. Eliska thought it must be a thunderstorm that often came at this time of the year. She rushed to the window to bolt the shutters. Gazing out, she stood petrified at the sight. In the field behind the cottage, massive explosions sprayed dirt and snow into the air.

Soldiers dodged for cover, running across the meadow. Screams rent the air as the exploding shells rip apart their bodies. Shells slammed onto the once quiet field, collapsing broad swaths of dry grass and snow into the coal mines below.

As the ground yawned open, the soldiers fell screaming into the abyss below; swallowed as if a giant whale gulped them down.

Czech soldiers charged into the firestorm. Polish soldiers, hidden in the woods, fired volley after volley at the incoming men. The splat of the bullets echoed across the meadow, ripping into the soft bodies of the advancing soldiers.

There was an insistent knock on the door as Eliska stood at the window, petrified. *Zuba may have come back early. He will know what to do.* She quickly opened the door to find an officer of the Czech army legion standing there. He was tall and broad of shoulders with a forced professional smile. He tipped his hat and said, "Good afternoon. I'm with the Czech 93rd Regiment, and we're evacuating the Polish from these houses. You must pack up and go. We need this house for an observation post."

"You are taking my home?" Eliska cried. "What right do you have to take my home?"

"There's a war on; this is now Czech land. We have orders to send the Polish back to their own country."

"I don't think I'm Polish; I was born in Litomysl. My husband is from Litomysl. That makes us Czech!"

"I'm sorry, I have my orders."

"You have no right!" Eliska screamed at the officer. "I'll not go!"

"Either you go, or we'll pack you up and move you. Do I have to call my soldiers?"

Eliska stood, hands on her hips, defiantly blocking the doorway. Her angry outburst woke Andela, whose lower lip quivered, and she cried. Eliska rushed to pick her up and hold her protectively to her breast.

The officer opened his binder, took out a pencil, and said, "What's your name please so that we can check you off our list."

"What business is it of yours? You take our home, and now, you ask us our names?"

The officer softened and hung his head, "I'm sorry, I have my orders."

"Does those orders make it right?"

"No, ma'am, it doesn't, but I can't do a thing about it."

"I suppose! You have your damn orders!" Eliska snapped back at him.

"Yes, ma'am, I do. Can I help you pack?"

"I can manage just fine. Give me a few minutes; we don't have much."

"Could I get your name? You must be Roma, but with a blond baby, maybe not."

"I am Roma and married to a Czech. A Czech, from Litomysl. He's not a Pole. I wish he were here. He'd throw you out!" Eliska said defiantly.

"I'm sure he would, ma'am. What's his name?"

"Zuba Palzek, if it's any business of yours!"

The officer raised his eyebrows, smiled, and said, "Then you must be Eliska."

"Yes, I am Eliska. How did you know? You have lots of things in your little black book. I suppose you know how many times we go to the outhouse?"

"No, ma'am, my mother told me about you."

"How does your mother know?"

"Because she's a Zuba's mother, too. I'm Petr Jr," The officer said softly.

Eliska was still angry, "So your family is just like mine! Drive us from our home! Such a brother!"

"I'm sorry, but I can help. We have set up a refugee camp for the Czechs. I could get you in there. They don't take Roma, but I can vouch for you, as my brother's wife. Your light skin and the blond baby will help too. When this is over, you might be able to come back here."

"If I leave, Zuba won't know where we are," Eliska said tearfully.

"Do you hear those artillery explosions? Those are not only ours, but the Polish army is firing back at us. They could hit this house," Petr Jr said. "What would become of you and Andela then?"

Tears continued to well up in Eliska's eyes. Her lip tremored, "But,. But,.. Zuba won't know where we are."

"I have a notice that I'll tack on your door; it tells what has happened and where you will be."

Eliska wrung her hands and pleaded, "But Zuba, he don't read so good, he'll worry about us."

Petr Jr wrapped his arms around Eliska and Andela. "It will be all right; I'll look out for him and you." Petr Jr. turned Eliska around. "You must hurry, the shelling will quit soon, and then the Poles will come out of hiding and shell us back."

Eliska swept their clothes in a one gunny sack; placed their dishes, kitchenware, and other keepsakes into another gunny sack. She grabbed Andela by the hand and Zuba's father's tuba in the other. Petr Jr picked up the gunny sacks, and they hurried away from the shelling. ~~~~~~

Chapter 35

SCHEMING

Karell Bar, Skoczow Poland, Fri, Jan 23, 1919

After playing their last set of music, Jacob and Hanzi sat plotting in the Karell bar. "Now, here's what you do, Hanzi," Jacob explained. "You go to Zuba and tell him you are sorry for treating him so bad. Tell him that a brother-in-law shouldn't do that. Tell him you never saw a Mack truck and want to see it. They parked them by the railroad depot. The bar is across the street."

"Is this the only way?"

"Can you think of a better one?"

"No, but I don't like this."

"You like six hundred korunas, don't you?"

"Ya, I guess so, but it doesn't feel right," Hanzi replied.

"He's a gadjo, isn't he?"

"Ya, but...."

"No buts! You want to earn six hundred korunas or not?"

Hanzi hesitated, "Ya, I guess so."

"Good, give me your two hundred korunas, and I'll go pay the bartender. You go call on Zuba."

Hanzi gave him his korunas and left for Zuba's room. Jacob slid to the end of the polished bar where the tattooed bartender was cleaning glassware. Jacob began slowly counting out the money.

"Not here, you damn fool!" The bartender said. "Go over to the corner booth and sit there. I'll come to you."

Jacob sat in the corner booth, and the bartender came over.

"What'll you have?"

"I want to get this business done with," Jacob replied.

"Order something, or the boss might think I'm trying to cheat him."

Jacob ordered a brandy. The bartender brought it and lingered a while, talking loudly, as Jacob again counted out the money.

"Do you want to make an extra two hundred korunas?" Jacob said.

"Sure, who doesn't!"

"When you take the big fellow, take that little curly-haired guy that's with him."

"You mean your buddy?"

"Ya, but he's not really my buddy. I don't need him to be messing things up later."

"And you won't have to pay him back either, eh?"

"There's that too."

"Good friends like you are hard to find."

"Never mind the smart mouth; do we have a deal?"

"What do I care? Done!"

Jacob passed the money to the bartender and left the bar.

While this was going on, Hanzi carried his accordion up to the hotel's second floor and knocked on Zuba's door. When Zuba answered the door, he was surprised to see Hanzi there. Zuba peeked out into the hallway expecting that Jacob might be hiding nearby. "No trouble -- now -- Hanzi," Zuba stammered.

"No trouble Zuba," Hanzi hung his head, "I am sorry for treating you so bad. A brother-in-law shouldn't do that. Just shouldn't do it. But you know me, I do funny things when Jacob is around."

"It -- was -- funny -- business -- all right," Zuba stammered. "Thanks -- you -- go now."

"I just wanted you to know, no hard feelings?"

"No hard feelings, -- now -- go!"

"I hear you drove one of those Mack trucks here, eh?"

"Ya, -- me fix em -- me drive em, -- good night -- Hanzi."

"Well, -- I have never seen a Mack truck, and I want to look at one."

"You probably - gonna -- see -- a lot of -- them around."

"I can tell Papa I seen one. Wouldn't you want to please him?"

"Why -- should me -- worry on -- that?"

"Well, Papa found out about your baby? Your sweet baby. Mama is upset because she can't be with Eliska and the baby." Hanzi said.

Hanzi continued, "If we can be friends, maybe Papa will soften up, and Eliska can come and visit. Eliska would like that."

Zuba pondered what Hanzi said. "Ya, peace -- in family -- be good."

"I have to leave first thing in the morning. Could we see your truck tonight? Is it outside the hotel?"

"No, it's -- by -- the depot."

"Can we go now?"

"Now? -- It's late -- me tired!"

"Please, Zuba! I must leave early in the morning! Do it now for Eliska and Mama. It could make them happy and mend the family."

Zuba thought for the longest time. He knew Eliska would want that. He looked up and down the hallway again, to make sure Jacob wasn't hiding anywhere.

"Just -- you and -- me? No Jacob?"

"No, Jacob, I swear."

"Let me -- get coat -- and -- my tuba."

"Leave the tuba!"

"In this place? -- It be gone -- when -- we get back!"

Zuba and Hanzi made their way along the snow-packed streets to the railroad depot. Lonely train whistles echoed in the still night air. Christmas wreaths still hung on the lamp posts.

On the far side of the depot, the lamps splashed yellow light on the shiny hoods of Zuba's pride and joy, his Mac trucks!

"Look how they shine -- in the lamplight, Hanzi. They can do the -- work of ten horses and -- faster too," Zuba proudly exclaimed.

"My, they are a wonder, a wonder I tell you, such big wagons all in a row. And no horse to pull them. Such a wonder. Such a wonder."

"Ya -- let's -- go back -- to the hotel."

"You know what, my brother-in-law, my good friend? We should toast our new friendship with a brandy. What do you say?"

"Me say -- Me tired -- go -- back."

They walked out of the depot yard and crossed the street.

Stepping into the light of a single streetlamp in front of a run-down bar, Hanzi turned to Zuba. "What do you say, my friend? Let's have a brandy. I'll even buy. What do you think of that? Pretty good, eh, my brother-in-law? Tight old Hanzi buys you a drink. Not bad, eh? Let's drink to peace in the family."

Zuba hesitated, then wiped a clean spot on the bar's dirty front window and peered inside. The lone customer was an old drunk nursing a drink and singing to himself.

"Well -- guess it might -- be all -- right. Just one drink!"

Entering the bar, they passed tables still littered with food particles and empty beer glasses. Stale cigarette smoke lingered in the air. It mingled with the spilled beer smell floating up from the floor. A spoiled, pungent aroma, reminiscent of day-old vomit, emanated from the tabletops. Standing at the bar was the cleanest choice. Hanzi ordered two brandies, and they stood, nursing their drinks.

"This is good, Zuba; you will be proud of what's coming."

"What -- is coming?"

"Well, peace in my family, what do you think?"

"Me think -- it late, and -- me tired."

The bartender came over and wiped the bar with his dirty bar rag, "Could you boys use some entertainment."

"Why sure, what do you have in mind?" Hanzi said.

"Well, I have a genuine African monkey in a cage, out back."

"A monkey? The hell you say! A monkey, eh? I never saw one of those. Have you Zuba? Can we see it too? Zuba, you want to look at a genuine African monkey, don't you?"

"No, don't -- want to see -- no monkey. Don't -- know what a -- monkey is," Zuba replied.

"How much to see the monkey? How much?" Hanzi cried.

"Only two korunas a piece," the bartender said.

"Two korunas is not bad. What do you say, Zuba? Let's go look at the genuine African monkey!"

"Me no -- pay two korunas -- to see no -- monkey."

"Tell you what," the bartender said, "it's late. I'll let the two of you in for the price of one. How's that for a deal?"

"Done!" Hanzi cried. "Here's the two korunas. Let's go, Zuba!"

"As long -- as me don't -- have to pay. But you look quick -- then we go -- back to the -- hotel -- ya?"

Hanzi paid the bartender, and the bartender jerked his thumb toward the side door. At the same time, he reached under the bar and pulled a small cord. "Through that door," the bartender said.

Hanzi and Zuba stepped through the side door. They ended up standing on the edge of a dark, snow-packed alley. They stood there waiting for their eyes to adjust to the light; when they did, they saw a pile of wooden crates before them.

"I bet you that is where the monkey is. Let's get a good look," Hanzi exclaimed. Standing, peering into the dark crates, they could see something moving in them. "Look, I think I see the monkey!"

As Zuba and Hanzi crowded closer, trying to see the monkey, two large men crept up behind them. In their hands, each gripped a sock with a bar of soap stuffed in the toe. An improvised blackjack! They silently came up behind Zuba and Hanzi and, with a quick swing of the socks, gave each man a sharp blow on the head.

"Good, down like a rock. Them socks work good, every time. Now quick, get them into the crates and lock um." The first man said.

"Let's look in their suitcases." The second man said.

"Na, they looks too poor to have anything worth taking. Probably dirty underwear. It's damn cold out here. Throw the suitcases in the crates with them. Let's load them, quick."

The two men closed the crates, lifted them on a railroad trolley cart, then pushed them to a boxcar and loaded them in. They positioned the grate alongside two other crates stacked against the back of the boxcar.

The men chuckled, and one of them said, "That's it, Captain Tamarra will be happy to get all four. Four times the money tonight. I didn't think the last two would ever show. Let's get a hot brandy and celebrate!"

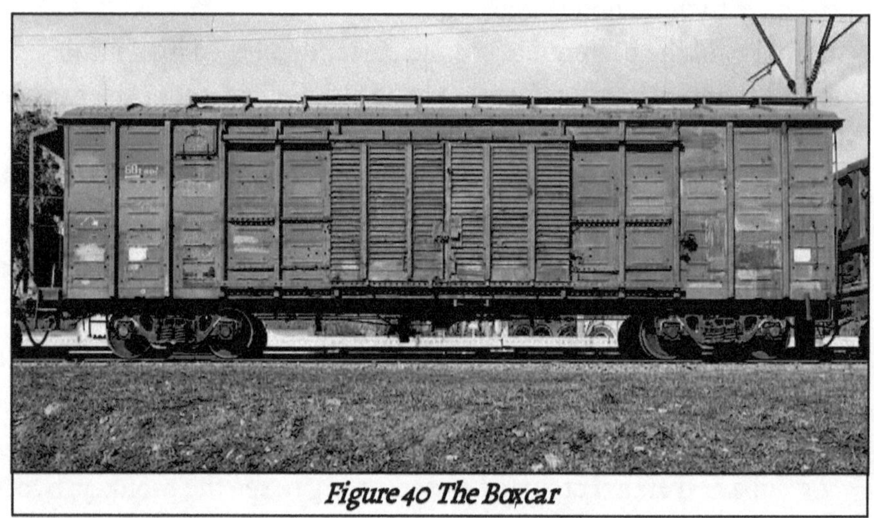

Figure 40 The Boxcar

In the silence of the rail yard, only a faraway whistle wailed a mournful melody. No sounds came from the dark crates on the cold boxcar. ~~~~~~

Chapter 36

SET SAIL

The Raspatau, Szczecin, Poland, Sat, Jan 24, 1919

It was two PM Saturday afternoon when the train pulled into the Baltic seacoast town of Szczecin, Poland. The locomotive engineer shunted the box cars onto a siding that ran right up to the loading docks. He parked the cars next to an outgoing freighter, the Raspatau. The deckhands quickly unloaded the crates that Zuba and Hanzi were in, onto the ship. Captain Tamarra and his first mate Rocco supervised the loading.

"Put those monkey crates in the hold where we can get at them," Rocco said. "We'll open them after we go to sea. It will be safer."

After they completed the loading, Captain Tamarra called the harbormaster to have the tugboats tow the ship out of the harbor. Once out in the open water, the tugboats turned around said goodbye to the Raspatau by bellowing their foghorns. The Raspatau answered with its own mighty horn and surged full steam out into the ocean.

Figure 41 Rocco and the Crew

On the bridge, Captain Tamarra and Rocco calculated the shipping route. Captain Tamarra said, "We'll stop in Copenhagen and pick up dried fish; then to England for a few days, then we'll head straight to New York and unload most of the cargo. We then go to Detroit, MI, to load trucks. We deliver them to Duluth, MN, where we pick up iron ore and bring the whole works back to Poland."

Captain Tamarra folded up the map and put it in his map case next to the wheel. "Rocco, after we're at sea for an hour, you can open the monkey crates. You better take 5-6 men with you. Remember when we had the big Russian? He damn near tore the ship apart. Oh, if any of them are dead, tie weights on em and toss em over the side," Captain Tamarra said.

"Aye, captain," Rocco said. He hurried off to get the manpower needed for the job.

Figure 42 Capt. Tamarra

When the hour was up, Rocco and his gang of six descended into the hold. They pried the boards off of the four crates. "Man, these monkeys smell," Rocco said. "Get the hose out, and we'll wash them down before the captain gets wind of them."

They opened each crate, and from each one, a dazed, smelly man crawled out. The men looked around anxiously. Hungry, thirsty, filthy, and utterly subdued.

"Get to your feet, you monkeys," Rocco roared as he turned the hose on each of them.

The men struggled to their feet. They shivered as the icy seawater hit them. They screamed out in pain when the salty water seeped into the open wounds inflicted when shanghaied.

After the bath was over, Rocco passed out plain seaman's dungarees and blue denim shirts. The men dressed in the ship's clothes, and Rocco gathered up the discarded soiled clothes. "You won't need these anymore; I'll burn them. You now belong to the Raspatau. The ship's name is printed on the back of your shirt. Behave yourself, and you won't get into any trouble."

Hanzi stood up straight, "Sir, I'm not supposed to be here. I'm Czech and not supposed to be here. Do you hear me? You have made a big mistake, and you will pay for it, I tell you."

"Whose name is on the back of your shirt, sailor?" Rocco demanded.

"I can't read it."

"It's Raspatau, smart mouth; you belong to me!" Rocco growled.

"Raspatau, I guess if you say so, but I don't belong here! You better let me go. I have friends all over that will help me. I don't belong here!" Hanzi insisted.

Rocco responded with a sharp blow from a crop whip across Hanzi's face. "Now, do you belong here? Or do you want to taste Sally, my whip again?"

"No, I don't, but this is kidnapping! Kidnapping! I tell you! You messed with the wrong Roma; I tell you!" Hanzi screamed as he glared at Rocco.

Rocco responded with another sharp blow across Hanzi's face. He raised Sally again to repeat the action when one monkey grabbed his arm.

"No -- hurt -- no -- more!" Zuba said, twisting Rocco's arm backward. The deckhands jumped in and set upon Zuba, knocking him to the floor. They landed blow after blow and kick after kick on the prostrate Zuba. Rocco stepped in and took pleasure in working the pain of his twisted arm out by hammering Zuba. Sally tap-danced, blow after blow, on Zuba's back.

Figure 43 Raspatau

"Stop that!" A commanding voice echoed down the ladder from the upper deck. "What the hell is the matter with you? We can't work these men if you kill them. They've learned their lesson," Captain Tamarra yelled. "Now show them what to do."

"Aye, Captain!" Rocco replied. He pulled a bloody Zuba up to his feet. "We aren't finished yet, big man. It's a long trip to New York. Lots can happen along the way."

"OK, you smart mouth, little, curly-haired bastard. And you, you big piece of seal dung. Come with me!" Rocco took Hanzi and Zuba to the engine room, where he ordered them to clean out the sludge tanks. "Finish up, then start on the toilet holding tanks."

Hanzi came close to Zuba, "Thanks for helping out. I could have taken em, though, but thanks anyway."

Zuba nodded sadly, "I might have been better -- if I let him hit you. I wouldn't hurt so much. -- We in big trouble. -- Can't stay here -- have to get home to Eliska and Andela." ~~~~~~

Chapter 37

NO NEWS

Refugee Camp in Karvina Czechoslovakia, Tues, Feb 4, 1919

Eliska sat on the edge of the army cot, rocking Andela quietly in her arms. She contemplated how she got here and where Zuba was.

The tent was home to several of the families from the slums. A constant din floated on the stale, canvas smelling air. An army of rampaging children cooped up too long, swirled dust around the rows of cots.

Privacy was a luxury, long lost in the uprooting of the families. Family squabbles became common knowledge, even though everyone pretended not to hear them.

The makeshift outhouses, set up outside the tents, were full to overflowing. Mothers constantly watched the children keeping them from playing in such distractions.

Clare Novak, her husband, and their six children had cots across from Eliska. The children raised a commotion, but Andela loved playing with them. The giggles and antics helped Eliska forget Zuba for a few minutes during the long days and nights of waiting.

The authorities had allowed the Roma to come to the big tents. Clare and her family were next to Eliska. Clare came over and sat beside Eliska. "How are you today, Eliska?"

Eliska was quiet as she kept rocking Andela. "I expected Zuba to be home nine days ago,"

"Now, now, don't worry. Yesterday, I read in the paper that a big battle is happening in Skoczow, Poland. He and the band probably hid in some, out-of-the-way place." Clare put her arm on Eliska's shoulder, "It should be over soon. The paper said the big shots are dealing with peace. I'm sure after that, he will be home."

"How will he know where we are? Zuba can't read so good... The notice might have blown away... He could be back now and is looking for us." Eliska exclaimed.

"He is a resourceful man; he will find you. I'll go to the supply store and get a new paper," Clare said as she left the tent. A few minutes later, she burst into the tent. "The war is over! The war is over! They signed up for peace last Sunday." The people huddled in the tent erupted in cheers of relief. Clare continued to read the paper. "It says we can go back to our homes on Wednesday. Why that's tomorrow. Returning home will be nice! I hope we have a house left."

Eliska hugged Andela tight. "Your Papa will be home. It's only twenty miles and might already be there!" Eliska picked up Andela and whirled her around, laughed with a fake laugh. "I bet he's lost; he never could find his way without me reading the map." She chuckled and hugged Andela again. "We go home tomorrow!" Eliska's face darkened; she turned to Clare. "Clare, is that for sure?"

Clare was quiet as she held the newspaper up to her face. She laughed half heartily. "Next time we go live in a tent, I gotta remember my glasses."

Eliska interrupted, "Does it say anymore?"

Clare hesitated, "They have a list of the dead here. About fifty Czechs killed, many more injured or missing."

Eliska's joyful mood evaporated. "Is there -- anyone we know?"

"Just the last names."

"Are.... they...?" Eliska paused, afraid to ask. Finally, rapidly, expectantly, she said, "They are the army men, I bet!"

"Maybe, just last names."

"Anyone..... We know?" Eliska asked hesitantly.

"It could be a mistake: Things get mixed up."

Eliska was silent for a moment. "Is Zuba's name on that list?"

"Not sure, but here's a Palzek on the list. It might be from a different Palzek family."

The blood drained out of Eliska's face. All her worries and fears were coming true. *Can he be dead?... He's not dead!... Roma can sense the death of a loved one. I never felt that.*

Eliska bit her lip, trembling. "He's not dead! ... I must go home! He'll be waiting for us! He's just lost, that's all!" Eliska whispered to herself, "He always gets lost!"

Eliska quickly filled her gunny sacks and put Andela's coat on; she grabbed the sacks and the tuba. "Hold on to Mama's coat, Andela; we're going home."

"They said tomorrow, Eliska," Clare admonished.

"I don't care. When Zuba comes back, I want to have a nice warm fire going and be cooking his favorite goulash. He'll be back real quick to us, you'll see."

Eliska and Andela left the refugee center and made their way back to their home in the slums of Karvina. As they skirted around the piles of fallen bricks and rubbish, they saw the damage that war inflicts on everything and everyone. The odor of death lingered in the air. Eliska covered her face with a scarf, and she slid Andela's babushka down across Andela's nose.

"It stinks, Mama!" Andela cried, "Let's go back to the tent!"

"It's better if we hurry and get past the dead dog over there."

"He's a fat one, isn't he, Mama?"

"Yes, dear, they blow up when they are dead," Eliska replied. An acid taste erupted in her mouth as her morning sickness returned.

"Mama?"

"Yes, honey,"

"Dat house got big hole in the wall, and the roof fall down. They gonna need to fix before it rains, won't they, Mama?"

"Yes, dear. Watch out for the boards on the street; they have nails sticking out. If you step on them, it could stick you in the foot."

"Look, Mama, fire burning that house!"

Eliska grabbed Andela's by the hand and pulled. "Keep going so we can get out of this smoke."

They scrambled along and stopped by a pile of rubble. Eliska could no longer hold her stomach in check. She laid the gunny sacks down, turned away from Andela, and vomited.

Andela clutched Eliska's hand and looked up at her, said, "You sick, Mama?"

"Remember I told you that when a woman is to have a baby, sometimes we throw up? We have a new baby coming. That's why I'm sick."

"Yes, Mama. Will Da Da bring the baby?"

"No, I will bring it."

"Will Da Da come with his new baby too?"

"No, dear, you ask too many questions. Let's hurry and get to our house."

They entered the street where they lived. Looking down the row of cottages, not one remained untouched. The humble little gray cottage where Andela was born was in shambles. That plain little cottage, their first home, now stood with its north wall gone and most of the roof missing.

Gasping for breath, Eliska set her gunny sacks at the door of the cottage and entered. She tipped up the table, brushed off a chair, and slumped on it. Surveying the damage, she thought, *Zuba and I can fix this! Just a little work and it will... will be.... As good.... as new. Zuba can......* She couldn't hold her anguish in any longer. She put her head on the table, and great sobs wracked her body. *"Oh Lord, how much more? Was my sin so great for you to punish me so?"*

Andela stood by sucking her thumb with her doll under her arm. She clutched Eliska's coat with the other chubby little hand and began to cry. Eliska quickly regained her composure. "Now, now, nothing to cry on. Let's go back to that nice tent; you can have fun playing with the Novak kids."

With one lingering glance around her beloved home, Eliska turned and picked up Andela. She grabbed her gunny sacks and desolately walked out the cottage door. As Eliska pulled her gunny sacks behind her, her rescued silverware, pots, and pans bounced inside the sacks clanging out her song of despair. ~~~~~~

Chapter 38

PAPA

Refugee Camp in Karvina Czechoslovakia, Tues, Feb 11, 1919
The houses in the village were so severely damaged that the government allowed the refugees to stay in the camp until repairs were completed. Eliska made daily trips to the destroyed cottage. She'd leave early in the morning and come back mid afternoon. Andela stayed with Clare Novak when Eliska made her daily journey. *"He won't be able to find us. I better be there when he comes back!"* Every day Eliska started out hopeful and came back dejected. When she entered the tent after her last journey, Clare Novak came up to her.

"Eliska, they say you have a visitor; he is in the processing building."

Eliska's heart leaped. She wrapped her shawl around her head and ran into the processing building. "Zuba, are you finally home? Where are you?" As her eyes adjusted to the darkened room, she noticed that on a bench at the far wall sat a black-hatted man. She rushed toward him, "Zuba, is it you?"

"No, child, it's your Papa," Bolda Danka said.

Eliska hesitated then approached, Bolda. "Papa, what are you doing here?"

"I come to take Hanzi's body home," Bolda said.

"Hanzi! What is he doing here?"

"He's not here. He is in Skoczow Poland at the band festival."

"That's where Zuba is."

"I know."

"How do you know?"

"Jacob was with Hanzi, and he saw Zuba. Jacob just came back with the news."

"What did he say about Zuba?"

"It's not good. Jacob said that he, with Hanzi and Zuba, was hiding in the basement of the Karell hotel when a shell hit."

Bolda halted and reached out and pulled his daughter close and said, "A wall collapsed and buried Hanzi and Zuba. Jacob escaped."

"But what about Zuba, Papa?"

Bolda hesitated again and then blurted it out. "Hanzi and Zuba are dead."

A wave of disbelief swept over Eliska. She backed up and beat her fists on her father's chest. "Zuba can't be dead! I didn't feel it! You're lying! We Roma can sense the death of a loved one!"

Bolda shrugged and answered quietly. "I don't lie. We don't always feel it. I didn't feel Hanzi's death either."

"Did Jacob see the bodies?" Eliska demanded.

"No, but he said the stone wall was over ten feet tall and fell right on them. No one could live through it."

"I don't believe it!"

"I'm sorry." Bolda cupped his daughter's chin and lifted her head so that their eyes met. He stroked her cheek as he had done so many times before when she was his little girl. "You must hurt badly. But I need to leave now. I'm going to Skoczow to get Hanzi's body."

"Wait, Papa, I'll go too?"

"It may be hard."

"I don't care; I have to be sure!"

Bolda hesitated, then shrugged, "All right."

"Let me get Clare Novak to take care of Andela."

"Is Andela your little girl?"

"Yes."

Bolda was silent for several moments, "Can I see her?"

"Oh, yes, Papa, yes, come with me."

Eliska took Bolda to the tent they were staying in. As they entered, Andela came running up. "Mama DA, DA, Home?"

"No, child, but I have someone special. Here's your grandpa."

Andela hid behind her mother's shirt and peeked around at the stranger. Bolda knelt and reached his arms out to her.

Andela hung firmly to Eliska's skirts, but Bolda coaxed a small, tentative smile from her.

"She is a pretty child."

"Ya Papa, and there's another one on the way."

"I see; when are you due?"

"Sometime toward the end of March."

"Are you sure you should travel?"

"No, but I have to find Zuba."

Bolda thought for a moment, then said, "Very well, let's go."

The trip to Skoczow, Poland, was just twenty miles. It took forever as Bolda dodged shelled outbuildings and military trucks speeding by. Bolda soothed Daisy, his horse, every time an army truck roared by. "Damn trucks, they frighten Daisy," he muttered under his breath.

They pulled up to the Karell hotel. There was a large hole in the wall closest to the bar. Workers were busy rebuilding that wall. Bolda stepped from the wagon and talked to the workers. "Did you find any bodies in the rubble?"

"Ya, three or four, I guess."

"Where are they?"

"They took the bartender to his home; others are at the City Center."

"How do I get there?"

"Head right down the street," the workman said, without looking up, pointed with his thumb,

"Diky (thanks)," Bolda replied.

Bolda turned the wagon and left. When he is out of earshot, one workman remarked. "Damn gypsies, scavenging around to find what they can steal."

Bolda and Eliska parked the wagon outside the City Center. Bolda firmly cradled his daughter's arm in his arm as they entered the vestibule.

Inside the stone building, rows of offices lined a central hallway leading to a large open rotunda. Curved ornate stairways, on each side of the domed rotunda, led to the second-story courtrooms.

Throughout the building, there was the hustle and bustle of activity. Clerks dashed by with armloads of documents. Judges in black robes grandly promenaded from the rotunda up the stairs to their courtrooms.

Bolda stopped a young clerk carrying a large armful of papers. "Those killed in the war, where did they put them?"

"In the ground! Where do you suppose?" The clerk snapped back and spat on the floor.

"Is there a list of the names?"

The clerk sneered, "Hell no, they were just parts and pieces, lots of strangers. Their names are a mystery."

Bolda grabbed the clerk's shirt on each side, raised him up to his tiptoes, and looked squarely into his eyes, "Have respect! Tell us where they buried them!"

Papers flew out of the clerk's arms and cascaded to the marble floor. He danced on his tiptoes and stammered, "Ya, Ya, they dug a big hole out to the beggar's cemetery. They put them there."

"How do we get there?" Bolda said, giving the clerk a hard shake.

"Just off the road that goes to Karvina."

Bolda let loose of the clerk's shirt and growled, "Next time, don't let your smart mouth buy you a pile of trouble you can't chew!"

The clerk, his face drained of color and expression, picked his papers up, arranged them in a jumbled heap, clasped them to his torn shirt, and scurried off.

Bolda reached out and held Eliska close. He stroked her head as she cried on his shoulder. They held each other, in silence, for several minutes. Their hearts were breaking at the thought of not finding their loved ones.

"Do you want to go to the cemetery?" Bolda said.

"What for? Zuba's not there!" Eliska insisted.

Bolda looked at his daughter with sadness in his eyes. He nodded solemnly, "Ya, I guess that's best."

As they returned to the refugee camp late in the afternoon, a steady stream of refugees flowed out the front gate.

"What is happening?" Eliska asked an old gray-haired woman pulling a cart.

The old woman said. "The government said we need to go back to our homes, so here we go."

"Are you going to your home?" Bolda asked.

"What home? The army wrecked it! I have nowhere to go."

Bolda thought for a moment. "I think you should come with me."

"But Zuba will be back!"

"He has family in Litomysl, doesn't he?"

"Ya, his Mama and brother."

"When he can't find you here, he might go there. I will tell the coal company so they can tell him where you are. He's bound to check there too," Bolda said, knowing it was a futile gesture.

"Ya, but I don't feel right leaving."

"What will you do? Where will you live? Think of Andela."

"Ya Papa, I guess that's best, but only till Zuba comes back."

They loaded Eliska's meager belongings in Bolda's wagon and started the long drive back to Litomysl. ~~~~~~

Chapter 39

A Poor Bargain

Danka Home, Litomysl Czechoslovakia Saturday, Feb 23, 1919

It's now ten days since Eliska returned to her parent's home. Florica was overjoyed to see her and was even happier to meet Andela. The time she spends with her headstrong daughter, and new grandchild has erased some of her sadness over losing Hanzi.

"Bolda, is today the day?" Florica asked. "I'm glad you brought Eliska here."

"Ya, it was right. I'll meet with the Kris (Judicial Council) to get their decision on Eliska."

"Thank you for taking a chance and bringing Eliska here. It is right,"

"We'll see what they say."

Bolda left, and Florica busied herself with housework. Eliska's twin brothers, Stevo, and Luca were roughhousing on the floor. Eliska was tending to Andela. An hour later, Bolda returned home.

"Good news the Kris has decided it's ok for Eliska to stay."

"That's wonderful!" Florica beamed and clapped her hands.

"There are conditions."

"Conditions? What conditions?" Eliska asked.

"You are to marry Jacob as originally planned."

"I can't marry Jacob; I am married to Zuba!"

"I think you know in your heart that Zuba is dead."

"No! I never felt it," Eliska replied sternly, "Zuba is not dead!"

"Hanzi left, and I didn't feel it. It doesn't always work that way. Sometimes the spirits of the dead get lost and can't contact us. That must be what happened," Bolda replied.

"Zuba is not dead!" Eliska shouted. "I know he is not dead. You'll see!"

A knock on the door interrupted them. Bolda opened it, and Jacob was standing there.

"I heard the Kris's decision, and I came right over," Jacob said gleefully.

"Come in," Bolda said.

Jacob entered and went over to Eliska. "Good news, eh? We'll get married, yes?"

"No!" Eliska snapped. "I am married to Zuba!"

"You heard the Kris's decision, didn't you?" Jacob said.

"I can't marry another when I am already married," Eliska replied, "I will never marry you!"

Jacob turned to Bolda. "Look here, Bolda, I paid you the full dowry, right?"

"Ya, you did."

"Did you return any of it?" Jacob said.

"No, you said it was all right because Eliska might come back to you."

"It's time you give me Eliska or give the dowry back."

"I can give some back, but I used half to go to Karvina," Bolda said.

"Well then, give the other half back. Eliska is damaged goods now, so I'll only pay half for her."

"Papa, I won't be bought and sold! I'm not a colored slave. Give him all of it back!" Eliska shouted.

"Be quiet, woman!" Jacob said. He grabbed her wrist and twisted her arm, hard. "Know your place! I am willing to take you and your bastard kid under my roof, and you tell me the right and wrong of it."

"You toilet! Leave her be," Bolda said, grabbing Jacob's arm. "You are in my house, and she is not your wife yet!"

"She will be my wife, or you and your whole family can leave. My uncles are on the Kris. How the hell do you think you can stay after they find out that Eliska won't marry me, and you kept the dowry?"

"You will have my decision tomorrow. Now get the hell out of here," Bold said. He grabbed Jacob by the collar, escorted him to the door, and slammed it hard. After he had left, Bolda exclaimed, "He makes me so damn mad!"

"Oh, Papa, I'm sorry to cause you so much trouble. I should leave," Eliska said tearfully.

"Child, why are you so proud and stubborn? Can't you see the pickle you are in? No husband, a child, and another on the way. Still, you insist on holding your head so high!"

"I know Papa, but Zuba is alive, and Jacob is mean. I would rather live without Zuba than with Jacob taking his pleasure with me."

"I must think hard; I have to decide, for the good of all," Bolda said. "I'm afraid there is no easy answer." ~~~

Chapter 40

RUNNING AWAY

On the Streets of Litomysl, Czechoslovakia, Fri, Feb 24, 1919
It was still dark when Eliska stepped out into the bitterly cold
February morning. A blanket of fluffy snow smothered the ground.
How lovely and peaceful! I wonder if God knows what a storm is in my heart?

Eliska placed her gunny sacks, filled with their belongings, outside
the front door, then went back for Zuba's tuba. On the last trip, she
wrapped a sleeping Andela tightly in a blanket, and as she quietly
tiptoed to the door, she felt a hand lightly touch her shoulder. "Where
are you going, child?" A bewildered Florica whispered.

"It's best for the family if I leave Mama," Eliska replied. "Then Papa
can make a deal with Jacob about the money. He will have no choice
but to honor it. With me gone, the Kris will say 'good riddance,' and
then it's done."

Florica looked at Eliska's swollen stomach. "Oh child, it's freezing
out, and another baby is due soon. Life is never the way we want it.
Why don't you marry Jacob and make the best of it?"

"I can't, Mama, I can't betray my husband. Even if I did, Jacob
would treat the children and me harshly."

"Please, Eliska, Papa can check on you from time to time."

"This is best. I don't wanna make Papa decide. It's okay, Mama. I'll
go to Zuba's mother's farm. I'm sure they will take us in."

"I'm sorry it had to go this way. We must think of the twins as well.
We have to be careful; without the clan, we are out," Florica replied.
"You've seen how the gadje treat the Roma, especially when we're
alone."

"Ya, Mama, I know."

"I can't help much, but you go out behind the house; there's an old
pushcart. The wood is sound, and the wheels are almost new. Take it
and put your things in it. Papa will never miss it until spring. It's the
best I can do to help you."

"Thanks, Mama. I love you."

Florica embraced Eliska, "God be with you and your child."

Two separate, solitary cart tracks straddled Eliska's footprints as she trudged ankle-deep through the fluffy snow lying deep on the streets of Litomysl.

Figure 44 In the Snow

~~~~~~

A chilly morning dawned. Floating feathers of snow danced, slipping softly by, as the sky glowed a rosy pink. Eliska trudged on. The snow crunched and creaked under her feet. A wobbly wheel squeaked every time it rolled. It was only an hour since leaving her parents' home, but Eliska's arms ached, her feet were numb with cold, and despair was knocking at her door. Andela sat up in the cart, "Mama... cold," she said through chattering teeth.

"We will stop soon," Eliska said as she struggled to keep the cart upright as she pulled it over piles of snow. She walked the deserted streets of Litomysl, stopping at the only open store, a general store.

Eliska picked up Andela, carried her into the store, and set her on a pickle barrel. As she unwrapped her, a short, pudgy farmer entered the store.
~~~~~~

"Good morning Mr. Dusek! How are you this chilly day? What will you have?" The storekeeper asked.

"I need nails, window glass, and boards," Antonie Dusek answered, laying a neatly written list on the counter. "It's a bit nippy out!!"

"Ya, the cats, keep their tails in their pockets, you can bet. Quite a list you got," the storekeeper said. "I'll get it ready for you right away. Not too much business this morning." He turned and entered the back room.

Antonie walked over to where Andela was sitting on the pickle barrel. He chucked her chin and chuckled, "Are they selling sweet pickles today."

Eliska hurried over and picked up Andela. "Sorry, Mr. Dusek."

"No need. That bright little face makes the sun want to hide."

"Thank you! Are you Antonie Dusek that lives by the Palzek farm?"

"Yes, I am. Who might you be?"

"I married Zuba Palzek. We're on our way to see Emilia right now."

"You must be Eliska. Emilia talked about you a lot."

"Nothing too bad, I hope," Eliska replied with a slight blush, worried that she might not be welcome.

"No, she spoke of you fondly. And this must be Andela. Emilia sure is tickled with her."

Relief washed over Eliska's face, "I'm happy to hear that. Would it be too much trouble for us to ride in your wagon back to the farm?"

"It'll be fine. But why are you going there?" Antonie replied. "Emilia is not there. Petr Jr's wife, Janel, convinced her to move to Prague with her. Janel's from there. She's a teacher. Emilia is helping with the children in her class and doing the housekeeping. She should like that."

"Why did she do that?"

"Emilia was confused and distraught when Petr Jr. was killed in the war. With Zuba lost as well, Emilia had nowhere to turn to or anyone to run the farm. She was half crazy with grief, wringing her hands and worrying about how to take care of the farm." Antonie said.

Antonie filled his pie, lit it, took a long draw on it, and continued, "Janel was concerned that something would happen to Emilia, so she took Emilia under her wing. Janel convinced Emilia to sell the farm to my boy and me. He will live there with his new wife. That's why we need the nails and such. We're fixing up before planting time."

Eliska sat down hard on the pickle barrel next to Andela. *The list of the dead with the Palzek name on it was Petr Jr, not Zuba! Oh, thank God!.... But I should be ashamed of my selfishness. Emilia must hurt, and I find no joy in that..... We can't stay with Emilia..... What to do now?*

"Zuba is not here; that's for sure, but he is not dead!" Eliska stated emphatically.

Eliska's reply struck Antonie like a hammer. "I didn't mean to turn up hard hurts, I'm sorry," he said

"It's not your fault; it's just...." Tears welled up in Eliska's eyes. She picked up Andela and left the store, loaded her into the cart, and once again pulled it along the street.

~~~~~~

Eliska passed the Exaltation Church as the church tower bells called out a hearty welcome. She remembered this church as the same one they attended on Christmas day. She pulled the cart around to the back of the Nativity scene, then hid the cart by covering it with pine tree branches from the manger scene. Taking Andela by the hand, they walked to the front of the crib and bowed to the baby Jesus.

"Bay bee cold," Andela said. She pulled her babushka off her head and offered it to Eliska.
~~~~~~

A puzzled look came across Eliska's face as she wrapped the babushka back on Andela's head. "We'll go inside and warm up, sweetie."

"Bay bee cold!" Andela insisted and pulled her babushka off again and held towards the manger. "Dere," she said, pointing a fat little finger at the manger scene.

An astonished Eliska looked over at the statue of the naked baby Jesus in the manger. "You mean that baby?" She said, pointing to the figure.

Andela nodded vigorously, "Bab bee cold!"

"Oh, you sweet child," Eliska laughed as she hugged Andela. She took the babushka from Andela's outstretched hand and placed it over the figure of Jesus in the manger. "I guess we can do without it for a while."

"Bye, Bay bee," Andela said, waving her hand.

They entered the church and stood before the altar of Saint Wenceslas. Not so much for prayer, but to warm their hands over the burning candles. As they sat in the last pew, the Mass ended, and Eliska was unsure of what to do next. She took her purse from her waistband and carefully counted out the money she had left. *One hundred korunas, not much. Where to go? ... -What to do? ... How could Zuba find them now?* An old dark woman, hobbling along on a cane, came up the aisle. The woman's dirty white hair hung limply over her prune-wrinkled face. She wore a mismatch of ragged clothes, and her exposed fingers stuck out of the holes in the ends of her mittens.

She interrupted Eliska with a plaintive cry, "Alms for the poor. Alms for a blind woman," the woman said as she groped her way along the wall.

"I'm poor myself," Eliska said, irritated by the woman's boldness. "What little can I do for you?"

Figure 45 Blind Woman

"Any little bit will help a poor Roma woman."

"You are Roma? So am I."

"I know."

"How did you know? You can't see me!"

"Only a Roma can see into another Roma's heart. No eyes needed."

Eliska, taken back by the bluntness of the woman, squirmed uncomfortably. *She's worse off than I am. But this is all we have!* Eliska fingered the coins in her pocket. *What would Zuba do?* Eliska hesitated, then something in her heart snapped. She counted out ten korunas and placed them in the blind woman's hand.

The blind woman bit on the coins and turned them over in her fingers as her lifeless eyes stared straight ahead. "Thank you and may Kali Sara (Black Sara) watch over you and yours. By the way, your baby is a boy." Then the old woman pointed to a door at the far end of the church. "Go there!"

Eliska grabbed Andela's hand and walked up the aisle toward the door indicated. She hesitated, stopped, then turned back to the old woman. "By what name do they call... you?"

There was no sign of the blind woman; the church was empty.

~~~~~~
~~~~~~

Chapter 41

A PORT IN THE STORM

Exaltation Church, Litomysl, Czechoslovakia Fri, Feb 24, 1919

Eliska approached the door at the far end of the church. Apprehensively, she opened it and peered into a classroom full of children being taught by a short, stout woman wearing a dark veil. Noticing Eliska in the doorway, she said, "Can I help you?"

"I.... don't know... I guess... not."

"My name is Sister Lucie," she said, then she turned back to the children. "Time for recess." The children put their caps and coats on and galloped out the door to the patio playground. "I don't know who needs the recess more, the kids or me," she chuckled. "Are you troubled, my child?"

"Nooo... I just... wanted to see about... getting... my little girl... into -- school," Eliska replied.

"How old is the child?"

"She'll be one in March."

"She's too young. We don't start them until six or seven. We need them out of diapers."

"I understand. Sorry to bother you," Eliska said, turning to leave.

"Wait, it so happens that we cooked too much breakfast this morning. Have you eaten? I hate to throw it out to the pig. It's a sin to waste food, and the pig is too fat already," Sister Lucie grinned.

"No, we didn't waste much where I come from either," Eliska said. She remembered the day when her milk dried up, and she went without food so Andela could eat.

Sister Lucie dished up two bowls of hot porridge and added canned apples to it. She brought two big glasses of milk and motioned to a nearby table.

"Here! Come! Sit! Eat!" Sister Lucie said.

"Well, if it is going to waste, anyway. Better us than the pig!" Eliska said, light-heartedly relieved, as she sat Andela at the table.

"What is your little girl's name?" Sister Lucie asked.

"Andela, mine is Eliska."

"She is beautiful, takes after her mother."

Eliska blushed, "I'm afraid I don't look so good since I came here."

"Can I ask where you are from?"

"We were in Karvina."

"Karvina! That's a long way! Isn't that where that awful war was?"

Upon hearing those words, Eliska's emotions burst forth: she sobbed, with tears dripping into her porridge.

Sister Lucie stood up and came to her and put her arms around her. "Now, girl, it's a long way from here."

"Ya, but the hard pains just keep coming."

"Would you tell me about it?"

With that caring invitation, Eliska tearfully described the loss of her family, of Zuba, and of losing their home. She unloaded all the troubles that had beset her since Zuba left for the Skoczow Band Festival. "The one bright spot is my little Andela, and my baby will be here soon."

"Do you have a place to stay?"

"No, we were going to Zuba's mother, north of Litomysl, but she sold the farm and left."

"I am sorry to hear that."

"Is there any place else? Your parents, perhaps?"

"No, my parents tried, but we're Roma, and I married a gadjo. I am not allowed in the community if I don't marry a Roma."

"Maybe, I can help," Sister Lucie replied.

"How can you help?"

"Well, I am a member of the Salesian Community volunteers. We teach and serve children. To do that, sometimes we must serve the parents too. The children are welcome to come to school as soon as they are of age."

"What will I do until then?"

"We can find you a place to stay until your baby comes, then after the baby is born, you will need a job to take care of your expenses. I don't mean to be hard, but I must. We don't run a mother's home here, and we have many other needs."

"When it's time for the baby, where can I find a midwife?"

"We can do better than that; we'll send you to the Litomysl hospital. Our volunteers will be there to help you," Sister Lucie replied. "You are keeping the baby, aren't you?"

"Of course!"

"Good! I've seen desperate mothers do things to their bodies to lose the baby. If you think that way, please don't. There is an adoption service that can find a home for your baby."

"You mean, give my baby away?"

"Yes, that could be arranged... To a good home."

"I would never give my child away," Eliska said. "How terrible."

"It's harsh, but the good of the child must be considered first."

"Shouldn't a loving mother be the first consideration?"

"Yes, but a desperate, loving mother will do anything to help her children survive. Sometimes she even turns to being used for men's pleasures." Sister Lucie replied sadly.

"I would never do that!"

"You know what fear and desperation are. Tough words to hear for any young mother, especially without a husband to help. These are the facts as I've seen them. I pray that this will not be the case with you." Sister Lucie paused, "Let's not worry about it until that time comes. Let's get you and Andela settled in a nice dry room. Will that be all right?"

Eliska pondered. *Nowhere to go. We need food. I can't go back to Papa.* Then she said meekly, "I guess so." *'Until that time comes' can mean putting off things that are best left unsaid or even thought about."* ~~~~~~

Chapter 42

OUT TO SEA

Open Sea–Raspatau, Mon, March 10, 1919

Hanzi struggled to lift the 80-pound sludge buckets, and when he was too slow, Rocco's crop whip, Sally, rained blows upon his helpless back.

"This stuff stinks -- worse than calf poop -- from eating green grass," Zuba sniffed as he lifted the oily buckets filled with the slimy sludge and carried them over to the sludge purifiers.

"Me must get back to -- Eliska and Andela. They can no get by without -- me to help. Could jump overboard, -- but can't swim. Need to get home."

"Not too bright, are you?" Hanzi chided Zuba. "Who gives a damn? This is it! We're stuck here.

"Quit talking and get to work," Rocco said, with a sneer in his voice.

"Is it OK -- me change -- jobs with Hanzi?" Zuba said.

Figure 46 Engine Room

"What do I care? Just do it!" Rocco replied.

"Why are you doing this? To get on my good side?" Hanzi said.

"I'm bigger and stronger -- than you are. -- Fill buckets, -- me lift -- to the sludge purifier," Zuba said.

He turned and looked at Rocco. "Why don't you pump -- right into the purifiers?"

"The pump broke right after we left Copenhagen," Rocco replied. "A fork would hold more water. Can't get anyone to fix it before we get to New York."

"Me -- fix. OK? –to look at it?"

"A big toad like you knows something about pumps? Ha!"

"I worked -- on big trucks at -- the coal mine."

"If you're not just trying to get out of this work, I may let you."

"I need tools -- big wrenches and–if me fix -- will you let up a little?"

"If you can fix the damn thing, I'll give you a day off."

"Two days off -- for me and -- Hanzi too."

"Who the hell do you think you are? Telling me what to do? I ought to crack you a good one across that thick head of yours."

"That thick head -- gonna fix your pump," Zuba replied. "Then you can work us -- someplace else. You don't -- catch -- too many new -- fellows in Copenhagen, you are -- shorthanded."

"Why do we always get the damn smart Aleck Pollacks on this ship?" Rocco said, shaking his head.

"We're Czech -- not Polish."

"All right, all right, I don't give a damn what you are. Fix the blasted pump--- get two days off."

Rocco brought Zuba the tools he requested. Zuba took the pump apart and cleaned it. "You need -- a new gasket," Zuba said to Rocco.

"We don't have a gasket, smart boy. I guess you're going back to pumping sludge by hand."

Zuba scratched his head, "Do you have strips -- of leather and -- raincoat?"

"Ya, but how will that fix it?"

"Let me -- worry about that."

Rocco fetched the items that Zuba requested. Zuba cut a new gasket out of the leather. When he finished, he fashioned two duplicates of the gasket from the raincoat and placed one copy on either side of the leather gasket. He slipped the makeshift gasket back on the pump and pulled the bolts tight.

"There -- turn it on," Zuba ordered Rocco. The pump whirled into action. A small leak trickled on the underside.

Figure 47 Turn It On

"Well, smart guy, that didn't work," Rocco sneered.

Zuba picked up the big wrenches again; he gave the bolts another hard twist, stopping the leak. "Needed -- adjustment."

"All right, you win, take the next two days off. Don't let the other crew members know. Pretend you're sick or something."

"You have a heart of rusty gold," Hanzi sneered.

Rocco's face blazed red. He whirled and slapped Sally across Hanzi's face. "I don't have to give you any damn time off, your smart-ass gypsy."

Zuba pulled Hanzi away from Rocco. "Sometimes, my brother-in-law's mouth goes when he should be thinking."

Rocco's face softened, "Ya. I got a brother-in-law that needs a slap across the head, most of the time."

~~~~~~

The next day Zuba and Hanzi stayed in their quarters. Zuba stared at the wall with a faraway look in his eyes.

"What's a matter with you? We have two whole days off!"

"Shut up and -- let me be," Zuba said while fingering his gold cross.

"That looks like Eliska's cross," Hanzi persisted.

"It is -- leave be!"
~~~~~~

"Well, you don't have to get upset. We better make the best of our situation. You may never see Eliska again."

"Don't say -- that!" Zuba snapped. "What you -- know? You wanted -- to cause trouble. How -- you know --- how me feel?"

Hanzi sensed that he had stepped over the line. "Look, I'm sorry. I didn't mean to upset you. It's nice to have a couple of days' rest, that's all. Why does that bother you so?"

"Today -- is," tears formed in Zuba's eyes as he continued, "today is -- Andela's birthday. -- one-year-old, -- me not there to kiss and hug her."

Hanzi was quiet, then shuddered and said, "I miss Mama and Papa too. I don't want to think on it. That's all. It's easier if I pretend I don't care and keep working."

"Ya, me don't -- think tomorrow -- be better. Maybe work -- not think on it."

"When we get to that New York place, maybe we can sneak off the ship. It can't be too far to go home." Hanzi said.

"How -- do that? We -- sail for 38 days. -- We don't even know -- where we be! -- can't understand -- what people say. How it be -- any better in New York? How we -- get home from there?" Zuba replied.

"Maybe we could find a Czech or something. Do you suppose they have Czechs in New York place? Even a Roma would help us?"

"Better not talk -- loud. If Rocco finds out -- it be Sally for sure -- on both of us."

"I want to go back to work," Hanzi said.

"Ya, me too. Sometimes the -- pain of a day off -- isn't worth it," Zuba replied. ~~~~~~

Chapter 43

HAPPY BIRTHDAY

Salesian Mission, Litomysl Czechoslovakia Tues, March 11, 1919

"Happy birthday to you," sang the children, as Sister Lucie placed Andela on a stool at the head of the class and brought in a large birthday cake. She said, "This always makes the children happy, even their teacher. I love birthdays, especially the cake."

Andela beamed, clapped her chubby hands, saying, "like -cak."

Eliska smirked, kissing Andela on the cheek, "I go goofy for cake too, honey."

The other kids jumped up and down as they dashed up and helped themselves to the cake. Sister Lucie came over and stood by Eliska. "How's the search for a job going?"

"I applied at lots of places. But some don't want me because I am Roma. They think I'll steal from them. What is a cook to steal?" Eliska replied. "Maybe take a chicken or ham bone home?"

"Some people have soft minds and hard hearts, Eliska, but many are not like that. They just need to taste your cooking! We love your cooking here, and I would keep you on, but we have our rules, and we don't have the money for it. The bishop has inquired, and I think he might have gotten a stiff neck from looking the other way."

"I understand," Eliska said, fingering her gold cross. *I wonder where he is? He would love to be here.* Tears flowed, and Eliska, not wanting to spoil Andela's birthday, got up and left the classroom. She entered the dark, cool church and sat in a pew.

Young Father Emilio, newly ordained six months ago, entered from the vestibule. His cassock hung loosely on his thin, tall frame; he was balding with dark hair and brown eyes. His quiet style hid a daily secret, a vice that most people with good noses were aware of.

He smoked his favorite cigar in the church office but limited himself to only ten puffs; then, he put the cigar out, saving the stub for another time.

After his customary ten puffs, Father strolled outside the church, saying his prayers, hoping that the outside air dissipated the cigar smell and would go unnoticed. After his walk, he entered the church to complete his prayers. He crossed himself and knelt in the pew ahead of Eliska. Father sensed the distress of the person behind him. Turning, he saw that Eliska was crying.

"Why so sad, child?" Father asked.

"Nothing you can do much about, Father," Eliska said curtly through her tears.

"How do you know if you don't ask?"

"Today is my Andela's birthday," Eliska said, sobbing.

"Well, it should be a joyous occasion. Is she ill?"

"No, Father, she is well."

"Well, what then?"

"Her Papa isn't here. He's gone for 48 days."

"Oh, you must be Eliska, whose husband died in that war."

"He's not dead!" Eliska replied angrily, "I know he's not dead!"

"Sometimes, it's hard to accept the death of a loved one."

"Do you have trouble hearing? HE IS NOT DEAD!"

Father Emilio was taken back by her outburst. He searched his memory, trying to find something wise to say. Finally, he said. "God works in mysterious ways, my child."

"He is out to lunch, father. Why would he be so cruel to make my husband be lost?"

"He will keep looking until he finds his sheep."

"All you people want with us sheep is to shear them."

That accusation plainly hurt Father Emilio. "You are staying here at the goodness of the church, aren't you?"

"Yes."

"Has anyone asked you for money?"

"No, Father, I guess not." Eliska lowered her head in embarrassment. "I should be more thankful."

"I'm sure your husband is in God's care right now, directing his steps."

"He better tell him quick. My Zuba don't read so good and doesn't know where we are gone to."

"I'm sure you will see him again."

"Father, he's not dead!"

"Yes, child, God's will be done."

"If His will brings my Zuba home."

~~~~~~

<div align="center">Chapter 44</div>

A CZECH SALE

Hotel Aplaus, Litomysl Czechoslovakia, March 29, 1919

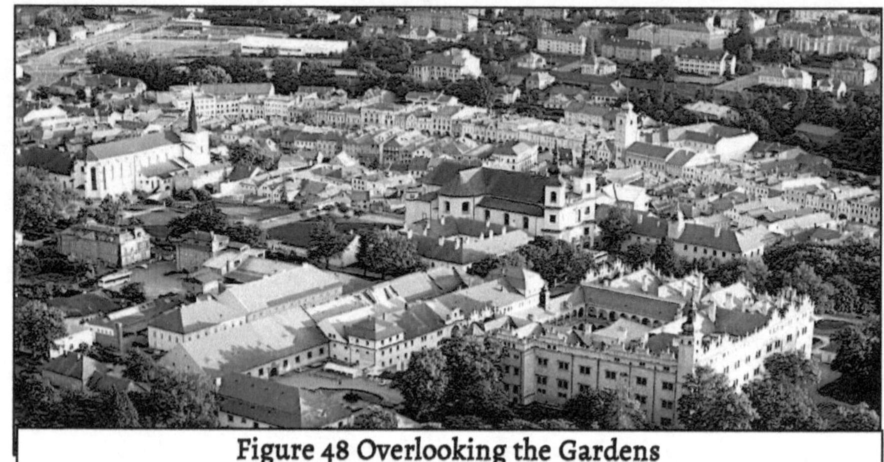

Figure 48 Overlooking the Gardens

Successful Minnesota businessman, Thomas Koupil, awoke early, stretched, and strolled to the window to check the early morning activity. From his elegant room, at the upscale Hotel Aplaus, he looked down on the stunning monastery garden where yellow daffodils and red tulips peeked through a late March snowfall.

Next door, rows of white tombstones, lined up in perfect symmetry, marched up to the nearby Piarist monastery. Across the street stood the grand Chateau.
~~~~~~

Thomas Koupil, a sales representative for Mack Trucks, made this his last sales call before going into business for himself. An arduous journey for him and his wife Marta, but very profitable. World War One created an enormous demand for coal and, subsequently, the vehicles to haul that coal. Thomas has sold a large order of trucks to the coal company in Litomysl.

Thomas stood in front of the window; his tall figure silhouetted by the early morning sunlight. He ran his slender fingers through his salt and pepper black hair as he turned and gazed at his sleeping wife, Marta. *I wish she had not come.... After six years of trying, this is the last chance of having a baby.*

Planning to go home soon, Thomas was looking forward to starting a truck dealership in Owatonna, MN. He bought the dealership with inheritance money from his father, a well-to-do Owatonna businessman. Owatonna was an easy commute from their home in Litomysl, MN, only ten miles south. Marta felt safe in the house as it was quiet, and Thomas came home every night.

Marta was too insecure to stay at home when he was gone too far away., She worried about medical care. However, Rochester, MN was only fifty miles from their home, where she could have had the best doctors on call, but that didn't satisfy her.

Thomas loved her dearly and would go to the ends of the earth for her, but sometimes it was hard to tolerate her paranoia. Especially now, as she was off her medication because of her pregnancy.

Thomas had planned this trip to make sales calls, but he made sure they were close to proper medical care. Marta stayed in the hotel while he talked to the coal companies. She paced the floor and peeked out the windows until he returned.

When she was younger, Marta's father had left town with a younger woman forcing Marta and her mother to live on the poor side of town. Her mother was delusional and institutionalized after she had a nervous breakdown. Six-year-old Marta then ended up at the County Orphanage and attended the local public school.

The children at that school taunted her threadbare clothes and tattered shoes. This scarred childhood left her desperate for acceptance and determined to have the better things in life.

At eighteen, Marta's life took a turn for the better when she married Thomas Koupil. Now, seventeen years later, swollen in pregnancy, she felt unattractive to Thomas even though he lavished his love and wealth on her.

Marta feared Thomas would find another woman while he was halfway around the world, so she clung to him, as only as an insecure person will do.

Now here at Hotel Aplaus, in the plush hotel bed, Marta raised herself on one elbow, the only position her big tummy allowed. "Is it morning already?"

"No, dear, I was restless and didn't want to wake you."

"Oh, help me up, will you? I must be sweating; the bed is wet."

Thomas helped her up, and her wet bedclothes clung to her. "You aren't sweating. Your water broke. It's time," Thomas said.

It was a short drive to the Litomysl hospital. Thomas went to the front desk to have Marta admitted. "I want a private room for my wife and your best doctor."

"I'm sorry, sir, we don't have private rooms, and our best doctor is our only doctor. If you want a private room, there's a clinic on the other side of town. Do you want the address?"

Marta moaned, "I need a doctor now. The baby is coming!"

"All right, at least can we have a private room?"

"We only have one room left. It's for two patients. There's a woman in there who just had a baby. The bed next to her is available. Will that do?"

"Yes, I suppose it will have to do. Now, get the doctor!"

"We'll get the room ready. From the look of your wife, she needs to go to the delivery room. I'll have a nurse take her right away, and I'll get the doctor. You can stay out here or wait in her room."

"I'll wait in her room."

Marta held her back and leaned against the nurse as they proceeded to the delivery room.

Thomas waited impatiently in Marta's hospital room. It was a sterile room painted in a light beige and smelling of disinfectant. Two beds, with a large curtain between them, graced the room. A young woman with long black hair occupied the first bed. She was resting comfortably, and her baby slept in a cradle in front of her bed. The card in the cardholder had 'Palzek' written on it.

Thomas sat in a deep, high-back chair decked out with mahogany-colored leather cushions. He began the long wait that all expectant fathers go through.

Sitting, pacing, praying, legs aching, and eyes blurring while his thoughts drifted back. *We lost two babies, one early in the pregnancy and the second right after the baby's birth. After losing the last baby, Marta showed no grief, a trait she learned in her childhood coping with tough times..... She is only 35 years old, obsessed about, and insisting on having a child of our own.... Wants a child before it is too late.... I suggested adoption.... She wouldn't hear of it! "It must be our baby! To prove our love for each other! Then the child will be someone I could trust and who would love me."*

The nurse entered the room later that afternoon. "You have a boy. It was a long delivery, and it stressed the baby."

She left and came back a little later, placing the baby in a cradle in front of Marta's bed. She made a card with 'Koupil' on it and put it in the cradle's cardholder. "There," she said, "side by side, they look alike, don't they?"

Thomas gazed at his baby lovingly. "They sure do, but ours is handsomer."

"A father would say that," the nurse said, laughing.

"How is my lovely wife?"

"Oh, she should be fine -- just a few more stitches. With a good rest, she'll be ready to dance a jig. We'll bring her in as soon as we're done. Congratulations!"

The nurses wheeled Marta in an hour later and transferred her to the bed. "Thomas, have you seen our baby?" she asked weakly.

"Yes. We have a handsome boy."

"Are you happy?"

"Yes, Marta, I don't know what to say, except we have the most handsome son I have ever seen!" Thomas said as he kissed her forehead. "Now get to sleep. I'll be here all night, so don't you worry."

Marta fell asleep at once. Thomas sat and pondered the events of the day. *I am a father, and Marta has her very own baby. She will be so pleased. -- I hope she copes better now that this has happened. –Marta always wanted a baby. I bet he will grow up healthy and handsome!* With a look of contentment on his face, he fell asleep in the soft chair.

At two in the morning, Thomas awoke, hearing the cry of a baby. A nurse came in and picked up the Palzek baby and took him over to his mother for nursing.

When finished, the nurse changed the baby's diaper and laid him back in the cradle. She checked the Koupil baby, and the baby was still sound asleep. "After a long delivery, it tires any baby," she whispered to Thomas.

Thomas fell asleep again. He awoke with a start an hour later. He got up and checked on his baby. The baby was still and blue. Thomas cautiously reached down to the baby's neck and felt for a pulse. He checked it several times, but he couldn't find a pulse. *Am I doing something wrong? ... This looks like the last baby we lost. Still and blue.... Marta can't handle another baby lost. -- Should I call the nurse? ... If the baby is dead, it won't matter. What will this do to Marta? ... If only I could prevent the pain that this will cause.*

Standing, with his arms folded, clutching himself in a protective shield, he looked at his baby, and he glanced over at the other sleeping baby. *Yes, they look alike.... I could..... The other mother is young; she can have another baby..... No, I can't! It's not right! But Marta will go to pieces this time.... might not even be able to get her back to the States.*

Thomas's mind raced. *Marta could end up in an insane ward like her mother. -- She is too old for another baby. This is a big problem.*

He wrestled with his conscience for several minutes and then again, checked the pulse of his baby and turned to the other baby. *They look alike. I want a son to follow me in the business..... No, it's wrong! The other mother isn't able to support the baby..... She is young.... Marta will never have another.*

Suddenly, Thomas decided. He changed the cradles one for the other. Then he pulled the Palzek card from the Palzek baby's cradle cardholder and put it in the cradle cardholder of his dead baby. He then took the Koupil card from his dead baby's cradle cardholder and put it on the cradle cardholder of the Palzek baby. ~~~~~~

Chapter 45

WHERE IS THE BABY?

Litomysl Hospital, Litomysl Czechoslovakia, March 30, 1919
Eliska woke with a start. Her breasts were full and painful. *Why haven't they brought the baby to nurse? It must be time.*

A nurse entered the room, along with a young priest.

"How are you feeling today, Eliska?" The nurse asked.

"Fine, how's the baby?' Why haven't you brought him to nurse?"

"Eliska, this is Father Emilio; he wants to talk to you."

"Hello child, we meet again. I am here to help you through a difficult morning." Father Emilio said.

"What are you talking about? I have a sweet baby boy! How can that be difficult?"

"Sometimes, God's ways are hard to understand."

"What hard way?"

"We can be grateful that we're in His care."

Eliska painfully eased out of bed, forced the priest aside, and hurried to her baby's cradle. "Where is my baby?" she demanded.

"I'm sorry, Eliska, what Father is trying to tell you is," The nurse cleared her throat and continued, "Your baby died during the night."

Eliska was silent for a moment. "No, you took him someplace else! If he died, I would have felt it!" Eliska snapped angrily.

"I'm sorry, Eliska, but it's true. I baptized the baby and gave him the last rites," Father Emilio said.

The nurse put her arms around Eliska, "It's true, Eliska."

"You're lying! I need to see my baby! Where is my baby?" Eliska screamed as she pushed away from the nurse.

"It may be best if she sees the baby," Father Emilio said.

Father Emilio and the nurse helped Eliska to the chapel. On the altar was a baby's cradle.

Eliska shoved the nurse away and walked hesitantly to the cradle. She unwrapped the blanket, revealing a still, blue baby. Eliska's knees gave out, and she collapsed on the floor. "It can't be my baby. It can't be my baby," she murmured.

The nurse helped her to her feet, and they turned to leave the chapel. Suddenly Eliska pulled away and stumbled back to the cradle and reaching under the baby's blankets; she cried, "Where is it? Where is the cross?"

"What cross?"

Eliska turned red-faced and angrily confronted the nurse and the priest. "My Zuba made a cross for our baby. I put it in his blankets! WHERE IS THE CROSS? MY BABY HAD A CROSS. WHERE IS IT?"

"I've never seen a cross," the nurse replied.

"It was here, I tell you! Where is my baby, and the cross?"

"God heals all wounds, my child," Father Emilio said, trying to comfort her. "You might have imagined the cross because I am here."

Eliska screamed and grabbed Father Emilio's cassock, scratched his face, and shook him. "I didn't imagine it. My child... my child!..... Where is......?" Suddenly, the color drained from Eliska's face; she passed out, still tightly clutching Father Emilio's cassock.

"Well, that went well, Father," the nurse said snidely. "Didn't they teach you at the seminary that grief counseling comes after the person accepts the death of a loved one?"

Father Emilio hung his head, "I must have been out that day. This is quite new to me. I guess I made a mess of things."

"Well, enough said, here, help me pick her up and carry her back to her room."

The nurse and Father Emilio took Eliska back to her bed.

In the other half of the room, Thomas Koupil sat watching his wife nurse their new baby. When they brought Eliska back into the room, his heart was even more troubled. *What have I done? This isn't right... But Marta will go to pieces if I tell the truth.... Best I leave things alone... But the girl is young... she will get over it... she can have another baby. What can I do now?*

Father Emilio and the nurse looked under the bed; Thomas walked over to them and asked, "Father, what are you looking for?"

"Eliska was raving about a gold cross that she had put in her baby's crib. She is delirious, but we'll look for it." Father Emilio replied.

Thomas turned and walked back to his baby's cradle. "Oh, I hope you find it." Then, inconspicuously as possible, he rummaged around the blankets in his baby's crib. His hand touched a metal object. He pulled it out to reveal a gold cross.

He looked at it sadly, swallowed hard, and placed it in his pocket.

~~~~~~

Chapter 46

PAINFUL TIME

Litomysl Hospital, Litomysl Czechoslovakia, Mon, Mar 31, 1919

Eliska cried fitfully and finally, at 3 AM, fell to sleep.

"Good morning, good morning," was the first thing Eliska heard as the sun peeked through the hospital curtains. Looking up, she saw the smiling face of Sister Lucie in the doorway.

Eliska, blurry-eyed, said a quiet, "Good morning."

"I have a sweet treat for you this morning," Sister Lucie replied.

"I'm not up to sweet treats."
~~~~~~

"Oh, this one you'll like," Sister Lucie said. She left and reappeared with a smiling Andela.

"Fool you, Mama," giggled Andela.

"Andela, my sweet, am I glad to see you!"

"Mama sleepy?"

"Yes, Mama had a rough time."

"Kiss fix?"

"It sure does! Fix me quick!"

Sister Lucie boosted Andela up on the bed, and Andela collapsed in Eliska's arms, kissing and hugging her. "Where baby, Mama?"

Eliska took a deep breath. "Baby's gone, looking for Dada."

"Oh good," Andela said, satisfied with the answer.

"They say you can come home today," Sister said.

"Good, the smell around here isn't too good."

"I'll go to the desk and take care of the bill. You dress. We can leave right away."

Figure 49 Andela

Sister and Andela left as Eliska got out of bed. *Stiff and sore, but relieved to get out of this place.* As Eliska was dressing, an old black woman came into the room with a mop and bucket and mopped the floor.

"Going home, I see," the woman said.

"Yes, I came expecting to take a baby home, but I'll take home emptiness."

"That will go. Your family will help."

"I have no family. I lost a son here, and no one cares."

"You are wrong; there's always someone who cares. What about Sister Lucie, Andela, and even the clumsy Father Emilio?"

"Yes, of course, but hard when all I can think of is what I lost."

"Are you throwing away what you have… longing for what you lost? I thought you Roma were good traders? It does not sound like a good trade to me."

"What do you know about the Roma?"

"I once was a Roma."

"Once was, you're not now?"

"It's different now. Better, no more pain."

Eliska finished packing her small bag. "How do you get away from the pain? I lost my husband and a son. The pain in my chest crushes my spirit."

"That will pass. You will see them again."

Eliska turned to check around the room for any missed items. "Yes, in the hereafter."

"No, you will see both before you die."

"How… can… you know?" Eliska asked as she turned around. There was no one in the room.

Eliska walked to the desk, where Sister Lucie signed the release papers. Andela ran up to Eliska. Eliska picked her up and winced as she did. Childbirth causes lots of lingering pain. She carried Andela over to the desk and sat her on it.

"Who is the old black woman mopping your floors?" Eliska said to the nurse.

"Black woman?" The nurse looked puzzled. "We have no black women here."

"But a black woman was here, in my room!"

"Sorry, no black women work here. None of the volunteers are black, either."

"But I….?"

"Are you Roma?"

"Yes."

"Sometimes, when we have a Roma here, they talk of a black woman that comes to them. I think it's superstition. They call her Kali Sara (Black Sara), an old wives' tale, told for ages."

"Come with me!" Eliska insisted as she took the nurse into her old room. "What do you see?"

"Not much.... Oh, I see the floor is wet. Someone mopped the floor. They do that every Friday, so it's clean when we have visitors on the weekend."

"You must have awful wet water!"

"Why, what do you mean?"

"Today is Monday!"

~~~~~~

<div align="center">

Chapter 47

SAILING HOME

</div>

Litomysl Czechoslovakia to Trieste, Italy, Thurs, May 1, 1919
During World War One, many of the ports in Europe were closed to American shipping. Italy was neutral in World War One, so the Mack truck company used Italian ports to deliver their trucks.

The train from Litomysl pulled into Trieste, Italy, right on schedule. Thomas and Marta Koupil stepped out of their private compartment onto the train's landing platform. Marta clutched their newborn boy tightly as they hurried to collect their baggage.

Thomas hailed a cab and entered with Marta and the baby. "Take us to the Trieste Maritime Station." Thomas declared.

They were to board the RMS Mauritania, sailing for New York City. RMS Mauritania was the fastest cruise liner available. So far, she had avoided the fate of her sister ship, the RMS Lusitania, which sank in May 1915, courtesy of a torpedo from a German U-boat.

Figure 50 Lusitania Sunk

"Do you have the boarding passes?" Marta inquired of her husband.
~~~~~~

"Yes, dear, long ago," Thomas replied. "And yes, we'll be in New York by May 15, and then we will board a cargo ship, the Raspatau, in New York. It may be uncomfortable, but I must pick up the new Mack trucks in Detroit. We'll go with them to Duluth and then drive them to Owatonna."

"Are you sure we'll be home for the church festival? I don't want to miss that."

"Yes, dear."

"Can we get the baby baptized, then?"

"Father Emilio baptized him in Litomysl."

"Well, does it hurt to do it twice?"

"You just want to show off the new baby."

"Well, what harm will that be? Mrs. Olvak is so smug about her two children. Now, I can show her what I accomplished by putting all my effort into one child."

"We should be home in the middle of June. Will that be enough time to get ready?"

"Yes, even enough time for a trip to Minneapolis to my favorite ladies' store."

"That could work," Thomas smiled. *Glad to see Marta so excited.*

"Oh, dear, I just thought of something. Do you think those nasty U-boats will give us any trouble?" Marta said.

"I think the war is over. I don't think we'll have any trouble. Peace talks are underway; they are negotiating the treaties now."

Guilt has a way of eating at you.

~ ~ ~ ~ ~ ~

Chapter 48

NO ANSWERS

Salesian Mission, Litomysl Czechoslovakia, Mon, May 15, 1919

May was in full bloom, but Eliska didn't care to celebrate her 19th birthday. *Days go by. Sleep is no reprieve. Is there a cure for an aching heart? Just another day with an ache in the pit of my stomach. Another gray day among a long string of gray days.*

In the kitchen, Eliska prepared the breakfast as the children cascading into the adjacent lunchroom. She had Andela perched on a stool by the table and had her pouring milk. Sister Lucie came in and leaned over to Andela and whispered in her ear. Andela's face lit up with a big, mischievous smile. She clapped her hands and cried out, "Mama, birthday!"

Andela's cheery manner roused Eliska out of her melancholy thoughts. *My birthday..... Remember Zuba and my first birthday together.*

She smiled a patient smile at Andela, "Thank you, sweetie."

Her thoughts wandered back to Zuba. *He brought me sweet buchtys.... We had lunch together under the lone tree in the coal yard.*

Father Emilio came into the kitchen, smelling of his morning cigar. "Nice to see you again, Eliska. We missed you at the Mass, Sunday," he scolded her.

"I am sorry, I'm not much of a church-goer. I tried, but the other people stare hard at me. Their eyes say you are Roma. Where is your husband? Go to your own church."

"Has anyone said that to you?"

"No, but I feel it."

"You are thinking up problems. You have enough problems. Isn't that enough of a load?"

Sister Lucie, seeing where the conversation was heading, tickled Andela and grabbed her little hand, "Let's go, sweetie, out to the classroom and see the other kids, OK?" The giggling duo skipped out of the kitchen.

Eliska resumed cooking, wiping her eyes on her apron. "I'm sorry, Father, I miss him so much. I don't know where to turn or who to trust." Father Emilio put his hand on her shoulder, "You might find peace in the church,"

Eliska reached out and put her head on his chest. "Why does this happen? All I did was love a gadjo. It was no sin. A priest married us. I've been a good mother. Where is God in this? If God can't find Zuba out in the open, how will he find me in a church?"

A perplexed expression crept over Father Emilio. He gently pushed Eliska away and looked her straight in the eyes. "I know I made a mess of consoling you before. I'll not use any more of the sayings they taught me at the seminary. All I can tell you is that love is what God is. Love that connects all of us. I don't have the answers; even the questions trip me up. I can't help people that are suffering. I do the best I can, which isn't that much."

"I'm sorry, Father, you can't have an answer where there's none."

"Don't tell my bishop!" Father Emilio joked. "Is there anything else I can do to help you?"

Eliska dried her eyes and chuckled, "Do you need a cook?"

"Well, no, I have one. I've tasted your cooking, and I'd be pig fat if you cooked for me!" Father Emilio scratched his head, "But I wonder.... I have a parishioner who is the manager of the dining room at the Chateau. He needs a cook. If I give you a letter of recommendation, will you see him?"

"Oh, yes, Father, yes!" Eliska wrapped her arms around Father Emilio and hugged him. Father Emilio's face glowed cherry red. He stammered, "Well, good. I wish all your problems were this easy to solve."

Easy to solve problems may not be the problems that need to be solved. ~~~~~~

Chapter 49

FREEDOM'S BEACON

New York Harbor, New York, USA, Thurs, May 15, 1919

The Raspatau sailed into New York harbor as Zuba and Hanzi were swabbing the decks. A harbor pilot came aboard to steer the ship to its berth. As the vessel crept into the port, off to the right was an enormous green statue.

Figure 51 Statue of Liberty

"What do you -- suppose that is?" Zuba said.

"It sure is big," Hanzi said in awe.

"Haven't you heard of the Statue of Liberty?" Rocco replied.

"Statue of Liberty, -- what does that mean?" Zuba pondered.

"The Americans say it's a symbol of freedom."

"You mean freedom to do as you please?" Hanzi said.

"I guess so, but what do they know?" Rocco replied. "Now get busy cleaning the passenger cabin. We have passengers coming aboard, a rich businessman and his wife."

"I wonder what it's like to be rich?" Hanzi said.

"I wonder what -- it's like to be free?" Zuba murmured.

"Never mind your babble. We'll be in Port Newark shortly. The cabin better be ready when we get there, or Sally will talk to you," Rocco snarled. "Do either of you speak English?"

"No, why?"

"Those rich people will need a steward. Someone to wait on them. But if you can't speak English, what good are you?"

The harbor pilot expertly steered the ship to its berthing dock. Once berthed, Zuba and Hanzi loaded cargo into the large mesh slings.

Then the crane operator raised the slings and lowered them onto the dock below. Down on the dock, it was alive with longshoremen, the air hanging heavy with the odor of their sweat.

Their sound of cursing echoed off the tin walls of the enormous warehouses, as they unloaded and toted the cargo inside.

"Do you suppose anybody on the dock speaks Czech?" Hanzi said.

"How -- we find out? We up -- here and they -- down there."

"We can write a note," Hanzi said.

"Ya, -- you do that -- me can't write no good."

"I can't much neither, but I'll try." Hanzi licked his pencil and scrawled, *'Pomozte nám, jsme se držel jako otroci'* (Help us, they hold us as slaves) on a piece of paper. He stuck it on the next load of cargo. The crane lifted the cargo over the railing and lowered it to the dock. A burly longshoreman unhooked the sling and hauled the cargo into the warehouse. He found the note and looked at it curiously, shrugged his shoulders, threw it down, and returned to work.

Rocco stood at the gangplank, talking to Thomas and Marta Koupil as they waited to board. A gust of wind blew Hanzi's note next to Thomas. He picked up the note, read it, and smirked. Turning the note over to Rocco, he said, "You have some boys that are unhappy."

"Ya, we always get soreheads about this time," Rocco replied. "That damn statue gives them ideas."

"Well, workers with ideas can be trouble, some work, most don't."

"Ya, that's a sure thing," Rocco replied. "Oh, we couldn't find you a steward that speaks English. This crew only speaks Polish and Czech, but I'll keep looking. I'd do it, but I've lots of other things to do."

"My wife and I speak Czech," Thomas replied. "Can you get us someone who is clean and trustworthy?"

"Ya, sure I can!"

Rocco scurried back on board and went over to Zuba and Hanzi. "Which one of you crapheads wrote that note?"

Zuba and Hanzi hung their heads.

"Well, it doesn't matter. The rich man needs someone to steward. He may not trust a Roma, but a big dumb Czech might do," Rocco said. "Zuba, go to cabin D. There are white steward clothes there."

Rocco continued, "That's what you will wear, and for God's sake, take a bath before you put them on. A skunk's behind would smell sweeter than you do."

"Me don't -- know -- what steward -- do?"

"You will wait on them hand and foot. Serve them their food and whatever they want. Do you understand?"

"Ya, me -- guess."

"And no more talk about freedom, do you hear?" Rocco snarled. "I'll be watching! If there's any trouble, your little curly-headed brother-in-law will talk to Sally. Understand?"

"Ya.

When Sally speaks, the entire crew listens. ~~~~~

Chapter 50

GETTING THE JOB

The Chateau, Litomysl, Czechoslovakia Tues, May 16, 1919

The Chateau is a Renaissance castle in the center of Litomysl. The Italians developed the Chateau style, and then the Czechs modified it. Originally, the building was a monastery and a brewery.

Figure 52 The Chateau

The main feature of the castle is the Sgraffito decoration on the outside. Sgraffito decorations, from a distance, resemble bricks but are really designs made from chipping away the plaster to reveal the undercoat.

Each design is different, tree leaves, people, biblical and mythical scenes, etc., all created by Italian masters.

Figure 53 Sgraffito

Figure 54 Sgraffito

There are nine buildings in the compound, plus across the road is a Piarist church and monastery.

The iron gates of the Chateau creaked as Eliska pushed them aside and walked into the well-groomed grounds. She caught her breath upon seeing the sprawling beauty. Apple trees were in full bloom; peonies and lilies made their presence known. Lilacs and roses painted the air with a sweet smell. Manicured lawns and sparkling fountains with nude statuettes vied for her attention.

Figure 56 Entrance to Chateau

The Chateau complex consisted of stables, a riding academy, a brewery and consumed several city blocks.

Eliska arrived at the main entrance and knocked on the massive wooden door. A

Figure 55 Nude Statuettes

butler dressed in black answered the door. "Yes, how may I help you?" he sniffed.

"I am here to apply for work."

"We don't take people off the street, madam," the butler sniffed again, "especially not Roma."

"Father Emilio sent me. I have a note from him," Eliska snapped.

The butler methodically unfolded the note, only using the tips of his fingers. "I see, umm, this is for kitchen help. Go to the servant's entrance, in the back of the house. See Karel Klimy, the kitchen manager."

The butler promptly closed the door in her face. Eliska turned away. Her shaking hands clasped the note as she made her way to the servant's entrance and walked in.

Off to the right, the kitchen was abuzz with activity. Pots and pans clanged, the smell of beef cooking emanating from them. Several cooks, dressed in white, prepared the noon meal.

Looking cautiously around, Eliska approached a woman kneading a pan of bread dough. "Where can I find Mr. Klimy, please?"

"He is over at the silverware section, counting the spoons or his nose hairs," the woman said, pointing at the silverware cabinet. "Oh, here he comes."

Karel, a short, thin, nervous man, was detail-oriented, well organized, and facetious about all things. His pride and joy was his turned-up, black mustache, which he continually twirled between his nervous fingers.

Karel flitted around the room, looking over his spectacles, giving orders to his helpers. "Here now, knead the dough slower... Make sure the cherries are fresh.... -The beef roast has lots of fat, trim more off... There are water spots on the silverware. Polish it."

He approached Eliska and asked sternly, "Why is this woman standing in my kitchen? What do you want?"

"Father Emilio sent me," Eliska said, handing Karel the note.

Karel examined the note. "Does he know cooking? He only knows cheap cigars and praying."

"I cook for him and the children at the school," Eliska protested. "They like my cooking!"

"We only cook the finest food for the finest people. We use Magdalena Dobromila Rettigova's Household Cookery Book, a famous Czech cooking manual. Have you read that?"

"No, but from what I've seen standing here, you use lots of butter, lard, cream, and syrup, as I do."

"Well, that's how much you know," Karel replied haughtily. "I cook for the elite here. I cook for the Thurn and Taxis family, and they have many important people come here. We have wedding receptions, big parties, a dinner theater, and a fine dining restaurant."

Karel looked Eliska over carefully. "I can see that you don't come from that type of people. Have you ever cooked for anyone important?"

Eliska's face hardened. She had all she could do, not to tell this pompous ass where to go. "I cooked for the most important people in the world! My husband! My daughter! And the kids at the Salesian school! I don't think your people are more important than that. I think I might be too good to cook in your high and mighty kitchen!"

Eliska turned and walked away. "I'll leave now," she said, looking back over her shoulder, "I'll tell Father Emilio that you could judge my cooking by looking at my face."

The fiery outburst from this brash young girl caught Karel unguarded. His mouth dropped open, and his glasses slid to the tip of his nose.

Karl was sweating profusely. None of his help had ever called him to task before, and he didn't quite know how to handle it. He didn't want Father Emilio to think badly of him, either.

Twirling his mustache, he cried out, "Wait a minute, wait a minute, maybe we can use you after all. It so happens we might have an opening at the Chudý Kuchyně (poor kitchen).

We cook a noon meal for the... umm... less fortunate of the community. I need someone to help there. You'd fit right in."

"I may be poor, but that doesn't give you the right to squint down your skinny little nose at me," Eliska replied and kept walking.

Karel ran after her. "Wait, I know good cooks are temperamental and demanding. Perhaps I was hasty in judging you so quickly."

"Never buy a horse that way; you will get took," Eliska snapped back and kept walking.

"I can pay you five korunas an hour," Karel hastily interjected, trying to keep up with Eliska.

"Can't work for less than ten korunas an hour," Eliska replied without looking at Karel.

"Seven korunas an hour," Karel said as he nervously moved his glasses back up on the bridge of his nose. *She gives me more trouble than any help I have ever hired.*

"I wouldn't work for less than fifteen korunas an hour," Eliska said.

"Wait a minute, wait a minute, that's not the way to haggle. You come down, and I go up. Then we meet in the middle!" Karel pleaded.

"All right, I said fifteen korunas, and you said seven korunas now. Ten korunas is about in the middle. Is it a deal?"

Karel stopped for a moment to catch his breath as Eliska kept walking. "Done!" He yelled. "And I hope you are worth it!"

"I am. When do I start?"

"Is right now too soon?" Karel said hesitantly.

"I can start now. Where do you want me?"

"Someplace out of my hair," Karel replied, smiling. "You better cook as good as you bargain."

"Better! Thank you."

Figure 57 Andela at Three.

You never know where you will find gold, under a rock or in a poor mother's desperate heart. ~~~~~~

Chapter 51

HARD TO PLEASE

Raspatau, Detroit, Michigan, US, Thurs, June 10, 1919

In Cabin A, the Koupils awoke and prepared for the day. Thomas shaved while Marta nursed their baby, Paul. Marta looked proudly at the baby. "He looks just like you, Thomas. Such black hair and broad shoulders."

"Ya, I guess," Thomas replied, wiping the last of the shave soap off his face.

"He has your brown eyes and your nose," Marta went on.

Thomas uncomfortably changed the subject. "We docked in Detroit, and I've got to get ready to see our new Mack trucks. The deckhands will load them, and I need to make sure they're hooked properly. The steward will be here shortly with your breakfast." He laid a dollar on the dresser. "Be sure to tip him."

"Yes, dear."

Thomas dressed in his best suit and tie, and a new straw hat topped him off. He left, and as he walked into the passageway, he met Zuba. "So, what's for breakfast, big man?"

"Sausage -- eggs -- coffee," Zuba stammered with his chin on his chest.

"Be sure to knock. Marta is nursing the baby and disturbing her isn't a good idea. Do you have any children?"

"Ya, -- a -- little -- girl -- and -- another one -- me -- think?"

"When you sign up for a long voyage, it must be hard to be away from your family."

"Me -- didn't -- sign -- me -- was -- took."

"Took? How is that?"

"Hit -- on -- head -- then, -- here me is."

"You mean shanghaied?"

"Me was – taken, -- don't -- know -- shang -- high."

"That's terrible. I'll speak to the captain as soon as we get done."

"Nooo -- doon -- do --. We -- will -- answer -- to Sally. -- me -- need to get -- to -- Czechoslovakia. -- Tell me -- how much -- it -- be to go -- back?"

"It costs one hundred dollars or twenty-five hundred korunas," Thomas said, then silent in thought, he rubbed his chin. "I have to unload. I want to talk more on this." He then hurried out to the deck.

Zuba knocked on the cabin door. *Mrs. Koupil, not an easy person to please. Demanding and cold. Hope she doesn't come to the door.* The door opened, and Marta ordered him inside the cabin. "Place the food on the table. It better be hot! Last night's dinner was lukewarm; I want it hot! Be quicker getting it to us!"

"Ya -- me -- sure -- try." Zuba placed the food on the table next to the cradle. In the cradle, the baby rested peacefully. "Pretty -- baby."

"I'm glad you approve. Now, my husband said to give you a tip." Marta pulled a quarter out of her purse and gave it to him. "Next time, try to earn it? You can leave now."

"Ya -- thank -- you," Zuba replied as he hastily retreated out of the cabin. *That woman could freeze ice. I wonder how she warmed up enough to make a baby.*

Zuba changed clothes and went up to the deck to help load the Mack trucks onto the deck of the Raspatau. Thomas Koupil was everywhere. He instructed the workmen how to how to set the slings, how to tie the vehicles to the deck, and how to secure any loose parts. "Big man, make sure you hook the chains to the axle and not the spring. Do you know what the spring is?"

"Ya -- next -- to -- the -- chain -- drive."

"Good, pull the binder tight, so the trucks don't bounce too much."

Zuba looked under one of the Mack trucks. "You -- have -- gearbox -- leak. Me -- get -- a -- wrench and tighten it." Zuba retrieved a wrench and tightened the bolts on the gearbox, then the leak stopped.

Thomas admired the quick work, saying, "You know your way around a truck, big man,"

"Ya -- me -- was a -- mechanic -- for -- the coal -- company at -- Karvina."

"You were! I sold twenty trucks to Josef Jelinek. Do you know him?"

"He -- was -- my -- boss -- in Litomysl."

"He told me he had a mechanic killed in the Czech-Polish war. They never found his body. Said he had a funny name. Ruba, Tuba, or something like that."

"My -- name -- is -- Zuba Palzek."

Thomas's eyes opened wide, and his mouth dropped open. "You must be the mechanic they lost! Do you play the tuba?"

"Ya -- a -- little."

Worry crossed Thomas' face. "Palzek? I met a Palzek in Litomysl. Do you have family there?"

"Yaa -- a mother and a -- brother."

"No, a young lady. I thought she might be your wife."

"No. -- Wife -- is in -- Karvina long way -- from -- Litomysl."

Thomas, relieved, said, "Well, here you are, shanghaied. Life has many funny little twists, doesn't it?"

"Ya, -- it--twist -- me -- good."

Thomas walked away, shaking his head. *I'm glad he isn't the father of our baby.* ~~~~~~

Chapter 52

THE SCHEME

Lake Superior, Duluth, Mn USA, June 10, 1919
Zuba, Hanzi, and the crew enjoyed a few hours off before they reached Duluth. Rocco told them to get their instruments out and play some snappy music for the crew. He felt that music softened the blow of arriving at the port and that the shanghaied men were less likely to jump ship.

After a lively polka finished, Otto, a large, heavily muscled man, sidled up beside Zuba. Otto was shanghaied with Zuba. A prior knife fight had left a scar above Otto's partially closed right eye.

His nose twisted to the left, resembling an overripe cucumber, courtesy of several barroom fights, one in which Otto had killed a man.

"Zuba," Otto whispered. "Youse works in dose rich folk's cabin, doesn't you?"

"Ya."

"I bet dey got lots of money and jewels yust a lying around, eh?"

"Me don't -- maybe."

"Youse goes to their cabin, tree times a day, don't youse?"

"Ya -- why?"

"Vell, dey is getting off in Duluth, right?"

"Ya?"

"Ve unload their luggage at the port. If you finds out which chest dey hides dere valuables in, so ve don't have to opens um all up. It be quick den, to helps ourselves. Dem not find dere things missed till dey unpacked at dere home. Ve be long gone by den. I bet dere be a couple of tousand-korunas worth of stuff wid dem. Ve get enough, ve jump ship, and catch a sail home."

"That -- not -- be -- right."

"Is it right dat dem rich people owns the ships like dis here one and forces us to work for nothing?"

"They -- don't own -- this ship."

"How you know? Would dey ride a crap bucket if dey didn't have a stake in it?"

"They -- have -- Mack -- trucks -- aboard."

"Ah hah! Even dey's richer than ve thought owns this ship and the trucks too. Taken off the backs of us poor folks."

"He -- nice."

"Ooh ya, how's dat wife, treat you nice, I suppose?"

"She -- she -- cold, -- not nice."

"Figures you is a tongue-tied mule, I betcha?"

"Ya -- me guess."

Hanzi jumped in, "What do you say, Zuba? A ride home would be great! We could go back. That would be something! How about it? Me and you. Jump ship! Go back home! That would be great! What do you say? Let's do it. Get their money."

Zuba was silent. *Got to get back to my family. Me don't owe these rich folks. They have lots of money, taken off the backs of us poor people.* Finally, he said, "Me -- think -- on -- it."

"Vell, youse better hurry, ve be in port in ten hours," Otto threatened.

~~~~~~

It was five in the afternoon when the Duluth harbor came into view. Hanzi came up on the deck and stood next to Zuba. "Well, what are you to do?"

Zuba hesitated, wrestling with his conscience, "Me guess -- need to be home."

"Good, do you know which trunk the money is in?"

"Ya."

"Which one?"

"It's in a small wooden -- box in chest number 4."

"Good, we'll get it!"

"Me already -- got it."

"You do? How much?"

"About two hundred dollars."

"How much for each of us?"

"Sixty dollars -- not enough to -- be home."

Just then, Otto came up to them. "Are youse going vith us, Zuba?"

"No! -- Me -- don't want -- to do it," Zuba said.

"You don't, does you? I tell you dis, goes along, or ve'll slit your throat in your snoring! Both of you! Does youse hear me?"

Zuba and Hanzi were silent; then Hanzi turned to face Otto. Looking him squarely in the eyes, he said, "We'll do it, don't you worry. We'll do it. You can bet on that. Right, Zuba? We'll do it, I tell you!"
~~~~~~

Otto walked away and stopped nearby, pretending to untie cargo, glaring at Zuba and Hanzi.

"Zuba, what are we to do?" Hanzi whispered nervously.

Zuba was staring at the deck. "We jump -- ship here."

"How?"

"Me -- load all -- Koupils things -- in truck number three. You get -- our things -- put in -- same truck."

"How do we get off the ship?"

"Turn your -- shirt inside out -- they not -- see the ship's name.

"Ok, then what?"

"There a space -- under box -- of truck where -- we hide. They unload -- trucks -- on the dock. -- We might -- get a chance -- to run for it there."

~~~~~~

<div align="center">Chapter 53</div>

JUMPING SHIP

Harbor, Duluth, Minnesota, USA Tues, June 10, 1919

A brisk north wind blew across Lake Superior, directly into the Duluth harbor. The Raspatau docked at Pier Four. A flurry of bare-chested, cursing deckhands poured forth from the ship's lower deck to muscle the cargo up from the hold and swung it to the dock below.

Figure 58 Duluth Harbor

Zuba and Hanzi hooked up the third and last Mack truck. Hanzi crawled under it and pulled himself up to the hiding place, under the truck box. Rocco walked by, giving orders and urged the men to a greater effort with an occasional word from Sally. "What the hell are you standing there for?" he said to Zuba.

"Mr. Koupil asked -- me -- help with -- the -- truck -- unloading -- OK?"
~~~~~~

"OK but hurry up! We want to leave as soon as the iron ore is loaded." Rocco snapped.

"Ya," Zuba replied. He waited until Rocco was away; then he carefully looked around; he signaled to the crane operator to lift and swing the truck to the dock. As the lift chains tightened, he rolled under the truck and pulled himself up into the hiding place next to Hanzi.

Figure 59 Ships Unloading Duluth Harbor

"Tight -- in -- here," Zuba said breathlessly.

"It wouldn't be if you didn't have all those pancakes for breakfast!"

"Figured -- not -- eat -- for a while. Shush -- somebody hear -- us."

The truck soared high over the ship; the operator swung it out and lowered it fifty feet to the dock. A sudden burst of north wind caused the truck to swing back and forth vigorously. Hanzi started to slip out in his perch. "Help me. I'm falling!" Hanzi shouted.

Zuba reached over and grabbed Hanzi's arm, "Hang -- tight." As the truck continued its slow descent to the dock, Hanzi frantically hung on. When they reached the dock, Hanzi was dangling in mid-air beneath the truck, only held on to by the lifeline of Zuba's strong right arm.

Rocco noticed the commotion, ran down the gangplank, sprinted down the dock toward them as Zuba and Hanzi crawled out from under the truck, dazed.

"Well, that worked great, didn't it, big man? Any more bright ideas?" Hanzi said.

"Ya -- time to run!"

When Zuba and Hanzi stood up, they came face to face with two burly harbor policemen. With billy clubs raised, they nabbed each man by the collar. "What are you doing? Entering the US without papers?"

The harbor policemen were taking them away when a breathless Rocco ran up. "Good, you caught them. They tried to jump ship. I'll deal with them. Take them back up to the ship."

The policemen escorted Zuba and Hanzi to the landing gangplank as Thomas Koupil came down. He blocked the walkway and addressed Zuba in Czech. "No se děje (What is going on?)."

Zuba with tears in his eyes said, "Berou nás -- zpátky být -- otroky ještě víc. (They -- taking us back -- to be slaves -- again.)"

Thomas held his position, head low and deep in thought; then, an idea hit him. "Wait a minute, gentleman; these men work for me. There must be a mistake."

"Work for you? Hell no! They belong to the ship!" Rocco snarled as he grabbed Zuba's arm.

Thomas reached out and squeezed Rocco's arm hard. "Well, if they belong to you, these policemen will have to check the hiring papers for all the men aboard the ship. We abolished slavery in the United States, and shanghaied seamen fit that description. So, do these men belong to the ship, or are they, my employees?"

Rocco felt Thomas tighten the painful grip on his arm. *How could a skinny man have such power in his hands?* He glared at Zuba and Hanzi and said, "I, I.... guess it's a mistake. They look like my men, but on a closer look, they aren't. Sorry for the mix-up."

"Good," Thomas said. He nodded to the policemen, "Thank you, gentlemen, for being so diligent. These tramp freighters are known to use shanghaied men."

"Are you sure these men are legal?" The policemen asked.

"Well, they work for me. Can you fellows start a truck?"

The policemen shook their heads, no.

Thomas continued, "Do you see those trucks over there?"

The policemen nodded.

Thomas pointed to Zuba, "He is my chief mechanic. He has a tough time with English, so I'll tell him in Czech to start the truck."

Thomas turned to Zuba. "Doufám, že víte, co jste řekl, víte, nebo oba jsou v průšvihu. Jděte spuštění vozíku (I hope you know, what you said you know, or we both are in trouble. Go start the truck.)."

Zuba motioned to Hanzi, "Come, help, -- remember -- me show -- you magneto lever?"

"I think so, on the steering column."

"Climb -- in truck -- me crank – you pull lever down, OK?"

"Ok."

Zuba walked to the front of the truck and gave the crank a mighty twirl. "Now!" He cried to Hanzi. The truck did not start. Zuba scratched his head thoughtfully; then, his eyes lit up. He crawled under the engine, reached up, and turned a valve.

Getting back up, he said to Thomas. "Plynové potrubí uzavírací (Gas line shut off.)"

Zuba went back to the front of the truck and gave the crank another mighty twirl. "Now!" He cried to Hanzi. The truck roared to life.

Thomas smiled at the policemen. "Now, gentlemen, do you think an illegal could do that?"

The impressed policemen shook their heads, no. They warily backed away from the mighty truck rumbling before them.

Thomas stood tall, head held high, and continued. "Do I look like someone who would jeopardize my lucrative business by harboring an illegal?"

The embarrassed policemen shook their heads no, again! They tipped their hats to Thomas and said, "Sorry, sir, just doing our jobs."

"And doing them very well, thank you for your help," Thomas replied.

Sometimes the best-laid plans of men and mice can't beat a lucky break.

~ ~ ~ ~ ~ ~

Chapter 54

Job Offer

Harbor, Duluth, Minnesota, USA, Tues, June 10, 1919

While Marta and the baby waited, Thomas Koupil walked around each of his three trucks, scrutinizing them. He ran his hand lovingly over their shiny new hoods as if he were caressing a baby. He then gave his approval to the harbor shipping clerk, verifying that no shipping damage occurred.

Zuba and Hanzi stood off to the side, wondering what would happen. Thomas turned to Zuba and Hanzi. "They held you as slaves; now, you are free to go if you wish."

Zuba and Hanzi looked at each other, bewildered. Their plan to escape was to get off the ship and catch a ride back home to Czechoslovakia.

Hanzi whispered in Zuba's ear, "Do you still have their box of money?"

Zuba nodded yes, guilty for taking the money, but he had to get back to his family.

"Let's take it and go."

"We – can no talk -- the words they say."

Hanzi wrung his hands, "So, what now?"

As with freed slaves, there's an immediate sense of joy. Joy, fast followed by bewilderment as to what to do next.

Zuba turned to Thomas, "We don't -- know what -- to do?"

"Look, I hired two guys to come up here and drive the trucks, but they didn't show up. I must get these trucks to Owatonna. Are you interested in driving them there for me? It will take two or three days, and then you can go. I'll take Marta and the baby in one, and each of you, drive one."

Zuba leaned over to Hanzi, "Can you -- drive -- truck?"

"Sure, how hard can it be?"

"It not -- horse!"

"I can do it, don't worry, I'm a quick learner. I can do it. Let me at it. I'll show you. Let's do it. What do ya say?"

Zuba turned to Thomas, "Me don't -- know."

Thomas didn't want to leave the trucks parked in Duluth. Too much damage or theft could happen before he returned. It would take several days to reach Owatonna and back again and finding someone who could drive these trucks would take even longer. His salesman's instincts kicked into high gear. He knew there was a good possibility of Zuba accepting his offer. "I'll pay you well. We live in the little community of Litomysl, MN, where there are lots of Czechs. They can get you on the right track and help get you back home. You could learn English, so you can get along better."

When he heard the familiar name of his hometown, Zuba's face lit up. "Litomysl! You -- have Litomysl here?"

"Yes, we do. It's a small place, but we like it. It's away from the hustle and bustle of Owatonna. A good place to raise kids. Lots of Czech farmers and a church too. What do you say?"

At the mention of the church, Zuba stomach sank. *I stole the Koupils money. But me need it for my family. They aren't in a good place. It's wrong, but what can me do? Must get home. My family needs me.*

Zuba was still shaking his head no when Thomas persisted, "Here's what I'll do; you drive the trucks to Owatonna, then come to work for me as a mechanic. I'll pay you fifty cents an hour. That's twelve korunas an hour in Czech money. What you say?"

"You got – no place to -- sleep?"

"I own another house in Litomysl; it's small but clean and dry. You can stay there. I'll throw that in for free if you work for me. What ya say?"

"What -- about -- Hanzi?"

"Is Hanzi a mechanic?"

"No, -- mouth runs all the time. He's -- Roma."

"I noticed, but we don't have Roma in Litomysl. Most folks there haven't ever met one. Probably don't care anyway if he is an honorable man."

"So, what -- about Hanzi?"

"He can stay with you."

"What he -- do while -- me work?"

Marta stood with her hands on her hips and called out curtly. "Thomas Koupil! We have been standing here in the cold for a long time. Are you still jabbering with those men? Let's go!"

"Oh, for goodness' sake, now Marta is getting impatient. We have to go." Thomas thought for a moment, "As much talking Hanzi does, he could be a salesman. If I put him on as a salesman, will you do it?"

"Me talk to -- him." Zuba walked over to where Hanzi was throwing pebbles into the harbor. "You want -- drive truck and -- sell trucks too?"

"Drive em, sell em, sure I do it. How many do you want drove? How many do you want sold?" Hanzi said jubilantly. Then he hesitated, "But I don't own no trucks?"

"Just sell, not buy."

"That's even better sell em even if I don't own them. Lots of profit!"

"It don't -- work -- that way."

"Zuba, whatever you think is best." Hanzi brushed his shirt, "I'm tired of standing here. The damn seagulls are pooping on me."

Zuba turned to Thomas, "Ya, we -- try -- a little while."

~~~~~~
~~~~~~

Chapter 55

HOBBLING TO OWATONNA

Duluth to Owatonna, MN, USA Tues, June 10, 1919

Thomas helped Marta into the cab of the first truck. "Zuba, get the trucks started. You follow me. We'll be on Highway twenty-three. That's the road over there, by the hotel. Stay on it, go south. I'll stop after we are out of town and wait for you. OK?"

"Ya," Zuba replied.

Thomas rumbled through the streets of Duluth, driving past hillside houses smutched gray from the coal soot hanging in the air. Soot from the smoke belched from the iron ore freighters entering and leaving the port. After laboring up the last hill of the town, Thomas pointed the truck south toward Minneapolis.

Zuba took Hanzi by the shirt sleeve and steered him to one of the waiting trucks. "Get in, -- we get started. -- You sure you -- run this?"

"How hard can it be? If you can do it, I can do it better. I know I can do it better."

After the truck started, Zuba walked to the door and looked into the cab. Hanzi was sitting on the passenger side, far from the steering wheel. "What you -- doing -- over there?"

"There's more room here. Where're the reins?"

"Reins? Truck no have -- reins, -- has steering wheel -- slide over and sit behind -- steering wheel."

Hanzi slid over. "Ok, giddap! Come on, let's go." Hanzi made a clicking sound with his mouth and bounced up and down on the seat. "What do you say to make this thing go?"

"Say nothing -- push the clutch down!"

"What's that?"

"On floor -- by your foot."

Hanzi pushed the gas pedal down.

The truck roared. "YAHOO! HERE WE GO! GIDDYAP! GIDDYAP! GIDDYAP!" Hanzi yelled, but the truck sat there.

"CLUTCH -- ON LEFT, PUSH IT -- IN FIRST!" Zuba yelled.

"OK, HERE WE GO, GIDDYAP! GIDDYAP! GIDDYAP!" Hanzi yelled. He paused and looked out the window at Zuba. "DID YOU FEED THIS DAMN THING THIS MORNING?"

"LET UP ON -- GAS PEDAL -- BEFORE YOU -- BLOW ENGINE UP!"

Hanzi let up on the pedal, and the engine calmed to a contented purr. Zuba stepped up on the running board and glared at Hanzi. "Me explain. -- See floor. -- First pedal on left -- that clutch, -- next pedal -- that brake -- and you – in love with next one, -- that gas pedal. -- OK?"

"Clutch, brake, and gas pedal. I got it, but why do I want to break it?" Hanzi said, perplexed.

Exasperated, Zuba said, "You no -- understand -- not break, -- brake, -- brake not break. Understand?"

"Break not break? That's as clear as horse manure."

"See, -- three pedals, -- clutch, brake -- gas. That brake pedal!" Zuba pointed to the second pedal from the left. "That -- for -- stopping!"

"We're already stopped," a frustrated Hanzi replied.

"After -- you -- go!"

"I haven't gone yet."

"When you -- go."

"OK, clutch, brake, and gas. That should be easy. Now let's get going." Hanzi grabbed the steering wheel, bounced up and down on the seat, and looked anxiously at Zuba.

"Put -- in gear!"

"How do I do that?"

"See -- tall lever -- in the middle -- on the floor?"

"Ya, you mean the stopping lever?"

"Not a -- stop -- stopping lever!"

"On a horse-pulled wagon, it is."

"For going -- not -- stopping. Brake -- for stopping. That shift lever!"

"Ok, to go, you pull the stopping lever, and to stop, you pull the brake pedal. Got it. Let's GO!" Hanzi said, as he pulled the shift lever. The truck shook with the noise of gears grinding.

"NO! NO! NO! -- YOU BREAK IT!"

"OK, I'll pull the brake pedal. That'll stop it!"

"YOU PUSH -- BRAKE PEDAL!" Zuba shouted at Hanzi. "TAKE YOUR HAND OFF -- SHIFT LEVER!"

Hanzi raised his hands and held them out in front of him, all the while pushing on the brake pedal. "That's done it! I'm getting the hang of this! I'll be a great driver! I can drive horses with the best of them. Now trucks will be a piece of cake!"

"You -- need -- more schooling. You no -- move the truck yet."

"If I had a good teacher, I could learn much easier," Hanzi cut back.

Zuba opened the door to the truck, "Slide -- butt over. Me -- show how. Pay -- heed -- what me say!"

"With the way you talk, we'll be here till tomorrow. Just get me going. I'll figure it out as I go."

"Then -- watch -- not talk."

"Good, that's a relief. A person can get old waiting for you to explain something. You should practice talking," Hanzi said. "Say two or three words quick, at a time. Real fast! Add a word or two more, every so often. Practice, I say, it's the best medicine for you. Don't you think that's a good idea? What do you say?"

"You -- use up all the -- words --, me -- won't -- have -- any left -- to -- say with." Zuba stammered as he slid under the steering wheel. "Watch. -- Push clutch -- in. -- See? That stops gears. -- Then grab shift lever -- put it in lowest gear -- like this." Zuba pulled the shift lever toward him and down. "That's -- 'Grandma' gear –the slowest and – most pulling power. That's -- how you start."

Zuba took a deep breath and continued, "Then you -- let the clutch out while -- pressing on the gas pedal. -- Off -- you go."

Zuba let out the clutch, and the truck lurched forward.

Zuba said. "When you -- want stop -- you press -- the clutch in with -- left foot and -- press brake in with -- right foot."

"You don't say whoa?"

"No, -- no need, -- truck stop -- if you press -- brake pedal. Got it?"

"I push the clutch in and give her the gas, and away we go."

"No, think -- again."

"Oh, I remember, wake Grandma up, so she can pull the truck. Poor Grandma."

"Well, kinda -- like that."

"To stop, I clutch Grandma and break her."

Zuba rolled his eyes, "If that's how -- you remember, OK? Now, when going -- shift -- to second gear, -- Mama gear -- up and -- to the right. When you -- go good -- shift to the fast gear, -- Papa gear, -- over, to the right and -- down. Can you -- remember?"

"Ya, when Grandma can't keep up, let Mama take over, and when Mama can't keep up, then Papa takes over."

"You got it, -- think, will you?"

"Ok, let's go. I can't wait to wake Papa up!"

Zuba stepped down from the truck, and Hanzi slid behind the wheel. "Now let's see, mash the clutch in," he muttered to himself. "Grab Grandma and pull her down and press the gas and let out the clutch."

The truck roared ahead. Away Hanzi chugged, weaving from side to side and knocking over piles of freight.

Dockhands shook their fists and recited colorful poems at Hanzi as they scattered in every direction avoiding the rumbling beast. No matter, Hanzi, like all good drivers, was firmly clutching the steering wheel with both hands. The fearful expression on his face gave ample evidence of his complete concentration.

Zuba climbed into the remaining truck and started after Hanzi, who was out of sight by this time. Duluth gradually faded behind Zuba as he tried to catch up with Hanzi.

Rounding a bend in the road, he saw the Mack truck ahead of him. Its front end is in the ditch and its rear end in the air. Hanzi was standing beside it, kicking the tires and cursing at the helpless truck. "You, worthless dog! You son of a snake! May the heavens push you into hell! You sorry excuse for a horse!"

Zuba stopped and got out of his truck, he walked over to Hanzi and 'fake' smiled and deadpanned, "You -- have -- problem?"

"Even a Granny without her glasses could see that, you slow-talking son of a bat!"

"Me no -- drive my truck -- in the ditch, -- did me?"

"Your teaching didn't say nothing about scaring any horses I met."

"Did the horses -- run you off the road?"

"Well, yes, sorta, they made me nervous, and I looked at them and wanted to stop the truck, and I said, whoa! But will it stop? Nooo! And the next thing, in the ditch, I go."

Hanzi dejectedly walked away from the truck. "Damn!" he said, turned and looked at Zuba, "Is it too late to hook a horse to the front of this contraption?"

~~~~~~

Chapter 56

LONGING

Ten Years Later Litomysl MN, US, Mon, July 1, 1929,
Ten years ago, Zuba and Hanzi made that fateful trip from Duluth to Owatonna and then to Litomysl, MN. They now live in the small house that Thomas Koupil provided.

"Zuba, why are you sitting there? It's time to be going; we'll be late for work!" Hanzi yelled at Zuba.

Zuba was quiet, quieter than usual. Sitting at the kitchen table in the small house, he fingered his gold cross as Hanzi looked over his shoulder. "Why are you playing with that cross again? You will wear it out!"

"Today -- wedding anniversary."

"What wedding? Where's the party?" Hanzi said jubilantly.
~~~~~~

"No, Eliska and me -- married twelve years now," Zuba said in a whisper.

"Twelve years now, eh? Time flies. Ten years ago, I taught you how to drive in Duluth. Remember that?" Hanzi joked.

Zuba didn't respond. His sad eyes conveyed a message of hurt and futility that words couldn't describe. Finally, he spoke, "Well, it doesn't matter -- we never save enough to -- get home."

"You said we have almost eight hundred dollars saved up now."

"Ya, but the prices -- go up in ten years. It be -- five hundred dollars -- each now. -- The longer we here, -- the more it costs."

"Why did you give the Koupils the money back? We could be home now."

"I never give -- money back. That be in -- what we save."

"You told me you gave the money back! Why did you lie to me?"

"Remember last week -- we play -- Owatonna ballroom?"

"Ya, sure! Great party!"

"Remember, you not earn enough -- to pay for your beer -- and beer you buy for your lady friends? -- You need to -- borrow from me."

"They were thirsty. You wouldn't want me to leave a pretty lady in distress. I'm not that kind of guy. Generous to a fault."

"That's what me tell you. -- Money run -- through your fingers -- water through a screen. If you knew -- we have money, you -- be after that too."

"Where is it?"

"In a safe place."

"Good, where?"

"Better for me to -- know than -- you figure out."

"Some friend you are, keeping secrets from me."

"You don't -- keep no secrets from me?"

"No, I don't do that."

Zuba stood up to his full six-foot, two-inch height and looked straight down at Hanzi. "Me always wonder -- when we be -- shanghaied. You say -- they not to -- take you. -- What you mean?"

A dead silence penetrated the room as Hanzi's breath left, and he looked up at Zuba apprehensively. His usual chatter and smart remarks deserted him. He surveyed the big man in front of him. Discretion being the better part of valor, he replied, "We better get to work."

~~~~~~.

Mornings at the Koupil's Mack garage in Owatonna were a frantic affair. Traffic passed by on Main Street. Lawyers walked by on the way to the courthouse. Customers come in wanting a truck fixed in a hurry. Work left over from the day before, needed finishing. This morning was no different when Zuba and Hanzi checked in for work.

"Good morning Mr. Koupil," Zuba greeted Thomas.

"Good morning Zuba, Hanzi, great day, isn't it?" Thomas held up a sales order and showed it to Hanzi. "Hanzi, Mr. Peterson is buying the truck you showed him. Excellent job! Keep up the good work." He took out a pile of work orders and handed them to Zuba. "Zuba, the customers are very pleased with how you tune their trucks. They say the trucks run better than when they bought them brand new. Fine job!"

Zuba and Hanzi grinned, as Thomas continued, "Things are going so well. I'm giving each of you a raise. Another two dollars an hour."

Hanzi wrung his hands with glee, "You must be doing all right, Mr. Koupil!"

"I am. Even put money in the stock market. The market keeps going up, so I'm putting in more every day. The First Farmers Bank gave me a loan for twenty new trucks, so I'm ordering them today. They will be ready by the first of the year. I have an old customer coming in next year, and we can sell him at least ten trucks. I hope to have them on hand by that time."

"That's good, Mr. Koupil," Zuba replied happily at the prospect of a wage increase.

"Well, boys, you were a big part of it. If I get the trucks sold, I'll make sure you get a big bonus."
~~~~~~

"Well, enough of this jabber." Thomas looked up to Zuba, "I have meetings till evening. You remember Paul, don't you? He was just a baby on the ship when you were our steward. He was born over in your hometown of Litomysl, remember?"

"Ya, me remember."

"Ok. Well, I have a favor to ask. Paul will be here today. Can you put him to work sweeping the floor and any other odd jobs you can think of? Marta is too soft and shelters him. I finally convinced her that he needed to learn the value of hard work. Will you do that for me?"

Zuba fidgeted nervously; he remembered the spoiled boy that made fun of him at the band concerts in the park. Paul and his buddy Lester had put firecrackers under the bandstand on the 4th of July. They repeated the merriment on July 7th and July 14th until running out of fireworks.

"I hope he -- no have -- no more firecrackers."

"No, I confiscated the last of those. I talked with Paul; I hope he understands what he did was wrong. But sometimes, I think a rock might hear me before he does."

"Might be you -- talking to -- wrong end," Zuba blurted out. He at once regretted that it had slipped out.

Thomas looked up in surprise and thoughtfully said, "You may be right, Zuba, but Marta would have a fit if I disciplined the way my father did. Well, if you don't want to, I understand. Paul is a little hard to handle."

"Is all right, floor needs -- sweeping and -- lots of other work to do."

"Thanks, Zuba, you really helped me out. Paul is outside. I'll send him in, put him to work."

Paul stomped into the garage. His fat belly hung out of his red and white striped shirt and over the white shorts he wore. Sullen anger showed on his round face, and his black hair was a tousled mess. A rolled-up comic book stuck out of his back pocket. Even though breakfast had been less than an hour ago, he was munching on a candy bar he stole from the lunch counter on his way into the shop.

He walked up to Zuba as he bent over the engine of a truck. "My dad said I get to watch you fix trucks."

"Good. You watch -- from over there. See that -- broom behind you? You sweep -- while watching."

"Sweep, that's crap work, that's your job! You work for us! Mom says Dad pays you too damn much."

Zuba stepped away from the truck and looked down at Paul. "I should -- sweep out -- your dirty little mouth."

Paul, fearfully, stepped backward. He tripped over the broom and landed on his backside on the floor. Zuba walked over to him and slid his arms under Paul's armpits. He picked him up with one smooth motion and held him straight out in front of him. Paul kicked at him. Zuba showed no pain as the kicks landed on his stomach. Paul was crying. "Put me down, you big ox, or I'll tell my mother."

Zuba held Paul aloof and looked him straight in the eyes. "You tell her -- about your dirty mouth. Tell her you -- disobey your Papa. Your Papa said -- put you to work! Go push -- broom -- don't -- raise a cloud of dust!"

Zuba set Paul down. Paul, still sobbing, reluctantly picked up the broom and swept.

Hanzi watched this. With a silly grin on his face, he said, "That went well, don't you think, big man? That should get us another raise, eh? Lucky if it doesn't get us fired."

"Children need -- respect their elders. -- Little hard -- work never hurt no one."

It was noon when the men entered the lunchroom. Paul followed them in and grabbed a candy bar from the snack counter. Zuba looked at Paul, "Don't steal -- candy bars. -- Eat lunch. -- Where is it?"

"I left it at home! What's it to you? Do you run the lunchroom too?" A surly Paul replied.

"No, when a boy -- do man work -- he should eat man food."

"Don't bug me!" Paul said, then suddenly stopped talking and looked at Zuba..... "I did.... man.... work?" he said incredulously

"Sure, you did. -- Work up a sweat -- didn't you?"

"Well, it's hot and humid in the shop," Paul said, smiling and wiping his brow. "You say I did a man's work? Just sweeping the crummy floors?"

"Don't matter -- if the work be honest, it be good work. When me and Hanzi were on that ship -- there was lots of dirty work."

"You were on a ship? A pirate ship?"

Zuba laughed, "No pirate ship -- just a bunch of shady characters."

Paul's eyes were wide in wonder, "Tell me about it!"

"OK," Zuba said, "but first here -- is one of my sausage sandwiches. A boy works like a man -- eat man food."

Paul wolfed down the sandwich while Zuba told him about how they were shanghaied. He told him about the trip across the oceans, and a vivid description of Rocco's whip, Sally.

As the men returned to work, Paul's mother, Marta, entered the garage. She took one look at Paul and exploded.

Marta glared at Zuba and said accusingly, "What have you been doing to this boy! He's sweaty and dirty as a pig!" She stood with fists doubled up, arms straight down at her sides, and glared at Zuba, "Explain yourself!"

Zuba, surprised by Marta's onslaught, eyed the floor, and mumbled a few words. "Mr. Koupil -- told -- me -- to --."

Before he could finish, Paul blurted out. "It's all right Mom, I was helping Zuba; he was getting behind, so I lent a hand, OK?"

Marta bent over and cupped Paul's dirty, sweaty face in her hands, and her face softened.

"Well, I suppose, but next time, take it easy," Marta said, stroking Paul's head.

Paul turned to Zuba and winked at him, "It's all right, Mom. When there's work to do, a man has to step up and do it."

Paul, head held high, turned, and strutted out of the shop. A dazed Marta followed, fondly looking after him. ~~~~~~

Chapter 57

THE PERVERT

Apartment House, Litomysl Czechoslovakia, Mon, July 1, 1929

Morning dawned on the small apartment house, two blocks down the street from the Chateau. The early morning sun poured in as Eliska sat at her kitchen table, fingering her gold cross. Streaks of gray peppered her dark hair, despair pressed her shoulders down, and a weariness surrounded her.

As Andela came into the kitchen, she saw that Eliska's head was bowed and her hands folded in her lap, tears streaming down her cheeks. "Mama, why are you crying? .... Oh, I remember! Today is you and Papa's wedding day again, isn't it?"

"Yes, dear, I wonder.... Where......?"

Figure 60 Andela

"He's not coming back. He might have gone to heaven." Andela blurted out innocently.

Eliska turned angrily to Andela. She took the eleven-year girl by the shoulders, looked into her face, and admonished Andela, very deliberately, as if she could say it exactly right, it was true, "Your..... Papa.... Is...... Not.... Dead!"

Andela put her arms around Eliska and hugged her, "You say that every year Mama."

Eliska sobbed, "He's not dead. I know it. Don't you ever forget it! You hear me?"

"Yes, Mama."

Eliska wiped her eyes with her apron. "Well, enough sad memories. We have work to do. Since Mr. Klimy bought this building and put me in charge, there's lots of extra work. I want you to sweep up the halls and the entryway."

Eliska went on. "And the sidewalks, don't forget them like you did last time. Mr. Klimy is very particular here and in his kitchen. You hear me?"

"Yes, Mama, you going cooking?" Andela replied.

"We have a big reception today for a bunch of big shots. And the kitchen for the poor is open too. Finish up, then come quick. Don't be playing with your bear! We have lots of chickens to dress and potatoes to peel. Don't forget now!"

"OK, Mama."

Eliska hurriedly got ready and stepped out into the warm July sunshine. *It was so warm in the little room above the stable, on our wedding day. We made enough heat by ourselves to heat the whole town in the winter; she chuckled to herself. A dull ache descended into her stomach. Mustn't think of such things..... Must keep going. Not to worry, things will work out. And...... And...... I.... Will see him again.*

Eliska tried to wipe the doubts out of her mind, but they always had a way of sneaking back to haunt her. She hurried the two blocks to the Chateau and entered the bustling kitchen.

Karel Klimy had arrived early. "A little late this morning, Eliska?" He knew full well that Eliska was never late except on July 1st. He didn't understand but didn't bother to ask her the reason; she was an excellent cook after all. He had put her in charge of the kitchen for the poor, and she was second to him, here in the big kitchen. "The Freikorps have a banquet today. They are always so arrogant; you'd think they didn't lose the war."

Eliska nodded, deep in thought. *The last time I saw the German Freikorps was at the dance hall in Litomysl. -- They grabbed me, and if it weren't for Zuba, Lord only knows what could have happened.*

"They'll drink lots of beer, slap the wait girls on the rump, and sing those damn songs. I sure won't miss them when they're gone. Thankfully, we won't have to put up with them for a while after that," Eliska said, shrugging her shoulders.

An hour after Eliska left, and as Andela finished the sweeping, a short, muscular man came up to her. He wore brown shorts and a tan shirt upon which several medals hung. He reached down and took her hand. "You are the sweetest little girl I've seen today. And so sweet. Is your Mama home?"

Figure 61 Fidorka Sugar Wafer

Andela shook her head no, as she tried to pull her hand free.

"Let's go for a walk to the park. I'll buy you Fidorkas (sugar wafer cookies)." the man said.

The man leered at her and squeezed her hand. "Let me go!" a frightened Andela cried.

"You should be nice to your elders," the man replied.

Andela's mind raced, trying to think of a way to have him let her go.

Remembering what her mother had taught her, Andela gave the man a swift kick to his exposed shinbone and defiantly yelled at him. "My Papa is home! Do you want me to call him?"

The man howled in pain, swore, and dropped Andela's little hand. "You little Hose Scheisse (pants crapper)! Don't call your damn Papa. I'll be back some other time." He turned and left, but after going several feet, he stopped, turned, and glared back at Andela. Andela glared back. She stood with her feet planted squarely, and with her hands on her hips, she stared him down. The man took a step toward her, then thought better of it. He whirled back around and left. Then, head held high; he hobbled away with an exaggerated military stride.

~~~~~~

Andela bound into the Chateau kitchen. Sneaking over to the cake that Eliska was frosting, Andela slipped her little finger into the cake, pulled a gob of frosting out, and licked it off. Eliska smiled playfully and swatted Andela's hand with the frosting spatula. The spatula left a gob of frosting on the back of her hand. "No, you don't!"

Andela giggled and licked the back of her hand, "Thanks, Mama!"
~~~~~~

"Where have you been? I told you to be here in a hurry!" Eliska scolded. "Were you playing with your bear again?"

Andela was suddenly quiet, "No, Mama, a man scared me, and I waited until he left."

"A man scared you? What man?"

"I don't know who he was; he is mean, though."

An overwhelming feeling of concern washed over Eliska. "Somebody from the neighborhood?"

"No, I didn't know him."

"What did he do?"

"He grabbed me, twisted my arm, and wanted to take me to the park and have Fidorkas."

Eliska bent over and hugged Andela. "Well, it's over now." Eliska turned away; *I must stay calm and not scare her any further.* "I am so glad you are here to help me. Can you put the silverware on the table?

Remember, the forks go on the left, and the knife and spoons on the right. Put them on the table in the way they use them. Dessert spoon to the inside, soup spoon to the outside." Eliska raised one finger. "And put them, nice and straight, OK?"

"OK, Mama."

Andela grabbed a handful of silverware and, as little girls do, bounced into the dining room. Eliska watched through the kitchen door until she was sure that Andela was placing the silverware correctly.

Satisfied, she returned to frosting her cake. *Who could this man be?.. What did he want with my little Andela? .... Other mothers in the neighborhood have told me stories.* She shuddered. Suddenly, from the dining room, she heard the clatter of silverware hitting the floor. *Oh no, she dropped the silverware. I'll have to rewash them. That careless girl will get a talking to!*

Eliska wiped her hands on her apron and started toward the dining-room door when Andela burst in, "Mama, Mama, that man is out there!"

"What man?"

"The man that twisted my arm."

Eliska grabbed a sharp butcher knife from the knife rack. "Show me!" She replied resolutely.

Andela pushed the dining-room door open and peeked out. "There, Mama, over talking to Mr. Klimy."

Eliska, knife behind her back, peeked through the half-open door and let out a gasp. *My God, that's Ales Baum! The one from the dance house that threw me into the air.* Hate built up as she clenched her teeth, then fear as she trembled. *It is one thing to hurt me, but you will never hurt my little girl! I'll take care of this once and for all.*

Eliska took a deep breath and turned to Andela. "Go over to the Chudý Kuchyně (poor kitchen) and see Radmila, the meat cook. She has jobs for you."

Andela left, and Eliska pondered. *What to do next? If I cause a scene now, I will lose this job, and we can't afford that. If I cut the bastard, I'll go to jail, and Andela will go to an orphanage.* She pointed the knife in his direction and glared. *We'll meet again, you son of a bitch, don't even think of my little girl!* ~~~~~~

Chapter 58

THE CRASH

Koupil Garage, Owatonna, MN, USA Thursday, October 31, 1929

Figure 62 The Crash

Two days before, on Oct 29th, 'Black Tuesday' exploded on Wall Street. Investors traded sixteen million shares on the New York Stock Exchange in a single day. Thousands of investors lost billions of dollars, wiping them out. After Black Tuesday, America and the rest of the industrialized world spiraled downward into the Great Depression 1929-39. This was the deepest and longest-lasting economic downturn in the history of the Western industrialized world.

<div align="center">~~~~~~</div>

For the last four months, Paul has been a daily visitor to the repair shop of the Mack dealership. After school, on weekdays, and all day on Saturday. He graduated from sweeping floors to changing oil and replacing spark plugs.

After finishing his work, he was Zuba's shadow. He constantly pestered Zuba about his days on the ship Raspatau.

Zuba told him again how Paul's dad, Thomas, rescued them. Zuba patiently answered his questions, but sometimes it got in the way of productive work. Paul arrived at his usual time of four in the afternoon, just after school.

He entered the lunchroom where Zuba and Hanzi were having their afternoon coffee. "Hey Zuba, what's on today's schedule?"

"Afternoon Paul, I thought -- you might -- help me out."

"Sure, what's to do?" Paul responded gleefully.

"You read real -- good, yes?"

"Oh, you betcha, I got a B+ in reading last week!" Paul said enthusiastically. "I can read a newspaper! Let me show you!" Paul grabbed the paper from the lunchroom table. "It says... a... market... crashed in New York." He looked at Zuba. "Do you suppose it's like our grocery market here in Owatonna?"

"If it crashed – I guess it they -- didn't build too good," Zuba replied, "You read -- words -- good."

"Thanks!"

"Me lost reading glasses -- can't make out -- words in this new -- Mack tune-up manual. They have a new way -- adjust the timing. -- Big words -- mix me up. -- me can't see no good. -- Can you read it -- tell what to do?"

"OK, Let me at it."

"Stay here -- read and when -- done -- bring the book and come to me, -- OK?"

Zuba and Hanzi then returned to work.

"You still haven't learned to read, have you?" Hanzi chided Zuba.

"No, I try, but those -- markings are chicken scratchings."

"How are we supposed to get home when you can't read?"

"Why don't you -- learn better, -- Mr. Smart Aleck?" Zuba shot back.

"Roma don't believe in that sort of thing. I get along just fine with what I can read, stop signs, and such. Didn't I sell five trucks last month?" Hanzi replied proudly. "So, no need for it!"

Thomas Koupil came into the repair shop, drawn and haggard. No evidence of his usual, impeccable dress style could be seen; his tie was askew; his shirt soaked with sweat. Walking up to Zuba and Hanzi, he lowered his head and his voice. "Boys, I'm ashamed to go back on my word, but I can't give you the raise I promised you."

Thomas's shoulders sagged, and he had a tough time lifting his head. Honoring his word has been a hallmark of his integrity.

Zuba's face held a dazed question. He looked at Hanzi and back to the forlorn Thomas Koupil. *"It must be -- bad -- have to cancel -- the raise. Me planning on raise to help get me back to Eliska.* What happen?"

"Remember I promised you the raise in July? Well, I put all my savings into the stock market. Last Tuesday, the market crashed, and I lost it all, thirty thousand dollars. I just came from the Farmers National Bank. The stock I bought was collateral for the loan for the twenty trucks, and now they want more. I must put up another ten thousand of collateral in a week, or they will call the loan, and we'll be out of business. I might have to pledge the savings we put away for Paul's education."

"What's this collateral thing?" Hanzi asked.

"It's where you get a money loan, give the bankers an equal amount called collateral, so they don't worry about you paying them back."

"If you have this cold -- at her -- all, -- why do you need the loan?"

"To buy the trucks."

"Aren't trucks good collateral?" Hanzi said.

"Yes, they are."

"Sounds like -- you can borrow -- money if you give -- them twice as much as you need," Zuba said, scratching his head.

"That's how it works, I guess. Sorry boys, I hate to go back on my word." Tears welled up in Thomas's eyes, "but there's no other way. You have been with me the longest; I promise you I'll make this right with you."

"Mr. Koupil, you -- been fair to us, if it weren't for you, we still be -- on that damn ship. We get by!" Zuba turned to Hanzi, "Right Hanzi?"

"Well, I could have mended the holes in my pockets with two dollars an hour extra. Especially on Saturday night."

"Never mind about -- damn girlfriends!" Zuba replied angrily. Then he turned to Thomas. "We be -- OK, Mr. Koupil."

"Thank you, Zuba. Please don't say anything to the rest of the men. And for God's sake, say nothing to Paul or Marta. OK?"

Zuba glared at Hanzi, "Ya, Mr. Koupil, -- we both understand!" ~~~

Chapter 59

THE BAND CONCERT

Town Square, Owatonna, MN, USA, Wed, July 1st, 1931

The hot July evening was heavy and still as a funeral home viewing room. Winds that had battered this Minnesota village now lay sleeping. Relief at last! Over the previous three days, a relentless, restless, dry south wind had pummeled a parched, Southern Minnesota. The sky had boiled up with thunder clouds as far as the eye could see. Only these weren't thunderclouds; they brought no rain to the drought-stricken community.

They were a dust blizzard. The clouds boiled up ten thousand feet high or more. They rolled on like an avenging juggernaut. When the dust fell, it penetrated everything, hair, nose, and throat. It carried a mottled mixture of black, brown, and gray, swirling Oklahoma dirt; blown all the way to Owatonna, Minnesota. The dust clouds would continue their horrific journey to Washington D. C. and finally alight on New York City. Even ships, three hundred miles off the New York coastline, were covered with fine brown silt.

The hot, persistent summer winds colored faces black. Neckerchiefs tied across the mouth showed a perfect outline of a person's mouth in dirty black. Itchy dirt seeped under windowsills and dyed the wash on the line, a murky gray.

Figure 63 Dust Blizzard.

The residents of the Great Plains had a new blizzard to contend with. A black blizzard! Dust fell like snow, piling up on the ground in huge drifts! Black powder dust seeped through every windowsill and door crack, making tiny, drifted streaks across the floors. Mothers kept their children busy indoors for fear of losing them in the winds outside.

Further South, hundreds of farmers left the land as fast as the land left them. Some said that the lucky ones couldn't leave, as they lay buried underneath the restless soil, taken by dust pneumonia.

Every Wednesday, the Owatonna farmers delivered fresh milk and eggs to town, attended church services, and stayed on to have a meal at Charlie's Cafe. After supper, the menfolk told the women that they needed to walk to work off that sumptuous meal.

The women folk accommodated this little charade, knowing that the men would saunter down the street to have a beer (or two) at the Blue Room tap or Walt's pool hall. It was a relief to the women to have them gone.

Figure 64 Buried Machinery

The gussied-up women, dressed in their best homemade flour sack dresses, chattered among themselves as they made their way to Central Park. There, after wiping off the dusty wooden benches, they demurely sat in front of the twenty-year-old bandstand. They fanned themselves, talking and waiting for the concert to start.

The community band was getting ready to play, thankful that the evening was quiet, as they didn't hold the last two concerts because of the black blizzards.

The band members cleaned off the benches and railings of the bandstand with rags brought from home. Zuba had his tuba out, and Hanzi was warming up on his accordion when the director, Karl Bennoy, arrived on the scene.

Karl Bennoy was an accomplished musician, educated at Harvard but gave up his first love to join his father's bank (Farmers National) in Owatonna. "I hope you boys practiced this week. It's been two weeks since we played," he said.

Figure 65 Farmers National Bank, Owatonna MN.

Zuba and Hanzi nodded yes. They had practiced and played every Sunday for church services in Litomysl.

Karl continued, "Can you fellas play the Praha (Farewell to Prague) polka?" Both nodded yes.

"Good, we'll start with that. Half the band are Czechs and live in Litomysl, so I figured you could play it."

Zuba had been moody since morning. Hanzi piped up. "What's a matter with you? You look funny! You didn't forget the Praha Polka, did you, big guy? Just watch me. I'll get you through it. We played it many times. I'll show you how. Old Hanzi to the rescue!"

Zuba snapped back, "Shut up for once Hanzi, -- me play it."

"What's a matter you? You don't have to take my head off. I was just...." Hanzi stopped short, "Today is July 1st, isn't it?"

"Ya."

"And you're thinking about Eliska again, aren't you?"

Zuba's chin was on his chest, and he turned away from Hanzi. He didn't want Hanzi to see the tears on his cheeks. Finally, he answered, "Ya, be our wedding day. -- Last time me played the Praha Polka -- was in your Papa's band at the dance house. Me never – want to play it since we been took."

Hanzi was quiet as he picked his accordion up and played "Dark Eyes," not knowing its effect on Zuba.

Zuba winced as thoughts of Eliska came rushing back. *That is the song that Eliska sang after they had made love.* He picked up his tuba and polished it here and there, using his big red handkerchief. When he was sure no one was looking, he wiped his eyes.

Hanzi looked over at him and caught him in the act. He understood and said, "That Oklahoma dust, I'll bet?"

"Ya -- me guess." ~~~~~~

Chapter 60

THE RAZOR'S EDGE

Apartment House, Litomysl Czechoslovakia, Sat, July 1st, 1933

Eliska slid a long dagger across her thumb, testing its sharpness. "Andela, are you ready to leave?" Eliska slipped the blade into its sheath, tucked it under a wide serape, and wrapped it around her waist. She carried the knife ever since Ales Baum reappeared in her life four years ago. *As God is my witness, I'll let nothing happen to Andela. Andela is fifteen and shows she is a young woman in all the right places. She turns many a boy's (and few men's) heads. That's worrisome. The Germans are having a special party at the Chateau. They drink till they get slobbering drunk, making their big heads even bigger. Andela will help serve today.*

Figure 67 The Dagger

Eliska finished dressing, "Let's go; we'll be late!"

"That's OK Mama, Mr. Klimy knows today is you and Papa's wedding anniversary. You are always late on that day."

"Maybe it's time I change," Eliska replied, but the old familiar sinking feeling deep in the pit of her stomach returned. *Where is he? Damn him! Why did he leave us? We have a daughter coming of age. We need a father's looking after. Where is he?*

~~~~~~

Brown-shirted Freikorps crowded the Chateau dining room as Andela went up and down the rows of tables, serving glasses of beer. Eliska flitted back and forth from her work at the cake station. She constantly peeped through the doorway of the dining room, checking on Andela. Every so often, someone offered a rousing shout, "Heil Hitler."

Eliska thought, *I wonder what the hell that means. A drinking game? These bastards are so arrogant.*

As Ales Baum entered the dining room and made his way to the head table, more "Heil Hitler" yells erupted. He raised his hands for quiet. "Gentlemen, a glorious day for Czechoslovakia, a glorious day for Germany, and a glorious day for the whole Aryan race. We elected a wonderful man Chancellor of Germany. Adolf Hitler! Heil Hitler!" The room erupted in cheers with the clinking of the beer glasses, toasting their recent victory.

The party became wilder and rowdier. Karel Klimy came over to Eliska, "We better serve the food to settle these damn fools down!"

Figure 68 Chateau Dining Room

"You're right, Mr. Klimy. I'll get the girls started right away. I hope they are wearing extra hard underpants. When they get pinched, it won't hurt so much."

The Chateau staff served the dinner; then, Ales Baum ordered Slivovice (plum brandy) and another round of beer to wash it down.
~~~~~~

Andela struggled with two large pitchers of beer as she went down the rows of tables serving the men.

Two brown-shirted boys, Eldric and Hartmut, not much older than Andela, grabbed her from behind and clutched her backside. She whirled around, spilling beer across the front of their uniforms.

They chided her, "See what you have done! You splashed beer over us! Now we must change our clothes." They grabbed Andela, Eldric on one arm, and Hartmut on the other. They raised her up and carried her down a hallway towards an adjacent room. "You can help us dress," they snickered mischievously.

Panic crossed Andela's face as she screamed, "Leave me alone!"

The rest of the Freikorps jeered and stomped their feet. "Now she will meet German superiority!" they hooted.

Halfway down the hall, as they passed a doorway, a hand grabbed Eldric by the hair and jerked his head backward. A thin dagger slid up and tickled his throat.

"Let her be!" Eliska said, with a slurred, fierce growl. "Or the rug will drink your blood!"

All the color drained out of Eldric's face. Hartmut pulled away, still holding tight to Andela. He whipped out his 12-inch dress sword and pointed it at Andela's side.

"You drop your knife. This one is a lot bigger than your knife," he smirked. "Then you can join us, you're a little old, but you will do."

"No, don't," Eldric said breathlessly, as he felt a trickle of blood down the side of his neck. "Her knife is razor-sharp."
"She wouldn't dare hurt you. I'll cut this one bad if she does," Hartmut replied. He backed away with one arm firmly crushing Andela's neck and the other holding the sword to her side. Suddenly, he stopped short as he felt the touch of cold steel on his cheek.

Karel Klimy stood behind him with a long-handled, two-handed kitchen meat cleaver. "Mine is bigger!"

Karel tapped the cleaver lightly on Hartmut's shoulder. The boy turned his head and stared nervously at the cleaver.

Karel raised the cleaver high, "Young fellow, you haven't lived long

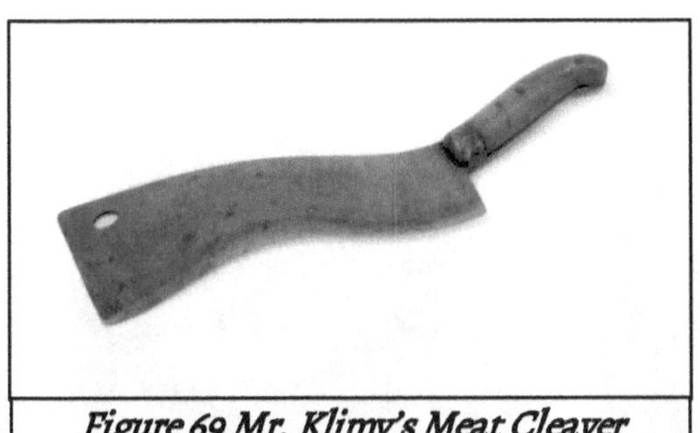
Figure 69 *Mr. Klimy's Meat Cleaver*

enough to acquire a thinking brain. This little knife has lifted off many a hog's head. They were brighter than you are. They knew they were going to die. Do you?"

Hartmut hesitated. Karel took a firm grip on the meat cleaver and lifted it even higher. "It loves to kiss the neck of a hog! And it will kiss yours! LET! MY! KITCHEN! HELP! GO! NOW!"

Hartmut let loose of Andela's arm and dropped the sword. Andela promptly turned and kicked him in the shins.

"You bastards, get the hell out of here before I call the police." Mr. Klimy yelled, still gripping the meat cleaver in its kill position.

"We were just having fun," the two men whined as they stumbled down the hall and re-entered the celebration. They never said a word to the other men as they were too ashamed to admit that a woman, and a short, skinny man, had bested them with a huge meat cleaver.

Karel adjusted his glasses with trembling hands, "Damn Germans," He leaned against the wall as the meat cleaver dropped from his hands and clattered to the floor.

Eliska ran to Andela and hugged her. "Are you all right?"

"Ya Mama, I'm OK."

Eliska hugged the shaking Mr. Klimy. "Thank you. You are very brave."

Mr. Klimy was sweating profusely. With a shaking hand, he pushed his glasses back up on his nose. "Brave hell, I didn't want to lose a great cook and kitchen helper. Too darn hard to train!" He laughed a relieved laugh with Eliska and Andela joining him.

Mr. Klimy's face changed to a somber shade of concern, "Watch your back. Those bastards are trouble." ~~~~~~

Chapter 61

PARISH FESTIVAL

Holy Trinity Church, Litomysl MN, USA, Tues, July 4th, 1933

Figure 70 Holy Trinity Church

Figure 71 Holy Trinity over front door

Hanzi yelled at Zuba from the cottage door. "Hurry, Zuba. You'll miss the picnic in the churchyard!"

"Don't be -- in rush -- it across the road."

"The ladies' picnic basket auction starts quick. Can't miss that."

"You mean you don't -- miss bidding on -- Beda Blaha's basket?"

"Well, she's gotta be an excellent cook. Look how round and plump she is. And those rosy cheeks, I bet her bottom is rosy too."

"Sounds you're hoping -- she cooked a rump roast," Zuba said, smirking like a contented cat with his first mouse.

"Never mind your smart remarks. I dig Beda. I can't pretend I'm a priest like you?"

When Hanzi said that, Zuba's mood shifted. He lowered his head and passed his fingers through his thinning gray hair. *Sixteen years, last Saturday, Eliska and I married. -- Maybe found someone else. Fine woman and a great mother. -- What right-thinking man wouldn't want her? Maybe married again and has ten kids. -- Maybe, no use in going back. -- me haven't saved enough to buy the ticket. Only eight hundred dollars left. Not right to use Mr. Koupil's money. -- Farm work slow, farmers have tough time -- corn so cheap they burn it in the stove.*

Hanzi slicked back his hair and twirled his mustache. He handed Zuba an old straw hat. "Here's your white hat!" Hanzi slipped a headband on, with a chicken feather sticking out, grabbed his accordion and Zuba's tuba, and yelled, "Let's run, big fellow! Hi, Ho Silver, Gettum Up Scout!"

"Hi, Ho Silver, what -- you blabber about?"

"The new radio show, The Lone Ranger and his horse Silver. I'll be the faithful sidekick, Tonto."

"Who's Tonto? What's a sidekick?"

"An Indian, riding a paint horse named Scout. He rides with the Lone Ranger. Pulls the Lone Ranger's butt out of trouble whenever he gets in a fix. Like I do when you run into trouble."

"'Me guess there – not be any -- curly, gray-headed Indians. -- Riding a painted horse? Ha! -- What color you paint -- dat horse?

Never mind! You know what I mean, a horse with different colors.

Different colors like -- pink and blue?

"No, a painted horse is black and white, you slow-tongued lizard!"

Sounds like -- Holstein cow. You know -- difference between cow -- and horse?

"Of course, I do! You look like a horse that's facing away from me."

"Now, no -- get spunky. me try to -- get this straight. If you ride a horse -- dat been painted and -- play a bad accordion -- you spook every cow -- in twenty miles!"

"I'll have you know; I'm the best accordion player in Litomysl, MN."

"How about -- Ole Sandstrom?"

"He lives closer to Owatonna, and he's a Swede. That doesn't count. He's 'a natural,' from milking cows. Strong fingers. The Squeezebox on an accordion is like a cow's udder. Squeezes out the sweetness."

"In Litomysl, we don't have -- over 50 people living here!" Zuba said.

"No other accordion players will move here once they find out about me! Are you coming?"

"Why? -- You say enough -- for both of us. -- You can do the band -- all by yourself."

"Let's run, big fellow, Hi Ho Silver! Gettum up, Scout! I'll sneak up on Beda Blaha's basket and check it out. See you over in the churchyard, partner. I'll be the one with the girls buzzing around me. Eeeeeh Haaaaaaw!"

Hanzi left in a rush, and Zuba soon followed, crossing the road to the church.

The parish members had set up several booths in front of, and on both sides of the church. The church ladies sold bratwurst, ice cream, cookies, handmade dollies, and artwork.

Under a sprawling elm tree, Hanzi leaned over the counter of the Beda Blaha's kissing booth. Smiling and making eyes at her, he was angling to pick up a free kiss from her. Hanzi was in luck, well only partially, selling kisses was slow for Beda, so she cut the cost of her kisses in half, but no free ones! It dismayed Hanzi, but he remained her only customer.

Zuba chuckled and murmured. "There flies away -- a week's pay."

As Zuba entered the churchyard, he saw fourteen-year-old Paul, tall, thin, and not a speck of baby fat left on him. Paul and his friend Lester ran over to him. "Hey, Zuba," Paul said. "Lester has a puzzle for you. Show him, Lester."

Lester held out his hands. "Zuba. This is an intelligence test!"

"What's a -- intelli -- gence -- test?"

"To see if you know anything!"

"Oh -- all right, -- go -- ahead."

Lester opened his hands. In one hand was a dime, and in the other, a quarter. "You can have one to keep."

Zuba picked the dime. Lester snickered and whispered to Paul, "See, I knew he was dumb. He took the dime. See you, Paul!" Lester went off.

Paul turned and winked at Zuba, "Works every time, doesn't it, Zuba?"

"Ya, I put dime -- with other dimes in pickle jar," Zuba laughed. "If I take quarter, -- nobody test me no more."

Paul and Zuba slapped hands.

"You bring -- tuba, Paul?"

"Sure did. I'll sit next to you and blow you off the bandstand."

Zuba laughed, "You dream -- again?"

"You'll see! See on the bandstand this afternoon!" Paul yelled as he dashed after Lester.

Zuba walked up to and sat down on a circular bench built around a massive oak tree. Thomas Koupil came and sat beside him, a haggard expression topped off his well-worn suit and a shirt with a frayed collar. "Good morning Zuba, how is it going?"

"Ok, -- Mr. Koupil. Be better -- me -- work for you again."

"I wish you still were. Things haven't been good. When the Farmers National Bank failed, I did too."

"I didn't know -- what happened?"

"Well, I had money in the bank, but the liquidators kept it. The worst of it was that the liquidators then called the loan. I had to sell out to pay it."

"They take your -- money, and you -- pay off the loan too?"

"Doesn't seem fair, does it?"

"Me sad to hear -- no want to pry."

"Zuba, you aren't prying. You are a valuable and faithful friend. I still owe you and Hanzi your last wages."

"Don't fret, -- me and Hanzi get along OK, -- No family like you. -- Your family, OK?"

"Well, no, Marta is still sickly; losing the business and the coming down of our status hit her hard."

"Things kinda, -- maybe, work out."

"Oh.... Well, maybe.... Have you seen Paul?"

"He just -- here. We play -- quarter game."

"That's good; he looks up to you. You're a great example to him. Did you notice how gaunt he is?"

"Ya -- grow spurt. Need -- little time outside, -- need fresh air -- sunshine, he kinda pale."

Thomas did not answer, his hands covered his face, and tears ran between his fingers.

"What trouble -- Mr. Koupil? Things -- be better." Zuba said.

"Paul is sick and needs an operation," Thomas blurted out.

Zuba exhaled, with a lump sticking his throat. "Well, you -- you -- you just -- get that operation!"

Figure 72 Mayo Clinic

Thomas winced and let out a sob, "It's tough. With the Depression on, everything must be cash. Cash I don't have. The Mayo Clinic in Rochester will cost $750."

There was no response from Zuba. *I have $750. Almost enough to go home. If I give up, I'll never get back to Czechoslovakia. But $200 is Mr. Koupils money.* After several minutes, he cleared his throat and placed his hand on Thomas Koupil's shoulder.

"You can -- get -- no other place?"

"No, I've tried. Everyone is broke or afraid to lend money that they may need later."

Zuba pondered the words. *Me need to go to Eliska and Andela. This may be last chance to go home.* Staring at the ground, he made circles in the dirt with his foot.

As Zuba pondered, the kids at the parish celebration played ring-around-rosie as the parents talked and laughed at picnic tables. Suddenly firecrackers exploded. The parish priest leaped into action and quickly caught the little villains and plopped them down, on a bench, next to the brat-stand, saying, "Now you little brats cool off! No more firecrackers near the church! You hear me, or I box your ears."

Embarrassed parents quickly rushed in and gave a quick swat to the troublemakers behind, as a punctuation of the priest's warning.

Zuba let out a deep sigh, sniffed back tears, as he cleared his throat, "Mr. Koupil-- me -- have -- $750. -- me give -- get Paul's operation."

Thomas was awestruck. With tears in his eyes, he grasped Zuba's hands, "Zuba, what are you saying? You saved that money to go to your family. You surely don't mean that?"

Zuba turned his hat over and over, thinking long and hard. Finally, he spoke, "Mr. Koupil, for -- fourteen years you and Paul -- my family." Zuba swallowed hard, "I don't know -- if -- me -have -- family anymore. -- Maybe, me give up -- going home."

"Zuba, you can't!"

"Me want. -- love Paul -- like son. -- He need help -- me help -- if me don't -- that wrong."

Thomas shook Zuba's hand vigorously. "Zuba, I'll never forget this, and I'll pay every cent back to you."

"Maybe pray -- operation -- fixes trouble."

Thomas replied, "I hope so." ~~~~~~

Chapter 62

FOUND OUT

The Chateau, Litomysl Czechoslovakia. Thurs, March.16,1939.
Ales Baum strode into the kitchen at the Chateau. In full gray SS uniform, his medals glistened and wiggled as he walked. "Karel Klimy, where the hell are you?" he yelled.

Karel walked out of the beverage room, wiping his hands on his apron. His glasses were precariously perched on the end of his nose, and his bald head shone from the heat in the kitchen.

"Here I am. What'd want?" Karel said, irritated.

"Need to inspect your kitchen staff. Bring every slacker out here! Now!"

"Oh, you want to inspect? Do you? What the hell for? We're in the middle of getting the banquet ready. Can't we do this at another time?"

"No, dammit! I must see that the food is prepared properly. If you have any damn gypsies or Jews on your staff, they need to leave," Baum ordered as he slipped his hand over his Luger pistol. "You hear me? Don't stand there with that stupid look on your face! Get your people in here, line them up, now!"

Karel shrugged his shoulders and motioned to the staff to join him. They lined up, and Baum strode down the line, stopping and leering at each one. Karel followed along at his side. Baum stopped in front of Eliska. "You look like a gypsy! Gypsies must report to the work camp!"

"My name is Eliska Palzekova; is that a gypsy name?" she snarled at him.

Baum next stepped in front of Andela, who was standing next to Eliska. Eliska protectively put her arm over her shoulder and drew her close. "Who is this?" Baum said, tapping his riding crop on Andela's shoulder.

Eliska jerked her head up, "My daughter Andela." Eliska's face held a fierce look of a mother she-lion. Her eyes shone out her intense hate.

Baum observed Andela closely, smirked, and tapped his crop against her breast. "She is perfect German breeding stock. Blonde hair and blue eyes. A great specimen. Make a brave German fighting man, a grand wife! Give us plenty of babies for the Fatherland."

Baum turned his gaze to Eliska and asked, "Are you telling me she is your daughter? You stole her, didn't you?"

Karel laughed, interrupting Ales, "We don't have time to play your silly games. Eliska and Andela have been with me for twenty years. My best workers. Lazy gypsies! Ha!"

Baum shook his head and eyed Eliska. "You look familiar. Have we met before?"

"If you have been to the Chateau before," Eliska replied without looking up. "I've cooked here for a while."

Baum extended his riding crop and reached in and pulled up the gold chain and cross that Eliska had around her neck. The same cross that Zuba had made her. When Baum saw the cross, he stiffened, "I'm sorry, I see you are a loyal subject. You support the cause."

Baum waved his hand and said, "Carry on! The Fuhrer arrives in an hour. Make sure everything is ready for the big occasion." He turned to walk away, then stopped, swung around, and raised his hand stiffly. "Today is a wonderful day. Czechoslovakia is a Protectorate of Germany, Heil Hitler!"

Baum then marched out of the room. "Heil to you, you ass!" Karel grumbled under his breath as the door slammed behind Ales. "Our damn weak-kneed politicians give that bastard Hitler, the Sudetenland. Then they give him the whole country. There will be hell to pay." He wiped his sweating brow with his handkerchief. "Everybody, to your duties! Finish up."

Eliska said to Karel, "Thank you for sticking up for us."

"Those damn Germans are always trying to run my kitchen staff. I know you are Roma! Makes no never mind to me. You work hard and are an excellent mother. What more is there to know."

Karel's words startled Eliska. "How did you know I'm Roma?"

"You are lighter-skinned than the average Roma, but I have a Roma wife, and I recognize the Roma ways."

"You have a Roma wife?"

"Yes, her name is Kizzy."

"Is she Florica Danka's sister?"

"Why yes, how do you know?"

"She is my mother's sister!" ~~~~~~

Chapter 63

THE WINDS OF HELL

Saturday, November 09, 1940, Toms Repair Litomysl MN

It was a lazy Saturday morning. Tom Koupil was catching up on some bookwork at the repair shop when Zuba and Hanzi came in.

"Good morning, Mr. Koupil, Hanzi said.

"Good morning Hanzi, Zuba. What are you boys up to? I thought I gave you a long weekend off, with Armistice Day coming up on Monday."

"We just drop in-- to get bottle of pop," Zuba replied.

"Beautiful weather, isn't it? It should get up to sixty degrees today." Thomas said, "What are you going to do with three days off?"

"We dance tonight, sing in church Sunday, and maybe picnic on Monday," Hanzi replied.

"Hanzi means-- Dance tonight, -- Go to confession then – maybe sing in church Sunday," Zuba deadpanned, "Me probably stay to -- home from picnic," Zuba said, "Me not gonna horn in -- No place be for -- me."

"Why?" Tom inquired.

"Loverboy -- Hanzi gonna take -- girlfriend -- Beda Blaha along."

"I tell you what, Zuba, why don't you come along. You like birds, don't you?" Hanzi said.

"Ya."

"Well, we could go to Straight River Marsh. Ole Larson said they have thousands of ducks, geese, swans, and all kinds of other birds out there. The most he has ever seen. You could fish too." Hanzi coaxed.

"You just want me -- to drive so you can -- neck in back seat. "

"Have I ever done that to you?"

"No, me – not want to neck with you." Zuba chuckled.

"Listen, smart-aleck; you know what I mean. When is the last time I was necking with a girl in the back seat?"

"Ya, what about-- Saturday night -- coming home -- from dance in Owatonna.?"

"I was sitting in the back seat being a gentleman, not wanting the girls to get lonely."

"Girls not -- get lonely. There was three -- of them."

"I didn't want to have them fight over me. If you would be a sport, you could have one or two, but nooo, Mr. Lonely Heart, you won't!"

"Me -- don't know."

"I'll have Beda make some extra fried chicken. Lots, maybe some pickled pork hocks and Czech Style potato salad too.

"Me see -- how tired -- me be -- Monday morning."

~~~~~~

Monday, November 11, 1940, Litomysl MN

It was Armistice Day, the remembrance of the end of World War I. On the 22nd anniversary of the war's end, two of the Allied powers were not at peace. France was under Nazi occupation, and Britain was under siege by the Germans. Newspaper headlines retold President Franklin Roosevelt's Armistice Day message, in which he denounced the world's dictators.

Across the Upper Midwest, temperatures had been well above normal through the first weeks of fall. On the morning of the 11th, temperatures were in the fifties across the area. At 7:30 in the morning, the temperature in Chicago was 55F. It was 54F in Davenport, Iowa. Highs the day before had been in the 50s and 60s across the entire region. Hunters took advantage of the holiday and the exceptionally mild weather to go to lakes and rivers across Minnesota and Iowa. They were to be rewarded with an overabundance of waterfowl. Many would later comment that they had never seen so many birds. The birds knew something most of the hunters didn't. They were getting out of the way of the winds of hell!
~~~~~~

"Hurry up, Zuba. I got the Chevy packed for a great day. A picnic with a beautiful, soft, squeezable lady. Get your lazy butt out of bed. The car is full of gas. I got to get the fishing poles in and dig some bait. You hurry up now, or I will play the accordion polka!"

"Oh no -- not the accordion polka that sounds -- like the -- Polish funeral march! Me -- get up quick!" Zuba laughed.

Hanzi pulled the car up to the little cottage door, and Zuba came out lugging a five-gallon fishing bucket, a couple of blankets, and two big winter coats.

"What do you want all that junk along for? It's a beautiful day!" Hanzi said.

"Need blankets -- for to sit on ground -- not get butt wet!"

"I already have a couple in the trunk of the car. But two big winter coats? We don't even have snow on the ground. It was sixty degrees yesterday. It's already fifty now." Hanzi said impatiently.

"Weatherman on -- WCCO said it might -- get cold later on."

"What do they know!? They miss every prediction they make. We got a rock in the yard that can do as good. If the rock is wet, it's raining, if snow is on it, it's snowing, and if the rock is gone, it's windy."

"Maybe – you get job as -- weather sorter outer feller. Could call you – Hanzi, the rock watcher. Bet you -- do a good job of – watching a rock. – It stays in place – not get away – like all your girlfriends."

"Never mind, dump that junk in the trunk of the car and let's go!"

"What the – big hurry?"

"I think maybe I pop the question to Beda today."

"What be – popping the – question mean?"

"To get married, you big dummy!"

"How you – pop a question? Put it – in a balloon – stick it with – pin?"

"Sometimes, you are as dense as a slab of rock."

"You be the rock watcher! – Better keep your eye on this slab of rock – or me may go back into the house – for nap."

After everything was in order, Zuba and Hanzi drove a mile out of town and turned into a neatly cared-for farm place of Carl and Annie Blaha. Hanzi beeped the horn, and Beda Blaha came running out of the house, her plump little body undulating with each step she took. She wore a blue and white checkered blouse that set off the gold of her hair and the blue of her eyes. A sturdy pair of work jeans that had seen several weeks of work and washing completed her dashing ensemble. As she and her sister were the only children of Arnie Blaha, they had spent a lot of time working the farm.

Beda's cheeks were flushed with excitement as she carried a picnic basket in the crook of each of her arms. "Oh, you sweet boys, this is going to be so much fun. Just one more trip to the house, and I will have everything we need."

Beda whirled and undulated back into the house, then stopped at the doorway of the house and yelled to Zuba, "My older sister, Margot, might go along if you want. What do you think, Zuba?"

Zuba slid down in the seat and looked pleadingly at Hanzi. "So, -- this why me come along. – this is another -- no see um date."

"No, Zuba, I didn't know about this at all. You can or not. Makes no difference to me." Hanzi stammered.

"Margot made a big batch of Bratislavsky Goulash for us," Beta yelled again.

"Bratislavsky Goulash! When's the last time you had that?" Hanzi said. "That's got to be good cause she's a healthy girl. What you say?"

"Healthy, she bigger -- than me! But if is gonna -- get us to -- marsh quick -- me can slip off and go fish -- be ok -- she come," Zuba said.

"Ya, tell her to come," Hanzi yelled.

The two Blaha girls undulated across the farmyard towards the car. Both had their hair put up in pigtails, wrapped in a circle, and piled high at the top of their heads. They carried buckets of goulash, blankets, jars of lemonade, coffee, and mincemeat pie.

"Look like -- they are cooking for -- threshing crew," Zuba remarked.

"It is nice of you handsome fellows to take us along," Margot said, her chubby cheeks glowing and her blue eyes shining. She was a larger version of Beda. She had bib overalls on and a red and white checkered blouse under it. A red neckerchief was haphazardly wrapped around her neck. She cooed excitedly to Zuba, "I was just telling Beda how handsome you fellows are and that some lucky girl is gonna have a big prize if they can hook and reel you in. What do you think of that Zuba?"

"Me think --"

Margot was not one to let a lapse in the conversation go unfilled. "You know it isn't often that you can find two hard-working girls like us. What ya think, Zuba?"

"Me think --"

"Now, me, I want a handsome hard-working man, a good eater, no cheater, and someone who is inclined to a lot of children."

"Me think -- incline might be too steep – for me to climb."

"I think it's important for a girl to tell a guy what she wants in a man before she reels him in."

"Me think – you might be – using the -- wrong bait.

"Well, never mind, where are we going?"

"Straight River Marsh just down the road," Hanzi said, "they have a new boat landing dock, picnic tables, and new outhouses with rolls of that new toilet paper. No corn cobs or Sears catalog, first-class joint!" Hanzi chuckled.

"Well, an outhouse is nice, but we can do without, if need be," Margot said.

"Me think – you might handle that."

~~~~~~

11:30 AM, Straight River Marsh, five miles South of Litomysl MN

It had rained some, but an occasional blue sky smiled through as the foursome arrived at the picnic site. The entrance road was rutted from the traffic of the many early morning duck hunters launching boats from the landing dock. Wave after wave of all kinds of waterfowl buzzed overhead, and the hunters were excited to have such easy pickings.

Zuba stopped the car close to the shore of the marsh. He got out of the car and motioned to a picnic table close by. "That – good place. Outhouse – close by."

The men walked twenty feet to the shore and set their fishing lines in. They came back as the girls put a sumptuous feast on the picnic table.

Beda babbled on, "You like fried chicken, pickled pork hocks, and Czech Style potato salad? Margot made the Bratislavsky Goulash and her special cheese-filled bread. Got sauerkraut, mincemeat pie, and fruit dumplings too."

When the feast was consumed, Hanzi laid a blanket on the grass, stretched out on it, and pretended to be asleep. Beda picked a cattail from the marsh and came over to Hanzi and tickled his nose. Hanzi grabbed her and pull her down on the blanket. He grabbed the cattail, squashed it good, and sprinkled the fuzzy cattail lint on her hair.

"Zuba, you want to take a walk along the shore?" Margot said, pulling on his arm.

"Maybe – eh – eh walk a little – not go far. Hanzi and Beda – make moo eyes – at each other – don't need us around."

~~~~~~

After Zuba and Margot left, Hanzi raised on one elbow and looked Beda deep in her eyes. He kissed her tenderly and then stammered, "Beda, do you ever think about getting married?"

"Oh yes, all the time."

"You think you could marry a Roma?"

"If he was a good man."

"If that Roma was to ask, you would consider me?"

"Are you asking or just fooling around?"

"I guess the fooling around time is over and maybe time to make it a little serious," Hanzi whispered.

"Are you serious?"

"Maybe, kinda, ya, I think so."

"Hanzi Danke! Are you asking me to marry or not!"

"I was trying to figure out what you would say before I asked you."

"Will, did you?"

"No, I guess not."

"So, there is only one way to find out."

"There is?"

"Yes, just ask me!"

"All right, Beda," Hanzi twirled his mustache and stammered on, "Beda,"

"You already said that!"

"Oh, ok Beda will you.... ah....... ah."

"Will you just say it!"

"Will you murmur me?"

"Maybe you better try that again. I don't know how to murmur you."

"Will you ma.... ma....... marry me.?"

"YES! YES! YES!!!!

~~~~~~

Meanwhile, Zuba and Margot are walking to the marsh.

Margot said, "Let's cut some walking sticks."

After they cut the walking sticks, Margot and Zuba strolled to the shore and checked the fishing lines, leaned against the walking sticks, and waited for a cork to bob.

"Nice afternoon, isn't it, Zuba?"

"YA, – nice blue sky – above – why the sky – green in the west?"

"Oh, just the sun, shining kinda funny."

"Lake – full of ducks – swarming with them."

"My Gramma Blaha said to watch the livestock. They will tell you about the weather. Maybe some rain coming."

"Ya, me – papa say – the same."

"Grandma Blaha used to talk on the blizzard of 1880."

"Didn't – get no blizzards – in Czechoslovakia – just snow. Got some windy – snowy days here – they call them blizzards. – What – the difference?"

"The blizzard I am talking about doesn't happen too often. Maybe once every forty or fifty years. Grandma Blaha says that the blizzards we have gotten recently are babies compared to 1880. Children froze in the schoolhouses. Cattle would put their back to the wind, and walk for miles until they couldn't go anymore, then froze to death, standing up. She called those types of blizzards 'the wind from hell.' The wind was so strong you could barely walk in it. Air full of watery mist, like trying to breathe syrup. The cold made it hard to breathe. Your wet breath and snow blowing at you could freeze your mouth shut. Your lungs felt like someone stuck red-hot poker in them. Tears froze in your eyes, and you couldn't see," Margot shuddered and went on, "Least that's what Gramma Blaha says. But she's old, and her memory isn't so good, so maybe not that bad."

"Me, hope not. – WCCO say –just be – a little rain and – get colder."
~~~~~~

"Zuba, on the way out here, I wasn't too nice., I'm sorry about talking so fast and not letting you speak. I was excited to have a date with a man."

"When me – get excited – no can – talk – even slow Maybe – we be two sides – of the same kinda coin. – Me sorry too – me talk at you – smart like."

"Thank you, Zuba." Margot lowered her head, and tears were dripping from her chin. "It's been hard with Mama sick and us taking care of the house too. Beda helps, but she's only sixteen and gets mixed up some. Papa can't afford a hired hand, so we help with milking and haying too." Margot's big hands shook as she steadied herself on the walking stick; her plain face was awash in pain and tears.

"Ya, things – hard but – get better. Everybody – has trouble."

"I know about you and your family, and I shouldn't have been doing that. It's just that when you are as big a girl as I am, it gets kinda lonesome when all the other girls are getting boyfriends and married.

Margot hesitated and finally regained her composure, "I know I stand almost as tall as you are. I'm strong and cook good. But boys don't seem to appreciate those traits."

"Me Papa – say that the wedding night – has lots of kisses but – only lasts a – couple weeks, – but good cooking – goes on forever."

"It's just that the boys seem to like the fancy girls, with pretty dresses and ribbons in the hair," Margot said.

"Fancy face – no make a fancy heart. -- A sweet heart – make a sweet face."

"Thank you, Zuba. You're a nice man," Margot said as she wiped the tears from her face. "Maybe we better get back. Do you see the sky getting all orange?"

"Ya sun – playing– tricks today."

<div style="text-align:center">~~~~~~</div>

The winds came suddenly. Fierce frightening and icy. Then more ducks arrived, hundreds, thousands, then tens of thousands. They came in unending waves and all species. All were flying about ten feet off the water. As the winds increased, the beds of rushes and cattails were flattened, and the big, mounded muskrat houses blew away.

~~~~~~

Zuba and Margot quickly gathered up the fishing gear and ran back to the picnic area. Hanzi and Beda were carrying baskets of food and blankets to the trunk of the car. Rain, mixed with sleet and snow, pelted them as they all piled into the car.

"We need –get out– go home," Zuba said as he started the car. He backed the car around and pointed it back the way they had come in. The road was wet with snow and sleet, and the ruts were quickly filling with water.

Zuba slipped the car into first gear and slowly inched forward. The car sputtered, and Zuba gave it the gas. The car lurched. They went ten feet down the slippery ruts, then sunk into a deep water-filled rut, and the wheels spun out. They were stuck!

"We stuck. – Need push. Hanzi come – drive. – me push."

"We can help too," the girls said in unison. Both jumped out of the car and put their shoulders to the rear fender of the car. Zuba was on the other side of the car with his shoulder against the other fender. He yelled to Hanzi, "All right – give it a go. Everybody push!"

Hanzi tromped town the gas pedal, the back wheels spun, throwing mud and water on the three pushers in the back.

"No – stop Hanzi – you are digging us – deeper. We be – hung up. – Gonna take – tractor to pull – us out now." Zuba cried.

"Maybe I can walk to a farmer. You better get back in the car. You are all muddy and wet," Hanzi yelled over the howling wind.

They all got into the car, closed the doors, and rolled the windows up tight.
~~~~~~

They dried off as they discussed the options. As it was, no one could come up with any good advice except wait till the storm subsided, then walk for a tractor.

At two in the afternoon, a black rolling cloud appeared on the horizon and steadily marched towards the stranded car. On the leading edge of the rolling cloud, a tornado erupted and danced across the road, just a half-mile in front of them. It ripped at the rain-soaked trees and pulled them out like a gardener pulls weeds in a garden. The storm then dropped the trees across the road they were supposed to leave on.

At two-thirty in the afternoon, the wind picked up in intensity, screeching out a wailing death song. It seemed to erupt from the bowels of hell to vomit forth a mournful wail. A wail that grew in crescendo to a thunderous roar. As the roar intensified, a wall of blinding snow rocked and buffeted the car. The snow sought every crevice in the car. A powdered mist of snow seeped in through the closed doors and windows and enveloped the car's interior. It floated peacefully down on the hapless occupants.

Looking out any window was hopeless. All one could see was white. It was as if someone had painted the windows white. Only a dim glow lit the interior of the car.

Lightning suddenly crackled and engulfed the car, dancing across the hood and racing its way to the ground.

"Oh God, we are going to die!" Beda screamed as she clutched Hanzi as firmly as she could. Hanzi pulled her close as he prayed to Saint Sara. All that is heard from the two other members in the car's front seat was a low murmuring of 'The Our Father.'

They sat trembling in the car, occasionally starting the engine to run the heater and shutting it down again to save gas.

Zuba, wrapped in a winter coat and a blanket, would get out of the car before starting it, to clear away any snow that may have blocked the exhaust pipe. "Don't want – have poison gas in car – if the pipe – blocked," he would say.

At three in the afternoon, Zuba cleared the snow and tried to start the car. It wouldn't turn over. It just grunted but wouldn't start. He wrapped up again, went outside, and lifted the hood of the car.

Peering down into the dim recesses of the engine cavity, he saw that the motor was packed, level full of snow. All driven in by the monstrous winds.

Climbing back into the car, Zuba announced that there would be no more heater as the engine was wet.

"What are we to do, Zuba?" Hanzi cried.

"Maybe me – go walk for help," Zuba replied

"No! Don't do that!" Margot cried, "Gramma Blaha always said never go out from shelter you will get lost and freeze.

"Maybe when – it lets up a little," Zuba said.

"It will be dark in another hour." Margot pleaded.

Beda cried through chattering teeth, "I need to go to the outhouse!"

"We can't even see where the outhouse is," Hanzi said

"It was just over there. If it lets up a little, we might see it." Beda pleaded.

"There's a five-gallon fishing bucket – in the trunk. I get that – for you. Not pretty – do in a pinch." Zuba offered.

"I can't do that in front of all of you," Beda cried.

"I'll get – bucket, anyway. – might be a long night. You get cold – faster if – sitting in wet clothes."

Zuba got out of the car and waded through knee-deep snow to the trunk. He returned to the car. He turned around to hand the bucket to Hanzi, and the backseat was empty. "Where be – Hanzi and Beda?"

"The wind let up a little, and Beda could see the outhouse, so Hanzi and her went for it. They should be back quick. I would think the outhouse would be pretty cold," Margot said. "If you don't mind, I will go in the backseat and use the bucket."

"Ya, –me shut – my eyes," Zuba replied.

At three-thirty in the afternoon, Zuba began to worry. *Wind blows like crazy. No see anything of Hanzi and Beda. Me hope they aren't lost. The wind is crazy again. Can't see much more than a foot.*

"Me got – couple big balls of fishing line. It pretty tough. – Maybe me tie them together – then around – my waist so me can find – way back to the car. It reaches maybe one hundred feet. Me try and find them." Zuba said.

"No! I will go! You have been out of this car several times. It's my turn! She's my sister, and if anything happens to her, I will never forgive myself. When we get back, we will need you to take care of the car." Margot cried.

"Ok, unwind string –as you go, then pull on it – to find way back. – Jerk it a couple times if – need help, then me follow – string to you. – Don't pull too hard. Its tough string – but can't take – too much pulling." Zuba instructed.

Margot tied the string around her waist, cut up strips of a blanket, and wrapped them around her feet. She then grabbed two blankets and went out into the storm, as Zuba played out the string.

At four in the afternoon, Zuba was worried. The string had lain slack for the last ten minutes. He peered out in the gloomy whiteness. Darkness was setting in, and he was all alone.

What now, O Lord, do me try to find them or stay here if they need help. Margot hasn't pulled the string for some time. Wonder if she is alright. Me could follow the string to find her. That's what me do. Zuba got out of the car, walked a little, and pulled on the string, hand over hand, until the empty end of the broken string was in his hand.

Zuba murmured, "Margot must have broken the string or cut it on something. Don't even know where to look for her. Me only ten feet away from the car, -- can't even see it. Eyes freeze shut." Zuba turned to return to the car, and something seemed to grab him around the ankle. *Must be a stick.*

Zuba reached down, and where the stick was thought to be, he found a hand clutching his ankle. Frantically he dug down into the snow until the snow-covered face of Hanzi appeared.

When he pulled Hanzi up, a low babble escaped Hanzi's lips. "White, white all over, up or down, all around. We don't know where to go."

Zuba brushed the snow away from Hanzi's face. "Where be Beda?

"Help Beda. She's here too." Hanzi murmured.

Zuba dug deeper and found Beda sleeping in a fetal position. He checked her and found a faint pulse. Tying the empty end of the string to Hanzi's wrist, and then, clutching the string, he carried Beda to the car's back seat. He then followed the string back out to Hanzi and carried him get back to the car too.

Zuba, Beha and Hanzi all sit in the back seat. Zuba ripped up a blanket to wrap around their feet. He then pulled off the front seat covering and stuffing, and covered Hanzi and Beda with it.

Hanzi held Beta close, trying to warm her up, even though he was freezing too. "He, he, he, here, ... my, my, my, sweet, I'll keep you warm...... Ol Hanzi to the rescue." He mumbled through chattering teeth.

The threesome huddled in the darkness of the longest night of their lives. Zuba tried to stay awake and urge them to keep wiggling their fingers and toes until he fell into a fitful sleep.

At most, it was 5 degrees below zero when the morning dawned, and the blizzard continued.

The pain in Zuba's feet woke him with a start, and he wiggled some life back in them. He woke Hanzi and urged him to do the same. "How be Beda?" Zuba asked.

"Pretty good. I think she is sleeping good, and we are warm under all these coverings. Should I wake her?"

Figure 72a - Chevy stuck in snow.

Zuba looked over at Beda. Her face had an angelic expression. She was sleeping the rest of the righteous. Her face had a bluish tinge to it, and her breath had frozen her lips together. "No Hanzi, -- let her sleep. -- Just keep your head covered. – It's pretty cold in here." Zuba sat and wiggled his toes and urged Hanzi to do the same throughout the entire morning into early afternoon.

When the storm subsided, Zuba heard a strange pounding on the roof of the car. His foggy mind wasn't sure of what was going on. *Angels calling us home.*

He opened his eyes to see a hand scraping the frost off the side window.

"Anybody in there," a voice called out. "I'm the Steele County sheriff. Do you need help?"

"Ya, We – awful cold. Can you scoop – snow away from door so we – get out?"

"Sure, I'll get my deputies to help." the Sheriff replied.

The Sheriff and deputies scooped snow away from the door and helped Zuba out of the car. His legs were stiff, and he was a bit shaky standing there. "Get my – friend and his girl – would you?"

The Sheriff helped Hanzi out of the car. Hanzi stood with a blank expression on his face as the Sheriff and the deputy carried Beda out of the car and laid her on a stretcher.

They checked her pulse and looked over at Zuba and Hanzi, and said quietly, "Did you know that she is dead?"

"Ya, I knew it....... this morning, but didn't want to believe it," Hanzi said. "We were....... going to get married, just asked her yesterday."

"We will put her on the hayrack with the three frozen duck hunters we found. The tractor will pull them to the road. We have an ambulance waiting there. You are lucky we were looking for the hunters. Normally, we wouldn't plow this road out until fishing season in the spring." The Sheriff said.

"We – missing another girl too, she left – in blizzard," Zuba said.

"We found something unusual," the Sheriff said.

A deputy came up and said, "We are ready to take care of ... things."

The deputy was pulling a sled, loaded down with shovels and ice chisels. Zuba followed them down to the dock.

The deputy walked out on the frozen marsh and stopped at the end of the dock. He pointed to the end of the dock. A lone figure was standing upright, the ice of the marsh frozen around her. He grimly said, "She must have wandered down the dock and stepped off into the marsh. Apparently, she got stuck in the deep mud on the bottom or couldn't figure out where she was. The ice froze around her. She stood there, up to her waist in water, and slowly froze to death. Her mouth is frozen open, screaming for help, her eyes frozen shut."

The deputy shook his head, "Poor girl, she would have fallen over if she hadn't been clutching on that walking stick. She has a fishing line, balled up in the other hand. Is this the girl you were talking about?"

"Ya, – is Margot," Zuba replied.

~~~~~~
~~~~~~

Donald Pawlitschek

Friday, November 15, 1940, Owatonna Hospital, Owatonna MN,

Hanzi's recuperated well at the Owatonna Hospital. His toes and part of his left foot had to be amputated. The doctors removed other spots of frozen flesh that were on his lower legs. Hanzi's mind was another story. He lay quietly in his hospital bed, hands folded on his chest, staring at the ceiling.

Zuba came in. "How you – doing, Hanzi?"

Hanzi kept staring at the ceiling until Zuba reached out and placed his hand on Hanzi's shoulder. "You hurt bad – I think."

"Oh, Zuba, I loved her so much. We were to marry, but this evil country stole her away." Hanzi said. Tears streamed down his face as he turned over and faced Zuba. "I wasn't even able to go to her funeral."

"Was big – crowd at – church. Just – come from there. Carl Blaha had – to be helped in. His wife is on –next floor above us. She doesn't know anyone – just babbles, "got to go home – to tuck the girls in."

Hanzi started sobbing. Zuba went to him and wrapped his big arms around him. He pulled Hanzi to his chest and said, "Me not know – how to make better. Only time and – God can do that. – OK if me – stay with you awhile?"

Figure 72b - 12ft high snowbanks

Footnote: When it was all said and done, up to twenty-six inches of snow had fallen in parts of Minnesota. Furious winds up to 60 mph whipped the heavy snowfall into drifts twenty feet high. One of the deadliest blizzards in Midwest struck without warning leaving death and devastation in its wake while carving a 1,000mile-wide path through the mid-section of the country. Especially vulnerable were the many unprepared duck hunters who found themselves in a life-and-death struggle for survival. The storm took its toll, killing forty-nine in Minnesota and 150 nationwide.

Chapter 64
PLANNING A NEW PROJECT

Tom's Repair, Litomysl MN, USA. Tues, June. 30, 1942

It's ten years since Thomas Koupil lost his business in Owatonna. It's nine years since Zuba's donation helped save Paul's life. Thomas has opened Tom's Repair, a blacksmith and repair shop in Litomysl, MN. He sharpened plow lathes and mended horses' harnesses. Zuba joined him to repair autos, trucks, and tractors. Hanzi oversaw oil changes and pick up and delivery.

Paul regained his strength after his operation, and now at age 23, he works daily in his father's repair shop. Today, Zuba and Paul have their heads together and plan to convert an old Mack flatbed truck into a delivery truck.

"Guess what, Zuba! We could pull a tractor or car up on it." Paul said.

"How?"

"If we could tilt the front of the truck bed up, winch the tractor up on the bed, lower the truck bed down, and off we go."

"Tilt it up? We have -- crank on a cable hoist."

"No cranking, we could use a Saint Paul hydraulic hoist, invented by Gar Wood up in Saint Paul."

Figure 663 The Wood Hoist Ad

"Me never heared -- of one of those. -- How you do dat?" Zuba said.

Paul laid out a large sheet of paper and drew the layout of the delivery truck.

Zuba watched, "It maybe work. -- Be strong enough?"

"Should be, the first hoist that Gar Wood built was to dump coal trucks, and that was heavier than a tractor."

"Where -- to pick up a -- hy -- raw -- lic hoist?"

"We'll have to buy it."

"Me bet they spendy, -- maybe we fix up with cable hoist. -- A couple in the junk pile -- behind shop. Make a good one -- out of two."

"They aren't safe; this is faster. I'll talk to Dad and see if we can afford it."

Rolling up the drawing, Paul left for his dad's crowded little office. When passing the lunchroom, he glanced at a revealing pinup calendar on the wall. *I should be more serious with Irene Larson. She kisses nice, and we really steamed up the windows in Dad's old 1930 Chevy last spring. I might do that.* He entered the office as his father rummaged through a file cabinet. Thomas looked up over his reading glasses at Paul. "So, do you two mechanical geniuses have the delivery truck figured out?" he said, smiling.

"Yep, here's the drawing!" Paul said, as he picked up a pile of papers from the desk and set them on a stack of car magazines on the floor.

"This better be good," Thomas laughed, "I just sorted that pile out."

"Oh, it's good, trust me," Paul said enthusiastically, rolling out the drawing.

"Hmm, I see a bunch of ant tracks."

"Here, I'll explain it." Paul then detailed how to build the delivery truck. "We have to buy a Saint Paul hoist, we have the truck and Zuba, and I will install it. What do you say, Dad?"

"Buy a Saint Paul hydraulic hoist? What's the cost?"

"About $500, I think."

"Wheeeeew...," Thomas whistled. "Well, times have picked up, but $500 is a bunch of money!"

"Well, we could buy a used hoist. They build them in Saint Paul. Or you can talk to Mr. Gar Wood about a dealership." Paul said.

Paul continued. "We could mount the hoist on the farm trucks and wagons, too, for dumping grain. Make extra money that way."

"Did you say Gar Wood?" Thomas said.

"Yes."

"I met a Gar Wood when I was selling Mac trucks on the Iron Range. He was selling Model N Fords. We had a drink together in a Duluth bar. I wonder if he's the same man."

The door to the garage swung open abruptly, and Marta, Paul's mother, limped in. As she approached, her crutches echoed a Tac, Tac, Tac, as they hammered on the cement floor. Polio was a cruel taskmaster; it doesn't care who you are when it attacks. A grim expression painted her pale face, not her usual grimness but much darker. Her flour sack dress hung limply on her thin frame, and she held an unopened letter in her shaking, twisted hand.

"I'm afraid to open this," she said, handing the letter to Paul.

Paul looked it over and saw that the return address, 'Selective Service, Washington, DC.'

He opened the letter and read it. "I'm 1A; I'll be in the army soon."

"Oh, God, No!" Marta sobbed. Thomas stood up and put his arms around Marta.

"It was your damn idea that he goes register at that damn draft board," Marta said, pounding her fists on Thomas's chest.

"There was no choice. Roosevelt made it a law, made last September."

"I don't care about politics and that damn Roosevelt. He is our only son! Will they take him?"

Thomas shook his head and spoke. "I'm afraid so. I don't like it any better than you. But Hitler has to be stopped. Without a shot, he grabbed our Czechoslovakia, and then took Poland, Denmark, Norway, France, Holland, and Belgium. He wants the whole damn world. God knows who he will attack next."

"Let him have it. It doesn't concern us!" Marta wailed convulsively.

"It's OK, Mom," Paul said, trying to console her.

"No, it's not! It will never be OK if I lose you!" Marta said as she hobbled, crying from the office.

Thomas took a deep sigh and wrapped his arms around Paul. "You know how upset your mother gets. I'm sorry you have to go."

Paul reread the draft notice, drew a heavy breath, and said, "It's OK, Dad. I'd thought about this for a long time. I'd rather be in the Air Force. If I can land a mechanic's job fixing airplanes, that's what I want to do."

"Whatever you do, son, I'm proud of you." Thomas shook his hand, stopped for a moment, and grabbed Paul holding him in a firm embrace.

Paul walked returned to Zuba. "Maybe Dad can't do the truck thing; I guess it doesn't matter now."

Zuba stood puzzled, with his mouth open, "What happened? I heard your -- mother yelling?"

"I'm drafted!"

"What drafted?"

"The government says I go to help out the army."

"It's that -- Hitler guy, ain't it?"

"Ya, nobody can stop him."

"So, the government -- thinks you can do it?"

"Well, I and a whole bunch of other fellas might."

<p style="text-align:center">~~~~~~</p>

Chapter 65

THE OPPRESSION

Litomysl, Czechoslovakia. Sat, August 1, 1942.

For an entire month, the streets of Litomysl were alive with German troops and the Czech police. An SS officer or a Geheime Staatspolizei (Gestapo agent) led each squad of police. They were ruthless after the Prague assassination of SS-Obergruppenführer and General of Police, Reinhard Heydrich. They pounded on door after door, paying particular attention to the Roma section of town, ordering every Roma to register by Sunday, August 2nd.

<p style="text-align:center">~~~~~~</p>

There was an early morning knock on Eliska's apartment door. "Open up for the police!"

Eliska yelled to Andela, "Pull your gold cross out of your blouse and let it hang." Eliska pulled her gold cross from her blouse and opened the door. In her free hand, she held her faithful dagger behind her back. A Gestapo agent, backed by three police officers, stood before her with rifles at the ready. "Are you the manager of this building?"

"Yes, what do you want?"

Even though it was 80 degrees out, the thin, expressionless man wore a long, black, felt overcoat. "Good morning, I am Bertham Egger. All gypsies are to register by sundown tomorrow." He smiled and continued, "It's important we contact any gypsies living here. This is for everybody's protection. Are any gypsies living here?"

"I don't think so."

"Let's see your records!"

"Yes, of course."

Eliska slipped the dagger back into its hiding place in her waistband and opened the door wide.

Egger entered, accompanied by two of the police. The third policeman stood guard outside in the hallway.

Eliska brought the rental list out and handed it to Egger. "See, we have Havelecek, Dolan, Hruska, and Matesek. My name is Eliska Palzekova, and this is my daughter Andela."

He slid his finger down the rental list carefully. Raising his head, he looked over his glasses. "Everybody working?"

"Oh yes, all of them, they pay their rent, on time too. Excellent Czech tenants!"

"Any homosexuals?"

"They have wives, other than that; I don't notice. I just collect the rent."

"Any Communists?"

"I don't talk politics with them. Just collect the rent."

"Any Jews?"

"Mostly Catholic. But I just collect the rent."

"Not much better. You don't know if they are Jews?"

"I don't talk religion with them either. Just…"

Egger interrupted, "Just collect the rent. I know!" He inspected the list over again, prolonging the suspense, taking all the time in the world. A tactic he had learned in the training school six months earlier in Germany. *The longer you prolong a visit, the more nervous they become.* He took out his black notebook and wrote in it. *Make sure you detail everything.*

Eliska bit the inside of her tongue, suppressing her nervousness.

Egger directed his attention to Eliska and peered at her intently. "What about you?"

"What about me?"

Figure 73a, Pavel, the Siberian Cat

"You're a gypsy, aren't you?" As Egger said that Eliska's black Siberian cat, Pavel, jumped off the couch and rubbed against Egger's leg. Egger reached down, picked up, and stroked the cat. "Must smell my cats. I love Siberian cats."

"He's a good mouser. Showed up on our doorstep one day. I named him after the son I lost." Eliska said.

Egger stroked the cat slowly, then looking over the cat at Eliska, he asked, "What gypsy tribe do you belong to?"

When Egger said that Eliska remembered her father's advice. *If you must lie to protect your loved ones, do it with gusto and keep as close to the truth as possible. Remember, it takes ten lies to cover up one.*

"Again, I ask you, are you a gypsy?" Egger demanded.

Eliska squarely faced the little man. She put her hands on her hips, and looking him straight in his bespectacled eyes, she blustered. "You accuse me of being a lazy gypsy? You better clean your dirty little glasses!"

Eliska went on, "I have a husband, fighting God knows what and in God knows where. We're doing the best we can to support the cause. How dare you accuse me of being a gypsy! Look again! Do you see a damn gypsy?" Eliska raised her head high and glared at him.

The indignant outburst took Egger by surprise; he wasn't used to that from the people he intimidated. He studied Eliska and then blonde, blue-eyed Andela. His eyes rested on their gold crosses, reflecting the sunlight streaming through the window.

"I see you are loyal German subjects. Please forgive me. I did not mean to insult you with your husband away at war. Not on the Russian front, I hope?"

"No, the last we heard, he was in Poland."

"Aw, guarding those pesky Poles. It should be a safer duty, so don't worry."

"Thank you, that makes me feel better." Eliska escorted him to the door. "Good day to you."

Egger gently placed Pavil on the floor, tipped his hat, and left. When he was out of sight, he stopped and wrote several notations in his notebook.

Eliska closed the door, slumped on a chair by the kitchen table, and rubbed her cold and shaking hands.

Eliska wiped the blood from her mouth after biting her tongue. She fingered her cross, scrutinizing it. "Andela, I don't know what these crosses mean to the Nazis, but from now on, we wear them on the outside of our blouses, understand?"

Andela placed a shawl over her mother's shoulders. "Yes, Mama, it might be the engraving on the cross," Andela said, examining the cross. "Where did this cross come from?"

"My grandmother from India gave it to me when I was a little girl," Eliska said, trembling. "I gave mine to your Papa; Zuba made replicas for me and you and the baby that died."

Even in the heat of August, the icy winds of oppressive fear chill the blood. Shivering is unavoidable as apprehension infects the mind.

~~~~~~

Chapter 66

THE ACCIDENT

Tom's Repair, Litomysl MN, USA, Mon, Aug 17, 1942

Paul arrived early. In the yard, the sun had burned bare spots in the parched grass. Sparrows played in the water tank outside Tom's Repair shop as if the rain were on a permanent vacation. The tank was a courtesy to the customers who still used horses to get around. It was already so hot that the squirrels were walking with their tails fanning themselves. Zuba and Hanzi were in the shop since early morning, working on a 1939 Chevy.

"What'cha doing, Zuba?" Paul shouted, struggling to get Zuba's attention over the roar of the Chevy engine.

"Gotta -- fix timing -- before it -- gets hot."

"I'm showing him how," Hanzi chimed in.

"Are we working on the hoist?" Paul inquired.

"Ya -- soon -- this -- done."

Zuba finished the timing and shut the car off.

"That does it. -- Make -- Ole Larson happy -- he grouchy man!"
~~~~~~

"You would be too if you were the only Norwegian-Lutheran in a community of Czech Catholics," Paul laughed. "His daughter Irene is friendly, though."

"I noticed you -- making cow eyes -- at her," Zuba chided him.

"Ya, she's got her hooks set for you, I see that," Hanzi boosted. "Women are my specialty. I've studied the matter thoroughly. Without getting hooked, that is. Well, I almost got hooked, but....... Beda........" Hanzi turned away and looked out the window.

"Irene is very nice, but it won't go anywhere. She's Lutheran, and I'm Catholic, and the two don't mix too well." Paul said.

"Me Czech, and my Eliska is Roma. -- That old, gray-haired, curly windbag is her brother. Our families weren't -- pleased with us getting together."

"My dad was furious; I tell you that. I didn't care for him much either. He's all right, just talks too much now," Hanzi filled in.

"Love -- a tight harness once -- hooked into it. We had -- our sweet, -- little -- Andela -- and --," Zuba couldn't continue. The lump in his throat choked him up. He pulled the grease rag out of his back pocket, took off his glasses, and wiped his eyes. "-- me think -- a -- gnat in -- eye. Mighty thick, -- this time of the year."

Hanzi turned away and looked at the ceiling. Paul understood and averted his eyes. "They sure fly into your eyes. I'll start on the hoist."

Hanzi and Paul strolled over to a table and examined the hoist plans. Next to the table, the delivery truck stood with the flat truck bed tilted up in the air, propped up in that position by two stout wooden poles. Today was installation day for the Saint Paul hoist.

Wood was so enthusiastic about the project that he sold the hoist at less than dealer cost and appointed Tom's Repair as the Southern Minnesota dealer. This truck was to be a farmer's demo model.

Paul and Hanzi studied the plans as Irene Larson, a cute girl with a blonde ponytail, entered the garage. Fair-skinned, Irene had blue eyes, with freckles caressing her nose. She was slim of build, with just a distant promise of breasts.

"Good morning honey, what are you doing here?" Paul said.

"Well, it's cool this morning -- I thought -- you and --." She stopped short. Her usual jovial mood when she was with Paul was absent. She glanced over at Zuba and Hanzi and back to Paul and whispered, "Can we talk outside? Please."

"Sure, honey, what's the matter?"

Outside, they stood in the shade, under a willow tree, on the south side of the shop. Paul put his arm around her shoulder, "Tell me what's wrong."

"Paul, Oh Paul," she stammered, "I think I'm pregnant!"

Paul rocked back against the tree. "Pregnant? Are you sure?"

"Yes, I missed two of my monthly visits."

"Oh," Paul was silent before replying. "Well, we talked about getting married, but I don't think your dad approves of me." Paul pondered, then slapped the top of his head with his hand. "OH, MY GOD! I'm leaving for the Air Force in December."

"Yes, that's why I am worried," Irene sobbed. Paul pulled her tight as she cried on his chest.

"What are we to do?" Irene said.

Paul thought for a moment. "I'll come over this evening and talk to your dad. Can you make it home by yourself?"

"Yes."

Zuba had finished the Chevy and started on the hoist as Paul re-entered the shop.

"Bout time you got back," Hanzi said. "Did that cute little gal say anything important, or did she run her fingers through your long black hair? I bet her hand slipped off with all that goo you have on it. What kind of hairdo is that? Everything swept together in the back! I bet a duck is flying around without its butt!"

When Paul didn't respond to his teasing, Hanzi made a pompous stand with hands on his hips, and then, in his most demanding, 'I'm the boss' voice, he declared. "Lots of things to finish by tonight. Move it. I'll be the manager."

Paul didn't answer; he stared blankly off into space.

Hanzi piped up, "He's lovesick! Had it several times myself, I can tell you. Boy, oh boy, did I ever. First, there was Helena, then Marina, then there was Kloes, and don't forget, ... poor sweet Beda Blaha. ...... We were to be married; you know.

Hanzi continued, "every time my feet get cold, I think of her." Hanzi stammered and suddenly had to blow his nose in his handkerchief. "What a wonderful assortment of women, and Beda was the best! If ever you love till it hurts, you will never forget it."

Hanzi was quiet for a spell and finally regained his composure. He put his hands on his hips and said matter-in-factly. "Lovesickness is a tough disease to have. It sneaks up on you and smacks you. When you lose it, you wish to get smacked all over again. It's the water, I tell you. The best cure is a jug of wine, and it passes. Great cure! Just make sure that another pretty girl isn't sitting on your lap when you take the cure! You're infected again." Hanzi teased.

Zuba crawled under the frame of the delivery truck. He reached in to tighten the frame bolts of the hoist with a socket wrench. "Darn, -- wrong wrench, Paul -- get -- inch and half socket!" Zuba called from under the truck.

Paul didn't answer. Hanzi poked him, "The inch and half socket?"

Paul looked up, startled. "What?"

"Do you have an inch and a half socket?"

"Oh yeah, it's here someplace," Paul said, rummaging through the tool drawer. "Oh damn, I left it in Dad's garage at home. I'll run and get it."

"No way, your head -- in clouds -- you -- be gone -- all day," Zuba yelled from under the truck. "Hanzi -- get it!"

Zuba crawled out from under the truck. "Let's attach -- hoist to the frame -- while waiting."

Zuba was on the left side of the frame, and Paul on the right, with the flatbed truck between them.

The front-end of the massive steel delivery bed tilted up, at a 45-degree angle, up over the truck frame, and they attached the back end to the rear of the frame and made it swivel. Heavy-duty wooden poles propped against the upright front-end of the bed, kept the bed from falling.

Zuba grabbed the hoist, "I'll hold the hoist while you put in the bolts."

Zuba held the hoist as Paul reached in to install the bolts.

"Hurry -- this thing is -- heavy!" Zuba snorted.

"Hard to reach that bolt," Paul replied, as he climbed up on the frame and laid across it to insert the bolt. Straining to reach the bolt, he pushed against one of the supporting poles, kicking it out of position. The pole fell on his head, knocking him unconscious. He lay spread across the truck frame.

Figure 73b Raised truck bed

"Watch -- out!" Zuba cried, but too late. The truck bed shuddered above Paul; the last support pole broke, and the huge bed creaked as it swung down. Zuba raised his arms high, stopping the bed, barely inches above Paul. The weight of the bed was tremendous, but Zuba stood there, a human stone pillar. *Paul! Wake up, please wake up. Can't bear this.*

The minutes ticked by slowly. Zuba's arms ached, pain seared down his back, into his legs and ankles. Sweat soaked his shirt to the waist, arms trembled, and still, he waited. *Please God, help me! No can bear it no longer.*

Hanzi limped into the garage. "Here's that inch and half socket! It was full of grease, had to wash it off, then I had to find the rachet and a breaker bar. Carl Slovance wanted me to grease his truck, but I came right here." Hanzi stopped jabbering and said to Zuba. "Why are you holding the box up? You got the hoist working!? Great job!

"Pull -- Paul out!" Zuba moaned.

Hanzi stood dumbfounded. "Where's Paul? What can I do?

"Other -- side -- is Paul. -- Pull out! -- me -- hold no longer!" Hanzi hobbled to the other side of the frame and strained to pull the much larger Paul to safety but without success.

"Pull -- out quick!' Zuba moaned.

Hanzi prayed to Saint Sara, and, with a mighty lunge, he pulled the unconscious Paul safely out onto the floor.

Zuba still held the delivery bed. *How me let it down and not get hit?* Hanzi slid beside him and held his arms up to the truck box.

"No, get -- away," Zuba yelled as he jumped back and let the truck bed fall, but Zuba, never too agile, could not escape. The delivery box collapsed, with a crash, striking Zuba on the head. He collapsed to the floor like a rag doll and lay there bleeding from the mouth.

Figure 74. 1936 Cadillac Ambulance

Hanzi hovered over Zuba. "Zuba, are you? My God! Are you dead? Oh, God, what to do? What to do?" As Hanzi knelt next to Zuba, Thomas walked in. Hanzi cried out, "We need a doctor quick." Thomas took one look, rushed to his office, and called an ambulance.

The ambulance arrived twenty minutes later. Paul was conscious, but Zuba was still unconscious on the floor. Hanzi placed a blanket over him and kneeled at his side. "Zuba, stay with us, don't go, please hang on." The ambulance attendants gently pulled Hanzi away and loaded Zuba into the ambulance. With sirens blaring, they raced for the Owatonna Hospital. ~~~~~~

Chapter 67

WAITING

Hospital, Owatonna, MN, USA, Tues, Aug 18, 1942,

The hospital in Owatonna was in the center of town, surrounded by older homes with neatly groomed lawns shaded by stately oak trees. The two-story hospital was a sizeable wooden building with adjacent small outbuildings that housed the ambulance service.

Thomas Koupil read and paced in the waiting room throughout the night. The doctors treated Paul, discharged him, and Hanzi drove him home. A headache was Paul's primary complaint.

Zuba, however, lay in a coma. The nurse checked him every 15 minutes. When they did, they noted the rapid eye movement under his eyelids. "That's unusual in a coma," the nurse wrote on her chart. Zuba heard everything as he lay imprisoned in the hospital bed, unable to speak or move. *People talking. Unable to respond. Drifting in and out of dreams. Sounds from the room and dreams mixed in a bewildering kaleidoscope. Visions of Eliska and little Andela intertwined with the sounds of the nurses attending to him. Eliska appeared to him. "You come home; we need you. Andela is growing up without a father. She needs you. I need you. Wake up and come home. I love you."*

Doctor Sullivan, a brain surgeon from the Rochester Mayo Clinic, arrived at midnight. He examined Zuba and assembled an operating team for immediate surgery. The surgery started at 2 AM. Before that, Father Nemac came and administered the last rites to Zuba, then Father spent time with Thomas, finally leaving as the morning sun peeked in.

For two hours, Thomas stared at the same Life magazine. It didn't improve his mood, as the magazine's pictures of army tanks were a constant reminder that a war was going on, and his only son was soon to join that war. In a way, Thomas was glad that Marta hadn't lived to see their son board the train to the boot camp. Her bout with polio not only crippled her legs but impaired her in other ways.

Even on crutches, Marta lashed out at Thomas and those around her.

She condemned Thomas for Paul leaving, losing the business, not having more children, and any other offenses, she imagined. Her rantings, night and day, had left him drained. Polio twisted Marta's demented mind along with her legs. Thomas sighed.... *She is at peace, ... I'm ashamed to say; I am too. I thought the troubles were over, but again, I've wrong.*

Thomas shook off the foreboding feelings. He stood up, stretched, yawned, and walked. Pacing the floor, he peeked through the slats of the Venetian window blind to squint out at the bright late summer sun. Again, he counted each slat, thirty-six to be exact, and each window had the same amount. Thomas bent over and touched the floor, then again started for the nurse's desk. The nurse saw him coming and shook her head; she already knew what he would ask. Her patient answer to his unspoken question was, "No news."

Finally, at ten AM, Dr. Sullivan left surgery. He walked over to Thomas, who was sitting with his head down, face in his hands. "Mr. Koupil?"

Thomas jumped up with a start. "Yes, I'm Thomas Koupil!"

"Zuba is out of surgery. It was touch and go. We lost him twice, but we revived him. Luckily, he has a stout heart."

Thomas asked. "Will he live?" *I know how stout that man's heart is.*

"We'll see in a week or two. He's in a coma, which is fine. It may be his body's way of healing. We drained blood from the brain and stopped the bleeding. He also has internal injuries and broken vertebrae in his back. He won't work again and will be lucky to walk."

"We just have to wait?"

"Yes, and pray," the doctor replied thoughtfully. "How heavy was the truck bed that he held up?"

"Well, I figure it was 1500 pounds. He held it for at least ten minutes."

"Amazing what the body does when it has to."

"He saved my son's life."

The doctor shook his head in amazement. "How old is he?"

"He was forty-four on April Fool's Day. We used to tease him," Thomas replied. "But I can tell you this much," tears welled up in Thomas's eyes... "that man is no fool! He couldn't talk too good, but he is the best man I ever met."

"I hope he's not too old to survive this." The doctor yawned and walked away, rubbing his neck. ~~~~~~

Chapter 68

NIGHT SWEATS

Apartment House, Litomysl Czechoslovakia Tues, Aug 18, 1942,

Eliska slept the whole night fitfully. *Her dreams were usually pleasant dreams of Zuba. But not last night. He called to her over and over, somewhere lost and in pain. She called back to him, "Come home. We need you. Andela is growing up without a father. She needs you. I need you. Wake up and come home. I love you."*

At four in the morning, Eliska woke with a start. Her nightgown was soaked with night sweats as she sat on the edge of the bed, shaking. Never had her dreams been so vivid or hopeless. Arising, she entered the kitchen and sat at the table, nursing a cup of tea and praying for? ... for what? She didn't know. A storm of emotions saturated her mind. *Since I lost Zuba, I've slid from crisis to crisis. Now, I have settled in at the Chateau and have a bit of a normal life.*

If normal is living under the heel of the Nazis, always worried that I might say the wrong thing. Maybe they find out we're Roma, or I might make the wrong person mad or suspicious of us.

So much pressure. Is it any wonder that my hair is gray? Wrinkles appear to frame my dimming eyesight. The joy in my heart washes away. I hang on to straws while a whirlpool sucks me down.

Eliska put her head on the table and sobbed. Her chest heaved, and a low moan escaped her lips.

~~~~~~

</div>
~~~~~~

Chapter 69

THE WEDDING

Holy Trinity, Church, Litomysl MN, USA. Sat, Oct 10, 1942.

The Holy Trinity Catholic Church dated back to 1878, when settlers in the Litomysl community built their first church. In 1940-41, they built the second stone structure. It was one of the largest stone churches in the nation. The members of the parish brought over six hundred loads of rock from their fields to create it.

Figure 75 Inside Holy Trinity Church

The bells pealed gaily as the bride and groom endured a shower of barley as they skipped down the steps of the Holy Trinity Catholic Church.

Paul, resplendent in his new suit, had his black hair slicked back, ending in his best imitation of a duck. His long legs allowed him to take two steps at a time as he descended the stairs, proudly waving to the crowd. Irene, his new bride, giggled as she clung to his hand, trying to keep up. Her freckles sparkled; her blonde hair glowed. Her growing motherhood never showed, secreted under a voluminous, off-white wedding dress. It was a tense affair with Irene Larson's Lutheran parents when the young couple informed them of their desire to marry. Angry words followed by lots of hand-wringing.

The impasse resolved when Irene told her parents of her impending motherhood. Sometimes a fight over religion is settled by the logic that a family needs to be together. Live in the same house, sleep in the same bed, and worship at the same altar.

Paul reasoned with the Larsons, "Isn't God everywhere? Does He care what we say to Him in love? Does He not recognize that each of his creatures cries out to Him in their unique voice, using their own tongue? Not just repeating words placed in their mouths, by a preacher?"

The Larsons had found some comfort from his sincere expression of faith and reluctantly gave their permission.

Figure 76 Entrance to Holy Trinity Church

Ole Larson and his wife Olga were the next in the receiving line. Feigned happiness covered the uncomfortable concern in their hearts as the couple approached. Olga hugged the bride tightly and then Paul, her new son-in-law. Ole hugged his daughter first and shook Paul's hand. Leaning over, he whispered in Paul's ear. "Treat her right, son, or you answer to me!"

Thomas Koupil was next. He hugged them. Tears welled in his eyes as he wished them well. "I wish Marta was here to see this."

Imitating his favorite movie star, Tyrone Power, Hanzi was resplendent in a freshly dry-cleaned suit. He had dyed his hair black, then combed it into a tangle of slick and shiny curls, smelling of his favorite rose pompadour gel. His little mustache tweaked to the perfect curl on each side, all firmly held together by the latest mustache wax. Stepping forward, he slapped Paul on the back, and kissed the bride.

"You're next, Hanzi," Paul teased. "Should I have Irene toss you the wedding bouquet?"

"Nah, throw it to someone that needs it," Hanzi said, shining his fingernails on his shirt. "I have my hands full, avoiding the marriage altar. I sure don't want the girls getting the idea that I am on the market."

"Your time will come," Paul laughed.

"Why buy the cow when the milk is free?" Hanzi smarted off, laughing. Irene blushed and urged Paul on through the receiving line. Paul turned back to Hanzi. "How is Zuba this morning?"

Hanzi's flippant attitude changed to a somber mood. He had spent the early morning at the hospital as he has done every morning since the accident. "Well, he's breathing better, still in the coma."

"I hope he comes to before I leave for basic training," Paul replied.

Hanzi swallowed hard, "Ya... me... too."

<p style="text-align:center">~~~~~~</p>

Chapter 70

HATE AND DESPAIR

Litomysl Czechoslovakia, Thurs, Dec 31, 1942

After the assassination of SS-Obergruppenführer General of Police, Reinhard Heydrich, the revenge of the Nazis started with martial law. Then, on June 10th, 1942, the Nazis razed the village of Lidice to the ground, and they shot its male inhabitants. The Nazi regime suspected that this village harbored local Resistance partisans and accused them of aiding Operation Anthropoid team members.

On June 24, 1942, Gestapo agents found a radio transmitter in Lezaky (35 miles north of Litomysl). It belonged to Operation Silver A, the group that had assassinated Heydrich. The SS troops and policemen surrounded Lezaky, removed the inhabitants, and reduced the village to rubble. They shot thirty-three villagers (both men and women).

~~~~~~

As the days crawled by, the weight of the occupation pressed down like a heavy boulder, crushing Czechoslovakia, squeezing the spirit out of the country. Fear hung in the air, like a stinking wet blanket from a dog kennel. Coffee shops, where men sat, laughed, and bantered, today echoed with forlorn emptiness. Wives, hanging wash, no longer laughed and talked to their neighbors across the back fence. Parents no longer talked at the supper table, fearing that their children might say something in school, bringing a late-night knock on their door. As the occupation wore on, there was more sickness, colds, and flu. Fear and apprehension infected the entire Czech body.

The policy of "Protective Custody" explained away the disappearance of many next-door neighbors. By a strange twist of morality or a deft way of avoiding responsibility, the Gestapo had the prisoner sign his own 'Schutzhaftbefehl,' (an order declaring that the person requested imprisonment). This, of course, wasn't before the prisoner had been "properly interrogated."
~~~~~~

The Nazis had honed the mantra of not trusting anyone to perfection. Developed in Germany and then brutally put it into action on helpless Czechoslovakia. The policy descended full fury, on young and old alike.

Not even the spineless politicians were immune. But it fell the hardest on the lower class. They were used to harsh conditions and better candidates for the work (slave) camps.

Friends watched friends. Neighbors watched neighbors. Children watched their parents. Workers watched other workers. Students watched teachers. A wrong word, a raised eyebrow at the wrong time, could mean condemnation. With the fearful help of so many, the small band of Gestapo agents and cooperating local police could hold the population in check.

A never-ending storm of hateful fear crept across the hapless country. Churches, once the center of the community, now stood empty. Prayers were silent, only said deep in one's heart. Confession, once a staple of Catholic life, was obsolete. Faithful Catholics feared that the seal of confession could be breached. The only confession available was to confess your neighbor to death. Love starved and died like a delicate petunia uprooted and dropped deep in the Sahara Desert.

<center>~~~~~~</center>

The last day of 1942 dawned with a thick white fog engulfing Litomysl, Czechoslovakia, painting everything the fog touched with white frozen crystals. The sun rose, trees sparkled, the fog burned away. Like a stage curtain opening, a royal blue sky framed the frozen landscape in a wonderland picture. A Currier and Ives white lithograph! God was encouraging his people with a glimpse of his promises.

Figure 76a Frosty Morning

Andela sat at the kitchen table. Her blonde hair hung straight; the redness of her eyes sets off her pale face. She stirred her porridge listlessly. She has been despondent since her latest love interest, Dalek, was killed in the massacre in Lezaky. There had been talk of marriage, and Eliska had tried her best to allow Andela to meet him when he was in Litomysl.

Eliska put on her oversized woolen coat and wrapped her head in her shawl. "Hurry, Andela, tonight's New Year's Eve. We'll be busy all day preparing. Even Aunt Kizzy is coming in to help. You run the poor kitchen today. More people turn up here every day."

Andela didn't answer; she continued stirring her porridge, staring at the swirls. Eliska, from behind her, bent down and encircled her with her arms and hugged her. "Honey, it's hard to lose someone you love. It hurts and may never stop hurting. It gets better. You will find someone else, but you always have sweet memories of your first love."

"Like you and Papa, Mama?" Andela sobbed.

The words slammed into Eliska, dredging up painful memories, memories lovingly tucked away deep in Eliska's heart. Her eyes filled with tears as she cleared her throat, exhaled, and murmured, "Just like Papa and me." Eliska thought about the years gone by. *There could have been others, but the Roma men are gone, and gadje men are uncomfortable with a Roma... Well, there's Mr. Slovak. He calls here, every week, when he trims the shrubs or scoops the snow. Nice man, a widower, he would be good to Andela and me... He asked me out to eat... It would be easier... I should? ... But Zuba's not dead! ... I couldn't be with another man when... I know he is...? Is he still alive? ... Why don't you come home? ... Why are you doing this to me? ... You could have come back last July for our twenty-fifth wedding anniversary!*

A hard knock on the door shattered Eliska's thoughts.

"Open the door; this is the Gestapo!"

Eliska brushed Andela's hair, then reached down, and pulled Andela's gold cross out of her blouse, and then pulled her cross out.

The second knock was more insistent.

"This is Bertham Egger. Open up; I know you are home!"

Eliska opened the door as she slipped her dagger in her waistband. "Hello, Mr. Egger. How are you?

Bertham Egger, backed by five Czech police officers, burst into the room. "We're searching the houses for the fools that dare defy the Third Reich. Have you seen any strange activity?"

"No. Why ask me?" Eliska said.

"I'm sure a loyal supporter such as you wouldn't harbor any Resistance fighter. But I have my orders; to search every building."

"Oh, by all means, search away. I'll cooperate fully."

"Thank You, Madam," Egger replied. He pointed to the bedroom and ordered the police to search there. He pulled out a black notebook. "Have you heard from your husband?"

"No, no word. I'm worried."

Egger carefully examined his notes, then looked up to Eliska. He smiled, but his eyes were as cold as the ice on the Lucina River. "You said he's stationed in Belgium, didn't you?"

Pavel, the cat, jumped off the couch and rubbed against Egger's leg. Egger smiled, picked him up, and stroked him. "You want a little attention, don't you? These Siberians need a lot of petting. You should do more of it." Egger's mood then changed, and again his stare dug into Eliska. "Belgium, you said, is that correct?"

Eliska felt the penetrating, lifeless stare reach deep inside her, searching every nook and cranny of her soul, searching for the slightest discrepancy, for a catch in her voice, for anything he could use to trip her up. Her face turned pale as she remembered what she had said earlier. "Oh, ah, no, Poland."

"Are you sure? I wrote Belgium in my book."

"No, you must have me confused with someone else."

"What unit is he within Poland?"

Eliska again searched her memory. "I don't know. Top secret, I guess. I suppose it's better if I don't know,"

Eliska sighed. "Wouldn't want to let the enemy find out where our troops are stationed. Don't you agree?" *Thank God for my father's advice.*

Egger checked his notes, then peered at Eliska with an all-knowing stare.

"Well, excuse me, I have to go to work," Eliska added. "I have a big party tonight, and I expect many of your German officers to be there. I must not be late. Will you be there?"

Egger set Pavil down and handed Eliska his card. "No," he replied curtly. "Remember, if you harbor the enemy, it's the firing squad. For the whole family! Don't get caught in the middle. If you see something strange, call me at this number."

"Oh, yes!" Eliska replied. *You are the strangest thing I've seen in a long time.*

Egger wrote more notes in his black book and left.

~~~~~~

Later That Same Day

The Chateau, Litomysl Czechoslovakia

The kitchen at the Chateau buzzed with activity. The gaiety of the decorated cakes lined up in a neat row across the counter belied the somberness of the occasion. The cooks prepared large bowls of sauerkraut, while five different pork cuts and sausages waited for the ovens. The wine steward tapped a keg of beer and brought out several cases of wine and a dozen cases of German schnapps. Karel hurried from workstation to workstation fussing about anything that came to mind.

Eliska was preparing a frosting at the cake station as Kizzy came up to her, "Have you heard the order?"

"What order? The Germans need us to cook something special, I suppose, like always."

"They call it the 'Preventive Fight against Criminality.' They say it solves the gypsy problem."

"What gypsy problem, what do you mean?"
~~~~~~

Kizzy pulled out a newspaper from under the counter and read it aloud. "Gypsies are to go to work camps at Lety, Hodonin, and Auschwitz."

"What will they do there?"

"Work, I guess. The Nazis need lots of slave labor to keep the war effort going. They take the whole family."

"Little kids too? They can't work much."

Kizzy shrugged her shoulders and replied fatalistically, "I suppose not. Who knows what they have in mind? The Germans always have something up their sleeves."

The afternoon went rapidly. German officers, with their wives, or girlfriends, arrived at six PM sharp. A German polka band was playing. Eliska's thoughts brought back images of her little family band of long ago. *A different world... We thought we had trouble, the Roma and gadje fought about who was the best... Small potatoes compared to now... Nazis are smart... They stir up old hatreds; then, they take over while we fight among ourselves.... They control every movement. Don't feel safe in our own homes.... Under constant worry, we might do something wrong to displease them.... We can't even sit on our front steps in the evening because of the curfew... Where is God in this?*

"Eliska, stop daydreaming!" Karel blurted out. "Are the cakes ready?"

"I finished the last one, Mr. Klimy."

Karel came close and examined the cake. "Great, and I told you, it's Karel, not Mr. Klimy. We are family!" he whispered.

"Yes, Mr.... er Karel. Should I cut the cakes?"

"Yes, get them ready to serve."

Eliska served the cakes as the rest of the staff took their break before cleaning up the kitchen. Kizzy fidgeted as she moved close to Eliska and whispered, "Eliska, follow me."

"What for? Why are you whispering?"

"Don't need the other staff to hear us. Some have German ears."

"They look like Czech ears to me!" Eliska laughed.

"Don't be smart!" Kizzy whispered curtly. She loudly said to Eliska, "I need your help to straighten up the storeroom." Then she waved to the other kitchen help. "Don't worry; we'll handle it! Relax and enjoy your break."

Eliska followed Kizzy across the lawn and entered an eerily quiet Chudý Kuchyně (poor kitchen). "I sent the staff home early," Kizzy said.

In a far, dark corner, on a wooden bench, sat an old bald man and a gray-haired woman. Two sacks rested at their feet. Threadbare coats hung on them, and a babushka covered the woman's head. The man had a tattered old wool cap pulled over his head.

"I was closing up when I found them. They came for the free food," Kizzy remarked,

"Get closer, Eliska." Kizzy grasped an apprehensive Eliska by the arm and pulled her closer.

In the dim light, it was hard to make out the faces, but when Eliska tiptoed closer, a nagging familiarity crept over her, then a wave of recognition swept her. "Oh, Saint Sara!" She cried as she rushed forward, "Mama! Papa!"

Florica stood up unsteadily and reached out to embrace her daughter. Tears streaked her cheeks. "Oh, my sweet Eliska, how I've missed you."

After the embrace, Florica nudged Bolda. "Here, I help you stand! Hug your daughter good! No more anger! This is family!" she ordered. Florica helped Bolda to his feet. She held on to him as she guided him over to Eliska. His legs were unsteady, but he spread his one, shaking arm wide to welcome his daughter into his arms.

"He don't talk too good, no more," Florica remarked. "He had a headache Christmas day, and the next day his arm don't work neither. Maybe eat too much at Christmas, but still no fix."

Eliska opened her arms wide and embraced both at once. When the embrace was over, Eliska said, "What are you doing here?"

"They come, take the Roma. There was fighting, but we hid till they gone. Tomorrow, they burn our houses."

"What about the twins?"

"Luca and Stevo joined the Resistance last May. In Poland."

"The Resistance? I thought the Roma wouldn't join the gadje in anything. We always try to make do. Run, not fight."

"Even a rabbit turns and bites when cornered," Florica observed. "Fear do strange things to people."

"Where are you to stay?"

"Don't know. I come, see Kizzy," Florica stammered. "She works where there's free food."

"Mama! It's cold! You can't stay outside!"

Florica shrugged her shoulders as she helped Bolda sit back down.

Bolda looked up dejectedly, "We... be OK. We... get by," he said through his drooping mouth.

Eliska glanced at Kizzy. What to do, etched their faces. Kizzy pondered, then spoke, "They could come with me, but the German's have their headquarters across the street. They would be caught."

Eliska thought for a moment, "You come with me. The Germans searched my apartment this morning; they won't be back for a while."

Just then, Karel entered, "I wondered where the two of you were?"

Kizzy introduced Karel to Bolda and Florica. "This is my husband, and this is my dear sister."

"What is going on?" Karel inquired. When Kizzy told him of what had happened, concern crossed Karel's face. "You realize what this means, don't you? If the Germans find them, we'll all be dead."

Kizzy was quiet, then she spoke deliberately. "You are harboring a Roma wife, A Roma niece, and a grandniece. How much deader can we be if they find Bolda and my sister?"

Karel considered what Kizzy had said. "You and that damn Roma logic." He pondered, then said, "All right, I'll help!" Then, in typical fashion, Karel laid out a plan on how to hide the Danka family. "This damn war can't go forever," he said. ~~~~~~

Chapter 71

BASIC TRAINING

Sheppard Air Base, Wichita Falls, Texas, USA Wed, Jan 14, 1943

Minnesota-born, Sgt. Palance, the drill sergeant, roared as he marched the troops across the vast drill field. "Hup! Two! Three! Four! Hup! Two! Three! Four! Quit your slacking! Get in step! Right turn, ho!... No. No. The other right, you stupid plowboys! How the hell are you gonna fight when you can't even walk together?... Koupil! Get your ass in step! You're bobbing like a fishing cork with a walleye on!"

They drilled from early morn, stumbled around the half-mile long drill field four times, endured an hour of calisthenics, and a ten-mile run, throughout drizzling rain.

The sergeant marched the soaked recruits into the open street, next to the drill field. "All right, you forgotten lumps of cow crap. Down the street on the double!" When they arrived in front of their wooden barracks, he shouted, "Trooooop Halt! Fallout to the barracks! Be back in five. Get ready for the rifle range!"

As Sgt. Palance waited, a staff car slowly inched along the road. It stopped, started, coughed, choked, quivered, and lurched ahead, then

Figure 67 Plymouth Staff Car

shuddered, stuttered, belched, and jerked to a halt next to Sgt. Palance. The driver got out, lifted the hood, and gazed anxiously at the maze of mechanical wonders sleeping within the engine compartment.

General Prochazka rolled down the window and stuck his chubby head out.

He blinked his eyes as the rain pelted him in the face. "Can you fix it, airman?"

The airman scratched his head and said, "I don't think so, sir. Don't know much about these damn things. Better get it to the motor pool."

"Hell's fire! I have to be at the briefing in ten minutes!"

Sgt Palance saluted smartly as he walked up, "Good morning, sir!"

"Good damn morning to you too, staff sergeant," the general said, returning the salute. "This wouldn't be a maintenance unit, would it? With fifty good mechanics?"

"No sir, just a bunch of plowboys, learning how to walk," the sergeant replied, as the airmen came running out of the barracks and formed up.

"All right, meatheads! Line up in three straight rows. And dress right an arm's length apart... Any of you men know anything about cars?" Sgt. Palance said as he surveyed the men.

"Hup," cried a voice from the back row.

"Front and center airman."

Paul Koupil stepped up to the front of the formation.

"Can you repair a car, Koupil?"

"I worked on cars in my dad's garage."

"Take a look at the general's car."

Paul went to the car, saluted the general smartly, and looked under the hood. He took out his handkerchief and wiped something. "Try it now," he said. The driver hit the starter button, sending the limousine to a quivering roar.

"Distributor got wet," Paul; said.

"Hot damn! You fixed it, son!" the general exclaimed as he stuck his head out the window. "What's your name?"

"Paul Koupil, sir."

"Thank you, Airman Koupil," the general replied. "Fall back in and ask the sergeant to come over here."

The sergeant ran up to the limousine. "Yes, Sir?"

"Sergeant, what can you tell me about the Koupil boy?" the general asked.

"Not much, sir. Marches like a turtle on a hot stove. Clumsy as hell."

General Prochazka laughed, "Good thing he's in the Air Force, isn't it? Anything else?"

"Well, sir, he'll probably get over it, but he's afraid of guns."

"Afraid of guns? Is he a conscientious objector?"

"No, sir, I don't believe he ever fired a gun before he enlisted. On the firing line, he holds his hands over his ears. I think the noise bothers him because he's a musician and afraid of hurting his ears."

"Have his records sent to me at headquarters, would you?"

"Yes, sir."

~~~~~~

A courier delivered a written summons to Paul, directing him to appear for an interview at the headquarters building. Nervously, Paul entered the building, walked to the master sergeant's desk, saluted him, and said, "Sir, Airman Koupil reporting."

The sergeant looked up from his paperwork. "How long have you been in the Air Force airman?"

"Two weeks, sir."

"I'm not a sir, you lunkhead. You call officers, sir. Understand? And no salute unless they are officers! The rest of us work for a living!"

"Yes, sir... ah... Yes, sergeant."

"That's better. Down the hall, the last door on your right is General Prochazka's office. Go there, knock first."

A clerk typed vigorously on a report as Paul entered the general's office. "Airman Koupil reporting as ordered."

"Go right in. The general is expecting you."

General Prochazka sat at his desk, finishing his breakfast. Bratwurst, eggs, and grits, with a dash of hot sauce, a taste he acquired while stationed in the South.

Paul came in the room and saluted, "Airman Koupil reporting, sir."

The general saluted back. "Glad you're here." He wiped his mouth with his napkin, "Damn, those are good, Koupil. Reminds me of my mother's cooking. I wish I could take that cook with me when we ship out."
~~~~~~

General Prochazka leaned back in his chair and rubbed his stomach. "You're Czech, aren't you?"

"Yes, sir. Grandparents immigrated here. Both my parents were born here."

"Same here," the general replied, letting out a slight burp. "Does your mother cook old country style?"

"I think so, sir."

"If I could just find a good Czech cook, I would put him on my staff," General Prochazka laughed. "You don't suppose she'd enlist, do you?"

"Hardly, sir, she passed away last year," Paul replied solemnly.

"Sorry to hear that, son. Do you speak any Czech?"

"Yes, sir, I picked up some from my father. Especially the swearing."

General Prochazka chuckled, "Then nothing you hear around here makes your ears burn?"

"No, sir, in the barracks, I add a few Czech sayings of my own, but the other men look at me cock-eyed. They don't understand the language. And the sayings don't translate too well into English."

General Prochazka chuckled again. "I know what you mean. When I get torqued, I fall back on my father's sayings. Confuses the hell out of my staff, but they can tell I'm mad, and they jump to."

Paul laughed, "My dad did the same thing around the repair shop. Drove the Norwegian help crazy."

General Prochazka's smile lit up his face to the far corners of his ears. Finally, he got to the point. "I hear you're a musician."

"Yes, sir, I play the tuba."

"You do? I need a tuba player in my regimental band. Are you interested?"

"Well, I wanted to work on airplane engines, sir."

"I can arrange that, Airman. The school is across the street. Also, I need a mechanic to keep my limo running. That would be your duties too."

"It's a heavy load, general. Band, school, and work on your car too. Not enough time for all that. I wouldn't know which to skip or which one to do."

"You seem to have a level head on your shoulders. Airman."

"Thank you, sir."

"Did you notice this star on my collar?"

"Yes, sir!"

"This star makes me a brigadier general. It means I make things happen. Don't you think I can arrange things for you to make this happen?"

"Well... yes, sir."

"Good, it's settled," General Prochazka rubbed his chunky hands together. "Finish your basic training, but you start in the band now. I'll make sure you have time for that."

General Prochazka pulled his desk drawer open. "Here, use these on the firing range." He handed Paul a set of earplugs. "I give a set to all of my musicians. Don't want to damage those ears, do we?"

"Thank you, sir."

"That's all, airman. I'll be in touch."

Paul saluted and left. The master sergeant came into the general's office. "Did you find yourself a tuba player, sir?"

General Prochazka nodded. "Yes, I did. He reminds me of my David."

"Have you heard any news about your son?"

"No, he was with Doolittle when they hit Tokyo. They flew into China and ditched the planes. With the Japanese all over China, I pray he escaped to the friendly Chinese."

The general was silent for a moment as he wiped the corner of his eye with his handkerchief, "Wait and pray, I guess. Being a general doesn't shelter your family." ~~~~~~.

Chapter 72

SMUGGLER'S ROOST

Litomysl, Czechoslovakia Easter Sunday, April 25th, 1943
The official doctrine of Hitler was to leave the churches alone. He feared that if he slammed down too hard on them, he would have a tough time keeping the population in line. He intended to replace the churches with his official religion, "Positive Christianity," as he quaintly called it.

Twenty-eight Protestant groups in Germany merged to form the National Reich Church in 1936. They elected a member of the Nazi party as Bishop of the Church and suspended non-Aryan ministers. Church members called themselves "German Christians," with the Swastika on their chests and the Cross in their hearts. It was a mix of paganism and Nazi doctrine while assimilating the Christian elements and gradually changing them.

Hitler officially declared his tolerance of religion, but he scattered nuggets of intolerance through his speeches and during private meetings. In his trusted henchmen's minds, he left no doubt that the churches, especially the Catholic Church, had to go. His henchmen saw it as their duty to eradicate any religion, not sanctioned by the state.

The Nazis killed the Jehovah's Witnesses in concentration camps because they wouldn't fight and refused to serve in the army. Next, they exterminated the Salvation Army, the Christian Saints, and the Seventh Day Adventists, along with any astrologers, healers, and fortune-tellers. These people did not have the more substantial power bases of the mainline religions. After the Nazis eliminated the smaller groups, they chipped away at the major denominations. The Catholic Church was now their immediate target.

Martin Bormann was the head of the Nazi Party Chancellery and the private secretary of Adolf Hitler. He was one of the most influential figures in the Third Reich and issued a secret decree to the regional party leaders of the Reich.

The order, as follows, was the true intentions of the Nazi regime toward the Christian churches.

"More and more, the people must be separated from the churches and their organs, the pastors. Just as the harmful influences of astrologers, seers, and other fakers, are eliminated and suppressed by the State, so must the possibility of church influence be totally removed. Not until this has happened does the State leadership have an influence on the individual citizens. Not until then, will the people, and Reich, be secure in their existence forever."

Alfred Rosenberg was the official Nazi philosopher and a proponent of "Positive Christianity." He planned the "extermination of the foreign Christian faiths imported into Germany." He wanted the Mein Kampf and the swastika to replace the Bible and the Christian cross.

~~~~~~

In Litomysl, the Germans watched the churches closely on Easter Sunday. Before the Germans came, over 60% of the Czech population was Catholic. Easter Sunday had always been a "standing room only" affair.

Only echoes filled the somber Exaltation Church this Easter Sunday, as Father Emilio said the Easter mass. Over the last few months, only a few brave, elderly parishioners had shown up, but they too had a habit of disappearing. So today, the empty pews wept a sad whisper of the joy of Easter.

The Nazis closed the Salesian mission school and took Sister Lucie to a re-education camp. She made the mistake of teaching that God's love was for all men, speaking out against the wrongs of the death and destruction caused by the Nazis.

Down the street, at the Chateau, the German officers commandeered the whole second floor. They used it as their quarters and playrooms entertaining their female collaborators. The Gestapo hesitated to upset these officers, so they conducted simple cursory searches and only if the higher-ups from Prague or Berlin were in the area.

Karel's plan to hide the Bolda and Florica Danka was to have them live with Eliska for a brief period. After everything was ready, he would transfer them to the Chateau.
~~~~~~

The Chateau was massive, and Karel had access to many unused rooms on the third floor. One room served as a storeroom for the kitchen, and the Dankas could stay there. Karel stacked the room high with boxes of napkins and kitchen supplies. Behind the supplies, he hid extra beds and furniture and made it a safe place for the Dankas to stay.

Figure 78 Looking Down the Chateau elevator room

The big problem was getting the Dankas into the Chateau and getting food, water, and other necessities to them.

Fortunately, the Chateau installed elevators in 1910. A German firm, Freisseler, ironically built them. They installed two. The first one, for guests only, was in the central part of the building leading from the lobby to the guest rooms.

They installed the second one off the kitchen. The staff used this elevator to deliver meals to the guest rooms and haul supplies up to the third-floor storage room.

Karel locked the kitchen elevator to everyone except Kizzy and Eliska. Fear of pilfering by the kitchen help was one reason for the locked elevator. The second reason, only understood by Kizzy, was that food was always in short supply in Karel's childhood home. He loved to come up and count the stacked-up boxes of food and supplies. It made him feel secure.

While he was there, the usually unflappable Karel sampled the plum brandy. He reasoned it tempered the stress of being the manager.

Karel trusted Kizzy and Eliska but not Radmila as she was born in the German Sudetenland in the north of Czechoslovakia. He suspected her of being a collaborator and carefully avoided expressing his political views when she was present.

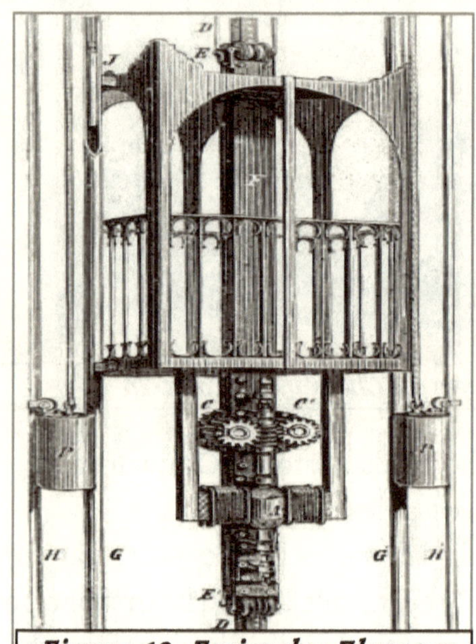

Figure 68 Freisseler Elevator

Sunday was a day of rest for Karel and his staff. No big Easter banquets, and the Chudý Kuchyně (poor kitchen) was closed. Karel decided to transfer the Dankas to the Chateau today, as it was increasingly dangerous for Eliska to hide them any longer.

Karel pulled up to Eliska's apartment building every Sunday afternoon for his weekly inspection, as it was his custom. A small garage and repair shop was behind the apartment building. To reach it, he drove through the alley alongside the building, then made a sharp left and turned into the garage after clearing the back corner of the building. Karel feared that his precious car would be damaged if he left it on the street, so he'd carefully park it in this garage and conduct his inspection.

Eliska hung wash, including every sheet and bedspread she owned, on two parallel clotheslines behind the apartment building.

The lines stretched from the building's back door, across the little yard to the side entrance of the garage.

Eliska and Karel waited until two in the afternoon, the usual time for a nap on Sundays, to move Bolda and Florica.

Karel parked in the garage and closed the garage doors. Eliska fervently opened the apartment building's back door and quickly guided her parents between the flapping sheets into the side entrance of the garage.

Karel had removed the back seat of the car and replaced it with a fake seat. It had just enough storage room underneath it to hold two persons. He tipped the fake seat up, and the Dankas laid down in the space below, then Karel lowered the seat back over them.

"Be quiet now. It won't take long. If I stop, don't make a sound until I give you the all-clear sign, which is, 'It's awful cold for an Easter Sunday'."

"Ya," a muffled Florica answered.

Eliska jumped into the passenger seat. "I'm going with you."

"No, if I'm caught, you know what will happen."

"You need help to get them into the Chateau. Neither walks too good, and Mama gets confused."

"I can handle it."

"I go, or you lose your best cook."

"Well, if you put it that way," Karel said fatalistically, "come on."

Karel started the car, drove through the alley, turned onto the street, and headed to the Chateau. As he rounded a bend in the road, two armored vehicles blocked his progress. Ales Baum, in his SS uniform, stood in the middle of the road. Flanking him was Bertham Egger, Gestapo, on one side and the other side, a man dressed in a shabby brown overcoat. Ales raised his hand and motioned Karel to pull the car over, which Karel did.

"Oh no! Damn!" Eliska uttered and hastily pulled out her scarf and sunglasses. She slid the glasses to her eyes and wrapped the scarf as far forward as she could.

Ales came to the car, "Out for a drive, are you Mr. Klimy?"

"Why, Ales, how good to see you. Do you have to work on this beautiful day? Haven't seen you at the Chateau for a while."

"I've been busy. Where are you going?" Ales Baum said tersely.

"To check on my property. I can only take so much leisure time, then I have to do something," Karel replied, smiling.

"Who is that with you?"

"This is my apartment manager and best cook. I just... picked... her up. We're making... special desserts today," Karel stuttered, "we... ah... refrigerate them for 24 hours. Big party tomorrow."

Egger and a man in the shabby brown overcoat came to the car.

"Search his vehicle," Egger ordered.

"Step out, open the trunk!" Ales commanded.

"By all means."

The men rummaged around in the car's trunk. They opened all the doors and scrutinized the interior.

The man in the shabby brown overcoat stared at Eliska. She lowered her head, so she didn't have to meet his eyes.

"It looks clean; you may go," Ales said, as the other men walked away.

"Thank you, Ales. Hope to see you at the Chateau soon. Everybody needs a day off, now and then. Especially when they tip as good as you."

"I hope so too. Lots of work to do, though."

"By the way, Ales, who is that man over there in the rumpled overcoat?"

"Just a damn gypsy, but a big help in finding other gypsies. He saved his ass by helping get rid of the gypsy settlement west of town. He led us to them; he knows every one of those worthless bastards."

"Loyal, eh? Good for something after all," Karel laughed offhandedly. "What's his name?"

"Jacob Conkova." ~~~~~~

Chapter 73

COME HOME

Owatonna Hospital, Owatonna, MN, USA. Mon, August 18th, 1943.

Hanzi pulled up to the hospital as the sun peeked over the precisely clipped hedge framed by the glowing background of the eastern sky. The nurses from the night shift were leaving as he limped into the hospital. Many greeted him like a long-lost friend.

"Hey Hanzi, big day," they said.

A black derby hat sat cockily over Hanzi's left ear, which he tipped as he flirted with every nurse he met. Gingerly climbing the long stairway to Zuba's floor, he stopped at the nurse's station, winked, and asked the nurse, "Zuba ready to go?"

"Yes, we have him dressed and ready to leave. It's a miracle; after a year, he comes out of the coma."

Hanzi yelled, "Thanks," as he quickly hobbled to Zuba's room.

Zuba, pale and thin, sat in his wheelchair, staring out the window. His eyes watered, and his right hand tremored.

"You're going home," Hanzi cried joyfully. "Won't that be something?"

Zuba nodded without saying a word. Hanzi grabbed the wheelchair. "Put your feet on the running boards, or they will get run over."

Zuba dutifully put one foot on the chair footrest but had trouble lifting his right foot. "Here, let me help you," Hanzi said, as he patiently lifted Zuba's leg into the footrest. Hanzi pulled a blanket up around Zuba's chin. "It's only 90 degrees out today, don't want you to take a chill," he chuckled.

Zuba looked up at him. A hint of a smile tickled the left corner of his mouth, breaking his blank expression. His wide eyes twinkled as he gave a jerky nod.

"Ok, here we go." Hanzi pushed Zuba up the hall to the elevator, all the while carrying on a nonstop conversation.

Hanzi jabbered on, "The Steele County Fair is on. What do you think of that? Suppose we go see the dancing girls? Bet you'd enjoy that? Or look at the horses or the pigs. You like pigs, don't you? We won't try any of the clip joints, though. A fellow could lose a bunch of money in those places." Hanzi wheeled Zuba out to the parking lot. He helped him into the 1939 Ford pickup with "Tom's Repair," painted on the door.

Hanzi pulled out, drove through the tree-lined streets of Owatonna, and turned on the gravel road, pointing the truck south to Litomysl. "Remember when I taught you how-to drive-in Duluth? Boy, were you ever green. Could have sold you one of those big ships for a koruna. Bet you're glad I took you under my wing, eh?"

Hanzi looked over at Zuba, who had his left hand above his eyes, shielding them from the hot August sunshine. "Sure, you are, I can tell by the jolly expression on your face. You don't have to salute me. I see, by your tears, you have fond memories. I wish you would stop your nonstop jabbering, though, gotta concentrate on my driving."

Hanzi arrived at Litomysl and stopped at Tom's Repair shop. Thomas rushed out and pulled his welding gloves off. He extended his hand through the open truck window. "Welcome, home Zuba!" Zuba grasped it with his working left hand.

Thomas helped Zuba out of the truck and over to a bench under the oak tree. "I am so glad that you're back. I owe you so much in so many ways. How can I ever repay you for saving Paul's life? Twice, once for the operation and now for the truck box. I'll be in your debt forever."

Zuba looked up at him. A faint smile crossed his face as he nodded.

"Don't worry about work or having a place to stay. You and Hanzi can stay here forever. I'll take care of it."

So, the days passed, sweltering summer days under the oak tree, and blustery winter days around the potbellied stove, in the corner of Tom's Repair. Hanzi jabbering away, joking with the customers, and always by Zuba's side. ~~~~~~

Chapter 74

LOSING YOUR LUNCH

Knettishall Air Force Base, England, Mon, May 1st, 1944

Patches of early morning fog drifted across the runway as Paul started work. A groundsman on a small tractor pulled a battered B17 into the hanger; Paul directed it to his repair station. After the colossal plane rolled to a stop, Paul opened the bottom hatch and swung up into the plane. Pieces of shrapnel lay strewn on the floor. Many of the airmen collected the shrapnel, but this crew, or at least those who survived, had other interests. They would swing down from the plane, walk to the side of the runway, kneel, and kiss the grass. They thanked God for surviving and apologized for what they had done. Then they grabbed a quick drink at the officer's club and then some much-needed sack time.

At the right waist position gunner's position, a gaping hole hovered above the dried blood on the floor. The 50-caliber machine gun needed replacement, but the mount remained in usable condition.

As Paul cleaned the gun position, he came across a mitten. He picked it up to throw it in his trash barrel; he realized that there was something more inside. Examining it carefully, he found a severed hand, still in the mitten. Suddenly, his breakfast was a heavy burden. He hurriedly dropped out of the bomber and vomited outside the plane: not his first time and not his last. After the first crummy time, he learned to get out quickly; it was easier to clean up outside than if he lost his cookies on the plane.

As he stood there, wiping his mouth, a youthful pilot walked into the hanger. "Kinda gets to you, doesn't it?"

Paul threw a hasty salute. "Yes, sir, always. It must be hell up there. You gotta be afraid all the time."

"We're usually too busy to be afraid. Walking to the plane before takeoff is the worst."

"What can I do for you, Captain?"

"Have a vibration in the plane at 30,000 feet, just before we reach the target."

"With all the bullet holes in it, it will probably vibrate at any altitude."

"It vibrates before we get hit. Can't find it. Think you can?"

"I'll check it over before you return. Been getting the same complaint from other pilots. We haven't been able to find the trouble, at least not here on the ground."

"Well, it worries me."

"The pilots have been calling it the Crappin Jitters," Paul explained. "Always happens before they crap on a target."

"Ya, I heard that too; just fix it, OK."

"Yes sir, I'll try."

Paul checked all the aircraft's components, including the engine, and everything checked out fine.

Four hours later, the pilot returned. "Find anything?"

"No, everything is up to spec. I don't have a clue why it does that."

"You should ride along."

"Aw... well, maybe... aw maybe not," Paul stammered, "I'd have to get General Prochazka's permission."

~~~~~~

Later that afternoon, Paul made a trip over to General Prochazka's office. He stopped at the adjutant's desk, saluted, and requested permission to see the general. The adjutant looked over the grease-covered mechanic. "Who sent you? The general is busy. He doesn't have time to see every grease monkey who walks through the door."

"Yes, sir, I'm sure. But this is important. What's it about?"

"The pilots say they were getting vibrations at the start of their bombing runs. They say that the plane goes into a shudder."

"Does it stop them from bombing?"

"No, sir, but the aircrews can be superstitious about their planes."

"What do you want to do?"

"I'd want to ride along on a flight and see if I can find it, sir."
~~~~~~

The adjutant considered it. "We don't want to overexpose the mechanics. You're too hard to replace."

As the adjutant was talking, General Prochazka came out of his office. Paul saluted him smartly, and the general returned it.

"Airman Koupil, how are you doing, son?"

"Fine, sir."

The adjutant chimed in quickly, "He is here to see you about a problem with the B17, sir."

"Oh, how is that?" the general responded.

Paul explained the problem.

"And so, you want to fly along, eh?" General Prochazka said.

"Yes, sir."

"Well, I hate to lose a good mechanic and a tuba player. Isn't there any other way you can figure out what the problem is?"

"I tried everything that I could think of, sir."

General Prochazka rubbed his chin and adjusted his glasses. *He reminds me so much of David.*

Paul interrupted his thoughts, "It's for the good of the men, sir."

General Prochazka took a deep breath and pondered this for a long minute. "All right, son, but if you get your ass shot up, you will answer to me, you hear?"

Paul laughed, "Yes, sir." ~~~~~~

Chapter 75

THE DEATH

The Chateau, Litomysl Czechoslovakia, Sat, May 1st, 1944
The Nazis deported the Roma and Jews to concentration camps and then tried to find anyone who was not "friendly" to Hitler's regime.

Eliska had a restless night with a premonition of impending doom. At four in the morning, she sat straight up in bed and screamed. Terrified, Andela rushed into her room, asking, "What happened?"

Eliska shook her head. "It's just a bad dream; I guess I go back to bed."

At six AM, Eliska left the apartment early and arrived at work before any of the other staff. A heaviness lay in the pit of her stomach as she donned her apron and a white cook's cap and started the morning chores. On a cart, she assembled her parent's breakfast tray with enough food to last all day. Scrambled eggs with mushrooms, roast beef Roma style, a large loaf of bread with a quarter pound of butter, a pitcher of water, and a small bottle of wine. She also included a bottle of Meruňkovice (apricot brandy). Her father had complained of not feeling well, and Meruňkovice was the traditional medicine for ailing bodies.

She wheeled the cart to the elevator, unlocked it, and took it up to the third floor. The elevator doors opened into the hallway next to the storeroom. Eliska peeked cautiously down the corridor, stepped out, and hurried to the storeroom. After surmising that there was no one around, she unlocked the door and pushed the cart in.

"Mama, Papa, it's Eliska," she softly called. "Here's a nice breakfast for you."

Florica came out from around the pile of boxes stacked in front of the cots. Her red eyes told a sad tale as she wrung her scarf in her hands. "Oh, Eliska," was all she could say before she broke and sobbed as she hung on to Eliska. "Papa... Papa is... gone."

Eliska hugged her mother, then sat her on a box and walked around the boxes. Bolda lay on his cot with the covers pulled up to his chin. His mouth and blank eyes were open, staring at the ceiling. He was already pale, and a blueness had crept around his lips. Eliska knew he was dead but checked his pulse to be sure. Determining that he was dead, she took two silver korunas out of her apron, reverently closed his eyelids, and placed one koruna on each eye. She rose and returned to her mother. Clinging to her, she said, "Mama Oh Mama, he's with O Del (God) now. His troubles are gone."

Eliska caressed her mother. "We must take care of him, Mama."

"Can we do it in the Roma way?" a bewildered Florica asked.

"I'll talk to Karel and see what we can do. Is there any way to reach the twins, Luca and Stevo?"

"They trusted only one gadjo, Josef Jelinek. He might know."

"Josef Jelinek, I remember him. I worked for him in the coal yard. He was gruff, but he took a chance on hiring me."

Florica sobbed, "He might be the one."

"I'll check it out. I'll be gone for a while; will you be all right, up here alone?"

"I'm not alone; Bolda's father and mother have been here since he took sick. They stay till after the funeral."

Taken back by this, Eliska knew that Grandpa and Grandma Danka had been dead for many years. *She recalled the Roma belief that deceased family members come for a loved one who was dying. They stayed with them until after the funeral and then took them away to the next world.*

"Can I light a candle for him, Eliska? He needs it to find the afterlife."

"Of course, Mama, in the candle box by the window. Just be careful."

"Even with the troubles, I know he died happy. Especially after seeing you again and your good heart. Do you remember yesterday when he asked you for forgiveness?"

"Yes, Mama, it made my heart skip."

"No, Roma wants to go to the next life with a troubled spirit."

Eliska went back to the kitchen.

Karel entered the kitchen, "You're here early, Eliska."

"I came to see if Mama and Papa were all right," Eliska replied, wiping her eyes.

"Doesn't look like it. What's wrong?"

"Papa's dead."

Karel was silent for a while. "I never planned on this."

"What are we to do?"

"Don't worry, I'll think of something. Is your mother all right?"

"Sad, but Grandpa and Grandma Danka are with her."

"What! Do you mean we have more Roma up there?"

"No, it's the old ways. A Roma belief that the relatives that have gone before will come back to guide their loved one home."

"Oh, just superstition, thank God."

"A superstition, but a comforting one all the same."

~~~~~~

Chapter 76

SEARCHING FOR HELP

Litomysl, Czechoslovakia, Mon, May 2nd, 1944

The coal-yard workers were leaving the yard, at quitting time, as Eliska made her way to the coal-yard office. She entered the office and inquired of a young lady at the reception desk. "Does Josef Jelinek still work here?"

"Oh, heavens no, he retired ten years ago."

"Do you have his address?"

"Ya, around here somewhere," she replied, rummaging through a pile of papers. "Here it is!"

Eliska wrote the address on the back of her hand and left. She walked to 101 Jirasek RD, Apt D. It was a short way from the Chateau. Entering the green painted building, she noticed the lack of upkeep on the property. *Never happen in my building.*
~~~~~~

Eliska knocked on the door. Once. Twice. The third time she knocked and yelled, "Open up, Mr. Jelinek, it's Eliska, remember me?"

The door opened a crack, and an old man peeked out. "Eliska, do I know you?"

"Yes, I worked for you. Eliska Danka and my husband, Zuba Palzek. Do you remember?"

"Oh yes, how are you? Come in, please," Josef swung the door open. "Would you care for tea? I don't get too many visitors."

"Yes, thank you."

Josef made the tea water on his little gas stove. "It's nice of you to visit. Where do you work now?"

"At the Chateau, and I manage the Klimy apartment building."

"Oh, down the street. It is nice of you to visit, but I don't think that is your reason for coming." Josef looked over his glasses, "Am I right?"

"Well, yes," Eliska hesitated. "My father died, and Mama had your name to contact my brothers."

"Now, why would this old man know where your brothers are?"

"Well, you were always a man who could tell which way the wind blew. I suspect you know the Resistance. My brothers are with them."

"If I did, that would make me a party to the Resistance. Is that what you are saying?"

"I don't know those things. I've exposed myself greatly to come to you. You know how the Nazis treat the Roma."

"Yes, I do," Josef said, stroking his stubby chin whiskers. "You must trust me."

"Yes, I used to. Now, maybe things have changed."

"You better be careful. That kind of talk could get both of us sent to a work camp," Josef said, coughing into his handkerchief.

"Some things are more important than one's life. My Mama grieves greatly." Eliska slid forward, grasped Josef's hands, and looked in the eyes, "We'll not be able to bury my Papa in the open. Hanzi, her other son, is gone, along with my Zuba. All she has left is the twins and me."

Josef coughed again. "I'm an old man with a thing called lung cancer. Too much damn coal dust, I expect death to be a welcome guest." Josef said.

The clock ticked monotonously on the mantle, Eliska waited nervously. Josef coughed, covering his mouth with a blood-spotted, gray cloth. He pondered before he spoke again. "So, you think I can find your brothers for you?"

"I don't know what to think anymore or who to trust. You always knew I was a Roma. You treated my Zuba and me fairly. He told me about the wages you didn't pay. And then you paid him in gold. Only an honest man would do that."

"I made the mistake of talking to a priest," Josef chuckled.

"Well, priest or no. I trust you. You could have lined your pockets and turned me in long ago."

"I'm not that kind of man, and I have no family to worry about. Never married and no kinfolk."

Eliska finished her tea and got up to leave. "Thanks so much for seeing me. I'm sorry that I bothered you."

"No bother, glad to see you. Sorry, I couldn't help. If you are in the neighborhood again, please stop for tea. I've enjoyed visiting with you," Josef said as he escorted Eliska to the door. "Good day to you Eliska, please stop anytime."

Dejectedly, Eliska walked back to the Chateau. *I've failed Mama and Papa again. Mama cannot bury Papa with the comfort of her family around her.*

~~~~~~

The following day Eliska was at the Chateau early. She met Karel in the kitchen, and he rushed up to her and said, "I have it all worked out. Here's what we do. I called Albert Cerny, an old friend. He's an undertaker and will come over and take care of the body. On Sunday, we can have a service in the storeroom, not so fancy, but I see no other way. We then move your Papa down the elevator and out to the cemetery in my car.
~~~~~~

Karel talked on, "The fake back seat works well, a bit undignified, but it's a good way. Albert has another funeral and will dig the grave extra deep and lower the first casket. He will then bury your Papa above that casket. The one below is a loyal German administrator. A Roma laid over a pompous German for eternity." Ironic, isn't it?

Fulfilling the Roma proverb, "You must dig deep to bury your daddy."

~~~~~~

Chapter 77

THE FUNERAL

The Chateau, Litomysl Czechoslovakia, Sunday, May 7th, 1944

Father Emilio slipped away from his German shadows after the last mass. He arrived at the Chateau kitchen door, and Kizzy promptly whisked him in.

But before going up the elevator, Kizzy said to him. "Father, I want you to put on your confessing scarf before we go any further."

"You mean my purple confessing stole?"

"Yes, everything from now on is as if we're in confession."

"Well, that's a little unusual."

"These are unusual times, Father."

"All right," Father said, as he pulled the purple stole out of his pocket, kissed it, and pulled over his graying hair, and put it around his neck.

Karel came in with Albert Cerny and directed him to the elevator with Kizzy and Father Emilio. "I'll stay here and make sure no one disturbs you."

Kizzy, Albert, and Father Emilio entered the third-floor storeroom where Albert had laid out Bolda on a large dining table. Florica sat on a chair by Bolda and rose to thank Father for coming. Father pulled out his funeral prayer book and started the service.

Halfway through the service, there was a loud knock on the door. The entire party assembled froze at the sound.
~~~~~~

The door opened, and Karel peeked in. "Sorry to disturb you, but we have a couple more guests."

He opened the door wide, and two men entered. They looked remarkably alike, sturdy young men with curly black hair, straight noses, and wearing the plain clothes of outdoorsmen.

Florica stood up shakily, "O Saint Sara. Stevo! Luca! My baby sons! You have come." The men advanced to their mother and wrapped their arms around her. "Yes, Mama, we heard. We would have been here sooner, but it isn't easy to move around."

"You honor your family, but you risk your lives. That makes me worry."

"It's all right, Mama, let us do the worrying."

Florica turned to Father Emilio, "Let's continue."

Father went ahead with the service and concluded by blessing the body. After the conclusion, he began taking his purple stole off.

Kizzy tapped him on his shoulder. "Father, remember our bargain!"

"Oh yes, I forget," Father said and kept his stole on. He walked to the door, pondering what had taken place. When he reached for the doorknob, he stopped, turned, and blessed those assembled and said, "You are forgiven." Then he left the room.

Florica trembled as she stood up, taking her twin sons, each by the arm, she said. "Come! Meet the rest of your family. This is Eliska; she is your older sister. You were two years old when she left. This is Andela, her daughter. You played with her when they were at our house. And here is my dear sister Kizzy. We wouldn't be here if it weren't for her. And the man that brought you up here is her husband, Karel. He's a gadjo but has the heart of a Roma. Roma or not, they sheltered Papa and me for a year and a half."

The twins came forward and hugged their family members. They sauntered over to Albert Cerny and reached out and shook his hand heartily. When they turned away from the others, Albert said, "I see you boys did a bang job up last week."

"Ya, the guns and the explosives really helped. How do you get them in?"

"My secret, I guess, but the Germans are squeamish about searching under a dead body in a casket," Albert chuckled.

Florica waved to the boys, "Come over, boys, sit and tell stories about your Papa."

The next hour they spent talking about Bolda. They caught up with Eliska and got to know their newfound relatives. When it came time to go, they cracked open a bottle of wine. Each took a full glass and spilled half, on the floor, in honor of the deceased and drank the rest. The twins were the first to leave. The rest followed. Eliska remained behind with her mother. Florica came to her, tears in her eyes, and hugged her tight. "Thank you! Was a good funeral. Papa is proud. Now, he can take his place in heaven. I'm sure he will talk to me in my dreams and tell me so."

~~~~~~

<div align="center">Chapter 78</div>

RIDE ALONG

Knettishall Air Force Base, England, Sat, May 12, 1944

In the ready room, Paul sat next to the radio operator. Paul was dressing in an array of insulated flight apparel. He donned alpaca-lined trousers and jacket and fur-lined boots that would make an Eskimo happy.

"Hi, I'm Paul Koupil."

"Jerry Norquist," the young man grinned with an amiable smile, reached over to shake Paul's hand. Jerry, just out of high school, has red wavy hair and freckles punctuated by teenage blemishes.

"Good to meet you," Paul replied. *He could pass for Irene's brother.* "Where are we headed?" Paul asked Jerry.

"Brux, I guess."

"Brux, where is Brux?"
~~~~~~

"Somewhere in Czechoslovakia. Make sure the heat cord is out. You need to plug in when we get in the air," Jerry replied.

"OK, I wish we had this back home in Minnesota; winters would have been warmer," Paul babbled nervously.

"Hell, you ain't seen a winter till you lived in Grand Forks, North Dakota," Jerry said, matter-a-factly. "Forty degrees below when I left for training. Had to start a fire under the car engine to warm it up enough to start it. Oil was stiff as Vaseline!"

"That's pretty damn cold."

"Yaa, a witch's breast feels warm up there," Jerry laughed. "We drive to Minnesota for a winter getaway. Mary Lo and I drove down to Crookston, MN, before I left."

"Crookston, MN is only 30 miles away, isn't it?"

"It's South! And East! Mary Lo is from there. She sure warmed me up!

"Mary Lo, your girlfriend?"

"Wife, we married a year ago. Got a little girl in the bargain too. Can't wait to go back and farm with my dad on our potato farm."

Paul finished pulling on his mitten inserts then his mittens. *Mother used to bundle me this way to play in the winter, the fall, and the spring. "No roughhousing!" she would say, "you could get hurt." I would reply, "How? If I hit the ground, I'll just bounce." I wonder what she would say if she saw me now?"*

"Here's your flak suit," Jerry said. "And here's an extra one to sit on."

"Why should I sit on that?"

"This old B17 is a tough bird, but flak or shrapnel has a nasty way of sneaking right on through the fuselage. If you're hit from below, your ass will be shredded wheat."

"Oh," Paul said with a visible tremble. "We'll be eight hours in the air?"

"Yep."

"How do you go to the latrine? I know you guys won't use the pee tube."

"Pee tube is too damn hard to hit with all these clothes on. Sometimes we are too busy to stop doing what we're doing. It's hard to stop and take care of things when the fighters buzz around you like flies on a dead hog. Also, the pee tube empties outside the plane. It hits the belly gunner's turret and freezes up, and he can't see. We prefer him being able to see."

"You have the chemical toilet in the back, don't you?" Paul added.

"Pull your pants down at thirty below zero? It's a disaster if we take evasive action. The damn thing is likely to explode with you on it. A lot of fellows have weak bowels when the flak starts. Or if a Messerschmidt is boring in on us," Jerry said.

Jerry continued, "and the ground crew must clean enough messes up, so we thought we might spare you guys a nasty cleanup."

"Thank you, appreciate that. I sure can approve of that."

"You married?" Jerry said.

"Right before I shipped out."

"Got any kids?"

"Yes, a boy, four months old. I've never seen him except for this picture," Paul said, pulling out a well-worn picture from his billfold.

"Good-looking kid. He should meet my girl! Here's her picture." Jerry said, showing off his little girl held by his wife.

"What are you, some sort of matchmaker? Paul said.

Jerry laughed an easy laugh, "Depends, you run something better than a potato farm?"

"No, we just have an out-of-the-way repair shop, that's all."

"Looks like you were kinda busy, weren't you? The first one can come at any time, can't they?" Jerry teased. He laughed and continued, "Sometimes quicker than nine months. Keeps the old wags, around town, up nights. They mark the wedding day on their calendars and check back when the baby comes."

Paul chuckled, "I'm sure it was a surprise, especially to my wife's parents."

"What do you put on him to keep him dry?" Jerry said.

"Who?"

"Your baby."

Paul's face lit up in recognition, "Oh, a diaper!" Paul continued, "Why do you ask?"

"We fliers have something similar, we call um, ah, a nappy, here's a couple," he said, as he threw Paul a bundle of oversized thick cotton diapers. "Keeps your butt warm too."

"Damn, I wish you had told me that before I finished dressing."

"It's our crew's dirty little secret. Keeps our ground crew happy too. Why do you think our flight crews head for the shower after a flight, city boy? We're always late for a briefing. Wouldn't want to offend the debriefing officer with our malodorous smells. We smell ripe as hell after we remove our flight suits."

After hastily taking his flight gear off, Paul strategically placed the nappy and put the flight clothes back on.

Jerry grinned at Paul, "If you ever tell anyone that we wear diapers, I'll kick your ass."

"Oh no! I won't!"

"Oh hell, I guess I don't care. Just get the job done. I'd give anything to go home and change my kid's diaper again," Jerry said longingly.

"Ya, I understand," Paul said wistfully.

"Makes me chuckle when I know that the officers are wearing them too. And guess what?... Theirs stink the same as the rest of us."

~~~~~~

The crew boarded, completed the preflight checks, and prepared to take off. Paul took a seat next to Jerry. Jerry already had his radio headset on, listening to the tower for the takeoff signal. His wife and baby's picture hung above his radio. He bunched his fingers together, touched them to his lips, and pressed a kiss to the picture. "Here we go!" Jerry yelled.

The captain pushed the throttle to the limit, and the plane raced ahead and struggled to rise above the trees that guarded the far end of the runway.
~~~~~~

Paul made the sign of the cross and lowered his head in prayer. The first prayer, his fear-laced mind could remember, was the table offering prayer. "Bless us, Oh Lord and… ah… and the gifts we are about to receive." He stopped short, embarrassed at his confusion. *If the Lord has given me this as a gift, I better try a different prayer.*

The B17 climbed steadily as the captain steered the plane to the predetermined assembly point. They circled until the entire group had assembled, then they turned, created a diamond formation, and flew straight for the target. There were fifteen planes in the squadron; each plane had thirteen, fifty-caliber machine guns pointed in every direction. Formed up in this diamond formation, the Germans called them 'Flying Porcupine.' Thousands of aircraft were in the air, bombers and escort fighters, racing for the target.

Figure 69 B17 Over Brux Czechoslovakia

The pilot climbed to 10,000 feet, and the crew put on their oxygen masks and hooked up the electrical connections to their heated flight suit.

The ball turret gunner was a small man, picked for this job because of his size. The turret entrance was too small for him to enter with his parachute on, so he laid his parachute carefully alongside the door to the turret as he slid into position. He wanted the chute to be within arm's reach if he had to leave the turret in a hurry. A minute can be a lifetime when a plane was hurtling earthward.

Today was their squadron's turn to fly in the "Purple Heart" section of the formation, or the back end. The lowest, rearmost, and the most vulnerable to enemy attack.

At 22,000 feet, the formation leveled out, flying at 220 miles per hour.

A half-hour before entering enemy territory, they removed the bomb's arming pins and test-fired the fifty-caliber machine guns. The sound, added to the roar of the four big 1200 horsepower Wright Cyclone engines, was deafening. Paul clapped his hands over his sensitive ears, even though his padded flight helmet helped muffle the sound.

Crossing into enemy territory, the crew slipped into their flak suits. The gunners searched the skies for "Little Friends," the American escort fighters flying over them, protecting them like a bunch of mother hens.

When the formation reached its Initial Point, they turned into the bombing run. The bomber group that Paul was in, quickly rose to their assigned 32,000 feet.

The bomber groups positioned themselves in their various pre-assigned altitudes. It is a careful plan, worked out by command headquarters to confuse anti-aircraft gunners on the ground. Once into their respective positions, they fly directly into "Hell's Merry Go Round."

Figure 70. Hell's Merry Go Round

Shrapnel (flak) reached up and exploded around the planes, ripping jagged holes in the fuselages; enemy fighters threw caution to the wind and swept through the formations, focusing their attention on the "Purple Heart" section.

The bombardier opened the bomb bay doors and released the safety lever; the captain gave control of the plane over to the bombardier. A shudder rippled through the ship as the "Crappin Jitters" struck! Paul went from station to station, trying to figure out the cause of the vibration. While doing this, the plane lurched upward, hit by massive doses of shrapnel bursts.

Unable to find the cause of the vibration, Paul crawled back to his seat and looked over at Jerry. He was slumped over his radio; red splatters covered the pictures of his wife and child; scarlet ribbons of blood snaked down the radio desk supports and dripped on the floor. Shrapnel had exploded through the wall above Paul's seat and lodged in what was left of Jerry's head; Jerry didn't know what hit him. He died instantly.

Paul pulled Jerry from the seat and laid him on the floor. He turned his back to Jerry and crawled to the other side of the plane and vomited. Dry heaving, Paul struggled to quiet his shaking body when a series of sharp "thumps" erupted over his head. A crazy Messerschmidt pilot ignored the shrapnel bursts and penetrated the "Porcupine" defense, making several direct hits in the plane, as the bullet holes above Paul's head testified.

Paul cowered in fear on the floor until he heard the top turret gunner scream in pain. Paul swallowed hard, stood up cautiously, pulled the gunner out of the turret, and lay him on the floor. The gunner babbled incoherently and held onto the stub of his shot-off leg. Paul hastily wrapped his flying scarf around the stub, knowing that it was no use. With four hours left to fly before returning to the airbase, the gunner would bleed to death within 30 minutes.

Frigid air carried a wisp of smoke as it snaked its way up from the open bomb bay. The bombardier yelled on the intercom. "Hang tight! Six minutes to go to the drop zone!"

Five minutes to go, shrapnel flew everywhere, a deadly hailstorm from hell.

Four and a half minutes to go, shrapnel smashed into the rear of the plane and tore a ragged hole in the tail fin.

Four minutes to go, the airmen's gasps muffled their confused prayers. "Our Father," "Our Father," "Our Father," "Our Father," "Our Father," Their terrified minds could not remember the rest of the prayer.

Three and a half minutes to go, the smell of hell's brimstone emanated from the cockpit.

Three minutes to go, silent wails hung in the air. "Drop the damn bombs, and let's get the hell out of here!"

Two and a half minutes to go, the belly turret gunner won't need his parachute. There's nothing left of the belly turret... or the gunner.

Two minutes to go, shrapnel punched through the bottom of the plane, the plane lurched upward, convulsing. The spent shrapnel sizzled and slid along the floor, coming to rest in small gray drifts against the inside walls of the plane.

One and a half minutes to go, a blast of searing shrapnel blew the right waist gunner across the plane. He landed in a crumpled, bloody heap at the left waist gunner's feet.

One minute to go, the left waist gunner convulsed with horror as he stepped, slipped, and fell into the remains of the right waist gunner.

The noise of the shrapnel bursts, the roar of the engines, the screams of the men all combined to create a realistic version of Dante's Inferno.

Thirty seconds to go... All the men silently screamed prayers. All except for young Davy, the tail gunner who sucked his thumb, murmuring, "Mama, Mama."

Twenty seconds to go... The navigator recited the 'Hail Mary' holding on to his rosary with one hand and his flak helmet with the other.

Fifteen seconds to go... not a dry nappy on the plane.

"BOMBS AWAY!" Six miles from the target, the bombardier released the bombs. The plane lurched upward as two thousand pounds of hell fell in the May sunshine. Silently they fell, sparkling with just a slight whistle... Quietly... Quietly... Hurtling down on the flame-ravaged fuel refineries below. In less than 45 seconds, the bomb load would crash into the refinery. Peacefully... Quietly... Softly in the sleepy sunlight... until the bombs slammed headlong into the already, fiery hell.

Figure 82 Bombs Away

During the bombing run, the bombers had drifted out of their Porcupine formation. They must now re-form at the rallying point, a location over East Czechoslovakia, before turning to fly home. Until they rallied back into the Porcupine position, they were vulnerable to attack by the enemy fighter planes.

The pilot shrieked, "GUNNERS GET TO YOUR POSITIONS, HERE COME THE KRAUTS!"

Paul took the dead, right waist gunner's position. He wiped the blood off the trigger and prepared to meet the fighters.

Sensing that there was no resistance from the top turret gunner, the Messerschmitt's charged down on the plane, slashing, firing, twisting, and squirming their way in, closing in for the kill. In front of Paul's gun position, bullets crisscrossed over the right wing. A fire ignited the wing and engulfed the right side of the plane.

"The wing is on fire. The fuel tanks will blow," The navigator called out.

"Bail out!" the captain ordered.

Paul had never jumped before. Dazed, he trembled as he struggled with his parachute, trying to figure out what to do. The bombardier grabbed him and slapped the blank look off his face. He looked Paul in the eye and yelled, "When you jump, wait till you're clear of the plane before pulling your chute!" He pointed to one of the handles, dangling from the front of the parachute. "Then you pull this. Wait for the chute to open. Count to fifty. If that doesn't open, here's your reserve chute handle. Pull it as a last resort. Don't pull both at once. They are liable to get tangled up, OK?"

"Ya, I think so," replied ashen-faced Paul.

"When you hit the ground roll, pull on one side of the chute straps to collapse the parachute. Now out the bomb bay! Good Luck."

It was one in the afternoon when Paul climbed down into the bomb bay. One look at the emptiness below, and he froze in trembling fear. He wrapped both arms around one of the bomb bay's supports. The bombardier, dropped into the bomb bay beside Paul, took a two-handed firm grip on the support strut and with one swift push sent Paul screaming into the frigid clear blue sky. ~~~~~~

Chapter 79

FALLING

Over Lezaky, Czechoslovakia, Sat, May 12, 1944

Paul plummeted toward the ground; even with a full flight suit on, he was bitterly cold. Shivering, he frantically pulled at the parachute handle, but his mitten-wrapped hands wouldn't fit into the handle. As a last resort, he bit on the end of the mitten, jerked his head back, and pulled it off. He fumbled for the handle, and the blast of frigid air instantly numbed his fingers. He couldn't breathe, at the altitude, as he had forgotten to put his emergency oxygen bottle on!

He fell... and fell... and fell. The thin air played tricks on him; he blacked out. *Mama, Mama, help me.* As his descent continued, a sense of euphoria settled over him. *This isn't so bad, is it? Hello Irene, Hi Mom, Dad, how are you? Zuba, are you better?* A thin, dark-haired woman beckoned to him. *"Wake up. You must awake. Wake! You must awake."*

Above Paul, the plane exploded, with the bombardier still gripping the strut. A massive fireball lit up the sky. Debris flew in every direction. The shock wave from the explosion blasted Paul like a punch in the face from a pot of scalding water. He screamed himself awake, flailing his arms as if he were a drowning swimmer. As he came to his senses, he realized he was still falling.

The blast warmed his hand enough so he could slide it into the main chute handle. With one mighty heave, he jerked the handle. "One two three," he counted. At the count of forty, he felt a tug on his shoulders and realized that his chute was open. Safe for now, but once on the ground, it might be a different story. *I wonder where I am?*

<div style="text-align: center">~~~~~~</div>

The Chateau, Litomysl Czechoslovakia Same Day.

Eliska finished serving the noon dinner and crossed the broad expanse of the Chateau lawn to the poor kitchen.

Andela was now second in command of the kitchen, and her doting mother was curious how she was doing.

As Eliska approached the hedge surrounding the lawn, a chill rolled up her spine. *This is May. The sun is out. Why the cold?* She continued to the door of the poor kitchen. As she entered, a small, wiry black woman dressed in rags came out. The woman nodded to Eliska and said, "You must reach out to your son."

"I only have a daughter, old woman. Why do you say that?"

"Your son needs you now. The son you had but lost needs you now."

Eliska's breath was ripped out of her; a bone-crushing ice wave slammed her to her knees. *Am I passing out? Why? Am I dying? What is happening? "Wake! you must awake. Wake, you must awake."*

As Eliska fell to the ground, an acrid smell filled her nostrils, and then an overwhelming feeling of warmth rolled over her. *Am I dying?*

Andela saw her mother fall and rushed out. She kneeled beside Eliska and cradled her mother's head in her lap, "Mama, are you all right?"

A stunned and shaking Eliska looked around. "What happened?"

"I found you lying here. Are you all right?"

Eliska sat up, rolled her head, and scanned her surroundings, then Andela helped her to her feet. "What are you looking for, Mama?"

"The old black woman. She was just here."

"There have been no poor here for at least a half-hour, Mama. And no black woman today."

"She... was... just here!"

"You have been working too hard, Mama. With grandpa's death and the pressure of the Germans, you need a rest."

"Ya, well tomorrow is Sunday, no work, I'll take off early today. See you at home."

~~~~~~
~~~~~~

Chapter 80

COMING TO A MASSACRE

Lezaky, Czechoslovakia. Sat, May 12th, 1944.

Paul dangled from his opened parachute as the charming countryside of Czechoslovakia floated by below him. Fields of wheat, barley, and corn, hugged each other, creating a green checkerboard that stretched out across the landscape and ended, kissing the outskirts of a small village. Paul pulled his chute lines and soared in the opposite direction. It was quiet below, no activity, and none as far as he could see. A warm spring breeze flapped his chute. Below him, he drifted across a sizeable green wheat field. His hands shook as he maneuvered his parachute lines. The ground rushed upward at him until he landed hard. He bent his knees and rolled in the green stems, ending at the edge of the field. He hurriedly collapsed the chute, wrapped it tightly, carried it into the nearby woods, and buried it.

Paul heard voices coming from the little village; he understood some of what they were saying, although understanding Czech wasn't his forte. He stayed low, crawling on his stomach. He slipped through the woods to get within 100 ft of the edge of the village. Halting behind a large elm tree, he took a quick look around the tree; then, he moved right up to the village's main entrance. A sign on the outskirts read, "Lezaky." The village lay in ruins. *Why would we bomb this little village?*

In the waning afternoon, he watched several villagers rummaging through the wreckage of the town. Two young women laid bunches of flowers at the town's signpost.

At an hour before sunset, German army trucks rumbled into the village. The Germans rounded up the villagers and marched them towards Paul's position; he hunkered low and slithered backward, away from the oncoming Germans. He slid down into a sewage drainage ditch that ran parallel to the village.

Paul lay on the ditch bottom, cowering in cold pungent mud as the chilly water flowed over him. He removed his flight suit but left on his regular uniform.

The German guards marched twenty villagers into the open field, right in front of Paul's hiding place. The sobbing villagers held on to each other. They stumbled along, forced on by the prodding of the sharp bayonets of the soldiers. The soldiers lined up the villagers in a single row. Four SS soldiers stepped forward and raised their M42* machine guns.

Figure 83 Hitler's Buzz Saw

Many of the villagers wrung their hands and pleaded; others screamed and lost their bowels, messing themselves; others crossed themselves with the sign of the cross and stoically knelt and quietly prayed.

A tall man, carrying a dark overcoat and wearing a black hat, suddenly stood up and ran straight towards Paul's hiding place; the man dropped his overcoat, in his desperate sprint for life; but before he made it ten feet, the guns ripped him apart. Crumpling like a wet towel, he landed face first in front of the drainage ditch.

The same outburst of machine-gun fire cut through other villagers, collapsing them where they stood. The officer in charge pulled his Lugar, and with a casual headshot, finished any villagers that were still moving or moaning. Upon completing this gruesome deed, he ordered the soldiers back onto the trucks, and they left.

Paul trembled with fear as a full moon rose in the East, and darkness crept over the wheat field. It was a quiet evening. A cool south breeze played in the treetops. The whippoorwills peacefully cooed, belying the fact of the atrocity that lay just beyond the ditch.

*M42*When these guns fire 1200 rounds per minute, they make a "ripping cloth" or a buzz-saw sound. The German soldiers called the gun, "Hitlersage (Hitler's Buzz-saw)" because the human ear could not tell when one shot stopped, and another began. A weapon of pure destruction!*

Paul, at last, summoned up enough courage to peek up over the ditch's edge. Right into the sightless eyes of the tall man! Paul stared, mesmerized by the look of fear, permanently etched on the man's face. Paul pivoted as his sensitive stomach deserted him again, and he dry retched into the ditch bottom.

As the moon came up, Paul laid still in the darkness and considered his next move. *Mechanics didn't leave the airfield... No training like the fliers have... I don't know what to do when you bail out over enemy territory... the Resistance... But how?... Czech collaborators?... How will I know which is which? I can't get too far with my Air Force uniform on... But if I don't wear it, could be shot as a spy... I can talk enough Czech to get by... but maybe not... The dialect might give me away... Better not speak... Just... maybe!... I could play like Zuba. Talk a little... better yet... not at all. That's it! Where will I get clothes?* His mind raced. *The man with the overcoat!... He's about my size! Oh, God! I must take his clothes!*

With his decision made, Paul cautiously crawled out of the ditch, up to and alongside the lifeless man. He examined the man's overcoat, finding no damage, but the clothes had several bullet holes in the back and through the front of his shirt. The man's trousers and shoes were bloody but otherwise workable. Gingerly, Paul stripped off the man's clothes. *Forgive me, God, for desecrating the dead, but I must do this.*

Paul carried the man's clothes to the ditch and washed the blood off in the muddy stream. He removed his clothing, including his soiled nappy, washed and wrung the dead man's clothes out, and put them on. Shivering in the chilly May evening, he climbed out of the ditch and walked south, knowing that north was Germany. In the northwest loomed a mountain range. *Maybe a good place to hide.* Paul walked for several hours until a new sunrise was born, casting a light orange glow on the eastern horizon. *Must find shelter until tonight, then find the Resistance.*

Paul found a stand of oak trees at the edge of a large hillock; he crawled into a group of low-growing bushes at the base of the largest oak tree; he covered himself up with dry oak leaves and fell into a fitful sleep.

He tossed and turned, repeatedly waking until the morning sun warmed his face. His troubled dreams tormented him; he called out several times; then, the tinkling of a bell woke him. Sitting up, he saw a small boy herding goats to pasture. *No need to worry. He can't see me.* He lay back again and was half asleep when he felt a cold metallic object against his cheek. Thinking a bug had crawled there, he swatted at it. "Nehýbej se (Don't Move)!" came the harsh command. Paul stiffened, turned, and looked straight into the muzzle of a rifle barrel held by a man about thirty years old. Paul tried to get up. The man said, "Budu střílet (I'll shoot)" and shoved the rifle hard into Paul's chest.

〰〰〰〰〰〰〰〰〰〰〰〰〰〰〰〰〰〰〰〰〰〰〰〰

Chapter 81

THE RIVERWALK

Apartment House, Litomysl Czechoslovakia., Sun, May 13, 1944
Eliska slept from Saturday afternoon until Sunday noon, and then she sat up in bed. She rose slowly, wiped the sleep out of her eyes, and peered through the open bedroom door at Andela mending clothes.

"Good morning! Oops, I mean good afternoon, Mama," Andela said cheerily, "Do you feel better?"

"Yes, much better," Eliska said, stretching her arms to the ceiling.

"Some of us have to work to make ends meet, and some of us keep their ends in bed all the day long," Andela teased.

"And some of us, if they are smart, don't tempt their mother. Her wooden spoon might meet their end!"

Andela chuckled and teased a little more. "I'm bigger than you are Mama, you couldn't spank me anymore."

"Don't you think, for one minute, my wooden spoon couldn't find your behind? You may take after your Papa in size, but I still can handle you." Eliska replied, laughing. *What was that icy feeling I had yesterday? Was it from my Zuba? Are you alive? Why didn't you come home? I miss you so.*

As Eliska sat at the table, Andela brought her butter and poured syrup over stale, leftover griddle cakes.

"Here, eat this. It's what's left for people who lie in bed the whole day."

"Thank you, Smart Aleck!" Eliska said. While eating, she brightened up. "Andela, today is a wonderful day to take the Riverwalk, along the Loucna River. I'll show you where Papa and I worked. The fantastic coal yards."

"Oh, Yaaay! We get to view the world-famous coal yard. I'd rather stay home and drink sour milk."

"It's a beautiful afternoon. Let's forget our troubles for a few hours."

"Oh, all right, Mama, I hope the boys are swimming in the river."

"Don't worry about the boys. You will marry soon enough."

"Mama, I was twenty-six last March. You were seventeen when you married Papa."

"I'm sorry, Andela, I didn't mean to hurt your feelings. It's hard when the young men your age are off fighting or dead. I know you loved Dalek. He got caught up in that awful business in Lezaky. But it's two years since that happened."

"Did you stop loving Papa when he died?"

"He's not dead!" Eliska replied angrily, then hesitated and softened. "I know he's... he's not dead," she murmured. "If he were, I'd move on."

"I didn't mean to bring the hurt up again."

"It's all right. The hurt is always lying there like a snake on a path. When you step on it, it nips at your heels." Eliska perked back up, "Enough of the gloomy talk, let's get out of here. Let the sunshine wash our troubles away."

Eliska and Andela put on their scarfs, wrapped light spring shawls over their shoulders, and left for the Loucna Riverwalk. A soft spring breeze rustled in the trees. Newly bloomed lilacs painted the air with the sweet smell of summer promise. Daffodils and tulips competed in a blatant contest of showmanship. Today, the police and Gestapo were sleeping off hangovers, so the people enjoyed the day even more. Collectively, the day gave off a huge sigh of relief.

Figure 84- Loucna River Walk

As they strolled the Riverwalk, the larks sang love songs in the trees. An ambitious male lark assembled an array of seeds in the crook of a tree, trying to entice a lady lark into his boudoir. Other male larks continually thwarted his amorous intentions by singing full-throated versions of their 'come-hither' mating songs and stealing the lady larks away.

"See that lark," Eliska said excitedly. "He thinks that if he feeds his love interest, he will have his way with her."

Eliska called up to the lady larks. "Hold out for love in the bargain." She chuckled, "He'll work harder, gathering seeds!" Eliska and Andela giggled and walked along the river.

Sandpipers danced a long-legged, jerking mambo along the mudflats of the Loucna River. Every foot or two, they punched a hole in the mud, pull their beaks back up, then stared cross-eyed at what the beak had pierced and gobbled down a fat water bug.

Mallards and their rows of ducklings swam by, contentedly bobbing for food, heads down in the sparkling water, butts in the air.

"Isn't this nice, Andela? Doesn't it pick up your spirit knowing God is alive and showing his love?"

"Ya, Mama, can we get cream ice?" Andela said excitedly. "I'll even buy. There's a sweet shop across the street."

Eliska smiled contently, putting her purse away. "Ok, if you say, but just a small dish."

They crossed the street and entered the sweet shop, ordered, and sat at a wrought-iron table on the plaza.

They shared the crowded square with other Sunday loungers; young couples making eyes at each other while sharing a dish of cream ice; families with kids, cream ice, smeared around their mouths; old folks enjoying the weather. A warm reprieve from the onslaught of oppression.

Eliska took a bite of her ice cream and sat back in her chair. "Such a peaceful Sunday. I wish this day could last a whole week."

From behind Eliska, an icy gruff voice greeted her, "Hello Eliska, how have you been?" Eliska turned and looked up into the cruel eyes of Jacob Conkova.

The blood drained out of Eliska's face as she felt the threat hidden deep in his voice. "How... have you been, Jacob?"

"You don't give a damn how I've been," Jacob sneered and stared at Andela. "Now, who is the lovely lady with you? I don't believe I know her."

"She is a friend from work."

"She could be your daughter. Am I right?"

"It's none of your business who she is."

Jacob smiled a knowing smile and continued. "Haven't seen you since you ran out on me," Jacob said snidely. "Oh wait, I remember you being in a car two years ago, I believe, that was you, wasn't it?"

"I did not run out on you. I was never with you."

"They promised you."

"I made no promise to you."

"Your father did."

"I guess my leaving caused you some hurt. I'm sorry your pride got tramped on."

"It upset my mother that you didn't keep your word."

"I am sorry your mother was hurt. She was a good woman, but I never gave you or her my word."

"Running out on me was bad, but hurting my poor old mother was unforgivable."

"You hurt your mother's memory when you betray your people."

"Well, a river under a bridge. Let bygones be bygones," Jacob said, smiling slyly.

Jacob glanced from Eliska to Andela and back again. "You haven't seen your brothers? I need to talk to them, urgent business to discuss."

"I haven't seen Hanzi since he disappeared in 1919."

"I told you Hanzi and Zuba were killed in Szczecin, Poland!"

"So, that's what you said," Eliska replied, not looking up.

"I mean the twin brothers."

"I don't know."

"Your Papa never paid the dowry back that he took for you."

"That's between you and him."

"He's disappeared. Don't you believe in tradition?"

"More than you. You condemn your people. You care only about yourself."

Eliska stood up to leave. As she turned to walk away, Jacob grabbed her arm and twisted her around, and pulled her close.

"You owe me, and I mean to collect," his brandy-soaked breath blew directly into Eliska's face.

Eliska reached up and raked her long fingernails across his face. "Here's your collection. Now, leave me alone."

Jacob howled, "You bitch!" He grabbed for his dagger, but before he could unsheathe it, Eliska had her blade at his throat.

In a voiced threat, razor-sharp as her dagger, Eliska said, "Don't tempt me to do something I wouldn't regret. If you ever touch me again, I'll cut you a new mouth," Eliska backed away and turned to Andela. "Let's go! This piece of dog crap has spoiled our day." They hurried away, stopping a block away, to make sure Jacob wasn't following them.

Andela, out of breath, said, "Mama, who is that nasty man?"

"A dirty bastard, I want to forget. I'll tell you when we're safe at home."

Meanwhile, Jacob nursed his wounded pride. People sitting at the other tables stole glances at him as he picked up his dagger. He ran his thumb over the dagger's edge and said to himself. *I could turn her in to the Gestapo, but that's too easy. I'll settle with her personally. She works for that Klimy guy. I'll find out what's what, then I settle it."*

~~~~~~

Chapter 82

THE INTERROGATION

The Woods, East of Litomysl Czechoslovakia., Sun, May 14, 1944

The men, who captured Paul, jerked him to his feet, tied his hands behind him, and pulled a blindfold tight over his eyes. They threw him into a car trunk, took off in a roar, bouncing along a dirt road for 15 minutes.

The men unloaded Paul in a wooded glen where the roar of chainsaws echoed out; they pushed him in the back with a rifle and shoved him into a tool shed. Inside, sawdust littered the floor, and on the walls hung chainsaws, handsaws, axes, and other assorted lumbering tools. Sunlight filtered into the room from a single window. In front of the window, a man sat at a lone table. With Paul's hands still tied, the men removed the blindfold and sat him at the table. Across from him sat an old bald man. He had pasty gray skin with a matching gray halo of hair above his ears. He held a sharp hand ax and was absent-mindedly chopping on the table.
~~~~~~

He nonchalantly looked up and finally spoke, "Sprichst du Deutsch? (Do you speak German?)" the man asked. Paul looked at him blankly. "Máte Speck česky? (Do you speak Czech?)." Paul recognized the words but didn't respond.

"He's either dumb or scared." The man guarding him said.

"Do you speak English?"

Paul stared blankly at the floor.

"Who the hell is he?" the other man growled. "Just shoot him, and we don't have to worry."

"Patience, young Danka," the old man responded. "Strip him. Let's see what he has on him."

They untied him and stripped Paul's clothes off. The men searched the pockets, and in the overcoat, they found the papers of the tall man.

The old man glanced at the papers. "It says you are Ales Pulkrabek. You have blond hair," the man coughed, spit bloody phlegm in his gray handkerchief, then looked at Paul's dark hair. "You have blue eyes, and your age is 53."

The man carefully folded the papers up and laid them beside him on the table. "Well, young man, sleeping under the oak tree must have been the fountain of youth for you. Now, your eyes are brown, and you might be 20 years old."

"Look at this." one man handed the old man a chain with metal tags attached.

Paul let out a silent gasp. *I forgot to take my dog tags off. That gives me away.*

The old man turned the tags over and over in his skinny, darkened fingers. He coughed again, "If I'm not mistaken, these are in English. Are you an Englishman, perhaps a flier?"

Paul stared blankly at him.

"An American, I think, there was a bunch of bombing over at Brux. You wouldn't be from a plane that was shot down, would you?"

Paul looked at the floor.

Both young men examined Paul's clothes, and they came to the table with his shirt stretched out between them. "Mr. Jelinek, look at this. See the holes in this shirt. Front and back," they said excitedly.

"Damn it; I told you never to use my name in front of a prisoner!" Jelinek snapped. He looked at Paul. "Lots of bullet holes in the shirt."

He looked Paul up and down. "But not a hole in you. Must be lucky. Or I suspect these are not your clothes. Am I right?"

Paul said nothing. The old man motioned to the two men saying in Czech, "Stevo a Luca tohoto muže ven a zastřelil ho (Stevo and Luca take this man outside and shoot him.)."

"Vy Němečtí bastardi ještě jste slyšeli o Ženevské úmluvy? Jsem (Paul Koupil, United States Air Force) muž prvotřídní Moje sériové číslo je uvedeno na psích známek. (You German bastards! Haven't you heard of the Geneva Convention? I'm Paul Koupil, United States Airman first class. My serial number is on the dog tags!)," Paul shouted at them.

"Aha! He speaks and Czech as well. Very interesting. But you aren't wearing the uniform of your country. You must be a spy," Jelinek chided him.

"I was shot down near Lezaky. Your soldiers shot villagers in a field. I took the clothes from a dead guy."

"What is the number of your aircraft group?"

"Go to hell."

"How are we to check you out if we can't get any details?"

"You'll shoot me, anyway, so get it over with."

"Once more. Where are you stationed?"

"Take a flying leap, jackass."

"You are not very cooperative. Stevo! Luca! Take him outside and show him the swimming pool."

Stevo and Luca untied Paul and picked him up by his arms and dragged his naked body out the door. They took him over to a deep pit filled with brackish water and knelt him beside it.

"Řekněme, že vaše modlitby (Say your prayers)," Luca said.

Paul made the sign of the cross and began the 'Our Father.' Stevo came up behind him, put his pistol to Paul's head, and... CLICK! He howled hilariously, "He sure as hell isn't one of those Nazi pagans.

Paul brought his head up, "That's what I told you two shit-heads."

Luca said, "That's Mr. Jelinek's little test. Works good. Welcome, we're Resistance fighters."

Paul stood still shaking, "Do you do that to all of your allies?"

"No, not always, sometimes we have a real bullet in the gun. Stevo gets a kick at scaring people," Luca said, laughing.

"Are you two twins?" Paul remarked.

Luca reached out his hand, "I'm Luca, and that's Stevo." Paul shook Luca's hand and then turned to Stevo.

Stevo reached out his hand, and Paul produced a haymaker right. His fist landed squarely on Stevo's jaw and sent him sprawling.

"We're even," Paul said as he reached out a hand to help Stevo up.

A dazed Stevo looked at the hand and the naked man standing before him. He hesitantly grabbed it and pulled himself to his feet. "You have a helluva right hook there, mister."

"Five years in the Golden Gloves at Owatonna, Minnesota." ~~~~~~

Chapter 83

HIDING PAUL

In the Woods Litomysl, Czechoslovakia., Mon, May 15, 1944
Josef Jelinek handed Paul a bundle. "Here are your new clothes. Get them on. We don't want the jolly lumberjacks around here to get the wrong idea."

"Where did the clothes come from?"

"Don't ask. We sorta borrowed them from a passing laundry truck. We burned yours. The bullet holes were a sure giveaway. Luca will take you to Litomysl," Josef Jelinek explained. "When you get to Litomysl, he will get your papers made. Without papers, you would be dead the first time a German patrol stops you."

"Can you get me back to the American lines?" Paul said.

"I don't think we can, but we'll mix you into the local population. We have several agents in the city. They will help you, but if they help you, it puts them in grave danger, so only in the most severe case should you contact them. Do you understand?"

"Yes, what am I to live on?"

"Luca has a sister that runs a kitchen. He will take you to her. She runs an apartment house too, where you can stay."

"Ok," Paul said, listening carefully.

"You said you're a mechanic?"

"Yes, cars, trucks, and airplanes."

"Good, but from now on, you know nothing about airplanes."

"All right, but why?"

"Poor Czech mechanics can't tell a propeller from a crankshaft. It might give you away. The best way to stay alive is to blend in. Speak nothing but Czech and little of that. Your accent isn't good."

"Fine by me."

"We want you to do us a big favor."

"What's that?"

"Luca's sister's name is Eliska. She's Roma too, but the Germans haven't figured it out. She can get her dander up, kinda like you. Can we trust you to take care of her and her daughter Andela?"

"Ya, I suppose I can do that."

"Good. You leave in ten minutes. Any questions before you leave?"

"How long do you think this war will last?"

"Till it's over! How the hell should I know! Just stay alive day by day," Josef responded.

"Sorry, I asked," Paul snapped.

"Let this be a lesson to you. Don't ask too many stupid questions. Don't lose your temper. Act slow, pretend you are dumb or slow-witted. The Nazis are masters at pushing the buttons exactly right so that you reveal your hand. Don't let that happen, or you will be dead," Jelinek explained. "Now, son, go with God." Josef Jelinek shook Paul's hand and waved goodbye. ~~~~~~

Chapter 84

FOOLING THE SS

Litomysl, Czechoslovakia. Tues, May 16, 1944.

A warm May sun beat down on a scrawny team of horses as they leisurely pulled a cart loaded with vegetables to Litomysl. Luca stoically drove the team with an occasional snap of the reins and a quick yell of encouragement. An old straw hat covered Luca's curly hair, and he wore his 'mucking out' boots, boots that a typical farmer wore. Luca told Paul, "Pretend you're taking a nap. If you look around too much, it arouses their suspicions. If you see something important, just a quick glance. Try to memorize it."

Paul pulled his hat over his eyes and pretended to nod off. *Sorry, I never got interested in spy comics. They may have come in handy now.*

When they reached the outskirts of town, a German checkpoint loomed before them. Lucas swore under his breath. "Damn, they changed the location again. We'll have to bluff our way through."

Lucas pulled to a stop at the checkpoint. A fat German sergeant came out. "What's in the cart?" he demanded.

"Lettuce, peas, spring onions, and fresh rhubarb."

"Get off, so I can look."

"Ya, OK," Luca replied.

Paul sat, hat over his eyes, petrified.

Luca reached up and gave Paul a swat. "Get off, dumb ass, get off so we can get going."

The sergeant laughed, "Got me a couple like that. Stumblebums! Can't find their way if I painted directions on the road."

Luca laughed, "You said it. He's too dumb to go into the army, so I get to babysit with him; try to get a crop picked with him, a stumblebum. My sister's kid, so what can I do? Takes after his lazy father. All he ever did was get my sister knocked up. Three times now. Sometimes I wonder if he hired that out."

The sergeant laughed again. "Looks OK, you can go."

"Good," Luca said, as he and Paul climbed back onto the seat. Luca reached behind the seat. "You eat sweet peas?"

"Oh yeah, sure, my mother made the best pea and ham soup."

"Can't help you with the ham, but here's a bucket of fresh peas you might enjoy," Luca said, as he handed the bucket to the sergeant. "If I see a pig, I'll chase him your way."

"Danke," the sergeant replied as he opened the barrier gate. "Got to find the onions now."

Luca again reached behind the cart seat and threw Sergeant Gruber two bunches of onions.

"Danke again," the sergeant replied, waving his hand forward.

Luca click, clicked the horses, and they went on their way.

"You sure kept your cool back there," Paul said.

"Cool? Hell, I almost wet my pants. Good thing Sergeant Gruber was on duty. We usually can slip things by him. I got his mind on his stomach, and he didn't even ask for our papers.

Luca and Paul delivered vegetables throughout Litomysl and finally stopped behind Fat Hilda's Cafe and took the vegetables in. Fat Hilda, who resembled a glorious blonde bowl of jello, came out from the corner of the kitchen. She wrapped her jiggly arms around Luca and lifted him up, squeezed his butt, and hugged him, "My little Luca, when are you gonna pick me up, carry me to the church and marry me?"

"Ah, sorry, Hilda, I have to keep all the girls happy."

"Don't you think I'd be woman enough?"

"Oh, hell yes, Hilda, too much. I'm afraid if you got me into bed, I'd tear up my gears making love to you; then I'd have to go around wearing a dress."

"You are such a snorter, my sweet," Hilda laughed, sizing Paul up. "Who's the big handsome friend?"

"Oh, some help, I picked up for the farm, kinda dumb, but he works cheap."

Hilda grabbed Luca again and lifted him up, kissing him on the mouth. "I could just take you home!" she laughed, then she whispered in his ear, "What do you need?"

"I need papers for him. Is the printer in?"

"Ya, in the basement, send him down, and you wait here. Unload: be useful," Hilda whispered to him. "One of my waitresses is a collaborator."

Paul took the stairs into the basement where the printer, a pale man with ink-stained hands, was chewing on a wad of paper and bent over a small ID card. The printer lined Paul up in front of a white sheet hanging from the wall and photographed him; then, the printer put together a set of documents that would fool the Germans. Within an hour, he had the film developed and the proper paperwork printed. Paul said, "Thanks, Mr.....?

"None of your business. It's better that way."

*Figure 85 - **Fat Hilda's Cafe***

~~~~~
~~~~~

Chapter 85

DODGING THE SS

The Chateau, Litomysl Czechoslovakia. Tues, May 16, 1944.
With the paperwork in hand, Luca and Paul casually drove the cart to the Chateau. Eliska met them, in the alley, at the loading dock.

"Good morning, Luca."

"Good morning Eliska, are you feeling better since Mama died so quick?"

"Ya, I think she wanted to join Papa. A broken heart can't keep beating. She knew Papa might need help to find his way."

Eliska looked up at Paul sitting on the cart seat. A tingle of warmth swept through her. "Who is this big handsome boy?"

"This is Paul Koupil. He helps us at the farm," Luca said as Paul tipped his hat.

"He does, does he?" Eliska said as she stared at Paul. "You look familiar. Have we ever met?"

"No, don't... think... so."

Eliska looked at him out of the corner of her eye, and a quizzical expression danced across her face.

Luca unloaded vegetables, "Can you put him up at the apartment?"

Eliska hesitated, "I'm not sure. What will Mr. Klimy say?"

"He's already approved it. Said to put him to work in the kitchen."

Eliska hesitated, "It's hard enough to stay ahead of the Gestapo, much less hide someone else... But we could use a big strong boy around. The apartment needs repair too."

"Good, it's settled," Luca said matter-a-factly.

Luca and Paul continued unloading vegetables. As they did, Ales Baum, with three German SS soldiers, came up the alley. They stopped and looked up at the loading dock.

"Fresh vegetables already?"

"Ya, time marches on. Crops are doing good this year," Luca replied without looking up.

"I haven't seen the two of you before. Show me your papers."

Luca jumped down, wiped his brow, and wiped his hands on his shirt. Pulling his papers out, he showed them to Baum. Baum looked them over suspiciously.

"Looks all right. What about him?" Baum said, pointing at Paul. Paul continued to unload vegetables.

"Is he deaf or something? Where're his papers?"

Luca stepped up to Baum. "You must excuse him. He's slow. Strong back, weak mind. Good help on the farm, though." Luca looked up at Paul. "Paul, stop that! Come here!"

Paul stood up and looked blankly at Luca.

"Now, dumkoff! Come here!" Luca said, pointing to the street.

Paul climbed off the wagon. "Da... vegetables... need unload."

"We'll get back to that. Do you have your papers?"

Paul looked at Luca, dumbfounded. Luca reached into Paul's pocket, pulled the papers out, and gave them to Baum. "See what I have to put up with? Have to tell him three or two times to do anything."

Paul stood fidgeting as Baum examined his papers. "It says you were born in Semanín?"

"Ya... Se... Manin."

"Where did you go to school?"

Paul shrugged his shoulders, "No... school... Mama... teach words."

"You work here long?"

"Too... long. Ah hee, a hee," Paul said, the corner of his mouth raised in a crooked grin, snorting at his little joke.

"That one's a real dunderhead," Baum said, handing back their papers. "Carry on."

Baum and the soldiers walked away. Eliska pulled Luca aside. "How can I use a guy as dumb as he is?"

Luca chuckled, "A fox is dumb alongside him." Luca put his arm around Eliska's shoulder. "He'll do fine."

~~~~~~
~~~~~~

Chapter 86

CHOP OFF THEIR HEADS

The Chateau, Litomysl Czechoslovakia., Tues, May 16, 1944

After Luca unloaded and left, Paul stayed behind with Eliska. "We need help today, dressing chickens. Have you ever dressed chickens?" Paul shook his head, no.

"It's easy. Chop off the head, dunk em in hot water, and pull the feathers off. Then open um up, pull the guts out. My daughter Andela will be there to show you how."

Eliska took Paul to a small, fenced-in yard behind the poor kitchen. Seated on short wooden stools were Andela and two other cook's helpers.

"Andela, this is Paul Koupil. Put him to work. He's a chicken dumb, I think."

"Ok, Mama." Andela wiped the feathers off her hands: pushed back her blond hair that had fallen in her face, and flashed Paul a coy smile. She motioned for him to come to the chopping block.

Figure 86 The Rooster

"Here's the ax. The roosters are in the crate over there. Grab one by the feet. Watch out for the spurs. Bring the rooster over here, take the ax and chop off his head. Hold on to him until he's done flopping. OK?"

"Ah... ya... I... do... that.

"Here, I'll do the first one." Andela took a big red rooster out of the crate and, with one blow, lopped the head off. When the rooster finished bleeding and flopping around, she threw him over to the helper who was running the scalding kettle. "That's all there is to it."

Paul tiptoed up to the crate.

"You don't have to sneak up on um, we already have them in the crate," Andela teased.

Paul opened the crate door and, after several attempts, pulled a rooster out. The bird flapped furiously and pecked at Paul's hand. "Damn, that hurt," slipped out.

With a cloud of feathers and raucous squawking from the rooster, Paul finally got the bird under control and took it to the chopping block. He positioned the bird on the block, raised the ax high, and came down with a mighty sweep of his arm. The rooster pulled his head back right before the ax hit, and Paul missed his target completely. Valiantly, he tried again, missed again, and again.

By this time, Andela and the other help were laughing uproariously. "What are you doing, chopping wood or roosters?" Andela teased him. "We only have the one chopping block. You should sneak up on him."

"How... I... do... that?"

"Don't look at him till before you hit him."

"Ok." Paul raised the ax and pretended not to look at the roster. Then, as the ax came down, he looked back at the rooster. The ax struck the rooster just right and OFF WENT HIS HEAD!

Paul gloated in his victory. He held the headless rooster high until the bird flopped around, spraying blood on Paul's face and clothes. Paul was dumbfounded at the sight of the blood. His mind raced back to his encounter with the blood of his fellow airmen over Brux. He trembled and dropped the bloody bird.

Unaware of the turmoil that the blood had brought back to Paul, Andela, and the kitchen help laughed and slapped each other on the back. Andela pulled two of the rooster's long red tail feathers out and stuck them in Paul's hat. "I dub thee Sir Rooster Koupil," she teased, "Your baptism is complete."

Paul regained his composure, gave his best victory pose, and bowed to Andela. "Thank... you... Madame."

Andela chuckled demurely. *He sure is a handsome man.* ~~~~~~

Chapter 87

FOUND OUT

Apartment House, Litomysl Czechoslovakia. Tues, May 16, 1944.

The sleepy sun bowed low in the western sky. The quiet Chateau kitchen was clean and neat, just as Karel demanded. Eliska put on her scarf and called to Andela. "Time to go. Tell Paul to come too."

"OK."

The threesome left the Chateau, walked through the gardens, and admired the spring flowers. After they had arrived at the apartment house, Eliska showed Paul his apartment. "Luca said, you are a mechanic."

"Yes... I can... a little."

"You can drop the act around Andela and me. We know you are as sly as a fox."

Paul let out his breath and dropped his shoulders. "Thank God! It's hard, keeping it up."

"You should stay on guard; you can't be sure of who you can trust. Come with me." Eliska took Paul out to a shed next to the garage behind the apartment house, "I have a lot of repair work that needs doing. I'm good with a wooden spoon, but a wrench or a hammer outsmarts me."

Paul looked around the repair shed and picked up a shiny wrench. "Plenty of good tools here. Someone knew what they were doing when they bought them."

"Oh, that's Karel Klimy, the owner of the apartments."

"The Mr. Klimy that runs the kitchens?"

"That's him, detailed to a fault, a good planner, a man you can trust."

Paul continued to inspect the tools when he came upon a large black suitcase. "What's this?"

"My husband's Helicon tuba. It was his father's." Paul opened the suitcase and took out the tuba.

Figure 71 Helicon Tuba

"It's beautiful," Paul said as he tenderly slid his hand along the bell of the horn.

"You know tubas?" Eliska asked.

"I played before the service and in the Air Force regimental band. A tuba, but different from this one. May I try it?"

Eliska hesitated; no one had played this horn since Zuba left. But, for some reason, it seemed fitting to allow it. She nodded yes.

Paul picked it up and played. "It has the same fingering as my horn." He smiled, contemplating the fingering, and played heartily. It was hard to solo with a rhythm instrument, but Paul performed a passable rendition of the Praha Polka.

Eliska clapped her hands along with the music. "I haven't heard that since my husband and I played in Papa's band. You play it the same as he did. How did you learn?"

"A Czech mechanic that works for my dad taught me. Or at least he had worked for my dad before the accident."

"The accident?"

"Ya, he saved my life. He held a heavy truck box over his head for ten minutes as I lay, knocked out underneath it. They pulled me out, but then the truck box fell and hit him. He ended up in the hospital and in a coma. The last letter I received from my dad said he was out of the coma, but his arm doesn't work, and he can't speak. Just sits and watches people in the repair shop."

"Sounds like a good man."

Paul's eyes clouded up, "Ya, best friend, even if he is older than I am."

Eliska came over and placed her hand on his shoulder. "Life is never what we want it to be. We keep going; hope for the best."

Paul wiped his eyes with the back of his hand and gently put the tuba away. "Is it OK if I play it again?"

"Anytime."   ~~~~~~

Chapter 88
THE INVASION BEGINS

The Chateau, Litomysl Czechoslovakia., Thurs, June 15, 1944

Karel came into the Chateau kitchen excited, carrying a newspaper.

"Why are you so chipper, Karel?" Eliska said

"The invasion has begun."

"What invasion? The Germans already invaded us."

"The Allies landed Tuesday, somewhere in France. A place called Normandy."

"Who landed?"

"Americans, English, Czech Free army, and many others are fighting the Germans."

"That's a long way from us."

"The Resistance doesn't think so; they're activating all members of the Resistance. They want us to tie up as many troops here as we can, so the Germans can't use them on the invaders."

"How are we to do that?"

"Who knows? But we'll do it!" Karel replied eagerly.

"Maybe a good plan... to make you dead."

"Time to do something. Enough is enough!"

"Well, I have work to do. Don't have a heart attack before I get back from the poor kitchen."

Eliska arrived in the poor kitchen as the kitchen help was cleaning up from the evening meal. Paul and Andela were up to their elbows in washing dishes. Andela giggled and teased 'Rooster Koupil' She placed a gob of soap suds on his nose, and then he put a gob of suds on her head, fashioning them into a semblance of a crown. "There you are my queen. My soapy, sudsy queen," Paul laughed and bowed gracefully.

"All right, you two, finish up and go home." Eliska scolded, smiling to herself. *It's good to hear Andela, happy again. Well, I better get serious.*

"Paul, come with me. Andela, you go home when you finish."

Eliska beckoned to a table in a far corner, and they sat down. "Paul, I think Andela is falling for you."

"She is? I thought we were just having fun. I don't have that kind of feeling for her. She's like a sister to me."

"Did you tell her that you are married, with a baby?"

"No, you said I shouldn't tell her too much about myself.

"I'll take care of that when I get home," Eliska said, then told Paul about the invasion and the plans to disrupt the Germans locally.

"What do they want me to do?" Paul said. ~~~~~~

Chapter 89

Join the Band

The Chateau, Litomysl Czechoslovakia. Thurs, June 15, 1944.

Paul was washing dishes when Eliska came up to him, "Luca wants you to join the community band. They perform at German parties. You can eavesdrop on all kinds of information if you listen. It might make more sense to you than the farmers in the Resistance." Eliska continued, "Practice is tonight at the Chateau. You can use my husband's tuba."

"OK," Paul said, wiping his hands. *Uneasy... meet new people? Eliska is so good to me; I can't refuse her.*

"Good! Tonight, at seven, in the Tauer room, right off the dining room. Andela will come to rehearsal as soon as she gets home." Eliska said. ~~~~~~

Paul entered the Tauer room, where the band rehearsed. Other band members were getting their instruments ready and checking the tuning.

Off to one side stood the player/director, Albert Cerny.

Albert was a slight man wearing a dark coat and pants; he had thick black hair that swept back from his pale forehead, creating a widow's peak, which pointed downward to a long hook nose perched upon a small lifeless mouth.

He greeted Paul. "Good evening. What can I do for you?"

"Eliska... Palzekova told me... you need a... tuba... player."

"Well, yes we do, but we don't take anyone. You must audition first. The Resistance killed our old tuba player for having too big of a mouth. Too bad, damn good tuba player."

"I... don't... know politics just... play... tuba."

"Good, that would be nice for a change. Can you play the Praha Polka?"

"Ya... sure."

Albert tapped his baton on his podium and called out to the rest of the band. "Let's get started. Mr. Koupil wants to join the band and is here to audition. Let's try the Praha Polka." Albert counted out the beat, and the band started. He picked up his trombone and sat next to Paul. It was a lively version of the polka, and the band members nodded their praise as they ended. "Great job! Solid beat!"

"Well, band, should we make him a member? If so, raise your hand," Albert said.

Most of the band raised their hands, but a few, wary of new members, didn't.

"Good, we have a new tuba player. Stand up, Mr. Koupil, and give us a word or two."

Paul stood and waved apprehensively.

"Thank... you. I... Got... no... words to... say."

Albert chuckled, "At last, a tuba player without diarrhea of the mouth."

Two hours later, Albert called the rehearsal to a halt. The musicians were packing up when Albert came over to Paul. "You play excellent, Paul."

"Thank... you."

"I know who you are and need to discuss a couple of things with you."

Paul hesitated, "How... you... know... what?"

"Luca asked his sister Eliska to send you to us. You met Luca, the vegetable smuggler, didn't you?"

"Sure, I did. Is there anyone who doesn't know who I am?" Paul said incredulously.

"None of the band knows. Just me. It's safer that way."

"What do you want of me?"

"You're an airplane mechanic, aren't you?"

"Ya."

"Do you know how to fly?"

"A little; I had to learn how to check out the planes better."

Albert continued, "Good, we captured an old Junkers F.13 passenger plane. It might help us in the coming days. We have the Junkers stored in a barn a short way from here. Needs work, but we're farmers and merchants. We know nothing about a plane. Will you look at it?"

"It might take a long time. I can't leave Eliska and Andela for long. I need to watch over them." Paul said.

"Understood, there will be someone watching them day and night when you leave."

"Sounds OK. You said a couple of things?"

"Yes, we're mighty short on weapons. Especially the ones we can conceal. Have any ideas?"

"Don't you have a gunsmith?"

"Used to, but he was the first one the Germans took away. The nearest one now is in Prague, and he may not be there anymore either."

"Did you ever hear of a zip gun?" Paul said.

"No."

"Do you have any small-caliber rounds such as a 22 or a 25?"

"I could find a few."

"Good, I used to teach a class on making a zip gun to our fliers. Just in case they were shot down. You must get close, though."

Paul picked up Albert's trombone and slid the slide back and forth. "Might be able to do something with this. Maybe use it once; after that, it may not be any good anymore."

"When the day comes, we will need weapons to get rid of those bastards."

"Let me take your trombone to the repair shop and see. No promises, OK?"

<center>~~~~~~</center>

Chapter 90

THE ABUSE

Apartment House, Litomysl Czechoslovakia. Thurs, June 15, 1944.

Paul walked back to his apartment, and as he passed Eliska's door, he heard a woman crying and another woman cursing. He knocked on the door, and an angry, red-faced Eliska came to the door, a dagger in her hand.

"What's wrong?" Paul said.

"Two damn SS soldiers had their way with my little Andela. I know who they are. They tried it before, and I warned them. Now, I'll cut their throats."

"May I come in?" Paul said.

Eliska opened the door wide, and in the far room, Andela lay on her bed sobbing unceasingly; her bruised cheek scratched, her left eye swollen half shut, and dried blood sat in the corner of her mouth. "Get him out of here, Mama; I don't want him to see me this way." Andela wailed.

Paul retreated to the kitchen as Eliska scurried around, making a poultice for Andela's swollen face. "This fixes her body, but her heart will never be the same."

"Do you know who they were?"

"Eldric and Hartmut! Freikorps bastards! They work for the SS. I should have cut their throats when I had the chance."

Eliska then went back to Andela, behind the closed door of the bedroom.

When she came out, a weariness hung over her like a willow tree bending under heavy snow. *How much longer? Oh Lord, how much longer before we break?* She hurried to the coat tree and put on her scarf and light jacket.

"Where are you going, Eliska?

"I have things to take care of."

"Eldric and Hartmut?"

"Yes, don't try to stop me."

"I won't, but I'm wondering, what am I to do with Andela when you don't come back?"

"I'll be back."

"You are one person with a small dagger. Can you dodge the guns at the SS headquarters."?

"I'll get those bastards for what they did to my little girl."

"Why don't you sit for a minute and think this through."

Eliska hesitated, then sat hard on the kitchen chair, "I'll get those bastards," she muttered again.

"I'm sure you will try. Again, what am I supposed to do with Andela when you don't come back? She needs you now more than ever," Paul said matter-a-factly.

Eliska slumped in her chair at the table. She laid her arms on the table, placed her head on them, and sobbed. Paul stood behind her and put his arms around her, whispering firmly, "I promise you this, Eliska, when the time comes, I will take care of it."

Eliska turned and put her arms around Paul and sobbed on his chest. "When the time comes." ~~~~~~

Chapter 91

WAITING

The Barn, West of Litomysl Czechoslovakia., Sat, Oct 20, 1944

Paul spent every available hour working on the Junkers F.13 passenger plane. He gerry-rigged repairs from parts scrounged from shot down and sabotaged German planes. Josef Jelinek observed his work closely, "Well, Paul, will it run?"

"It's quite a job. Lots of parts are broken or missing."

"Let us know what you need, and we'll try to get it."

"How about a new engine and props?"

"I can swim, but I can't walk on water," Josef joked.

"I'll get it going, it only takes time."

"We might have time. The invasion has made deep penetrations, and Hitler doesn't have much fuel left. He can't last long." Josef said.

"Good! How's the Resistance holding up?" Paul asked.

"We're still making hit-and-run strikes. We keep them guessing as to the size of the Resistance."

"Are you losing many men?" Paul asked.

"Some, but more join every day. Everybody wants in on the kill; I wonder where they were a year ago?"

"Hiding under a rock, I suppose. Can you blame them? It looked hopeless."

"Gotta go. Let me know when the plane is ready." Josef said, leaving the room.

"Roger."

Paul finished work before the sunset and hurried to return to Litomysl before curfew. As he slipped through an alley, he heard a scream. He peeked around the building corner and saw several German soldiers dragging a woman out into the street.

A man sprang into the street, ran towards the soldiers, screaming, "You bastards, leave my wife be!" He raised a pistol, aimed, and fired twice.

A German soldier fell, and the rest of the soldiers fired back, killing the man. He slumped to his knees, dropped on his face, dead. His gun, mingled with his life's blood, slid away and fell into a storm drain.

"Find that pistol," the German officer ordered. The soldiers searched diligently but couldn't find it. The officer finally gave up. "If we can't find it, neither can the Resistance. Let's go! Bring that traitorous bitch!

After the Germans left, Paul crawled to the storm drain and pulled off the drain cover. He extended his long arm in and felt along the edge of the drainpipe. Feeling the cold steel of the pistol, he retrieved it and slipped it in his pocket.

Paul returned to his apartment building and spent the next four hours in the repair shed. After considerable tinkering, he had remodeled Albert Cerny's trombone into a weapon. He closed the repair shed and returned to the apartment house.

In the central hallway, he stopped and knocked on Eliska's apartment. Eliska sneaked a peek before opening the door to him. Andela, her blonde hair pulled back in a clump, sat at the kitchen table, sewing.

Paul cheerily said, "Andela, you are pretty tonight. How do you feel?" Andela didn't acknowledge him.

Eliska took Paul aside. "Paul, I'm worried; it's four months since her ordeal. She eats little and speaks less. She's lost somewhere."

"Did the doctor help her?"

"He gave her pills, but she won't take them."

"May I talk to her?"

"I guess it won't hurt."

Paul sat across from Andela, reached out, and took the sewing from her. He clasped her hand with one of his hands and lifted her chin with the other hand so that their eyes met. "Andela, I know you are hurting. What they did to you shouldn't be done to anyone. It wasn't your fault and nothing to be ashamed of."

Paul stroked Andela's cheek. "You are as beautiful and wonderful as you always were. Nobody can take your spirit away. Only you can throw it away. Don't let them win."

Andela looked at Paul, tears washing her cheeks. "No boy will want me after this."

"That's not true; any sensible man would be happy to have you by his side."

"Would you?"

Paul, startled by the question, looked at Eliska.

Eliska nodded, "Tell her."

"I'd love to have you by my side if I was able?"

"If you are able! Are you looking for an excuse to wiggle out of what you said?"

"Andela, I have a wife and a baby boy in America. I love them with my whole heart. If it wasn't for that...." Paul's voice trailed off. *I didn't want to tell her this harshly, but it came out that way.*

Andela raised her head, eyes wide, "I didn't know. I thought you were avoiding me because of what happened."

"I didn't know what to say to you. Your mother knew. She was about to tell you when you got home that night. I didn't want to tell you after what happened and hurt you more."

"I hurt, but not as much as you, not talking to me."

"I'm so sorry, Andela. I care for you, but like a sister."

Andela dried her eyes and looked up at Eliska. "Do you have any soup, Mama? I'm hungry."

~~~~~~
~~~~~~

Chapter 92

TIME TO KILL

Apartment House, Litomysl Czechoslovakia, Wed, April 18, 1945

A late-night knock-on Paul's apartment door interrupted his sleep. He bolted upright in bed, warily grabbed his pistol, and opened the door to see the grinning face of Stevo, Eliska's brother. "We need you now."

"What's up?"

"We're getting ready to strike. We need to discuss the plans with you."

"Ok, have you got someone to stay and look after Eliska and Andela."

"Done! My American friend."

"You are sure, chipper."

"Gonna kill Germans and Czech collaborators, always makes an enjoyable day."

"It's time now? How is that?"

"Hear the rumbling off to the west."

"Ya, all day. Must be a storm coming," Paul replied.

"Storm hell! It's a Russian hurricane! That's their artillery, less than one hundred miles away." Stevo rubbed his hands together, "And a hotshot American general is pushing in from the East with a bunch of tanks and is kicking the crap out of the Germans."

"It must be Patton."

"We'll hit em on the Heir Fuhrer's birthday, April 20th. Josef called for an all-out effort."

"Good, be right with you."

Paul dressed and followed Stevo out of the apartment house. Crossing the back lawn, Paul noticed a shadowy figure leaning against the repair shed. He reached into his pocket for his pistol. Stevo grabbed his arm and stopped him. "Don't worry, that's Jacob Conkova. He will watch Eliska."

~~~~~~
~~~~~~

Chapter 93

THE CONCERT

Loucna River Front, Litomysl, Czechoslovakia. Fri, April 20, 1945.

The day dawned sunny and bright; the last of the snowdrifts trickled away, and spring bloomed its heart out. The Germans planned a big party at the Loucna River Park to celebrate Hitler's birthday. As a bonus, they were cheering the recent death of Franklin Roosevelt, the hated President of the United States. The community band was to perform, and several dignitaries were attending, including many German officers.

The Loucna River Park had a large cobblestone patio with small elm trees framing it. Artfully arranged purple hyacinths, and white crocuses, resembled colorful soldiers, aligned in neat rows, waving their petals, and marching to the beat of a spring song. The tulips bloomed blatantly. A shelter house was nestled on one side of the patio, and the Chateau staff had set up gayly decorated party tables in it to serve refreshments.

The guests were in full Nazi dress uniforms, oblivious to the world collapsing around them. Noticeably absent were the Czech friends that had catered to the German's for so long. Rats were leaving a sinking ship!

Albert Cerny concocted a unique concoction from his undertaker's business. After the first imbibe, when the taste of the schnapps had dulled the party goer's senses, Eliska mixed the mixture into the drinks.

"Maybe it won't kill em," Albert confided in Eliska, "but they'll have a hell of a time fighting when they can't get five feet from the outhouse. It's hard to run out and shoot someone, with your pants around your ankles," Albert smirked, "If they die, I won't have to use too much more embalming fluid."

On the far side of the patio was the bandstand, its balcony, shaped like the prow of a ship, jutted out over the swollen Loucna river.

At the bandstand, Andela took out her battered old cornet, oiled the valves, and adjusted the tuning.

Andela was slowly returning to her old self, but was apprehensive whenever she saw a German uniform. Today could be a trial for her, and Paul wished that he had not encouraged her to return to play in the band. Eliska thought it was best, as she was afraid to leave Andela home alone.

Off to the side of the bandstand, Paul showed Albert Cerny how to use his trombone weapon. Paul put the instrument to his lips and slid the slide out. He flicked a hidden switch, and a ten-inch thin dagger, more like an ice pick, flipped open and locked tight at the end of the slide.

Paul said, "In the right position, this will work. If you drive this in at the base of the skull upward, that is a kill spot. You should be able to drop a man with one thrust. Otherwise, you will be in trouble."

Albert picked up the trombone and tried it several times. "I must call out the right music to make this work."

The celebration had started at eleven-thirty in the morning. The band played at two in the afternoon. By then, several German officers, full of schnapps, wandered around like rudderless ships in a whirlpool.

One drunken soldier staggered up onto the bandstand. Noticing Andela, he came over to her, and in broken Czech and German, propositioned her. Andela pushed him back, but he was persistent. The band finished the number as the German stood behind Andela and tried to massage her breasts.

Albert Cerny, sitting behind Andela, called out the 'Tiger Rag.' It had several nice glissandos in it, and the band played a rip-roaring rendition. Albert liked it because of the long trombone slides on the chorus of 'Hold That Tiger.' The German was again trying to fondle Andela. Now was the opportune time; Albert flipped the switch; the dagger came out and locked in place. As hard as he could, he pushed his trombone slide to the limit.

The dagger penetrated the back of the German's neck, below the base of his skull, sliding upwards and coming out of his left eye socket. He collapsed like a wet noodle and fell right next to Andela. She didn't stop playing. With a swift kick, she pushed him over the bandstand wall into the raging river below. As he floated down the river, Andela whispered: "Have a nice day, you bastard." And the band played on. ~~~~

Chapter 94

THE BATTLE

Litomysl, Czechoslovakia Fri, May 4, 1945

In Prague, it was quiet, even though the Russian army was knocking at their gates. But it wouldn't be for long. Early Friday morning, the Czech Free Forces captured a Prague radio station, and the first call went out for the Resistance forces to join the battle.

The little city of Litomysl endured two weeks of repercussions from the results of the birthday party. The Resistance misjudged how long it would take for the German military to collapse and their rebellion too early, and now they suffered the consequences.

In retaliation for the poisoning at the birthday party, the SS conducted no-knock raids throughout Litomysl, searching for the suspected saboteurs and Resistance.

At the Chateau, they burst into the kitchen and sprayed it with bullets. Finding no one there, they searched and found the elevator. Two of the SS troops took the elevator to the third floor and opened the storeroom door. When the first SS man opened the door, Karel, with a mighty swing of his meat cleaver, cleaved his head asunder. Karel stood paralyzed as the second SS man raised his rifle to fire, but behind the SS man, Kizzy stepped up and skewered him with a meat hook. Karel and Kizzy ran towards the elevator, but a third SS man stepped came up the stairs. Realizing that his time was up, Karel raised the meat cleaver and charged.

The SS shot him in his stomach. Karel dropped his cleaver and lost his glasses. He fell to the floor, frantically crawling, trying to find his glasses. Kizzy rushed to his side, helped him stand, and they both struggled to the open stairway. As the bullets ricocheted about them, they jumped over the railing, fell three stories to the floor, and died in each other's arms.

The Germans tracked the embalming fluid to Albert Cerny. At his funeral home, they broke through every entry door at the same time.

Searching diligently, they found Albert hiding in a casket. Pulling him out, they spread-eagled him across his embalming table, tied his arms and legs to the table, and tortured him. In his last defiant action, Albert spat in their faces; he died with a bottle of embalming fluid jammed deep in his throat.

As the Russians got closer, the Germans reassigned troops to Prague for the defense of that city. In Litomysl, several of the remaining troops shed their uniforms, donned civilian clothes, and slunk away. Only the die-hard Freikorps, SS, and Gestapo remained. They roamed the city like hungry wolves, exacting frustrated revenge.

<div align="center">~~~~~~</div>

Gestapo headquarters, Litomysl, Czechoslovakia Sat, May 5, 1945
Jacob Conkova arrived at Gestapo headquarters early, and Helmut escorted him to Ales Baum's office.

"What the hell do you want?" Ales said as he burned papers in the stove.

"These Roma that have eluded you for a long while!" Jacob sneered.

"What use is that now?"

"Oh, this will tickle you. They worked right under your nose at the kitchen of that Klimy guy you killed."

"Is that so? What's it gonna cost this time?

"You have been such good customers; this one is on the house."

"You are a jewel, so speak up!"

"First, have Mr. Egger to come in here, so at least I get the credit for turning them over to you."

"All right, smart ass!" Ales turned to Helmut, "Call Mr. Egger in, will you?"

After a few minutes, Bertram Egger entered the room. "So, gypsy, what do you have?"

"I have two Roma women that have made a fool of your young Ales here, time and again," Jacob replied.

"Well, talk, or do I have to persuade you?" Ales said.

"Do you recall that Roma girl, the one you had fun with, at the dance a few years ago? The one I was with when she kneed you in your jewels?"

"Ah, yes, I do. What about it?

"She and her daughter work in the kitchen at the Chateau!" Jacob said.

"She does? Damn! Now I remember, I thought she looked familiar. We'll arrest her right away." Ales snarled.

"Not so fast. Her brothers are in the resistance. I have been friends with them, gathering information for you. You can set a trap for them and catch the whole damn bunch." Jacob said, rubbing his hands together.

Bertram Egger got up close and jabbed Jacob in the chest. Egger's cold, lifeless eyes bore into Jacob as he declared, "This wouldn't be a trap, would it? You don't want us to pay you for this information? How come? Are you switching sides?

"No, it's a personal score. I've waited to get even. I was to marry Eliska Danka, and she turned on me."

"You better not be lying; we have a lot of ways to deal with you if you cross us." Egger said, "Where does she live?"

Jacob told them where Eliska and Andela lived, and the Nazis planned the raid for the following day.

"Conkova, can you get word to the brothers about us raiding these women?" Egger said.

"Glad to," Jacob replied.

Egger set it up so it would look easy for someone to attack them after they arrested Eliska and Andela. "Ok, here's what we'll do. I expect that the two brothers will attack as we bring them to Gestapo headquarters," Egger said. "The best place is a block away; bring them that way, and I'll have extra men stationed nearby so they can respond quickly when the Resistance attacks. A little ambush within an ambush."

~~~~~~

Chapter 95

THE SHOWDOWN

Apartment House, Litomysl, Czechoslovakia, Sun, May 6, 1945

On Sunday morning, Ales Baum, Eldric, Hartmut, and Bertram Egger burst into Eliska's apartment. Eliska whirled and raced to reach a butcher knife on the kitchen counter, but before she could grasp it, Ales grabbed her by the hair, spun her around, and slapped her hard across the face. Andela grabbed a hot frying pan full of bacon grease and threw it in Bertram Egger's face. He screamed in pain as he grabbed his face. Andela raised the pan to hit Eggers, but Helmut backhanded her in the mouth. She flew against the table, falling on the floor.

After they subdued Eliska and Andela, they took the two women, kicking and screaming, into the street. "You are saboteurs and gypsies. How we missed you is beyond us. Now it's time to pay," they said as they marched them to the SS headquarters.

A block from the headquarters, Fat Hilda's delivery truck pulled up and parked at the curb. Fat Hilda got out and opened the delivery van's back doors. An old, bald man got out. He grabbed a large tray of pastries and carried them towards a small shop. The old man limped and spat out bloody dark phlegm.

As Baum and company advanced, crashing glass from across the street clattered to the sidewalk.
~~~~~~

They looked up, and hurtling down from a third-story window, was a man wearing a shabby brown overcoat. He sailed through the air, and as he reached the second floor, a rope attached to his neck ran out of slack, stopping him short. He dangled there, kicking, jerking, a slow twisting rag doll. Jacob Conkova had informed his last!

The Freikorps stood bewildered by this savage twist.

The old man dropped his tray of pastries; his free hand produced a pistol. He aimed carefully and shot Bertram Egger through the throat.

Bertram clutched his throat, gurgled, and fell to the sidewalk gasping for breath. His dazed expression pleaded out a prayer or a welcome to the devil, as the case may be. He held his neck as his blown-away jugular vein drained his life into the cobblestones.

The old man leveled his pistol on Ales Baum, but the younger Baum was faster, his Luger barked, and the bullet struck Josef Jelinek in the chest. Josef died on the cobblestones, a crimson pool forming under him.

Paul Koupil leaped out of the alley, and behind Eldric, he shot him in the back of the head. Ales Baum whirled and aimed his pistol at Paul. As he did, a shot rang out from the third-floor window that Conkova had fallen from. The bullet ripped through Ales Baum's heart and backbone. He was dead, collapsing to the street. Paul leveled his pistol at Hartmut and pulled the trigger. Click!... Bad Ammo! Click!... Misfire again!

Hartmut sneered and pointed his pistol at Paul. Suddenly, a flash of pain crossed Hartmut's face. Eliska had drawn her hidden dagger and slashed him deep into the lower part of his back.

Whirling in pain, Hartmut struck Eliska across her face. She fell hard, hitting her head on the street. She moaned and lay on the cobblestones bleeding out of her mouth. Andela quickly covered Eliska's body with her own, shielding her from Hartmut, who was pointing his pistol at Eliska's head. Before he could pull the trigger, Paul grabbed him from behind.

As Paul held him, a shot exploded into Hartmut, passing through him, lodging in Paul's side. Paul screamed and dropped Hartmut. Hartmut fell to the ground, next to Andela, moaning and holding his chest.

Seconds went by, and the fight seemed to be over, but Hartmut, in a last gasping act, revived and raised himself on one elbow and leveled his pistol at Paul. When he did, Andela saw the danger; leaped on him; grabbed his gun arm; held on with one hand while with her other hand, she searched the cobblestones for her mother's fallen dagger. She wrapped her hand around the dagger; raised it high; plunged it deep, slicing through Hartmut's throat. Hartmut twitched his last breath.

In less than ten seconds, six lives flew to their glory or hell.

Stevo leaned out of the third-floor window. "Everybody alive?"

"Yes, dammit, look where you're shooting. Your bullet passed through this bastard and hit me," Paul said.

"Sorry bout that. Such gratitude, I save your sorry ass, and this is the credit I get."

The gunfire had aroused the Germans in the SS headquarters, and they came running down the street.

"Get the hell out of there. We've got company coming." Stevo yelled.

Paul helped Eliska to stand. Paul yelled up to Stevo. "You coming?"

"Soon! More target practice! I don't only shoot friends, you know!"

Paul and Andela put their arms around Eliska and ran through the alley to a waiting car. "Jump in! Let's get out of here." Luca yelled.

"What about Stevo?"

"He'll be all right; he's got out of tighter spots than that," Luca said, letting out a confident laugh. "It's the Germans who need to worry."

"Stevo hung that the awful man, Jacob Conkova, didn't he?" Andela said.

"Sure did. Jacob was a collaborator. Turned in many a good Roma."

"If he's a collaborator, why was he guarding Eliska the other night?" Paul said, "I don't understand."

"She was safe. We had someone watching him," Luca smirked. "There's an old Roma saying, 'Keep your friends close, keep your enemies closer.' We knew he was a turncoat. We fed him false information, and we killed many Germans in the bargain. Time to retire him."

"What now?" Paul said, holding his side.

"We'll get you and Eliska, patched up, then out to the hanger, and figure a way to leave here. No need to stay for the damn Russians." Luca said.

Luca drove them to a Resistance doctor. He dug the bullet out and bandaged Paul's side. He wrapped Eliska's head and put a couple of stitches in her face. "Make you grin funny, but it will be all right," he said.

Luca raced through the empty streets to Eliska's apartment. "Gather up your things. We won't be back." Luca yelled.

They loaded up the essentials and drove to the barn.

"We must figure a way out of here," Luca pondered.

"We'll fly the Junkers F-13 out," Paul said.

"Are you crazy? Everybody in the country is shooting at German planes. We wouldn't get ten miles. Russians on one side, Americans on the other. Which way do we go?"

"Let me think about it. Now, I need sleep."

<div align="center">~~~~~~</div>

Chapter 96

READY TO RUN

The Barn, West of Litomysl Czechoslovakia. May 9, 1945.
The promise of a new day was born, melting old nightmares away.
A warm breeze, smelling of clover, flowed through the land. The
meadowlarks chirped, good morning, as a faint glow lit the eastern
sky. A signal that the earth was still alive, but many of its residents
are now underneath it. Three days have passed since the rescue
ambush in Litomysl had freed Eliska and Andela.

On this early morning, no one stirred in the barn except the
pigeons cooing in the rafters. A solitary figure quietly lifted the barn
door latch and entered. He carried a long rifle and a pistol in his belt.
He crept toward the sleeping residents of the barn and stiffened
when he felt a touch of cold steel pressed against his neck.

"Damn Luca, you scared the crap out of me," Stevo said.

"Well, you could have banged a bass drum with the noise you make.
You couldn't sneak up on a dead cow," Luca said, playfully slapping
him on the rear. "Bout time you drag your lazy butt back here. Good
hunting?"

"Ya, only a few Germans left, but the damn Ruskies are here.
Getting drunk, puking in the streets, and ransacking the homes.
Horny bastards, even eighty-year-old ladies aren't safe."

"We're leaving," Luca said.

"How the hell do we do that, flap our wings, and fly away?"

"No, but that will," Luca said, as he pointed to the Junkers F-13.

"Holy Saint Sara, that almost looks like an American plane!"

"Paul painted his Air Force markings on it. Lovely blue, Eh?"

"The girl painted on the nose is better," Stevo said. "Crazy
Americans, they paint pictures of girls on their airplanes. We paint
horses."

The conversation had awakened the other sleepers, and they rose one by one, Paul called out to Stevo. "Shoot any more of your friends, Stevo?"

"You won't let me live that down, will you?" Stevo jabbed back. "If wasn't for me, you'd be petunia fertilizer now."

"I suppose you're right, but it hurts a lot to be rescued by you," Paul laughed half heartily. "What do you think of the plane?"

"Pretty, especially the girl on the nose. Where are we going?"

"Poltava, Ukraine!"

"Poltava, Ukraine, where the hell is that?"

"About 800 miles west."

"That's Russian territory! They'll shoot us!"

"Not if we make it to the American airbase."

"You have an airbase in Ukraine?"

"Yep, flew there in April 1944, when we opened the base. General Prochazka took the whole band there to show the Russians we had class. They couldn't figure out how we could fly a band around when they had a hard time feeding themselves."

By now, Eliska, Andela, Luca, and Stevo had crowded around Paul.

"I might walk. I don't trust them flying machines," Eliska said.

"Me neither, I'd rather face more Germans than fly in that thing," Stevo observed.

"Nothing to it. Once we're in the air, you can sleep the whole way."

"A nightmare, I think," Eliska replied.

"Seven hours, and we will be there," Paul assured them. "But I have a minor problem."

"As if we didn't have enough problems," Luca smarted off. "What's the problem?"

"Well, if my calculations are right, the range of the Junkers F-13 is six hundred and fifty miles."

"So?"

"It's eight hundred and fifty miles to Poltava, Ukraine."

"Seems a little short."

"Well, that's with six male passengers, we have five passengers, and two are women. Eliska and Andela weigh about the same as a stout man, so we only weigh about four passengers. We should make at least an extra one hundred miles that way. Now one hundred plus six hundred and fifty that's seven hundred and fifty miles."

"Still not eight hundred and fifty miles, sounds short," Stevo said nervously.

"I'll check the fuel consumption on the way, and if at the halfway mark, we aren't doing too well and need to get rid of extra weight.... We throw Stevo out," Paul replied as he winked at Luca.

"Maybe leave him here," Luca joked. "Something tells me you might have a card or two up your sleeve."

"Ya, a couple of things. If we can get a tailwind, we cut fuel consumption."

"What's a tailwind? Passing gas?" Stevo asked.

"No," Paul chuckled, "It's the wind that will push us along, like a sailing ship. If we catch a wind blowing out of the East, we will save fuel."

The group stood around Paul, murmuring in approval, nodding their heads, but none of them understood a word he said.

"If we dump the extra weight, and I make carburetor adjustments, it could work."

"If it doesn't work, what then? Eliska asked hesitantly.

"Then we walk."

The group was silent. Then Eliska spoke, "Do you mind if we say a Roma prayer before we leave?"

"Pray away!"

"Good, when the East wind blow, we go."

~~~~~~
~~~~~~

Chapter 97

RACE TO THE WEST

The Barn, West of Litomysl Czechoslovakia, May 15, 1945

Figure 87 Junkers F-13

It rained hard the early morning of May 15th. Smashing, pounding rain, as if God were trying to purge the earth of blood, hate, and tears.

At eight in the morning, the sun came out, and the ground dried quickly. At ten in the morning, a gentle breeze from the East washed the meadow in front of the barn.

Eliska walked into the barn, "The East wind blow, time to go."

Andela skipped up to Eliska and hugged her. "Happy birthday, Mama."

Eliska blushed. "With the excitement, I forgot it."

"I even have a cake for you."

"A cake, out here?"

"Well, not as good as you make. I found cornmeal in the horse tack room. Mixed a little molasses from a bottle, and here it is! Right out of my fancy mix bowl!" Andela presented her with a small cupcake-sized hand full that she scooped out of a horse's water bowl.

"Thank you, princess!"

"You're welcome, my queen," Andela bowed and glared at the three startled male faces staring at her. "Do you think you are the only ones that figure things out? Want some?"

Paul, Luca, and Stevo crowded around her. They stuck their fingers in the water bowl, plucked a gob out, and licked off their fingers.

"My Lord, what is this?" Paul said, spitting it out.

"Cornbread and molasses cake."

Paul grabbed the molasses bottle and read it. "This is horse worming medicine."

"Maybe we won't have worms for a while," Luca snickered.

"You boys leave her alone. It's the thought that counts," Eliska chided.

In the distance, the rumble of Russian army trucks carrying supplies to Prague echoed through the woods. "It's only a matter of time before the Russians fan out to the countryside to inspect their new prize," Paul declared as he walked over to the airplane. "Let's get her ready to leave."

They pulled the Junker F-13 out of the barn and faced it into the East wind. Paul fueled up and tested the engine. They loaded their meager belongings as Eliska loaded Zuba's tuba.

"Can't we leave that here? It takes up too much space," Luca remarked.

"No, it goes, or I stay," Eliska replied fiercely.

"It's all right; we may need something to trade for a horse if we're short of Poltava," Paul joked, "I'll stow it in the cargo hold."

Paul had made triangle-shaped, wooden wheel chocks and placed them in front of each wheel. He tied a rope to each chock and ran the other end of the rope into each side of the plane, into the cabin's side windows. At ten-thirty in the morning, everybody was aboard.

Figure 72 Back Cabin of Junkers F-13

Luca and Stevo sat behind Paul's pilot position. Eliska and Andela sat behind them in the back passenger seats.

"After I start the plane, I'll rev the engine up. When I yell pull, Luca and Stevo, you pull the ropes as hard as you can; that will pull the chocks out from the front of the wheels. When the plane jumps ahead, drop the ropes. I don't want them to get tangled in the plane, understand?" Paul looked in his pilot's rear-view mirror at four, dumbfounded, pale faces staring at him. He reached back and slapped Luca and Stevo on the chest. "Understand?"

"Ya, you say pull... we pull... you jump ahead.... We drop the ropes... then we cover our heads!" Luca stammered.

"How about you, Stevo?"

"Ya, I pull hard. Why don't you take um out now?"

"I stepped it out to those trees out there. It's five hundred and fifty feet. We need one hundred feet more to get this thing off the ground. So, we rev it up and get a running start."

"OK, you rev it up, you say pull, we pull the hell out of um; we bury our heads and pray," Stevo replied nervously.

"Do it, and we'll be fine. Let's go!" Paul pushed the throttle forward. The plane roared into action. It strained, held back by the chock blocks; it shuttered, the tail raised off the ground, and the nose dipped downward. "Now, PULL!" Paul yelled. Luca and Stevo sat petrified. Paul turned to them and again slapped them on the chest. "PULL! DAMMIT! PULL!" Luca and Stevo responded, in kind, and yanked as hard as they could. As the chocks pulled free, the plane shot forward, lurched down the cow pasture runway. Bumping and shaking; one hundred feet gone;

At two hundred feet, the trees at the end of the runway menaced like towering green sentinels;

At three hundred feet, the trees were giant green sentinels;

At four hundred feet, the four passengers made the sign of the cross, calling on Saint Sara to protect them;

At five hundred feet, the plane roared a throaty salute from its Mercedes, 158 horsepower engine and lifted off the ground.

At five hundred and twenty-five feet, the plane was fully airborne.

At five hundred and fifty feet, it still had ten feet more to clear the nearest tall tree.

Paul twisted the plane, one wing up and one down. A robust east wind at the top of the trees pushed the plane higher, clearing the tallest tree by inches with a souvenir of leafy branches hanging from the landing gear.

Paul let out a deep breath, "Whew!" He looked in the rear mirror. All the passengers had their eyes tightly closed. "Piece of cake," Paul said.

Stevo warily opened one eye, "I'd rather eat Andela's cake." The cabin erupted into relieved laughter.

~~~~~~

Flight to Poltava, Ukraine.

Paul made a one hundred and eighty-degree turn, caught the East wind at the plane's tail, and set course for Poltava.

After flying for an hour, Paul's frightened passengers summoned up enough courage to open their eyes and peek out the windows.

"Oh, Saint Sara! Look at the little trees down there! If we go any higher, we can shake hands with Mama and Papa!" Eliska exclaimed. *Life was strange, living under the horror of the Nazis. I lost Zuba, our first home. Josef Jelinek, Karel, Kizzy, Mama and Papa, Sister Lucie, and our sweet baby. He would be twenty-six now.* The steady drone lulled her off into a fitful sleep.

Paul flew on, the East wind getting stronger and stronger; they were making good time, already four hours into their flight.

On the horizon, dark clouds formed. *That's the reason for the strong East wind. The storm system is pulling us into it.* Paul looked in his rear-view mirror at his chicks. *They're asleep. Seat belts fastened. Gonna be rough.*
~~~~~~

Paul flew at five thousand feet, then climbed, trying to gain height over the thunderheads looming ahead; six thousand feet; seven thousand feet; eight thousand feet; nine thousand feet; finally capping out at nine thousand, five hundred feet.

Paul thought, *If I go higher, we'll need oxygen.* He adjusted the fuel mixture for the low oxygen air that they were flying thru.

As they approached the storm, the east wind grew violent. It pushed the plane toward the fury that loomed ahead. The plane's airspeed climbed as it raced toward the fitful monsters yawning ahead.

And then, they were in the middle of it. Rain and hail pelted the windshield. Lightning flashed around the plane and danced off the wingtips. Paul struggled to keep the plane on a level course. His limited instruments weren't working.

Eliska awoke screaming. "The black woman said, go higher, go higher!"

Paul looked in the mirror at the frightened woman. *Something she said felt right, even if it made no sense without oxygen masks.*

Paul took the plane to ten thousand feet, then eleven thousand feet, then twelve thousand feet. The passengers were awake and panting. Flashes of lightning blinded Paul. He shook his head and blinked away tears as he struggled with the controls.

Paul flew on. The devil storm tossed the plane up, down, and side to side, shaking the plane in its wrathful grip. With a last, great, shaking rumble of thunder, the storm spit them out into sunny, peaceful airspace. Paul dropped the plane to eight thousand feet and reset the course to their destination. It was four-thirty in the afternoon, six hours since they took off. Must be getting close. Paul tapped the gas gauge, less than a quarter tank left. "It'll be tight if we are not too far off course or lost too much time in the storm."

At five in the afternoon, no airstrip was in sight. "Watch for aircraft and which way they are going. We might get a fix on the airfield from that." Paul said. Five pairs of eyes searched the horizon in all directions.

"Over there," Andela shouted. All eyes strained to see.

"It's a B17, and it's heading in for a landing. Its gear is down." Paul said, as he swung the plane to the left and followed.

"We don't dare follow too close, or they may shoot." As Paul said that, their plane sputtered and then resumed its flight. "Damn, we're out of fuel." The plane sputtered several more times before they saw the airfield.

The first B17 descended for the landing, followed by a second B17. "Can't land until they are out of the way," Paul said.

~~~~~~

By this time, an antiaircraft crew had sprung into action. The war was over, but they were still vigilant. The tower personnel trained their binoculars on the Junker. "What the hell is that? It's a German plane with Air Force markings, and they are coming in to land."

They called General Prochazka, and he entered the tower.

"What should we do, sir? We're ready to shoot," the tower controller said.

General Prochazka scanned the plane with his binoculars. "I don't see any guns. Only an American pilot paints a girl on the nose. Let it come in but have your men surround it when it lands."

Paul made another pass around as the engine died. "Here we go, can't wait any longer," he said, and glided the plane down. It landed hard; bounced once; right-wing scraped the runway, Paul struggled to control it; it bounced twice; left-wing almost touched the runway; it bounced three times and settled to roll across the landing mats. Paul braked the plane to a stop at the end of the runway.

"Whew!" Paul sighed.

"I need to use the outhouse," Luca said.

"It's too late for me," Stevo said, sheepishly.
~~~~~~

Paul stepped out of the plane to face several rifles, and a machine gun pointed at him. A lieutenant raised his pistol toward Paul. "State your business and make it good."

"Airman Paul Koupil is reporting in, sir," he yelled as he saluted. "Have a few refugees needing help."

"Get down, and no funny moves."

"Yes, sir!"

Paul helped his bewildered passengers' de-plane. The lieutenant escorted them to the briefing room. As they entered, General Prochazka looked over the ragged bunch. "Which one of you is the pilot?"

"I am, sir," Paul said.

General Prochazka came up to him and looked him over. "You remind me of a chubby mechanic that used to fix my car. Lost him over Brux, though."

"Well, sir, the lost is found!"

"Hot damn son, it's great to see you."

"Glad to be seen."

"Who are these folks?"

"These people saved my life. More than once! Let me introduce them. They don't speak English, though, only Czech. I'll translate."

"Translate hell; I was born in Tabor, South Dakota. All my folks spoke was Czech."

Paul then introduced Eliska, Andela, Luca, and Stevo.

"I'm delighted to meet you. Thank you for taking care of Paul." General Prochazka said, gallantly shaking their hands. He laughed and jerked his thumb toward Paul, "I told him if he got his ass shot up, he'd answer to me."

Paul whirled around and patted his backside. "Everything hooked together and in one piece, General!"

"So, I see, well, I'll forgo that. You folks can clean up. Will you join me for supper?" the general offered.

"Be happy to, sir."

The general ordered new clothes brought for them. "We only have the Air Force clothes, but they will do until we find you better ones. I'll have your belongings transferred to the officers' quarters, where there's plenty of room. We used to have fifteen hundred men here; today, we have three hundred. I'm here to close this base, give it back to the Ruskies after we pulled their acorns out of the fire."

After a slow soak in the shower and new clothes, Paul felt like a new man. Eliska and Andela shared a room, and Luca and Stevo shared another. They also soaked in the showers, a luxury they had never known. They dressed in the starched and pressed Air Force uniforms and went into the dining room.

"Well, aren't you snappy? If the Air Force had such beautiful girls, I would have enlisted sooner," Paul teased.

"Andela is the pretty one. I'm an old lady," Eliska said, blushing.

"Pretty enough, in my esteemed opinion," Paul declared as he kissed her on the forehead.

"Nobody has called me pretty in a long while."

General Prochazka overheard the conversation and held his arm out to Eliska. "Can I have the honor of escorting this beautiful lady to the table?" he said, nodding to her.

Eliska giggled a schoolgirl giggle, "Yes, I suppose," and took his arm

The supper progressed as the Air Force cooks served the meal. Paul explained everything that had happened to him and how the others had helped him. Finally, the supper ended.

General Prochazka wiped his mouth, folded and laid his napkin alongside his plate, saying, "I'm sorry I can't give you better food. These Air Force cooks grind up a fine steak and make a poor meatloaf out of it." He continued, "I'd give anything to have Calf's Liver with Onions and Bacon, Bratsky Goulash, or sweet buchtys."

Paul looked over at Eliska and winked. "General, what'd' you say if I could put those things together for you, in the Czech style?"

"It'd make my day. And a promotion for you too."

"Well, general, Eliska is the finest cook I have ever known. She was the top cook for the Chateau in Litomysl. Andela is her assistant."

The general's chubby face lit up. "The Chateau! My folks used to talk about that. They even visited once, real fancy, they said."

Eliska smiled, "The kitchen is still a kitchen!"

"Would you do some cooking?"

"I need the proper ingredients."

"I'll get them!"

"And no interference from your cooks?"

"Cooks, what cooks? I have garbage collectors! No interference from me."

"Is tomorrow at noon too soon?" Eliska replied. ~~~~~~

Chapter 98

A Fine Meal

Mess Hall, Poltava, Ukraine, May 16, 1945

The next morning Eliska and Andela arose early and commandeered the base kitchen. Paul, Luca, and Stevo came along to help. Paul interpreted for the rest of the kitchen staff.

At eleven-thirty in the morning, General Prochazka walked into the mess hall. Gorgeous odors drifted from the kitchen. He sniffed the air. "Now that's the ticket!" he declared, entering the kitchen. Eliska waved her wooden spoon at him. "Don't need another cook! Shoo! You, boss your airplanes, I boss the kitchen."

General Prochazka retreated, turned on his heel, and sat at the nearest table. "Reminds me of my mother," he chuckled.

Promptly at noon, the meal started. Luca and Stevo worked as servers. Course after course flowed from the kitchen; at one in the afternoon, the general surrendered. "Enough, I can't eat another bite!" he groaned, holding his stomach.

Eliska came out with a pleased smile on her face. She put her hands on her hips, a wooden spoon sticking out of her left hand. "A gallant effort General, but did you save room for sweet cake?"

"Eliska, if I eat another bite, I'll bust. But if you wrap it up, I'll take it to my quarters! I haven't ever tasted food so good."

Eliska brought the whole cake out and sliced it. Paul, Andela, Luca, and Stevo joined them at the table. Paul started the conversation, "General, what can we do for these folks?"

"Well, the State Department has a 'Displaced Person Program,' we might get them into. It will take a while. Most of Europe is displaced."

"Can you hurry it up?"

"No, I'm afraid not. I have very little pull with the State Department. I can get you on the waiting list, though."

"Can we get them to the States? They can stay with me in Litomysl?"

"Well, I have the authority to hire civilian help," he said thoughtfully. "Just... well." The general tapped his fingers on the table and was deep in thought. He snapped his fingers, "I have it!" He stood up and, with an expansive, sweeping motion of his arm, said, "We can ship my kitchen help home early, then you folks cook." He proceeded, "I'll take you to England and then home to Sioux Falls, where we are regrouping. Sioux Falls is only a few hours from your home, isn't it?"

"Yes, sir, but I don't want to cause you trouble, general?"

"Trouble hell, they can keep the uniforms on until Sioux Falls. I have my B17 for my staff and me. I'll recommend them for special status refugees for the help they gave me. We'll make it work!" He snorted, "I was going to retire, anyway. Go home and run the farm with my wife."

He grinned a satisfied grin, "And I'll have Eliska's sweet cooking for at least a month."

Paul studied Eliska, "What do you think?"

Eliska hesitated, "I kinda thought... maybe... I might go back to Litomysl. Maybe my... husband finds his way home."

"How long has it been?"

Eliska shrugged her shoulders and said, "Twenty-six going on twenty-seven years.... I guess."

"I'm sorry, that's a long time."

"I need to return. Zuba gets lost all the time. Couldn't read or write, so I know he can't find me."

Paul sat in stunned silence. *Could it be? Is it possible?* "Did you say your husband's name is Zuba?"

"Ya, Zuba Palzek."

"Why are you called Palzekova?"

General Prochazka spoke up, "The Czechs add 'ova' to the end of a name to signify a married woman. It's the same as Mrs., for Americans."

Paul pondered. *I don't want to raise false hopes.* "What does he look like?"

"Big guy, blond hair, strong, and the bluest eyes you ever saw."

"That describes many people," Paul said.

"Oh, you'd never forget him! He had trouble talking, but his heart was like a soft bowl of vanilla pudding. Yet, he was strong when he had to be but would help you any way he could."

"Sounds like a good man."

"The best," Eliska replied wistfully.

Paul pondered in silence. *If that doesn't describe Zuba, nothing will. But I don't want to raise any false hopes for her after all these years. If she comes with me and it is him. Great! If not, no harm done.*

"Eliska, things in Czechoslovakia will be tough for a long time. Come with me to Litomysl, Minnesota. There are lots of Czech people there. Meet my father and my friends. Spend some time. If you don't want to stay, I'll pay for your way back home. Will you do that?"

Eliska was quiet. *Mama and Papa are gone.... Andela may be better in this place than back in Czechoslovakia. Won't be afraid anymore. The brothers can't go back. They will treat them as Roma again.... I'll get them settled in this new place... then I go back.* "Can I go back without going on an airy plane?"

Paul laughed a relieved laugh, "Absolutely. If that's what you want."

"I might do that!"

"Good," Paul said, hugging her. "Don't be afraid. I'll be there for you." The others crowded around her. "We will, too; we're family."

~~~~~~

Chapter 99

ENGLAND

Knettishall Air Force Base England. Thursday, June 28th, 1945.

The general's private plane was refueled and made ready for the last leg of the journey, first to Newfoundland, then to New York, and then Sioux Falls, South Dakota.

Eliska wasn't as fearful in the massive B17 as she had been in the little Junkers that she had cut her flying teeth on. "Like sitting at your kitchen table," she had commented as she stepped off in England on the flight from Poltava, Ukraine. The size and the luxury of the General's B17 awed his guests.

"It's big enough to put ten buggies and twenty horses in," Stevo commented.

The indoor outhouse especially impressed Luca. After using it, the flushing surprised him. "Where does it go when it goes down?" he asked an amused airman. "Out the bottom of the plane," the airman replied.

Luca thought for a while, then said, "What happens if a farmer is hoeing below, and he is in the way?"

"Don't ask!" was the crewman's answer.

Luca chuckled, "Bet it ruins his day."

~~~~~~

Chapter 100

HOME

Sioux Falls, South Dakota, USA Tues, July 3, 1945

On a bright starlit summer night, the big plane landed in Sioux Falls, South Dakota. After unloading and saying goodbye to General Prochazka, Paul and his chicks boarded a Greyhound bus for the two-hundred-mile trip home. They arrived in Owatonna, Minnesota, at six in the morning, on the Fourth of July.

Paul had wired his father, Thomas of their arrival, and he was waiting at the bus depot with a large, twelve-passenger limousine. He held the baby, "Paul Zuba Koupil," while Paul's wife Irene ran headlong into Paul's arms. Thomas wasn't far behind. He hoisted the little boy up high, displaying him for all to see. Paul didn't know who to hug first or to let go of last. As he spied his son, the son he had never seen, a look of wondrous joy washed over his face. He picked him up and looked him over lovingly. The boy squirmed, cried, and reached for his grandpa.

"It takes time, son," Thomas said, as tears streaked his cheeks, "He doesn't know you."

Paul's chicks stood patiently as the joyous family reunion went on. After they liberally passed hugs around, Paul turned toward them and motioned them to come and join them. He introduced them to Thomas and Irene. When Paul introduced Eliska to Thomas, she thought she had met him before. Thomas was also puzzled. *Where have I met her?*

Thomas held up his hands for quiet, "Anybody hungry?" Everybody nodded vigorously. "Charlie's bus stop cafe is around the corner. Best breakfast in Owatonna, If fact, it's the only breakfast in Owatonna on the Fourth of July!"

They sat around a big circular table at Charlie's; Thomas and Paul helped the others read the menus; they placed their orders and ate.

Eliska picked up Paul Jr., squeezed him, and bounced him on her knee. "You have a very handsome son, Paul."

Paul laughed, "I can't take the credit for that; his mother is pretty as a summer rose."

Irene blushed, "It's time we get going, don't you think?"

Thomas paid the bill and loaded them into the limo for the trip to Litomysl. Entering Litomysl, cars were parked on both sides of the street and in the approaches to the cornfields. Hundreds of people lined the road, many waving red, white, and blue American flags. Paul was their favorite son! The church band played a faltering version of 'Stars and Stripes Forever.' Two street urchins livened up the party by tossing firecrackers under the car. As they exploded, Paul, Eliska, Andela, Luca, and Stevo, all ducked to the limo floor for cover.

Thomas, sensing the turmoil, shouted to them. "To je v pořádku! To je v pořádku!" (It's all right). Two fathers jumped from the crowd and took the offenders by their collars and marched them away.

Thomas stopped the limo at the entrance to the Holy Trinity church, where a reception was planned. When Paul stepped out, he saw Zuba and Hanzi sitting in the shade under the oak tree next to Tom's Repair. He excused himself from the others and crossed the street and ran up to them. Hanzi rose slowly, a bewildered look on his face. Paul slapped him on the back and hugged him, lifting him off his feet. "Great to see you, Hanzi."

Hanzi, for once, could not speak. Paul approached Zuba; Zuba stared at Paul, a faint smile lifting one side of his mouth. His eye watered as Paul knelt before him, "Do you remember me, Zuba?"

Zuba nodded his head slightly and reached out his good left arm to pull Paul closer. "Pau, -- Pau," Zuba uttered. He lifted his hand and rubbed it across Paul's face. "Bi -- Bi, -- big," he uttered again. Paul hugged Zuba tightly. He backed away and looked into his eyes. "I have someone I want you to meet. Be right back."

Paul hurried back across the street to where Eliska was standing, chatting with several women. "Eliska, come and meet my best friend who saved my life."

Eliska followed Paul across the street. Halfway across, she stopped; trembled; her breath left her, and she felt faint. *It must be the heat. It can't be. He's too old.*

Paul supported her by the arm and helped her move closer. Hanzi, a shocked look painted his face, stood protecting Zuba. Eliska looked at him and gave him a big hug. "I thought you were dead! Go, see your brothers!" she said, pointing to Luca and Stevo.

Eliska then stepped around Hanzi and leaned over the seated Zuba and cupped his face in her hands. She took his old, battered hat off and kissed him on the forehead, and said, "Look at you, remember me tichý žába (Silent frog)?" Zuba glanced at Eliska without recognition. His eyes showed that he was searching for the answer, but his mind couldn't match the memory.

"It's me love, your Eliska," Eliska intoned.

Zuba, bewildered, rolled his questioning eyes up to her, then to Paul.

Paul called out to Thomas, "Dad, will you bring Andela here?" Thomas brought Andela to stand in front of Zuba.

"Andela, meet your father," Eliska said. She picked up Zuba's working hand and placed it in Andela's hand. "Do you recognize your little babushka, Andela?" Eliska said.

Zuba became agitated and irritated. He didn't understand why he couldn't match the memories she stirred up with what he saw. *Who is the gray-haired lady? Who is the blonde woman?* He shook his head back and forth as if trying to shake the recognition loose. A low moan escaped his lips. "Knoooo -- you?"

Eliska reached into her leather pouch and retrieved a small bottle she had carried for twenty-seven years. She opened it, poured lavender splash water on her wrist, and held it to Zuba's nose. A jolt of recognition seared through him.

Eliska reached into a Zuba's shirt and found his cross and drew it out. She opened her blouse and pulled out the gold cross that he had made for her. Andela came closer and showed him her cross.

The same crosses that had saved their lives twice before, with strange markings, with the little-crooked crosses engraved on them.

Zuba could no longer hold back the dam of long-suppressed painful memories; the memories broke free, washed through Zuba, and burst forth through his watering eyes. He looked into Eliska's tear-filled eyes. "El, -- iss, -- kaaa," he moaned as he wrapped his good arm around her and pulled her close, burying his gray head in her bosom. A low moan again echoed up from deep within his heart. "Loo ve -- yooo."

"My love... My love," Eliska replied, holding him close and stroking his head. "So much I love you. I lost you. Here I find you."

Thomas Koupil watched this unfold. His breath left him, and his knees shook. Upon seeing the crosses with the engravings, he knew he couldn't be silent anymore. He left and went to the repair shop. He opened a small drawer of his desk, reached in, clenched his hand around the contents, and went back to the gathering.

Outside, Andela sat next to Zuba, stroking his forehead; Zuba, still confused, stared at Eliska and back at Andela; each time, expecting that if he looked back again, they would disappear, as they did in his dreams, so many times before.

Eliska kneeled and laid her cheek on his lap, fearing that if she didn't stay close, she'd lose him again. Zuba kept stroking her back and murmuring, "El -- is -- kaaaa. -- El -- is -- kaaaaaa."

The jubilant crowd sensed that something profound was happening; they stopped their chattering and fell silent. They were aware of Zuba's story and how he had lost his family. The crowd made not a sound, as they gathered around the family reunion.

Men who hadn't cried at their own father's funeral now stood with tears forming in their eyes, as a smile kissed their weather-beaten cheeks.

These same hardened men, beaten up by the times and trials they lived through, took their hats off. The gentle summer breeze rustled through the trees and tousled the sparse hair on their white foreheads. These tough men reached out and cradling an arm around their wife's shoulder, pulling her close.

The wives, in their best flour sack dresses, dabbed their eyes with hankies and pulled their children even closer.

The sparrows nesting in the eaves of the repair shop chirped, and the silent crowd watched. Honeybees sipped the last nectar of the spent summer flowers, and the hushed crowd waited. The smell of bratwurst drifted from the church booths. Still, the silent crowd waited.

Finally, Zuba spoke, "BA -- BA -- bee?"

Tears welled up again as Eliska shuddered and answered quietly, "The baby.... died right after.... he was born."

Zuba looked hopelessly up into her eyes. "BA, -- BA -- bee -- die?"

"Yes, my love, a boy."

"BA- bee -- die -- ooh -- Nooo?" as Zuba's confusion melted and the impact of what he heard, the longing thru the years, the angst of his predicament, broke through his defenses, and he wept.

A shaking voice broke the deafening silence. "He did not die!"

Heads turned as Thomas Koupil stepped forth. He walked up to Paul and stood before him. Thomas unwrapped his hands; gently separated two gold chains from which hung a gold cross; a gold cross with crooked little engravings on it; the engravings of a good luck symbol from India. Thomas placed that cross, from long ago, around Paul's neck.

Paul stood in stunned bewilderment; his emotions exploded in a cascade of feelings; a faintness crept over him; his breath sucked out of him. He gazed into Thomas's eyes, and then Paul knew.... That this was the truth. *Zuba is my father?...... Eliska, my mother?........ Andela, my sister? No wonder I had been such a fondness for Eliska and Andela...... No wonder I love Zuba so much.*

Thomas trembled as he looked to Eliska. "My wife was in labor in the next bed. Ours.... died...... Yours didn't.... I... I switched the babies." Thomas hung his head and sobbed, "I am so sorry."

Eliska was quiet; anger flashed across her face. She bit her lip and walked away from Thomas. She stopped behind a large oak tree. *How can you do this to me? What were you thinking? All this pain, all this time!*

Eliska sobbed; the collected pain of the last twenty-seven years broke loose from her heart. *Years drained my youth — years when I could have had a son by my side.* The constant fear, hunger, and longing all flowed from her into a pool of hate. She gritted her teeth, swore under her breath, and stared off into space until she felt a tug on her shirt sleeve. She pulled her sleeve away. Another tug and Eliska's anger flared, "What the hell do you want of me?"

Another tug, and Eliska's whirled to face her tormenter, "What the hell do.......?" Eliska was face to face with a beautiful dark-skinned girl.

The little girl took Eliska's hand and, while rubbing it, smiled at her. "Be of good heart. It is as it should be. Hate is dead. It is, as I said, isn't it?"

Shocked, Eliska nodded through her tears. "Yes... But how... Who are..., Are you, Sara E Kali?"

"Love and forget!" the girl kissed Eliska's hand, waved, and walked away.

Eliska's sobbed herself clean of hatred, clean of fear, and clean of remorse. Her mood matched this peaceful Minnesota morning.

Eliska wiped her eyes, gained her composure, and returned to the gathering. She took Paul by the hand and returned with him to Zuba and Andela. Hugging them closely, she turned to Thomas. "I... I... felt something for Paul the first time I met him, but I didn't understand."

Eliska tenderly put her hand out to Thomas and pulled him close. She reached up to Thomas's face and lovingly touched his cheek, "I forgive you."

Thomas looked up, mouth open, astonishment gripped his face, "You forgive me? After what I did to you?"

"The little girl let me see," Eliska replied.

"What little girl?" Thomas said, looking around.

"It's from a Roma's heart; I guess you wouldn't understand. When you cared for my Zuba and our son, you did it out of love. You preserved that love while I lived in a land where love died... My anger.... Has died. How... is that wrong?" Eliska said.

Eliska grasped Thomas's hands and pulled him close. "I believed... I prayed... No, I hoped... for many years that Zuba and our son were alive." Eliska shook her head. "You didn't take my Zuba away! You saved him. You gave love to our son, knowing that he wasn't your own. You raised a fine man that came and rescued us when we needed it the most. He brought our love back. He gave us a grandson. How is that wrong?" Eliska put her arms around Thomas, hugged him, and said. "Love forgets, God forgives."

~~~~~~

Figure 89 Cross with Crooked Little Engravings. A Swastika! A Good Luck Charm From India.
~~~~~~

Donald Pawlitschek

Rest in Peace

In a small country cemetery, surrounded by Minnesota cornfields, stands two lonely stone markers. If you look closely, you see that the markers have leaned, ever so slight, towards each other. Forever locked in love.

The Tombstones Read:

Zuba Palzek

Born April 1st, 1898 – Died Sep 1, 1965
Unlock your tongue to sing God's story,
Hold your head up high.
Your tuba sounds God's glory.
Days of joy are nigh

Eliska Palzekova

Born May 15, 1900 - Died Sept 2nd, 1965
Love shows the way
Love lightens the heavy load
Love brightens the dreary day
Love straightens the lonely road

~~~~~~

What does a headstone reflect?

A date that starts with birthing and ends with dying?

Or is it the dash between the years that make a life worthwhile?

When they gaze at your lonely carved stone, what will they remember?

The birthing?.............. The dying?................ Or the Dash?
~~~~~~

Epilog

A joyous impossible reunion. Love lost and found again. Zuba and Eliska regain their family and have a grandson. They spent their remaining years together, watching their family grow.

Paul and Irene will have four more children.

Andela will marry a local farmer boy and produce three children.

The tendrils of love twine on. The example Zuba and Eliska set is a legacy for future generations to emulate and strive for.

ABOUT THE AUTHOR

Don Pawlitschek is a dyed-in-the-wool promoter and entrepreneur.

- Over two thousand auctions, appraisals, real estate sales, consulting assignments, and funding projects completed nationwide since 1980!
- Minnesota Licensed Auctioneer
- Bonded Western Surety bond
- Certified Auctioneer CA
- Certified Personal Property Appraiser Instructor-CPPAI
- Certified Personal Property Appraiser-CPPA
- Certified Real Estate Auctioneer-CREA
- Certified Management and Fund-Raising Auctioneer-CCFRA
- Certified Online Internet Auctioneer-COI

Figure 92-Don Pawlitschek

- 30 yrs., a Real Estate Agent, Broker, and Investor Agent,
- Designed a plastic hog flooring slat with strength enough to span eight feet, ventilate and flush manure. He was issued Patent No. 4,135,339 on Jan 23rd, 1979.
- Listed in Who's Who since 1985.
- Recorded eleven albums; He wrote, directed, and acted in a TV pilot called "Crime Does Not Pay." Made for the family audience, it featured his family, places of interest from the Upper Midwest, acts he had on his shows, their act, and other features.
- Has written eighty stories, poems, and comedy routines
- He released his first full-length novel. He writes under the pen name of Popps Dundee.
- Photographer, producing an annual family album and has shot candid shots at several weddings.
- He owns a small recording studio and has performed and recorded several albums of country and fifties music.
- In 1992, as a concert promoter, he formed the company Butterfly Stew and promoted shows at various Civic Centers, such as Saint Cloud, Sioux City, Sioux Falls, Lacrosse, WI.
- He had a full range of acts, heavy into country music. From Nashville, he had Connie Smith, Jean Shepard, Bobby Rice, and Jack Greene (1967 male vocalist of the year). From Hollywood, he had Donna Douglas (Ellie Mae of the Beverly Hillbillies).
- Performs benefit auctions, is a public speaker, and performs in and directs the musical group Sugarloom to appear before hundreds of thousands of people since 2016. In 2021 he appeared to one hundred and forty thousand people. He also performs as a solo artist.
- Father of five children and nineteen grandchildren, each one his favorite. Has been married to the same woman since 1965. Thank God she is kind enough to put up with his comings and goings.

SOME SAMPLE POEMS.

The Love of The One

Organize and Separate, Dedicate and Differentiate

Separate paths lead to different gods, with neither truth

nor reason. They all grow hate in every season.

Love evolves, love solves, lies perpetuate, while leaders

call for hate.

When we finally know that God is one, total love will show

that our race is run.

The soul surrounds the body shell, reaching out to all it meets.

It is only God that it desperately seeks.

Neither earth, nor sun, fish nor fowl, can detach from the

Son's call.

After the battle is over and the stag grazes peacefully in the

clover,

the moon and stars will sleep, unblinking overhead.

When the sparrow's song awakes the morning, we will

sing the song of our great dawning.

The love of The One is the love of all.

Our journey of discovery will never reach a solution,

as love neither has a beginning or a conclusion.

The word foe, we no longer say, as 'friend' is the only way.

Aching hearts will find the true togetherness of mankind as,

we are all The One.

Cow Pie

Sometimes when you ponder and pause
and doubt the existence of Santa Claus.
It helps to take off your shoes and kick your feet up high.
But be careful along life's road, not to step in a cow pie.
Now, I know cow pies are fun to squibble between the toes.
And Lord knows they are handy to clear the sinuses of the nose.
Just remember, God made the sky up high and the humble cow pie.
So, when you are feeling all chipper and spry,
make sure your shoes aren't covered in cow pie!

Cow Pie Productions made this card.
Hallmark has no claim to fame cause this card puts them to shame.
It costs only four buffalo chips in fine stationery stores everywhere!

Hang in there and keep dreaming!

One thing about life I have found is that you never stop learning, or you shouldn't. Don't be afraid to try something new, although at my age, skydiving is out, and it's too late to be a Chippendale dancer. Buffet diving and a Chunkendunk dancer would be more appropriate. Someone suggested lap dancing, but I no longer have a lap, so what's a guy to do?

Remember, life happens, whether or not you are home!
It's never too late to hallucinate!
Web Site www. printcastnews.com

Order Page
To Order an autographed copy of this book, *The Dash*, send $23.00 (shipping and tax included) for each book. Include this order form.
Volume orders are available—Call 507-546-3448 for info.

Number of books. ______
Price per book $23:00
Total to enclose _________

Name:

____

Address:

____

City:

____

State: _______________

Zip _________________

Phone: __________________________________

Email address: _____________________________

Autograph it to: ____________________________________

____

Mail to -PrintCast News LLC
18014 499th Ave
Lake Crystal, MN 56055
507-546-3448